LISA KLEYPAS

Devil in Disguise

The Ravenels meet The Wallflowers

PIATKUS

First published in the United States in 2021 by Avon Books,
an imprint of HarperCollins Publishers
First published in Great Britain in 2021 by Piatkus

1 3 5 7 9 10 8 6 4 2

A CIP catalogue record for this book
is available from the British Library.

ISBN 978-0-349-40772-2

Printed and bound in Great Britain by
Clays Ltd, Elcograf S.p.A.

Papers used by Piatkus are from well-managed forests
and other responsible sources.

Piatkus
An imprint of
Little, Brown Book Group
Carmelite House
50 Victoria Embankment
London EC4Y 0DZ

An Hachette UK Company
www.hachette.co.uk

www.littlebrown.co.uk

To the marvelous Eloisa James,
who got me through 2020.
Thank you, my treasured friend!
Love always,
L.K.

Devil in Disguise

Chapter 1

London, 1880

"MacRae is as angry as a baited bear," Luke Marsden warned as he entered the office. "If you've never been around a Scotsman in a temper, you'd better brace yourself for the language."

Lady Merritt Sterling looked up from her desk with a faint smile. Her brother was a handsome sight, with his windblown dark hair and his complexion infused with color from the brisk autumn air. Like the rest of the Marsden brood, Luke had inherited their mother's long, elegant lines. Merritt, on the other hand, was the only one out of the half-dozen siblings who'd ended up short and full-figured.

"I've spent nearly three years managing a shipping firm," she pointed out. "After all the time I've spent around longshoremen, nothing could shock me now."

"Maybe not," Luke conceded. "But Scotsmen have a special gift for cursing. I had a friend at Cambridge who knew at least a dozen different words for testicles."

Merritt grinned. One of the things she enjoyed most about Luke, the youngest of her three brothers, was that he never shielded her from vulgarity or treated her like a delicate flower. That, among other reasons, was why she'd asked him to take over the management of her late husband's shipping company, once she'd taught him the ropes. He'd accepted the offer without hesitation. As the third son of an earl, his options had been limited, and as he'd remarked, a fellow couldn't earn a living by sitting around looking picturesque.

"Before you show Mr. MacRae in," Merritt said, "you might tell me why he's angry."

"To start with, the ship he chartered was supposed to deliver his cargo directly to our warehouse. But the dock authorities turned it away because all the berths were full. So it was just unloaded four miles inland, at Deptford Buoys."

"That's the usual procedure," Merritt said.

"Yes, but this isn't the usual cargo."

She frowned. "It's not the timber shipment?"

Luke shook his head. "Whisky. Twenty-five thousand gallons of extremely valuable single malt from Islay, still under bond. They've started the process of bringing it here in barges, but they say it will take three days for all of it to reach the warehouse."

Merritt's frown deepened. "Good Lord, all that bonded whisky can't sit at Deptford Buoys for three days!"

"To make matters worse," Luke continued, "there was an accident."

Her eyes widened. "What kind of accident?"

"A cask of whisky slipped from the hoisting gear, broke on the roof of a transit shed, and poured all over MacRae. He's ready to murder someone—which is why I brought him up here to you."

Despite her concern, Merritt let out a snort of laughter. "Luke Marsden, are you planning to hide behind my skirts while I confront the big, mean Scotsman?"

"Absolutely," he said without hesitation. "You like them big and mean."

Her brows lifted. "What in heaven's name are you talking about?"

"You love soothing difficult people. You're the human equivalent of table syrup."

Amused, Merritt leaned her chin on her hand. "Show him in, then, and I'll start pouring."

It wasn't that she *loved* soothing difficult people. But she definitely liked to smooth things over when she could. As the oldest of six children, she'd always been the one to settle quarrels among her brothers and sisters, or come up with indoor games on rainy days. More than once, she'd orchestrated midnight raids on the kitchen pantry or told them stories when they'd sneaked to her room after bedtime.

She sorted through the neat stack of files on her desk and found the one labeled "MacRae Distillery."

Not long before her husband, Joshua, had died, he'd struck a deal to provide warehousing for MacRae in England. He'd told her about his meeting with the Scotsman, who'd been visiting London for the first time.

"Oh, but you must ask him to dinner," Merritt had exclaimed, unable to bear the thought of a stranger traveling alone in an unfamiliar place.

"I did," Joshua had replied in his flat American accent. "He thanked me for the invitation but turned it down."

"Why?"

"MacRae is somewhat rough-mannered. He was raised on a remote island off the west coast of Scotland.

I suspect he finds the prospect of meeting the daughter of an earl overwhelming."

"He needn't worry about that," Merritt had protested. "You know my family is barely civilized!"

But Joshua replied that her definition of "barely civilized" was different from a rural Scotsman's, and MacRae would be far more comfortable left to his own devices.

Merritt had never dreamed that when she and Keir MacRae finally met, Joshua would be gone, and she would be the one managing Sterling Enterprises.

Her brother came to the doorway and paused at the threshold. "If you'll come this way," he said to someone outside the room, "I'll make introductions and then—"

Keir MacRae burst into the office like a force of nature and strode past Luke, coming to a stop on the other side of Merritt's desk.

Looking sardonic, Luke went to lean against the doorjamb and folded his arms. "On the other hand," he said to no one in particular, "why waste time with introductions?"

Merritt stared in bemusement at the big, wrathful Scotsman. He was an extraordinary sight, more than six feet of muscle and brawn dressed in a thin wet shirt and trousers that clung as if they'd been glued to his skin. An irritable shiver, almost certainly from the chill of evaporating alcohol, ran over him. Scowling, he reached up to remove his flat cap, revealing a shaggy mop of hair, several months past a good cut. The thick locks were a beautiful cool shade of amber shot with streaks of light gold.

He was handsome despite his unkempt state. *Very* handsome. His blue eyes were alert with the devil's own intelligence, the cheekbones high, the nose straight and strong. A tawny beard obscured the line of his jaw—perhaps concealing a weak chin?—she couldn't tell. Regardless, he was a stunner.

Merritt wouldn't have thought there was a man alive who could fluster her like this. She was a confident and worldly woman, after all. But she couldn't ignore the flush rising from the high-buttoned neck of her dress. Or the way her heart had begun to pound like a clumsy burglar trampling the flower bed.

"I want to speak to someone in charge," he said brusquely.

"That would be me," Merritt said with a quick smile, coming around the desk. "Lady Merritt Sterling, at your service." She extended her hand.

MacRae was slow to respond. His fingers closed over hers, cool and slightly rough.

The sensation raised the hairs on the back of her neck, and she felt something uncoil pleasantly at the pit of her stomach.

"My condolences," he said gruffly, releasing her hand. "Your husband was a good man."

"Thank you." She took a steadying breath. "Mr. MacRae, I'm so sorry for the way your delivery has been botched. I'll submit paperwork to make sure you're exempted from the landing charges and wharfage rates, and Sterling Enterprises will handle the lighterage fees. And in the future, I'll make sure a berth is reserved on the day your shipment is due."

"There'll be no fookin' future shipments if I'm to be

put out of business," MacRae said. "The excise agent says every barrel of whisky that hasn't been delivered to the warehouse by midnight will no longer be under bond, and I'm to be paying duties on it immediately."

"What?" Merritt shot an outraged glance at her brother, who shrugged and shook his head to indicate he knew nothing about it. This was deadly serious business. The government's regulations about storing whisky under bond were strictly enforced, and violations would earn terrible penalties. It would be bad for her business, and disastrous for MacRae's.

"No," she said firmly, "that will not happen." She went back behind the desk, took her chair, and sorted rapidly through a pile of authorizations, receipts, and excise forms. "Luke," she said, "the whisky must be transported here from Deptford Buoys as fast as possible. I'll persuade the excise officer to give us at least 'til noon tomorrow. Heaven knows he owes us that much, after the favors we've done him in the past."

"Will that be enough time?" Luke asked, looking skeptical.

"It will have to be. We'll need every barge and lighter vessel we can hire, and every able-bodied man—"

"No' so fast," MacRae said, slapping his palms firmly on the desk and leaning over it.

Merritt started at the sound and glanced up into the face so close to hers. His eyes were a piercing shade of ice blue, with faint whisks at the outer corners, etched by laughter and sun and sharp windy days.

"Yes, Mr. MacRae?" she managed to ask.

"Those clodpates of yours just spilled one hundred and nine gallons of whisky over the wharf, and a good portion over me in the bargain. Damned if I'll be letting them bungle the rest of it."

"Those weren't our clodpates," Luke protested. "They were lightermen from the barge."

To Merritt, her brother's voice sounded as if it were coming from another floor of the building. All she could focus on was the big, virile male in front of her.

Do your job, she told herself sternly, ripping her gaze from MacRae with an effort. She spoke to her brother in what she hoped was a professional tone. "Luke, from now on, no lightermen are to set foot on the hoisting crane platform." She turned back to MacRae. "My employees are experienced at handling valuable cargo," she assured him. "They'll be the only ones allowed to load your whisky onto the crane and stock it in the warehouse. No more accidents—you have my word."

"How can you be sure?" MacRae asked, one brow lifting in a mocking arch. "Will you be managing the operation yourself?"

The way he asked, sarcasm wrapped in silk, elicited an odd little pang of recognition, as if she'd heard him say something in just that tone before. Which made no sense, since they'd never met until this moment.

"No," she said, "my brother will manage it from start to finish."

Luke let out a sigh as he realized she'd just committed him to working through the night. "Oh, yes," he said acidly. "I was just about to suggest that."

Merritt looked at MacRae. "Does that meet with your approval?"

"Do I have a choice?" the Scotsman countered darkly, pushing back from the desk. He tugged at the damp, stained fabric of his shirt. "Let's be about it, then."

He was cold and uncomfortable, Merritt thought, and he reeked of cask-strength single malt. Before he returned to work, he needed the opportunity to tidy himself. "Mr. MacRae," she asked gently, "where are you staying while you're in London?"

"I was offered the use of the flat in the warehouse."

"Of course." A small, utilitarian set of rooms at their bonded warehouse had been installed for the convenience of vintners and distillers who wished to blend and bottle their products on the premises. "Has your luggage been taken there yet?"

"'Tis still on the docks," MacRae replied curtly, clearly not wanting to be bothered with trivial issues when there was so much to be done.

"We'll collect it right away, then, and have someone show you to the flat."

"Later," he said.

"But you'll need to change your clothes," Merritt said, perturbed.

"Milady, I'm going to work through the night beside longshoremen who won't give a damn how I look or smell."

Merritt should have let the matter go. She knew that. But she couldn't resist saying, "The docks are very cold at night. You'll need a coat."

MacRae looked exasperated. "I have only the one, and 'tis drookit."

Merritt gathered "drookit" meant thoroughly soaked. She told herself that Keir MacRae's well-being was none of her concern, and there was urgent business requiring her attention. But . . . this man could use a bit of looking after. Having grown up with three brothers, she was well familiar with the surly, hollow-eyed look of a hungry male.

Luke was right, she thought wryly. *I do like them big and mean.*

"You can't very well leave your luggage sitting out in public," she said reasonably. "It will only take a few minutes for me to fetch a key and show you to the flat." She slid a glance to her brother, who joined in obligingly.

"Besides, MacRae," Luke added, "there's nothing you can accomplish until I've had a chance to organize the men and hire extra barge crew."

The Scotsman pinched the bridge of his nose and rubbed the corners of his eyes. "You can't show me to the flat," he told Merritt firmly. "No' without a chaperone."

"Oh, no need to worry about that, I'm a widow. I'm the one who chaperones others."

MacRae gave Luke an expectant stare.

Luke wore a blank expression. "Are you expecting me to say something?"

"You will no' forbid your sister to go off alone with a stranger?" MacRae asked him incredulously.

"She's my older sister," Luke said, "and she employs me, so . . . no, I'm not going to tell her a damned thing."

"How do you know I won't insult her virtue?" the Scotsman demanded in outrage.

Luke lifted his brows, looking mildly interested. "Are you going to?"

"*No*. But I could!"

Merritt had to gnaw the insides of her lips to restrain a laugh. "Mr. MacRae," she soothed. "My brother and I are both well aware that I have nothing at all to fear from you. On the contrary, it's common knowledge that Scots are trustworthy and honest, and . . . and simply the *most* honorable of men."

MacRae's scowl eased slightly. After a moment, he said, "'Tis true that Scots have more honor per man than other lands. We carry the honor of Scotland with us wherever we go."

"Exactly," Merritt said. "No one would doubt my safety in your company. In fact, who would dare utter one offensive word, or threaten any harm to me, if you were there?"

MacRae seemed to warm to the idea. "If someone did," he said vehemently, "I'd skin the bawfaced bastard like a grape and toss him onto a flaming dung heap."

"There, you see?" Merritt exclaimed, beaming at him. "You're the perfect escort." Her gaze slid to her brother, who stood just behind MacRae.

Luke shook his head slowly, amusement tugging at the corners of his lips before he mouthed two silent words to her:

Table syrup.

She ignored him. "Come, Mr. MacRae—we'll have your affairs settled in no time."

KEIR COULDN'T HELP following Lady Merritt. Since the moment he'd been drenched in 80-proof whisky on the docks, he'd been chilled to the marrow of his bones. But this woman, with her quick smile and coffee-dark eyes, was the warmest thing in the world.

They went through a series of handsome rooms lined with wood paneling and paintings of ships. Keir barely noticed the surroundings. His attention was riveted by the shapely figure in front of him, the intricately pinned-up swirls of her hair, the voice dressed in silk and pearls. How good she smelled, like the kind of expensive soap that came wrapped in fancy paper. Keir and everyone he knew used common yellow rosin soap for everything: floors, dishes, hands, and body. But there was no sharpness to this scent. With every movement, hints of perfume seemed to rise from the rustling of her skirts and sleeves, as if she were a flower bouquet being gently shaken.

The carpet underfoot had been woven in a pattern beautiful enough to cover a wall. A crime, it was, to tread on it with his heavy work boots. Keir felt ill at ease in such fine surroundings. He didn't like having left his men, Owen and Slorach, out on the wharf. They could manage without him for a while, especially Slorach, who'd worked at his father's distillery for almost four decades. But this entire undertaking was Keir's responsibility, and the survival of his distillery depended on it. Making sure the bonded whisky was installed safely in the warehouse was too important to let himself be distracted by a woman.

Especially this one. She was educated and well-bred, the daughter of an earl. Not just any earl, but Lord Westcliff, a man whose influence and wealth was known far and wide. And Lady Merritt was a power in her own right, the owner of a shipping business that included a fleet of cargo steamers as well as warehouses.

As the only child of elderly parents, Keir had been given the best of what they'd been able to provide, but there had been little in the way of books or culture. He'd found beauty in seasons and storms, and in long rambles over the island. He loved to fish and walk with his dog, and he loved making whisky, the trade his father had taught him.

His pleasures were simple and straightforward.

Lady Merritt, however, was neither of those things. She was an altogether different kind of pleasure. A luxury to be savored, and not by the likes of him.

But that didn't stop Keir from imagining her in his bed, all flushed and yielding, her hair a blanket of dark silk over his pillow. He wanted to hear her pretty voice, with that high-toned accent, begging him for satisfaction while he rode her long and slow. Thankfully she had no idea of the lewd turn of his thoughts, or she would have fled from him, screaming.

They came to an open area where a middle-aged woman with fair hair and spectacles sat in front of a machine on an iron stand.

"My lady," the woman said, standing up to greet them. Her gaze flicked over Keir's unkempt appearance, taking in his damp clothes and the lack of a coat. A single twitch of her nose was the only recognition of the potent smell of whisky. "Sir."

"Mr. MacRae," Lady Merritt said, "this is my secretary, Miss Ewart." She gestured to a pair of sleek leather chairs in front of a fireplace framed by a white marble mantel. "Would you like to sit over there while I speak with her?"

No, he wouldn't. Or rather, he couldn't. It had been days since he'd had a decent rest. If he sat for even a few minutes, exhaustion would overtake him.

He shook his head. "I'll stand."

Lady Merritt gazed at him as if he and his problems interested her more than anything else in the world. The private tenderness in her eyes could have melted an icehouse in the dead of winter. "Would you like coffee?" she suggested. "With cream and sugar?"

That sounded so good, it almost weakened his knees. "Aye," he said gratefully.

In no time at all, the secretary had brought out a little silver tray with a coffee service and a footed porcelain mug. She set it on a table, where Lady Merritt proceeded to pour the coffee and stir in cream and sugar. Keir had never had a woman do that for him before. He drew closer, mesmerized by the graceful movements of her hands.

She gave him the mug, and he wrapped his fingers around it, relishing the radiant heat. Before drinking, however, he warily inspected the half-moon-shaped ledge at the rim of the cup.

"A mustache cup," Lady Merritt explained, noticing his hesitation. "That part at the top guards a gentleman's upper lip from the steam, and keeps mustache wax from melting into the beverage."

Keir couldn't hold back a grin as he lifted the cup to his lips. His own facial hair was close-trimmed, no wax necessary. But he'd seen the elaborate mustaches affected by wealthy men who had the time every morning to twirl and wax the ends into stiff little curls. Apparently the style required the making of special drinking mugs for them.

The coffee was rich and strong, possibly the best he'd ever had. So delicious, in fact, that he couldn't stop himself from downing it in just a few gulps. He was too famished to sip like a gentleman. Sheepishly he began to set the cup back on the tray, deciding it would be rude to ask for more.

Without even asking, Lady Merritt refilled his cup and prepared it again with sugar and cream. "I'll be but a moment," she said, before going to confer with the secretary.

Keir drank more slowly this time, and set the cup down. While the women talked, he meandered back to the desk to have a look at the shiny black contraption. A typewriter. He'd seen advertisements of them in newspapers. Intrigued, he bent to examine the alphabet keys mounted on tiny metal arms.

After the secretary left the room, Lady Merritt came to stand by Keir's side. Noticing his interest in the machine, she inserted a small sheet of letter paper and turned a roller to position it. "Push one of the letters," she invited.

Cautiously Keir touched a key, and a metal rod rose to touch an inked ribbon mounted in front of the paper. But when the arm lowered, the page was still blank.

"Harder," Lady Merritt advised, "so the letter plate strikes the paper."

Keir shook his head. "I dinna want to break it." The typewriter looked fragile and bloody expensive.

"You won't. Go on, try it." Smiling at his continued refusal, she said, "I'll type your name, then." She hunted for the correct keys, tapping each one firmly. He watched over her shoulder as his name emerged in tiny, perfect font.

Mr. Keir MacRae

"Why are the letters no' in alphabetical order?" Keir asked.

"If you type letters that are too close together, such as *S* and *T*, the metal arms jam together. Arranging the alphabet this way helps the machine operate smoothly. Shall I type something else?"

"Aye, your name."

A dimple appeared in her soft cheek as she complied. All Keir's attention was riveted on the tiny, delectable hollow. He wanted to press his lips there, touch his tongue to it.

Lady Merritt Sterling, she typed.

"Merritt," he repeated, testing the syllables on his lips. "'Tis a family name?"

"Not exactly. I was born during a storm, on a night when the doctor wasn't available, and the midwife was in her cups. But the local veterinarian, Dr. Merritt, volunteered to help my mother through her labor, and they decided to name me after him."

Keir felt a smile tugging at the corners of his mouth. Although he was half starved and had been in the devil's own mood for most of the day, a feeling of well-being began to creep over him.

As Lady Merritt turned the roller to free the paper, Keir caught a glimpse of her inner wrist, where a tracery of blue veins showed though the fine skin. Such a delicate, soft place. His gaze traveled along her back, savoring the full, neat curves of her, the trim waist and flared hips. The shape of her bottom, concealed by artfully draped skirts, he could only guess at. But he'd lay odds it was round and sweet, perfect to pat, squeeze, stroke—

As desire surged in his groin, he bit back a curse.

He was in a place of business, for God's sake. And she was a widow who should be treated with dignity. He tried to focus on how fine and cultured she was, and how much he respected her. When that didn't work, he thought very hard about the honor of Scotland.

A little lock of hair had slipped free of the complex arrangement of loops and swirls at the back of her head. The dark tendril lay against the back of her neck, curling at the end like a finger inviting him closer. How tender and vulnerable the nape of her neck looked. How good it would feel to nuzzle her there, and bite softly until she quivered and arched back against him. He would—

Bloody hell.

Desperately hunting for distractions, Keir glanced at their surroundings. He caught sight of a small but elaborately framed painting on one wall.

A portrait of Joshua Sterling.

That was enough to cool his lust.

The secretary had returned. Lady Merritt discarded the piece of typing paper in a little painted metal waste bin, and went to speak with her.

Keir's gaze fell to the contents of the bin. As soon as the women's backs were turned, he reached down to retrieve the typed page, folded it into a small square, and slid it into his trouser pocket.

He wandered to the painting for a closer look.

Joshua Sterling had been a fine-looking man, with rugged features and a level gaze. Keir remembered having liked him a great deal, especially after they'd discovered they both loved fly-fishing. Sterling had mentioned learning to fly cast in the streams and lakes around his native Boston, and Keir had invited him to visit Islay someday and fish for sea trout. Sterling had assured Keir he would take him up on the offer.

Poor bastard.

Sterling had reportedly died at sea. A shame, it was, for a man to have been taken in his prime, and with such a wife waiting at home. From what Keir had heard, there were no children from the union. No son to carry on his name and legacy.

He wondered if Lady Merritt would marry again. There was no doubt she could have any man she wanted. Was that why she planned to give her younger brother charge of Sterling Enterprises? So she could take part in society and find a husband?

Her voice interrupted his thoughts.

"I've always thought that portrait made my husband appear a bit too stern." Lady Merritt came to stand beside Keir. "I suspect he was trying to appear authoritative, since he knew the painting was intended for the company offices." She smiled slightly as she contemplated the portrait. "Perhaps someday I'll hire an artist to add a twinkle in his eyes, to make him look more like himself."

"How long were you married?" Keir was surprised to hear himself ask. As a rule, he rarely asked about people's personal business. But he couldn't help being intensely curious about this woman, who was unlike anyone he'd ever met.

"A year and a half," Lady Merritt replied. "I met Mr. Sterling when he came to London to establish a branch of his shipping firm." She paused. "I never imagined I would someday be running it."

"You've done very well," Keir commented, before it occurred to him that it might seem presumptuous, offering praise to someone so far above him.

Lady Merritt seemed pleased, however. "Thank you. Especially for not finishing that sentence with '. . . for a woman,' the way most people do. It always reminds me of the Samuel Johnson quote about a dog walking on its hind legs: 'It's not done well, but one is surprised to find it done at all.'"

Keir's lips twitched. "There's more than one woman who successfully runs a business on Islay. The button maker, and the butcher—" He broke off, wondering if he'd sounded condescending. "Although their shops can't be compared to a large shipping firm."

"The challenges are the same," Lady Merritt said. "Assuming the burden of responsibility, taking risks, evaluating problems . . ." She paused, looking wry. "I'm sorry to say mistakes still happen under my leadership. Your shipment being a case in point."

Keir shrugged. "Ah, well. There's always a knot somewhere in the rope."

"You're a gentleman, Mr. MacRae." She gave him a smile that crinkled her nose and tip-tilted her eyes. It made him a wee bit dizzy, that smile. It fed sunshine into his veins. He was dazzled by her, thinking she could have been some mythical creature. A fairy or even a goddess. Not some coldly aloof and perfect goddess . . . but a small and merry one.

Chapter 2

THE SKY HAD BEGUN to darken as they went back out to the wharf, and a lamplighter moved along a row of gas lamps. Merritt saw that the barge had departed for Deptford Buoys for another load of whisky. Its cargo had been unloaded and carried to the dock entrance.

"That's mine," MacRae said with a nod to a lone leather traveling trunk, repaired with a number of leather patches, that had been set amid a group of whisky casks.

Merritt followed the direction of his gaze. "Is there more?" she asked, thinking surely there had to be.

"No."

Afraid she might have given offense, Merritt said hastily, "I call that very efficient packing."

MacRae's lips twitched. "You could call it no' having very much to pack."

As they went to retrieve the trunk, they passed a group of longshoremen and warehousemen gathered around Luke. The sight caused Merritt to glow with pride.

"My brother's a very good manager," she said. "When he started at Sterling Enterprises, he insisted on spending the first month loading and unloading cargo right beside the longshoremen. Not only did he earn their respect, he now understands more than anyone about how difficult and dangerous their work is. Because of him, we've installed the latest safety equipment and procedures."

"It was also your doing," MacRae pointed out. "You hold the purse strings, aye? There's many a business owner who would choose profit over people."

"I could never do that. My employees are good, hardworking men, and most of them have families to support. If one of them were injured, or worse, because I didn't look after their safety . . ." Merritt paused and shook her head.

"I understand," he said. "Distilling is a dangerous business as well."

"It is?"

"Aye, there's a risk of fire and explosions at nearly every part of the process." They reached the trunk, and MacRae glanced over the crowd and across the wharf. "My men have gone to Deptford Buoys for the next load of casks, it looks like."

"I'm sure you wish you'd gone with them," Merritt said, trying to sound contrite.

MacRae shook his head, the creases at the outer corners of his eyes deepening as he looked down at her. "No' at the moment."

Something in his tone implied a compliment, and Merritt felt a little thrill of pleasure.

Grasping the trunk's side handle, MacRae hefted it to his shoulder with ease.

They proceeded to warehouse number three, where the whisky casks were being loaded, and walked around to a locked door at the side. "This leads to the upstairs flat," Merritt said, inserting and turning the key until the bolt slid back. "They'll be your private rooms, of course. You'll be able to come and go at will. But there's no connecting door to the warehouse storage. That part of the building can only be accessed when you and I are there with a revenue officer, each of us with our own key." She led the way up a narrow flight of stairs. "I'm afraid the flat has only cold running water. But you can heat water for a bath on the stove fire plate."

"I can wash with cold water the same as hot," he said.

"Oh, but not this time of year. You might catch a chill and come down with fever."

Now MacRae sounded amused. "I've never been ill a day in my life."

"You've never had fever?" Merritt asked.

"No."

"Never a sore throat or cough?"

"No."

"Not even a toothache?"

"No."

"How remarkably annoying," Merritt exclaimed, laughing. "How do you explain such perfect health?"

"Luck?"

"No one's that lucky." She unlocked the door at the top of the stairs. "It must be your diet. What do you eat?"

"Whatever's on the table," MacRae replied, following her into the flat and setting the trunk down.

Merritt pondered what little she knew about Scottish cuisine. "Porridge, I suppose."

"Aye, sometimes." Slowly MacRae began to investigate the room as they talked. It was simply furnished with a table and two chairs, and a small parlor stove with a single fire plate in the corner.

"I hope the flat is acceptable," Merritt said. "It's rather primitive."

"The floor of my house is paved with stone," he said dryly. "This is an improvement."

Merritt could have bitten her tongue. It wasn't at all like her to be so tactless. She tried to steer the conversation back on course. "You . . . you were telling me about your diet."

"Well, mostly I was raised on milk, potatoes, dulse, fish—"

"I beg your pardon, did you say 'dulse'? What is that, exactly?"

"A kind of seaweed," MacRae said. "As a lad, it was my job to go out at low tide before supper and cut handfuls of it from the rocks on shore." He opened a cupboard to view a small store of cooking supplies and utensils. "It goes in soup, or you can eat it raw." He glanced at her over his shoulder, amusement touching his lips as he saw her expression.

"Seaweed is the secret to good health?" Merritt asked dubiously.

"No, milady, that would be whisky. My men and I take a wee dram every day." Seeing her perplexed expression, he continued, "Whisky is the water of life. It warms the blood, keeps the spirits calm, and the heart strong."

"I wish I liked whisky, but I'm afraid it's not to my taste."

MacRae looked appalled. "Was it Scotch whisky?"

"I'm not sure," she said. "Whatever it was, it set my tongue on fire."

"It was no' Scotch, then, but rotgut. Islay whisky starts as hot as the devil's whisper . . . but then the flavors come through, and it might taste of cinnamon, or peat, or honeycomb fresh from the hive. It could taste of a long-ago walk on a winter's eve . . . or a kiss you once stole from your sweetheart in the hayloft. Whisky is yesterday's rain, distilled with barley into a vapor that rises like a will-o'-the-wisp, then set to bide its time in casks of good oak." His voice had turned as soft as a curl of smoke. "Someday we'll have a whisky, you and I. We'll toast health to our friends and peace to our foes . . . and we'll drink to the loves lost to time's perishing, as well as those yet to come."

Merritt stared at him, mesmerized. Her heart had begun to beat much too fast, and her face had turned hot for the second time that evening. "We'll drink to the loves yet to come for your sake," she managed to say, "but not mine."

MacRae's head tilted as he regarded her thoughtfully. "You dinna want to fall in love?"

Merritt turned to wander around the flat. "I've never cared for the phrase 'falling in love,' as if love were a hole in the ground. It's a choice, after all."

"Is it?" MacRae began to wander as well. He paused at the open archway of the main room to view the connecting bedroom, which contained a bed, dresser, and washstand. In one corner, a folding screen concealed a portable tin slipper tub and a modern water closet.

"Yes, a choice one must make according to common sense. I waited to marry until I found someone I knew would never break my heart." Merritt paused with a bleak smile before adding, "Of course, my heart was broken anyway, when his steamer sank in the mid-Atlantic. Nothing would ever be worth going through that again."

She looked up to find MacRae's gaze on her, as pale and bright as a flicker of moonlight. He made no comment, but there was something curiously comforting about the way he looked at her, as if there were nothing she could say that he wouldn't understand.

After a long moment, he turned and continued to explore the flat. Although the rooms were quite plain, Merritt had insisted on furnishing them with a few small luxuries: a soft tufted wool rug and upholstered chair, thick Turkish toweling and good white soap for washing. There were extra cotton quilted blankets for the bed, and white muslin curtains for the windows.

"You dinna think it will mend?" MacRae asked, and she realized he'd been thinking over what she'd said about her broken heart.

"It has already. But like most things broken and mended, it will never be the same."

"You're a young woman yet," he pointed out, "still of an age for breeding. Will you no' want bairns?"

Merritt blinked at his forwardness, before reminding herself that country folk were blunt about such matters. She decided to be equally frank. "I did, but as it turned out, I'm barren."

MacRae absorbed that without expression. He examined the cast-iron hand pump at the kitchen sink, running his fingers over the lever. "There are always little ones who need taking in."

"I might consider that someday. But for the time being, I have more than enough to occupy my time."

She paused. "What about you? Is there a sweetheart waiting for you back on Islay?"

"No."

"Why not? You're on the early side of your thirties, running a thriving business—"

"I wouldn't say 'thriving.' No' yet." At her questioning glance, he explained, "After my father passed away—five years ago, come January—I took charge of the distillery, and discovered Da had been as bad at business as he was good at making whisky. The books were a shamble, and we were deep in debt. Now the debts have been paid, and the distillery equipment upgraded. But with so much to be done, I've had no time for sweethearting. To be sure, I've no' met the woman who could tempt me away from a single life."

Merritt's brows lifted. "What kind of woman will she be?"

"I expect I'll know when I find her." MacRae took up the trunk and carried it to the bedroom.

"Shall I light the stove, and put on a kettle of water for you to wash with?" Merritt called after him.

Silence.

After a moment, MacRae leaned around the side of the archway to regard her with a frown.

"Thank you, milady, but I won't be needing that."

"Oh, dear. Well, washing with cold water will be better than nothing, I suppose."

"I'm no' going to wash," he said shortly.

"It will take only a few minutes."

"I've no reason to go to the docks all primpit up."

"I wouldn't call it primping," Merritt said. "Just basic hygiene." Seeing his stony expression, she added,

"Arguing about it will take the same amount of time as actually doing it."

"I can't wash with you in the flat; there's no door between this room and the next."

"Very well, I'll wait outside."

MacRae looked outraged. "Alone?"

"I'll be perfectly safe."

"The wharf is crawling with navvies and thieves!"

"Oh, come, you're making too much of it. I'll wait on the stairs, then." Now determined, Merritt fetched a large enameled jug from an open shelf, set it in the cast-iron sink, and reached for the pump handle. "But first, I'll fill this with water."

"That pump won't work unless you prime it first," MacRae informed her with a scowl.

"Yes it will," she said brightly. "This is a modern design, with a special valve that maintains a permanent prime." She took hold of the lever and pumped energetically. The cylinder sputtered and creaked and began to vibrate with accumulating pressure. She was perplexed as the spout remained dry. "Hmm. The water should be coming out by now."

"Milady, wait—" He headed toward her in swift strides.

"It's no trouble at all," Merritt said, putting more effort into pumping the lever. "I'll have it started soon."

But the lever became almost impossible to push down, and then it seemed to lock at an upright angle, while the entire assembly groaned and shuddered.

She let out a yelp and hopped backward as pressurized water spewed from the cylinder cap.

Fast as a leopard, MacRae reached the pump and

grappled with it, averting his face from the forceful spray. With a grunt of effort, he screwed the cylinder cap on more tightly, then struck the assembly base with the heel of his hand. The last of the water gurgled and gushed from the faucet into the sink.

Merritt hurried to fetch a dishcloth from the cabinet. "I'm so sorry," she exclaimed, coming back to him. "I had no idea that would happen, or I'd never have—" She broke off with a squeak of surprise as he shook his head like a wet dog, sending droplets everywhere.

MacRae turned toward her. With dismay, Merritt saw the water had gone down his front. The shirt was plastered over his torso, and his face and hair were dripping.

"Oh, dear," she said, apologetically holding out the dry dishcloth. "You're all drookit again. Here, take this and . . ." Her voice faded as he ignored the offering and kept coming toward her. Mildly alarmed, she leaned back to avoid contact with his wet body. Her breath caught as he gripped the edge of the sink on either side of her.

"You," he said flatly, "are a wee bully."

Merritt parted her lips to protest, but as she looked up at him, she saw amusement sparkling in his eyes.

Somewhere amid a chaos of heartbeats and nerves, she felt laughter trying to break through, and the more she tried to hold it back, the worse it became.

"Poor man . . . you haven't been dry since you s-set foot in England . . ."

Gasping, she began to dab at his face with the dishcloth, and MacRae held still. Water dripped from the locks hanging over his eyes, a few drops landing on her. She reached up to push his hair back. It felt like rich satin, the ends curling slightly against her fingers.

"I'm not a bully," she told him, continuing to wipe his face and throat. A few more giggles burst out, making her clumsy. "I was being h-helpful."

"You like telling people what to do," he accused softly, his gaze tracing over her features.

"Not at all. Oh, I feel so misjudged." But she was still laughing.

MacRae smiled, a flash of spendthrift charm amid the tawny beard. His teeth were very white. He was so gorgeous that Merritt's fingers went nerveless and she dropped the dishcloth. Her insides were singing with giddy excitement.

She waited for him to step back. But he didn't. She couldn't remember the last time she'd stood so close to a man that she'd felt the touch of his breath on her skin.

A question hung suspended in the silence.

The temptation to touch him was too overwhelming to resist. Slowly, almost timidly, she reached up to his bearded jaw.

Her stomach went light and she felt oddly weightless, as if the floor beneath her feet had suddenly disappeared. The illusion seemed so real that she gripped his arms reflexively, his muscles whipcord-taut beneath the wet layer of his shirt. She looked up into his eyes, the searing pale blue of hottest flame.

Her touch had spurred his breathing into a new, ragged rhythm.

"Milady," he said gruffly, "I'll be relying on your common sense now. Because at the moment, I have none."

Merritt's mouth had gone dry. Attraction pulsed all through her, making her fingers tighten rhythmically on his arms like the kneading of a cat's paws. "Wh-what about the honor of Scotland?" she managed to ask.

His head dipped lower, and she felt the brush of his lips and the coarse velvet of his beard against her forehead. An erotic sensation, rough and smooth all at once. She closed her eyes and wilted against the sink.

"The problem is . . . Scotsmen have a weakness." His murmur went through her skin and thrummed at the quick of her body, as if her spine had been replaced by a violin string.

"They do?"

"Aye . . . for bonnie dark-haired lasses who try to boss them."

"But I wasn't," she protested faintly, and felt the curve of his smile.

"A man knows when he's being bossed."

They stood together, motionless, with him braced over and around her.

His body was so close, so big and powerful. She wanted to explore the masculine terrain, charting every hard inch with her mouth and hands. It shocked her, how much she wanted him. Since Joshua's death, those needs had been set aside.

But something about Keir MacRae had made it impossible to ignore them any longer.

Carefully he clasped her chin and tilted it upward. Her blood was racing. He stared down at her intently, his eyes bright with glints of frost and fire.

When he spoke, his low voice was flicked with wry humor.

"You'll have your way, lass. I'll go wash in the other room, since you've already made a start of it for me. As for you . . . dinna move. Dinna touch anything. Because I doubt a lady would want to see a dobber like me dashing about in the a'thegither."

Which, Merritt thought dazedly, showed how little he knew about ladies.

MacRae pumped more water into the jug and carried it into the bedroom.

As he went into the next room, Merritt bent to retrieve the dishcloth and did her best to mop up the puddles on the floor. At the sounds from the next room—the clink of the porcelain basin at the washstand, the repeated sluices of water, some brushing and scrubbing—her imagination ran wild. She tried to distract herself by tidying the kitchen.

"Where are your men staying?" she eventually asked, wringing out the sodden dishcloth.

"They've taken rooms at the waterside tavern," came his reply.

"Shall we have someone carry their belongings there?"

"No, they did that themselves when the barge docked, and took their supper at the public house. They were like to starve to death."

"What about you?" She reached out to close the curtains over the window near the sink. "Have you had anything to eat?"

"That can wait 'til the morrow."

Merritt was about to reply, but she froze, her hand

suspended in midair. The window happened to be positioned to mirror the opening of the next room with remarkable clarity.

The naked form of Keir MacRae was reflected in the glass as he crossed the bedroom.

She went hot and cold all over, riveted as he bent to take a pair of trousers from the leather trunk. His movements were easy, graceful with a sense of coiled power, and that body—

"You're going to work through the night without any dinner at all?" she heard herself ask.

—with those long, elegant expanses of tightly knit muscle and sinew—

"I'll be fine," he said.

—was magnificent. Fantasy wrought into flesh. And just before he fastened the trousers, she couldn't help noticing the man was incredibly well-endowed.

Oh, this was beneath her, ogling a naked man. Had she no dignity? No decency? She had to stop before he caught her. Dragging her gaze away, she struggled to keep the conversation going.

"You would work more efficiently if you weren't weak from hunger," she called out.

The reply from the other room was slightly muffled. "I dinna have time for loafing at a public house."

Merritt's gaze darted back to the reflection in the window. She couldn't help it.

MacRae was pulling a shirt over his head and pushing his arms through the sleeves, his torso flexing and rippling with muscle. It was the body of a man accustomed to pushing himself without mercy.

This was the most interesting and exciting thing to

happen to Merritt in years. Perhaps in her entire adult life. Before her marriage, she would have been too shy to enjoy it. But now, as a widow who occupied a solitary bed . . . the sight of Keir MacRae's body made her achingly aware of what she'd once had and now missed.

Sighing, Merritt pulled the curtains closed and moved away from the window. Although she was unable to summon a full measure of her usual good humor, she tried to sound cheerful when MacRae came back into the room.

"Well," she said. "That's much better."

He looked refreshed and far more comfortable, wearing a knit wool waistcoat over the collarless shirt. His hair had been brushed back, but it was already falling over his forehead in shiny amber ribbons. The reek of whisky and sweat had been replaced by the scent of white soap and clean skin.

"I'll admit, 'tis preferable to smelling like a tavern floor." MacRae stopped in front of her, a glint of mischief in his eyes. "Now that you've taken charge of me, milady, what's your next command?"

The question was casual, with a hint of friendly teasing. But she was stunned by the reservoir of feeling he'd unlocked in her, so vast she was drowning in it. A feeling of pure longing. And until this moment, she'd never even known it was there.

She tried to think of some clever reply. But the only thing her mind could summon was something impulsive and silly.

Kiss me.

She would never say something so brazen, of course.

It would appear desperate or mad, and it would embarrass both of them. And for a business owner to behave in such an unprofessional manner with a customer—well, that didn't bear thinking of.

But as Merritt saw his blank expression, a horrid realization made something inside her plunge.

"Oh, God," she said faintly, her fingers flying to her mouth. "Did I say that out loud?"

Chapter 3

MACRAE SWALLOWED HARD BEFORE replying in a mere scrape of sound. "Aye."

Merritt was flooded with the deepest, fiercest blush of her life. "Could you . . . do you think . . . you might pretend you didn't hear?"

He shook his head, his own color rising. After what seemed an eternity, he replied huskily, "No' if it's something you want."

Was he asking for permission? Encouragement? She couldn't seem to catch up to her own heartbeats. Every inch of skin was on fire. "I don't suppose it . . . might be something you would want?"

She was always so composed—she was known for it. But at the moment she was all dither and turmoil, standing there in front of him.

Her mind flailed for a way to end the awful tension. She would make light of it. She would tell him it had been a frivolous comment at the end of a long day, and she hadn't meant it, and then she would laugh and—

MacRae drew closer and took her head in his hands. His thumbs caressed the edge of her jaw, the light rasp of calluses causing gooseflesh to rise everywhere. Holy Moses, he was really going to do it. She was about to be kissed by a stranger.

Too late to make light of anything now. *What have*

I done? She stared up at him with wide eyes, the dissonant notes of nerves and tension joining in a long, sweet chord of desire.

The crescents of his lashes, dark with gold tips, lowered slightly as he looked down at her. There was no place to hide from that piercing gaze. She felt so terribly exposed, every bit as naked as he'd been a few minutes ago.

His head bent, and his mouth found hers with a pressure as soft as snowfall.

She'd thought he might be rough or impatient, maybe a bit clumsy . . . she'd expected anything but the gently teasing caress that coaxed her lips apart before she was even aware of it. He tasted her with the tip of his tongue, a sensation that went down to her knees and weakened them. She felt herself list like a ship unable to right itself, but he gathered her firmly against him, his supportive arms closing around her. The tender focus on her mouth deepened until it had gone on longer than any kiss in her life, and still she wanted more.

He kissed her as if it were not the first time but the last, as if the world were about to end, and every second was worth a lifetime. He feasted on her with the craving of years. Blindly she caught at his mouth with hers, while her fingers tangled in his hair. The textures of him—plush velvet, rough bristle, wet silk—stimulated her beyond bearing. She'd never known desire like this, a swoon that kept deepening into more and more exquisite feeling.

All too soon, his mouth lifted, and to Merritt's eternal embarrassment, she whimpered and tried to pull him back to her.

"No, darlin'," he whispered. "You'll turn me to a live coal on the floor."

His mouth drifted to the tender angle beneath her jaw and nuzzled gently.

She tried to remember how to breathe. How to stand without her legs collapsing.

"Milady," she heard him say quietly. When she didn't, couldn't, respond, he tried again. "Merritt."

She loved the sound of her name on his lips, ghosted with a slight burr. Tipping her head back, she stared into his cool, bright eyes.

"No' for the world would I do you any harm," MacRae murmured, "or have it rumored that you've lowered yourself." Carefully he released her and stepped back. "That's why this will never happen again."

He was right. Merritt knew that. Reputations had been destroyed with far less cause than this. Even with the protection of a powerful family, she could still be harmed by scandal and alienated from good society. And she had no desire to live as an outcast. She liked having dinner with friends, attending dances and plays, and riding in the park. She liked going to church, attending holiday festivals, and belonging to women's clubs and charity organizations. The public sympathy she'd received since her husband's passing had allowed her to make some unconventional choices, such as running his company herself. But all that sympathy could be squandered in one careless moment.

She let out an unsteady breath, smoothed her skirts, and worked on recollecting herself.

"We don't have much time if we're to find something for you to eat before we return to the loading dock," she said, rather amazed at how normal she sounded.

MacRae gave her an adamant look. "I've already said I'll take no dinner, and that's my last word on the matter."

THE WEE BULLY had her way, of course. She towed Keir in the opposite direction of the warehouse dock, promising it wouldn't take long; they would purchase something from a street seller. Something that had already been made and could be eaten right there in public. He would feel much better, she assured him, and then her mind would be eased on his behalf.

Keir didn't object as strongly as he could have, partly because he was so hungry, his insides were fit to rattle like an empty churn. But mostly it was because this was the last time he would have this woman to himself, and despite his worries over the whisky shipment, he wanted a few more minutes with her.

He was still stunned by what had happened in the flat.

He was sure he hadn't kissed her the way a gentleman would. Thankfully, she hadn't seemed to mind. He'd tried to hold back, but it had been impossible. That mouth . . . sweet as honey from the comb. And the way she had molded bonelessly to him. She'd felt so exquisite in his arms, so fine and lush and warm.

He would relive that kiss in a thousand dreams. It had been as unlike anything that had happened in his life before, as it would be from everything that came after.

As they made their way through the filthy environs of the South London docks, he kept Merritt close beside him. It wasn't at all a place for her. The pavement was littered with refuse, the wicket gates and walls were plastered with faded advertisements and obscene images, and the windows of slop shops and public houses were covered with grime. Noise came in layers: steam cranes and sounds of construction, ships' bells and blasts, jingling carts, hooves and wheels, and the endless din of human voices.

"How invigorating," Merritt exclaimed, glancing around the scene with satisfaction.

He responded with a noncommittal grunt.

"Being in the thick of things," she continued, "where ships have docked with cargo from all over the world: pine from the West Indies, oranges from Seville, and tea from China. Yesterday one of our warehouses was stocked with ten thousand bundles of cinnamon, and the smell was *glorious*." She let out a satisfied sigh. "How busy and alive this place is. Look at all these people!"

"Aye," Keir said, gazing dourly at the milling crowd around them.

"The excitement of London always makes the family estate in Hampshire seem dull and quiet. There's nothing to do but fish, hunt, or walk through the countryside."

Keir almost smiled at that, thinking she'd just described his ideal day. "You dinna go back often?" he asked.

"Hardly ever since . . . well, since I had to start managing Sterling Enterprises. Fortunately, my family comes to London all the time." They came to a penny pie shop, and she exclaimed, "Here we are." Patrons had lined up in front of the shop, the queue extending along the pavement. Appetizing smells of hot pastry crust and fillings of minced beef or sweetened fruit drifted out from the doorway in a rich current. "This place is one of my favorites," Merritt said. "The pie maker keeps a clean shop, and always uses good ingredients." She assessed the size of the crowd with a slight frown. "Bother. The queue is too long."

"Are you sure—" Keir began, his gaze riveted on the little pies being carried out by customers. Each pie, with its flaky lid punctured at the top to let out fragrant steam, had been nestled in its own paraffined cardboard box. He could have eaten a dozen of them, boxes included.

"I'll take you to a food stall where we'll find something much faster," Merritt said, striding purposefully along the street.

They walked past offerings displayed on trestle boards and tables . . . puddings, sliced beef, boiled eggs, paper scoops filled with pickles, olives, salted nuts, or hot green peas glistening with bacon fat. There were roasted potatoes wrapped in waxed paper, crisp slivers of fried fish, smoked oysters crusted with salt, and cones of hardbake sweetmeats or brandy balls. Just a few minutes earlier, Keir had been willing to overlook his hunger in favor of more important concerns. Now that he was surrounded by this profusion of food, however, his empty stomach informed him that nothing else would happen until it was filled.

Merritt stopped at a stall featuring sandwiches, bread and butter, and cake.

"Evenin', milady," the stallkeeper said with a respectful tip of his hat.

"Mr. Gamp," she said warmly. "I've brought this gentleman to try the best ham sandwich in London."

"Smoked Hampshire ham, that's the secret," the stallkeeper said proudly as he set out a pasteboard box. "That, and the missus bakes the bread herself. Barm-leavened, to make it soft and sweet." Deftly he cut one of the sandwiches on the board into triangles. The sturdy slices of bread had been filled with a plump stack of thinly sliced ham and a layer of watercress.

"How much?" Keir asked, swallowing hard at the sight.

"For tuppence, you'll get a sandwich and a mug of beer," Gamp replied.

It was twice as much as the same meal would have cost in Islay. Keir handed over the money without a quibble.

After ceremoniously placing a wrapped sandwich in the pasteboard box, Gamp added a pickle and an individual loaf of currant cake, and said to Merritt, "Extries for any friend of yours, milady."

She beamed at him. "You're too kind, Mr. Gamp."

Keir went with Merritt to stand beneath the eaves of a top-heavy building, where he proceeded to wolf down his food. Ordinarily he would have felt self-conscious, eating in front of a lady—while standing on a public street, no less—but he was too hungry to care.

After he'd finished the sandwich and drained the beer, Keir was filled with fresh energy. He felt as if he could stock every cask of the whisky shipment into the warehouse singlehandedly.

He went to drop the empty mug into a bin beneath Gamp's stall table, and admitted to Merritt, "You could say, 'I told you so,' and you'd be in the right of it."

She laughed. "I never say, 'I told you so.' It never helps, and everyone hates hearing it."

Flecks of light danced over her cheeks, scattered by the nearby perforated iron firepots at the stall. It made her appear to sparkle like a creature out of Scottish lore. Beautiful women were often dangerous in those stories: disguised as a water spirit or a witch, to ensnare a hapless male and lead him to his fate. No escape, no mercy. As a young boy, Keir had always wondered why the men hadn't tried to resist.

"Ah, weel," his father had explained, "they're enchanters of men, bonnie women are, and when they beckon, we can't help but follow."

"I wouldn't!" Keir had said indignantly. "I'd stay home and take care of Mither."

There had come a chuckle from the stove, where his mother had been frying potatoes. "A good laddie, y'are," she'd called out.

His father had grinned and stretched out before the hearth, lacing his fingers together over his middle. "Someday, lad, you'll ken exactly why a man falls to temptation, even knowing the better of it."

And, as in most things, Keir thought ruefully, his father had been right.

IT WAS ONLY a short walk back to the wharf, past houses and shops with light glowing from windows and in glass cases of streetlamps. Merritt began to dread the moment when they reached the warehouse and this peculiar but delightful interlude with a stranger would be over. How long it had been since she'd felt this giddiness, as if she were being courted. She'd forgotten how much she'd liked it. How odd that the man to remind her was a rough-and-ready whisky distiller from a remote Scottish island.

MacRae accompanied her to Sterling Enterprises, and stopped with her just inside the entrance. "When will you go home?" he asked, as if he were concerned about leaving her there.

"I'll take my leave after I meet with Mr. Gruinard, the supervising exciseman," Merritt said. "He has an office here in the building. I'm sure I can persuade him to wait at least until noon tomorrow before interfering with the bond terms."

The hint of a smile lurked in the corners of his lips as he stared down at her. "How could anyone refuse you?"

That tempting forelock of hair had fallen over his forehead again. Merritt had to clench her hand to keep from reaching up and stroking it back. "You mustn't hesitate to come to me if there's anything you need," she told him. "Recommendations for places to go, or introductions to someone—or if there's a problem with the flat—I'm here most days, and of course my secretary or Luke will provide assistance—"

"I don't expect I'll be troubling you, milady."

"It would be no trouble. Just walk over here from the flat whenever you like, and . . . we'll go to the penny pie shop."

He nodded, but she knew he had no intention of taking her up on the invitation.

That was probably for the best.

But as they parted company, Merritt had a sense of being abandoned, deprived of something . . . not unlike a puppy whose owner had just left the house. What was the word for it? Forlorn, she decided. Yes. She was feeling forlorn, and that would not do.

Action must be taken.

She just wasn't certain what that was yet.

DURING AN HOUR of negotiations with Mr. Gruinard, Merritt managed to gain a few small but valuable concessions. Now she could finally go home. It had been a long day, and she was eager to sit by the fire with a pair of soft slippers on her feet. But no matter how tired she was, the cogs of her brain wouldn't stop turning, and she knew already she would be in for a night of poor sleep.

She decided to have her carriage stop at warehouse number three on the way home. After all, as a caring older sister, she was concerned for her brother's welfare, and as a responsible employer, it was her place to find out how work was progressing.

And if, in the process of speaking to Luke, she happened to catch sight of Keir MacRae . . . well, that was entirely incidental.

The warehouse was a hive of activity. A steam-powered crane creaked and groaned, and occasionally hissed as if with a sigh of relief, after lifting cargo to the upper level of the building.

Curses and grunts of effort filled the air as the warehousemen worked. Even with ramps and hand trucks, it took brute effort to maneuver and rack the whisky barrels.

Merritt entered the building as inconspicuously as possible, taking care not to block anyone's path. Nearby, men strained to push heavily loaded hand trucks up a ramp, where a warehouse gauger stamped each cask. At least a half-dozen workers with tin drinking cups had gone to the corner, where stone jugs of water had been set in barrels of sawdust and ice.

Her presence was quickly noticed by one of the foremen, who offered to escort her to the upper floor where Luke was working. They went up on a hand-powered lift, operated by a working rope at the front of the cage. During the ascent, Merritt gazed around the warehouse, but even from her elevated vantage point, there was no sign of Keir MacRae.

She found Luke on his hands and knees, marking the floor with chalk to indicate where to store the next load of casks. "Would you like to hear some good news?" she asked as she approached him.

A slow grin crossed her brother's sweat-streaked face at the sight of her. He stood and dusted his hands together, creating little clouds of chalk. "Tell me."

"I just met with Mr. Gruinard, and he said even if we don't have all the whisky stamped and stocked inside the warehouse by noon, as long as the casks are set inside the bonded yard—"

"The one we're only allowed to use for timber?"

"Yes, that one—Mr. Gruinard will make an exception and let us use it as a temporary holding area for the whisky until we finish the job."

"Thank God," Luke said fervently. "Well done, sis." He gave her a quizzical glance. "Is that all?"

"What do you mean, 'Is that all?'" Merritt asked with a laugh. "Isn't it enough?"

"Well, yes, but . . . there was no need to tell me in person at this hour. You could have sent a note, or let it wait until morning."

"I thought you'd want to know right away. And I wanted to see for myself how you were doing."

"I'm so touched by your concern," Luke said. "Especially since you've never taken such trouble over me before."

"What twaddle," Merritt exclaimed good-naturedly. "Two weeks ago, I brought soup and tea to you—here in this very warehouse—when you had the sniffles!"

Setting his hands on his hips in a relaxed posture, Luke said in a dry undertone, "Let's not pretend this visit has anything to do with me. You came here hoping for a glimpse of a certain bearded Scotsman."

She lowered her voice as she asked, "Did he say anything to you?"

"About what?"

"About *me*."

"Why yes, we stopped in the middle of work to gossip over tea. Then we made plans to visit the milliner and try on bonnets together—"

"Oh, hush," Merritt whispered sharply, both amused and annoyed.

Luke regarded her with a slow shake of his head. "Be careful, sis."

Her smile faded. "I'm sure I don't know what you mean."

"I'm referring to the mistake you've apparently already decided to make." Taking in her offended expression, Luke added, "Don't misunderstand me—MacRae seems as good-natured and steady as they come. A brick. But there's no part of your future that would naturally align with any part of his. On top of that, after the way you've flouted convention in recent years, London society is dying to catch you in a scandal. Don't provide them with one."

To receive a lecture on conduct from a younger

sibling—who was no saint himself—was bad enough. But it was even worse to see the concern in Luke's gaze, as if he suspected something had happened at the warehouse flat. Was it that obvious? She felt as if she were walking around with a large scarlet letter stitched across her bodice.

She kept her tone light even though her chest was tight with anger. "Why in heaven's name am I being lectured for something I haven't done?"

"It's not a lecture. Just a reminder. The devil never tries to make people do the wrong thing by scaring them. He tempts them."

Merritt's forced laugh came out as brittle as overcooked toffee. "Dear, are you claiming Mr. MacRae is the devil in disguise?"

"If he were," Luke replied quietly, "I'd say the disguise has been pretty damned successful so far."

She flushed deeply, and strove to keep her voice calm, even though she was seething. "If this is all the thanks I'll receive for my efforts with Mr. Gruinard, I'll take my leave now."

Turning on her heel, she began to make a smart exit, heading to the stairs instead of waiting for someone to operate the lift. The effect was ruined, however, as she crossed in front of a ramp leading to an upper row of barrel racks, and heard a muffled shout.

Pausing in confusion, Merritt glanced toward the noise and saw a heavy barrel rolling toward her.

Chapter 4

BEFORE ANOTHER SECOND HAD passed, Merritt felt herself snatched up and hauled out of the barrel's path. Momentum spun her in a half circle until she was brought abruptly against a tough, unyielding surface.

Dazedly she realized someone was holding her. Her senses gathered pleasurable impressions . . . the deep warmth of a masculine body . . . a sturdy arm around her back . . . a low murmur close to her ear.

"Easy, lass. I have you."

A lock of her hair had slipped free of its pins. The little hat that had been attached to the top of her head with a comb had been knocked askew. Slightly disoriented, she looked up into Keir MacRae's smiling blue eyes.

"Thank you," she said breathlessly. "I should have paid more attention to where I was going. How—how did you—"

"I'd just finished stocking a rack, and was coming to say good evening." Gently MacRae stroked back the loose curl over her eyes, and caught the hat just as it began to slide off her head. He regarded it quizzically. "What's this?"

"My hat." It was little more than a knot of feathers and a puff of gauze affixed to a velvet base. Merritt took it from him and fumbled to fasten it back in place.

His lips twitched. "A hat is for shielding you from sun or rain. That wee thing is no' a hat."

Her toes curled deliciously at the soft teasing. "I'll have you know it's the latest fashion."

"It reminds me of a lapwing."

"A what?"

"A bonnie wee bird with a spray of feathers at the back of her head." His arm was still behind her back, holding her securely. It felt too good, being this close to him. She realized the reason she'd been so cross with Luke was because he'd been right: She was heading for trouble. Running headlong toward it, in fact.

Luke had caught the stray barrel and was in the process of rolling it back up the ramp, while a foreman spoke sternly to a young warehouseman. The scarlet-faced young man, still in his teens, cast a distraught glance at Merritt. "I'm so very sorry, milady, I—I beg your pardon—"

"Dinna fash yourself, lad," MacRae said easily, making certain Merritt was steady before letting go of her. "Her ladyship suffered no harm."

"It was my fault," Merritt said. "I should have been more alert."

"No one's alert at this hour," Luke said, rolling the barrel back up the ramp and righting it with a grunt of effort. "Try rolling the barrel on the brim instead of the side," he advised the young warehouseman. "It's slower but easier to control. I'll show you, but first—" He glanced at Merritt over his shoulder, the crease of a frown appearing between his dark brows. Reluctantly he asked, "MacRae, would you be willing to escort my sister out to her carriage?"

"Aye, of course," MacRae said promptly.

Merritt smiled and reached out to take MacRae's arm. "I'd rather take the stairs than the lift."

As they proceeded down the long, enclosed staircase, Merritt told him about her meeting with the excise officer. MacRae was gratifyingly impressed by her negotiating skills, and thanked her for buying the extra time. They would need it, he said, as progress had been steady but slower than he would have liked.

"You must be exhausted," Merritt said in concern.

"'Tis weary work," he admitted, "but there'll be an end of it tomorrow, and I'll have a good sound sleep."

"And after that?"

"Sales meetings the rest of the week, with businesses who are after buying whisky for independent bottling."

"They would put their own labels on it?"

MacRae nodded, looking rueful. "It's no' something I'd prefer," he admitted, "but it's profitable, and there are many improvements needing to be made to the distillery."

They stopped at the bottom of the stairwell, and Merritt turned to look up into his shadowed face.

Time for good-bye, she thought, and the forlorn feeling came over her again.

"It sounds as if your days are occupied," she said, trying to sound casual, "but what about the evenings? Have you made plans? I could give a small, informal dinner at my house, and introduce you to some lovely people. I promise you would enjoy yourself—"

"No," MacRae said hastily. "Thank you, but I'll have been keeping company with new folk all day."

"I understand." Merritt hesitated. "Perhaps it should be just the two of us. I have an excellent cook.

She'll make something simple. Not tomorrow night, of course—you'll want to rest. But the next night, you must come to my house for dinner. We'll have a quiet, relaxing evening."

MacRae stayed unnervingly silent. He stared at her steadily, his eyes a flicker of starlight in the shadows.

He was going to refuse. How could she persuade him?

"You did say we would have a whisky someday," she reminded him. "This will be the perfect opportunity."

"Merritt—"

"Which reminds me—I wanted to ask about the name stamped on your whisky casks. The very long one that starts with P."

"Priobairneach."

"Yes, what does it mean?"

After a moment, MacRae said, "In English it means something like 'sudden excitement.'"

She smiled at that. "Will you bring some for me to try?"

But there was no answering smile. "Merritt," he said quietly, "you know why I cannot come."

As she pondered how to reply, she thought of a conversation she'd once had with her father, the most sensible man who'd ever existed. They'd been talking about various problems she'd faced after taking the reins at Sterling Enterprises, and she'd asked how he knew whether a risk was worth taking.

Her father had said, "Before taking a risk, begin by asking yourself what's important to you."

Time, Merritt thought. *Life is full of wasted time.*

She hadn't realized it until now, but her awareness of squandered time had been growing during the past year, eroding her usual patience. So many rules had been invented to keep people apart and wall off every natural instinct. She was tired of them. She had started to resent all the invisible barriers between herself and what she wanted.

It occurred to her this must be how her mother often felt. As a strong-willed young heiress, Mama had come to England with her younger sister, Aunt Daisy, when no gentlemen in New York had been willing to offer for either of them. Wallflowers, both of them, chafing at the limitations of polite behavior. Even now, Mama spoke and acted a little too freely at times, but Papa seemed to enjoy it.

"Mr. MacRae," Merritt said, "for the past three years, I've managed a shipping firm, attended hundreds of business meetings, and filled out paperwork for days on end. Other than my younger brother, my closest companion has been the company accountant. This evening, I met with a government excise supervisor for nearly two hours. As you might guess, none of this was the stuff of my childhood dreams. I'm not complaining, only pointing out that far too much of life is filled with responsibilities we haven't necessarily asked for. Which is why I feel perfectly justified in having dinner with a friend."

"Friend," MacRae repeated, now looking sardonic. "Is that what I am?"

"Yes, why not?"

He moved closer to her in the stairwell, his shadow falling over her. The glow of a gas lamp silhouetted his head.

"You would no' call me that," he said softly, "if you understood the temptation you are to me."

There it was—the truth laid out before them.

Merritt decided to ignore it.

"Temptation can be resisted," she said reasonably. "One makes a decision and sticks to it. I'm sure I'll be able to rely on your honor, as well as my own. Let's enjoy each other's company—discreetly, of course—without complications. Dinner will be at eight o'clock. My house is not far from here, number 3 Carnation Lane. Red brick, with white trim, and ivy on the—"

She broke off as her helpful directions were extinguished by the sweet, hot shock of his mouth on hers.

It was not the kiss a friend would give. It was heat and demand, fused in a raw sensuality that demolished her balance. Her gloved hands slid up to grip his broad shoulders. The kiss went on and on, exploring deliciously, wringing sensation from her mouth. One of his hands wandered over her back, stroking her spine into a pleasured arch. Her breasts felt full and tender, and she longed for him to touch them . . . kiss them . . . oh, God, she'd lost her mind.

She felt how hard he was all around her, every muscle taut. His breath rode roughshod on every powerful rise and fall of his chest. Reaching down, he gripped her hips to pull them high against an unmistakably rigid, swollen shape. She thought of how it would feel to lie spread beneath him, with all that hardness inside her, and a faint moan slipped from her throat.

MacRae licked at the sound as if he could taste it, and broke the kiss to rest his forehead against hers. Their panting breaths mingled.

It was hard to speak with him still clasping her hips against his. Every part of her was throbbing. "I suppose you think that proved a point," she managed to say.

"Aye," he said gruffly. "Dinna tempt me to prove it again." But he ducked his head to steal another kiss . . . and another . . . nuzzling and biting gently at her lips as if he couldn't help himself. He let out a shaken sigh and held her tightly, and said something in Gaelic that sounded like a curse.

Slowly, almost painfully, he eased their bodies apart and went to brace his hands against the wall of the stairwell. Lowering his head, he took several long, deliberate breaths.

Realizing he was willing his arousal to subside—and not finding it easy—Merritt felt a responsive quiver deep in her belly.

Eventually he pushed away from the wall and reached for the door, and held it open for her.

The cold night air drew a tremor from her as MacRae escorted her out to the carriage.

Upon seeing their approach, the footman hastened to open the carriage door and pull down the folding step.

Before entering the vehicle, Merritt paused to say one last thing to MacRae. She was pleased by how casual and ordinary she was able to sound, with all her thoughts in chaos. "I'll expect you at my house the day after tomorrow."

His eyes narrowed. "I dinna say I would come, you wee bully."

"Don't forget the whisky," she said, and hastily entered the carriage before he could reply.

Chapter 5

AFTER A SMALL FORTUNE in whisky had been stamped and delivered safely into the bonded warehouse, it had taken every last spark of Keir's remaining energy to climb the stairs to his flat. He'd slept all through the afternoon and night, and had awakened feeling refreshed and ready to take on the world.

The day's meetings had required the purchase of a new coat, since the one he'd brought needed to be laundered and was so old it probably wouldn't survive the washing. First, he'd gone to the penny pie shop, where he'd eaten his fill of pies for breakfast and asked where he might find some ready-made clothing.

For the first time in his life, Keir bought a garment stitched by machine. The black wool peacoat, styled after the ones worn by sailors and longshoremen, was double-breasted and cut short enough to allow the legs freedom of movement. It fit well enough, although the sleeves were too short and the middle too loose. He proceeded to a public house for a meeting with the manager, who intended to place a large order after his lawyer reviewed the details of the independent bottling contract.

His next meeting was on the west side, in the St. James area. At the suggestion of one of Islay's well-to-do residents, an elderly lawyer named Gordan Catach, Keir had decided to approach a prominent gentlemen's club with the intention of selling a special lot of forty-year-old single malt.

"The most famous clubs are White's, Brooks's, and Boodle's," Catach had told him. "Any of those would have the means to pay a steep asking price. But if I were you, lad, I'd first try Jenner's. It doesnae have so high a pedigree as the others, but 'tis the one everyone wants to belong to. Some gentlemen—higher-ups, mind ye—spend as long as ten years on the waiting list."

"How's that?"

"Jenner's offers the most luxury, the finest food and liquor . . . there's even a smoking room where they'll hand-roll a fresh cigar to suit your taste. The club was started lang ago by a professional boxer. His daughter married the Duke of Kingston, who owns the place now."

Keir, who couldn't have cared less about some doddering old aristocrat, responded with an indifferent shrug. "'Tis no' unusual for a duke to own prime London real estate."

"Aye, but the interesting part is, Kingston ran the club himself for a time." To make sure Keir understood the significance, Catach added, "Noblemen *never* work. To their minds it lowers them, ye ken, and costs them the respect of common folk as well as their peers."

"He must have had no choice," Keir mused.

"To be sure. But the duke made Jenner's what it is, and enriched himself in the process." Catach had shaken his head with a mixture of admiration and envy. "A charmed life, that one's had. They say in his youth, Kingston was as wicked as the devil himself. The bane of every man with a pretty wife. Then he married a rich woman and settled into a respectable middle age. For Kingston, the wages of sin have been nothing but gold and treasure."

"He sounds like a selfish pult," Keir said flatly. "I'll no' be selling my whisky to such a man."

"Dinna be a dunderclunk, lad. You won't be meeting with the duke himself. He gave over the running of it to someone else lang ago. Now, you'll want to write to the club steward. He'll have the charge of placing orders with tradesmen and superintending the cellar."

At Catach's urging, Keir had struck up a correspondence with Horace Hoagland, the managing steward of Jenner's, and they'd agreed to meet when Keir came to London.

Keir did his best to appear relaxed as he entered Jenner's with a small wooden case containing whisky samples. He might appear a primitive lout to these people, but he was damned if he'd act like one. Still, it was difficult not to stand and stare slack-jawed at his surroundings. Jenner's was more opulent than any place Keir had ever set foot in, with acres of white marble, plasterwork covered in gold leaf, rich soundless carpeting, and a canopy of crystal chandeliers overhead. The club was centered around a cavernous central hall with a grand staircase and marble balcony railings extending along the upper floors.

Thankfully there were no snouty aristocratic patrons in sight, only servants busy cleaning and polishing things that already looked clean and polished.

"Mr. MacRae." A stocky middle-aged man, dressed

to the nines in a fine dark suit of clothes with shiny buttons, approached him immediately. "Horace Hoagland, the club steward," he said, extending his hand. "A pleasure to finally meet you."

The steward's friendly demeanor put Keir at ease, and they exchanged a firm handshake.

"Welcome to Jenner's," Hoagland said. "What do you think of the place?"

"'Tis very grand."

The steward smiled. "I count myself the luckiest chap in the world, being able to work here." He led the way to a series of rooms with box-paneled ceilings and leather Chesterfield couches, and deep chairs arranged around small tables. Freshly ironed newspapers and sparkling crystal cigar dishes had been set out on the tables. "I have a special fondness for Islay single malt," Hoagland remarked. "Years ago, a Scottish cousin made a gift to me of a bottle from the MacRae distillery." He sighed reminiscently. "Smooth as cream, with a finish like a charred apple orchard. Extraordinary."

"My father loved what he did."

"He taught you his methods?"

"Since I was knee high," Keir assured him. "I started by carrying bags of malt to the kiln, and went on to learn every job in the distillery."

They sat at a table, where a round tray of clean drinking glasses had been set out. Keir unlatched the wooden sample box he'd brought, revealing a row of miniature bottles, each containing a dram of whisky.

"This is the batch you wrote to me about?" Hoagland asked, staring at the samples with frank anticipation.

"Aye. After my father's passing, my men and I took

inventory at the distillery and found a hidden cellar where he'd stashed a hogshead of single malt. It had been sitting there untouched for forty years." Keir uncorked one of the miniature bottles and poured the amber liquid into a glass. "We finished it in first-fill sherry quarter casks for a year, bottled it, and named it Ulaidh Lachlan—Lachlan's Treasure—in honor of my father."

"How many bottles in total?"

"Two hundred ninety-nine," Keir replied.

Hoagland swirled the whisky in the glass, moved it close to his nose, and inhaled deeply. He took a taste, paying attention to the soft, rolling feel of it in his mouth. The subtle variations of his expression revealed the progression of flavors . . . the opening of dry, dusty wood and salt brine, like lifting the lid of a pirate's treasure chest . . . the richness of bread pudding . . . finishing with a surprising meringue lightness and a touch of smoke.

The club steward was silent for a moment, staring at the remaining contents of the glass. "Isn't that something," he murmured. "A rare handsome whisky. I don't believe I've ever tasted its equal." He tasted it again, savoring it. "How round the malt is."

"We bottled it at cask strength."

Hoagland took another sip, closing his eyes to better appreciate it, and released a long sigh. "How much for the lot?" he asked.

"All of it?"

"All two hundred ninety-nine bottles."

"Three thousand pounds," Keir said readily.

Hoagland looked resigned rather than surprised. It was a fortune—at least ten times what ordinary whisky would cost. But they both knew this was no ordinary whisky. They both knew, also, that Keir could easily find another buyer.

"For that sum," Hoagland said, "I'll expect you to throw in the rest of those samples."

Keir grinned and nudged the wooden box toward him.

Hoagland parted his lips to say something, but paused and looked over Keir's shoulder, his face brightening. "You're in luck, MacRae," he said. "The Duke of Kingston himself just entered the club rooms. It's possible you'll have the honor of meeting His Grace, if he comes this way."

Having never seen a duke before, Keir resisted a strong temptation to twist in his chair and take a look. "I was told Kingston didn't have the running of the club anymore," he remarked.

"No, indeed. But the duke still considers Jenner's the jewel in the crown of his empire, and he never goes long without stopping by." Still gazing at Kingston, Hoagland glowed as if in the presence of some celestial being. "His Grace is speaking with the head waiter. No other gentleman of his status would take such notice of an inferior. But the duke is a most gracious man."

Keir was vaguely annoyed by the man's reverence, which seemed a hairsbreadth away from fawning.

"Ah—yes—he's walking over here," the steward exclaimed, and pushed his chair back to stand.

Keir wondered if he should stand as well. Was that something only servants did, or were commoners obliged to rise to their feet? No—he wouldn't stand to meet the duke like a boy answering a question from the village schoolmaster. But then he thought of how his father had always cautioned, "The proudest nettle grows on a dung heap."

Reluctantly he began to ask the steward, "Should I—"

"Yes," Hoagland said with quiet urgency, his gaze riveted on the approaching duke.

Keir pushed back his chair and stood to face Kingston.

From what he'd been told about the duke's past, Keir would have expected a florid old dandy, or a rheumy-eyed satyr. Anything but this elegantly lean man who moved with the supple ease of a tomcat. His clean-shaven face was a marvel of bone structure: a gift of male beauty that could never be outlived. The dark gold of his hair was silvered at the temples and sides, and time had weathered his complexion here and there with fine lines. But the signs of maturity only made him seem more powerful. The sheer presence of the man caused the hairs on Keir's arms to prickle in warning beneath the too-short sleeves of his ready-made coat.

"Hoagland," Kingston said in a voice like expensive liquor on ice, "it's good to see you. Your son is better, I trust?"

"You're very kind to ask, Your Grace. Yes, he's recovered fully from his tumble. The poor lad's grown so fast, he hasn't yet learned to manage those long arms and legs. A rackabones, my wife calls him."

"My boy Ivo is the same. He's shot up like a weed of late."

"Will he grow as tall as your other two sons, do you expect?"

"By force of will, if necessary," the duke replied dryly. "Ivo has informed me he has no intention of being the youngest *and* the shortest."

Hoagland chuckled and proceeded to make introductions. "Your Grace, this man, Mr. Keir MacRae, has brought whisky samples from his distillery in Islay. Will you try a dram? I recommend it highly."

"No, it's a bit early for—" The duke broke off as his gaze moved to Keir.

Keir found himself staring into blue eyes, as light and piercing as winter frost. The man's stillness reminded him of a golden eagle sighting prey on the island.

The oddly charged silence made Keir more and more uncomfortable. Finally, the duke dragged his gaze from Keir's and turned his attention to the perplexed steward, who was looking back and forth between them. "On the other hand," Kingston said in a careful monotone, "why not? Pour one for me, Hoagland."

"Yes, Your Grace." Nimbly the steward uncorked a dram bottle and emptied it into a clean glass.

The duke reached for the glass without ceremony, not bothering to swirl or sniff the contents. He tossed back the fine whisky with a stiff movement of the wrist, as if it were a dose of patent medicine.

Keir watched in mute outrage, wondering if it had been intended as an insult.

Gazing down at the empty glass in his hand, the duke appeared to be collecting his thoughts.

Hoagland was still looking from one of them to the other, appearing more baffled by the moment.

What the bloody hell was going on?

Kingston's head finally lifted, his expression inscrutable, his tone friendly. "You were born and raised on Islay?"

"Raised," Keir replied cautiously.

With undue care, the duke set down the glass. "A superlative single malt," he commented. "Less peat and far more complexity than I'd expect from an Islay whisky."

Slightly mollified by the praise, Keir said, "My father was never one for the big peaty whiskies."

"He's no longer with you?"

"Gone these four years past."

"I'm sorry to hear it. And your mother?"

"Gone as well."

After another unaccountably long silence, the duke picked up the empty dram bottle and regarded the label. "MacRae," he said. "A fine old Scottish name. Do you have family in England?"

"None that I know of."

"Have you been to England before?"

"Once, on business."

"You've found satisfactory accommodations, I hope?"

"Aye, a flat at one of the Sterling warehouses."

"Have you met Lady Merritt?"

The mere mention of her name softened the tension in the atmosphere almost miraculously. Keir felt the small muscles of his face relaxing. "Aye, I've had the honor. A kind and bonnie woman, she is."

The duke's sudden easy smile was like the sun giving off light. "I've known her since the day she was born."

Keir's brows lifted slightly. "You were there during the storm?"

"She told you about that? Yes, I was one of the volunteers who went out in search of a midwife or doctor. It didn't look promising when one of us brought back a veterinarian, but to his credit, it all turned out well."

"I'd say the credit should go to Lady Merritt's mither," Keir said.

Kingston grinned. "You're right."

Hoagland wore a distracted expression as he beheld the two of them. "Mr. MacRae," he ventured, "shall we proceed with a partial payment and delivery agreement?"

"A verbal agreement will do for now," Keir replied. "I have another meeting soon, and I dinna like to be late." He paused, thinking over his schedule. "Shall I come back Friday?"

Hoagland nodded. "Any time before noon."

Keir responded with a businesslike nod. "I'll be off, then." He turned to find the duke's intent gaze still on him. "A pleasure, Your Grace."

"I'm glad—" the duke began, but fell abruptly silent. He looked away and cleared his throat as if he were just now feeling the sting of the whisky.

Keir tilted his head slightly, regarding Kingston with a frown. Was the man not well? Had he recently received bad news?

Hoagland intervened hastily. "Like His Grace, I'm glad to have made your acquaintance, MacRae. I look forward to our next meeting on Friday."

Chapter 6

THE REST OF THE day went well. Keir met with a hotel manager and then a tavernkeep in Farrington, both of whom had agreed to contracts for private bottling. After that he went to collect his men, Owen and Slorach, and accompanied them to the Victoria Railway Station, where they would take an express up to Glasgow, and from there proceed to Islay.

Slorach, a dour and wizened Calvinist of sixty-five, was more than eager to leave London, which he regarded as an unwholesome den of sin and beggary.

Owen, on the other hand, a lighthearted lad barely out of his teens, was reluctant to go back to Islay. "There are many things I havnae done yet in London," he protested.

"Aye," returned Slorach dryly, "and 'tis well that you'll be gang back to Islay before the doing of them." Turning to Keir, the elderly man said ruefully, "He'll be griping all the way home. But I gave my word to his mither I'd keep him out of trooble." Looking grim, he added, "'Twould be my preference to take you back with us."

Keir grinned at him affectionately. "Dinna worry, I'll be keeping myself out of trooble."

"London's no place for the like of you, young MacRae. Dinna tarry one day more than you must."

"I won't."

After seeing the pair off, Keir went in search of a hansom cab. As he walked past construction scaffolding, a steam-engine excavator, a factory, and a tenement building, he reflected that Slorach's reaction to the city of five million was entirely understandable. There was too much activity and noise, too much of everything, for a man accustomed to the cool green quiet of a Scottish island.

But as Keir thought about seeing Merritt that night, he was filled with anticipation. He yearned for her company, as if she were a drug. No, not a drug . . . a spark of magic in an ordinary life. A good life, which he happened to love.

But he knew down to his soul how much of a danger Merritt was to him. The more he came to know her, the stronger this yearning would grow, until any chance of happiness had slipped away like sand through his fingers. He'd spend the rest of his days consumed by desire for a woman who would always be as distant from his reach as the most far-flung star.

Still . . . he had to see her one last time. He'd allow himself that much. After that, he'd finish his business in London and return to Islay.

Five hundred miles wouldn't be nearly enough distance to put between them.

Eight o'clock sharp, she'd said.

As Keir walked by a barbershop with a sign that advertised "penny cut, ha'penny shave," he paused to look through the window. The shop was a tidy, prosperous-looking place, with framed mirrors on the wall, shelves filled with bottles of tonic, and a leather chair with adjustable head and foot rests.

Maybe he should spruce himself a bit before dinner tonight. He ran a hand through his overgrown hair. Aye . . . the wild locks could do with some taming.

Cautiously he entered the shop.

"Welcome, sir," said the barber, a jovial-looking man with an intricately curled mustache. "Cut and a shave?"

"A cut," Keir replied.

The barber gestured to the chair. "If you will, sir."

After Keir sat, the barber adjusted the head and foot rests, and handed him a card printed with a dozen little illustrations of men's heads.

"What's this for?" Keir asked, looking at it closely.

"To choose a style." The barber pointed at a few of the labeled drawings. "This is called the Favorite . . . and this is the French Cut . . . this is the Squire . . ."

Keir, who hadn't been aware there was a choice beyond "short" or "not short," scrutinized the little drawings. He pointed to one in which the hair was close-cropped and tidy. "That one?"

"A good choice," the barber said, walking around the chair to assess his head from different angles. He tried to tug a fine-tooth comb through the heavy, slightly curly locks, and paused. "Hmm. This is going to be the work of two haircuts on one head."

After washing and rinsing Keir's hair in a porcelain sink with a spray connected to rubber tubing, the barber shepherded him back to the chair and fastened a cloth around his neck. A long session of snipping and shaping followed, first with scissors, then with clippers that cut layers into the locks with each squeeze of the spring-tension handles. Finally, the barber used a razor to neaten the back into a precise line.

"Shall I trim your beard, sir?" the barber asked.

"Aye."

The man paused, viewing Keir speculatively. "You might consider a full shave," he suggested. "You certainly have the chin for it."

Keir shook his head. "I must keep the beard."

Looking sympathetic, the barber asked, "Pockmarks? Scars?"

"No' exactly." Since the man seemed to expect an explanation, Keir continued uncomfortably, "It's . . . well . . . my friends and I, we're a rough lot, you ken. 'Tis our way to chaff and trade insults. Whenever I shave off the beard, they start mocking and jeering. Blowing kisses, calling me a fancy lad, and all that. They never tire of it. And the village lasses start flirting and mooning about my distillery, and interfering with work. 'Tis a vexation."

The barber stared at him in bemusement. "So the flaw you're trying to hide is . . . you're too handsome?"

A balding middle-aged man seated in the waiting area reacted with a derisive snort. "Balderdash," he exclaimed. "Enjoy it while you can, is my advice. A handsome shoe will someday be an ugly slipper."

"What did he say, nephew?" asked the elderly man beside him, lifting a metal horn to his ear.

The middle-aged man spoke into the horn. "Young fellow says he's too handsome."

"Too handsome?" the old codger repeated, adjusting his spectacles and squinting at Keir. "Who does the cheeky bugger think he is, the Duke of Kingston?"

Amused, the barber proceeded to explain the reference to Keir. "His Grace the Duke of Kingston is generally considered one of the finest-looking men who's ever lived."

"I know—" Keir began.

"He caused many a scandal in his day," the barber continued. "They still make jokes about it in *Punch*. Cartoons with fainting women, and so forth."

"Handsome as Othello, they say," said a man who was sweeping up hair clippings.

"Apollo," the barber corrected dryly. He used a dry brush to whisk away the hair from Keir's neck. "I suspect by now Kingston's probably lost most of those famed golden locks."

Keir was tempted to contradict him, since he'd met the duke earlier that very day and seen for himself the man still had a full head of hair. However, he thought better of it and held his tongue.

Upon returning to his flat, Keir heated enough water to scrub and wash thoroughly, using plenty of soap. He dressed in clean clothes, shined his shoes, and made himself as presentable as he could. A brief consultation of a map of London revealed that Carnation Lane was only a few minutes' walk away. Before leaving, he tucked a half-pint glass bottle of Priobairneach in the inside pocket of his new coat.

The evening was cool and damp, the moon reduced to a pallid glow behind a murky haze. The wharf had quieted, with lighter barges, eel boats, and packets now moored, the spars of a large ship pointing upward like the ribs of a clean-picked carcass.

Keir walked away from the docks toward the main thoroughfare, passing small alleys and byways that were deeply shadowed from overhanging eaves. Laborers and shopkeepers had locked up and gone home for the night, and now a different sort of people had begun to emerge: prostitutes, swindlers, beggars, street musicians, sailors, navvies. Vagrants with gin bottles slouched in doorways, while others huddled in stairwells. A group had built a little fire of rubbish beneath the stone arch of a canal bridge.

Streetlamps were few and far between in this place, and so far, there hadn't been a glimpse of a constable or anything resembling law enforcement. Keir kept to the side of the old wood block pavement as a group of drunken revelers staggered past, howling out a drinking song. A slight smile came to his lips as he thought of what his father had always said whenever someone was that far gone: "The lad has a brick in the hat tonight."

As Keir began down the street again, he had a creeping, tingling sense that something wasn't right. A shadow slid across the pavement—projecting from behind him—moving too fast. Before he could turn to see what it was, he felt a shove against his back. The force of it sent him into a dark alley, and he slammed into the side of a brick building.

Keir hadn't yet drawn a full breath when a strong hand gripped the back of his neck to pin him against the wall. Enraged, he began to twist around, and felt a blow on the right side of his back.

He swung to face the attacker, using a raised forearm to break the restraining grip. Too late, he saw the flash of a knife in the man's free hand. The knife came down to strike Keir's chest in an overhand stab, but the blade was deflected by the glass bottle in his coat pocket.

Grabbing the attacker's wrist and arm, Keir forced the elbow to bend, and turned sideways to gain leverage. Then it was a simple matter to twist the man's arm as if he were ripping the wing from a roast chicken. The crunch of a dislocated shoulder was accompanied by a howl of agony, and the knife clattered to the ground.

Keir stepped on the knife deliberately, and gave him a mean look. *Now* it was a fair fight. "Come here," he growled, "you sneakin', bawfaced shitweasel."

The attacker fled.

Panting, Keir reached down and picked up the small folding knife. A curse escaped him as he saw the streak of blood on it, and he reached around to feel the sore place on his back.

The cowardly bastard had managed to stab him.

Even worse, he'd made Keir late for dinner.

Chapter 7

ALTHOUGH MERRITT WAS AWARE that Keir MacRae might not accept her dinner invitation, she had decided to be optimistic. She and the cook, Mrs. Chalker, had worked out a simple menu: savory dark beef stew, a loaf of cottage bread, and for dessert, a marmalade cake coated with sugar glaze and tender bits of candied peel.

At half past eight, when there was still no sign of MacRae, disappointment began to creep through her. She wandered restlessly through the small house she and Joshua had bought from a retired sea captain. The house, with its charming cupolas, gables, and a telescope on the upper floor, was situated on a gentle hill from which one could view the sea. Merritt loved the freedom and privacy of having her own household, but there were times when loneliness would catch up to her. Such as now.

She went to sit by the parlor fire and glanced at the mantel clock. Eight forty-five.

"Bother," she said glumly. "I shouldn't have tried to coerce the poor man into coming." She frowned and sighed. "More cake for me, I suppose."

The cheerful jangle of the mechanical twist doorbell vibrated through the silence.

Merritt's nerves jangled with relief and excitement, and she could barely restrain herself from leaping up like a schoolgirl. She took a deep breath, smoothed her skirts, and went from the parlor to the entrance foyer. Her footman, Jeffrey, had answered the door and was speaking to someone on the other side of the threshold.

"You may show in my guest," she said lightly.

Jeffrey turned to her with a perturbed expression. "He won't come in, milady."

Puzzled, Merritt went to the doorway and motioned for the footman to step back.

There MacRae was, disheveled and hatless, but breathtakingly handsome. To her pleased surprise, his hair had been cut and shaped to his head in short layers of amber and gold. He had the cool, sensual allure of a lost angel painted by Cabanel.

Was it her imagination, or did he seem a bit pale? Was he nervous? Was he ill?

"Come with me," she urged.

But MacRae shook his head, looking uncomfortable and apologetic. "I can't stay. But I dinna want you to be kept waiting . . . if you were expecting me . . ."

"I was definitely expecting you." Merritt glanced over him with concern. He was pale, his eyes dilated into dark pools. "Come sit with me," she urged, "even if only for a few minutes."

"My apologies, milady, but . . . I have to go back to the flat."

Realizing something was wrong, Merritt kept her voice gentle. "May I ask why?"

"There was a wee scruffle on the way here, and I . . . need to rest a spell."

"Scruffle," she repeated, looking at him more closely. "You were in a fight?"

MacRae's mouth twisted with chagrin. "As I was walking away from the wharf, a thief pushed me into an alley. I drove him off."

Merritt's worried gaze traveled over him from head to toe. There was a liquid drop of red on the pale stone of the outside landing, right next to his shoe. Was that . . . blood? Another drop landed beside the first with a tiny *splat*.

Galvanized by sudden panic, she moved forward to take hold of him. "You're coming in. Yes, you are. Don't even think of arguing." Afraid he might not be entirely steady on his feet, she began to slide an arm around him. Her hand encountered a wet patch on the back of his waistcoat. She didn't have to look to know what it was.

"Jeffrey," she said over her shoulder to the footman, trying to sound calm despite her alarm.

"Yes, milady?"

"We need Dr. Gibson. Don't send a message—go find her in person, and tell her to come without delay."

Jeffrey responded with a nod and left promptly.

MacRae looked down at her in exasperation. "For God's sake, I dinna need a doctor—"

"You're bleeding."

"'Tis just a wee scratch."

"A scratch from what?" she demanded.

"A knife."

"In other words, you have a *stab wound*?" She towed him toward the parlor, her worry exploding into fear.

"I've been hurt worse during peat cutting, and carried on with the work of a day. I need to pour a splash of whisky on it, is all."

"You need to be seen by a doctor." Merritt paused at the parlor doorway to grasp a bellpull and ring vigorously for the housemaid. By the time she and MacRae had reached the couch, the young woman had appeared at the doorway.

"Milady?" the maid asked, taking in the scene with a wide-eyed glance.

"Jenny, fetch clean towels and cotton blankets as quickly as you can."

"Yes, ma'am." The housemaid scampered away.

MacRae scowled down at Merritt. "You're making a mickle into a muckle."

"I'll be the judge of that," she said, having no idea what a muckle was, and reached up to tug off his coat.

"Wait." MacRae reached inside the coat pocket and pulled out a small glass bottle with flat sides. "For you," he said. "The Priobairneach. And well it was for me that you asked me to bring it, or—" He broke off, evidently thinking better of what he'd been about to tell her.

"Or what?" Merritt asked suspiciously, setting the bottle aside. She saw a slit in his coat fabric that could only have been made by a very sharp blade. "My God," she exclaimed in alarm, "you were almost killed!"

"The blade struck the bottle," he said, wincing as Merritt tugged the coat down and pulled the sleeves from his arms.

After she tossed the coat to a nearby table, she hurriedly unfastened the waistcoat and started on the half placket of his shirt.

Disconcerted to find himself being undressed in the parlor, MacRae began to lift his hands, although she couldn't tell whether he intended to help or stop her.

"Let me do it, Keir," Merritt said tautly.

He went still at her use of his first name. His hands lowered to his sides.

She pulled the waistcoat away from him, and bit her lip as she saw the blood-soaked shirt over his back.

"England is hard on a man's clothes," Keir ventured.

"It certainly is on yours." She pointed to the couch, a long, low piece with a sloped head and a half back. "Sit right there."

He hesitated. "If the lads on Islay saw all this fuss over a wee scratch on my back, they'd toss me into Machir Bay like fish bait."

"Sit," Merritt said firmly. "I'll use physical force if necessary."

Looking resigned, Keir obeyed.

Carefully Merritt eased the sleeves from his arms and removed the shirt, exposing a sleek expanse of muscle and sinew. A fine steel chain around his neck led to the center of his chest, where a tiny gold pendant shone among the glinting fleece.

She turned to rummage in a nearby embroidery basket for some linen napkins she'd never gotten around to monogramming. As she knelt to hold the compress against the wound, she saw to her relief that the blood wasn't gushing, only oozing slowly.

"I'll warrant this isn't what you'd be doing if a fine English gentleman had come to dinner," he muttered.

"It certainly would be, had the English gentleman been attacked with a knife."

The housemaid hurried back into the room, and nearly dropped a large bundle of supplies at the sight of the half-naked man on the couch. Merritt took a blanket from her, spread it over the upholstery, and helped Keir lean against the sloped head of the couch. After draping another blanket over him, she wedged a small cushion behind him to hold the compress in place. Keir submitted with a wry quirk of his lips, as if she were making too much of the situation. In a moment, however, the weight of the blanket and the warmth of the nearby fire caused him to relax with a sigh and close his eyes.

"Jenny," Merritt said, turning back to the housemaid, "we'll need a can of hot water and . . ." Her voice faded as she realized the girl was mesmerized by Keir MacRae to the exclusion of all else. One could hardly blame her.

Keir looked like a drowsing lion in the firelight, all tawny and golden. His loose-limbed posture was unconsciously graceful, with the edge of the blanket dipping enough to reveal the broad winged shape of his collarbone and the sharply hewn musculature of his chest and shoulders. Flickers of firelight played among the newly shorn locks of his hair, picking out streaks of champagne and topaz. He could have been a young Arthur, a warrior-king just returned from battle.

"Jenny," Merritt repeated patiently.

The housemaid recalled herself with a start, tearing her gaze away from the figure on the couch. "Ma'am?"

"We'll need a can of hot water, some carbolic soap from the medicine cabinet, and a washbasin."

Jenny gave her a sheepish glance, bobbed a quick curtsy, and hurried out of the parlor.

Merritt's gaze fell on the small bottle of whisky Keir had brought. She took it to the parlor sideboard and poured two drinks, approximately an ounce each.

Wordlessly she returned to the couch. At the sound of her approach, Keir opened his eyes, saw the glass of whisky she extended, and took it gratefully. He downed it in a gulp and let out a controlled sigh.

Merritt sat beside him and took a cautious sip. The whisky went down her throat like smooth fire, leaving a soft, smoky glow. "It's very nice," she said. "Much smoother than the whisky I've tried before."

"It was made in tall copper still," he said. "As the whisky vapor floats upward, the copper draws away the heavy compounds. The longer the vapor spends with the copper, the more it unburdens itself. Like a good conversation."

Merritt smiled and took another sip. It was light, warm, bracing—no wonder people liked it so much. "Tell me how your whisky is made," she said. "What do you start with?"

"We cart in the barley and soak it in water from a local spring . . ." He went on to explain how they spread it onto malting floors to let it germinate, then dried it in a massive eighty-foot-long kiln fired with peat. By the time Keir had reached the part where the malt was crushed by metal rollers and poured into a giant metal vat called a mash tun, the housemaid had brought the rest of the supplies.

Merritt coaxed him into leaning against the sloped side of the couch so she could wash the bloodstains from his back. Although he was tense at first, he gradually relaxed at the feel of the hot cloth stroking over his skin. A spell of intimacy descended as he continued to talk about the distillery, while Merritt cleaned the area around the wound. Silently she admired his powerful shoulders and the wealth of muscle layered along his back in deep oblique slants. His skin was tough but satiny, gleaming like pale gold in the firelight.

She wasn't quite sure how this had happened. A chain of events had somehow led to having a large, half-naked Scotsman in her parlor. She was astonished to reflect she'd already seen more of Keir's body—and become more familiar with it—than she had with Joshua before their wedding. Even more surprising was how natural this felt. She hadn't realized how much she'd missed taking care of someone. Oh, she had family, friends, and a thousand employees to look after, but that wasn't the same as having her own person.

Not that this man was hers, of course.

But it felt like he was.

"Are you listening?" she heard him ask.

Briefly Merritt consulted the small portion of her brain that had been paying attention. "You were just describing how you run the liquor into the pot stills."

"Aye. Then it's heated from beneath to start the vapor rising . . ."

How perfectly the hair had been trimmed at the back of his neck, a precise line she longed to trace with her fingertips. Gooseflesh had risen on his skin in the wake of the damp cloth, and she drew the blanket over the beautiful expanse of his back.

She looked up as she heard the front door opening and muffled voices coming from the entrance foyer.

The footman came to the parlor door, and said, "Dr. Gibson is here, milady."

Merritt rose quickly to her feet. Seeing that Keir was preparing to stand as well, she said, "No, lie still."

Garrett Gibson entered the parlor, hefting the bulky doctor's bag with ease, as if her wand-slim arms had been reinforced with steel threads. She had the tidy, clean-scrubbed freshness of a schoolgirl, with a wealth of chestnut hair pinned up in braids from which no strands were permitted to stray. Her incisive green eyes softened with affection as she set down the bag and exchanged a brief embrace with Merritt.

Only a woman with great confidence and determination could manage to become the first—and so far, only—licensed female physician in England. Garrett possessed both qualities in abundance. Since no medical school in England would admit a woman, she had studied the French language so she could earn a medical degree at the Sorbonne in Paris. Upon her return to England, she'd acquired her medical license by finding a loophole that the British Medical Association closed as soon as they realized she'd managed to slip through.

Merritt had become friendly with Garrett over the course of many social occasions, but this was the first time she'd ever required her professional services. Ordinarily Merritt would have sent for the older physician her family had always relied on, but Garrett had been trained in the most modern and advanced surgical techniques.

"Thank you for coming," Merritt exclaimed. "Forgive

me for having interrupted your evening—I do hope I haven't made your husband cross."

"Not at all," Dr. Gibson assured her. "Ethan had to take a train up to Scotland to attend to some business that suddenly cropped up. Little Cormac is already down for the night, and he's in the nanny's care."

Merritt turned to introduce her to Keir, and frowned as she saw he'd risen to his feet.

He gave her an obstinate glance, pulling the blanket more closely around his shoulders.

"Dr. Garrett Gibson, this is Mr. MacRae," Merritt said, "who shouldn't be standing, since he was just stabbed in an alley."

Dr. Gibson came to Keir quickly, who gave her a hard stare. "Have a seat, my friend. In fact, why don't you lie on your front and let me have a look at the injury?"

"'Tis more of a scratch than a stab," Keir muttered, lowering himself to the couch. "All it needs is a dab of whisky and a bandage."

There was a smile in Dr. Gibson's voice as she replied. "Whisky can indeed be used as an antiseptic, but I'd recommend it only as a last resort, since pouring it into an open wound could damage exposed tissue. I'd much rather pour it into a glass and drink it neat over ice."

"You like whisky?" Keir asked.

"Love it," came her prompt reply, which Merritt could see had earned his instant liking.

"Mr. MacRae is a distiller from Islay," she told Garrett. "He's visiting London on business."

"Will you tell me exactly what happened?" Garrett

asked Keir, and listened to his account of the attack while she washed her hands over the basin. "I'm surprised the thief tried to rob a man of your size," she commented, extending her soapy hands while Merritt poured clean water over them. "You're not what anyone could consider an easy mark."

"And the devil knows I dinna have the look of a man carrying valuables," Keir said wryly.

Garrett knelt beside the couch to examine the wound, gently manipulating the skin around it. "A single-edged blade," she commented. "Quite sharp. It made a V-shaped notch and gouged a little shelf beneath the skin—as if you began to turn just as the knife struck."

"Aye," came his muffled reply.

"Well done," the doctor said, still inspecting the wound. "Had you not reacted so quickly, the blade would very likely have severed an artery near your kidney."

Merritt was chilled by the realization of how close he'd come to death. "He dropped the knife in the scruffle," Keir said.

"Tis in my coat pocket."

Garrett's eyes were bright with interest. "May I see it?"

At Keir's nod, Merritt went to his discarded coat and carefully fished the knife from the pocket. She brought it to Garrett, who deftly pried it open.

"A stag handle with a slip joint closure," the doctor observed aloud, "and a three-inch drop point steel blade fortified with nickel bolsters."

"You're an expert on knives?" Merritt asked.

Garrett sent her a brief grin. "Not an expert, but I am keen on them. My husband, on the other hand, is a connoisseur and has an extensive collection." Her attention returned to the knife, and she squinted at the metal-capped pommel. "How curious. There's a serialized number here—along with what appears to be a hand-stamped identifying number. It could be British army issue. Or navy, if this is a marlinspike . . ." She pried out a skinny steel hook. "A hoof pick," she said triumphantly. "Definitely army. Cavalry or mounted infantry."

Keir gave her a dubious glance. "The man in the alley was no' in uniform."

"He may have been a former soldier, or this knife could have been stolen from one." Garrett folded the knife. "Now, as for the wound . . . I'm afraid it's going to need stitches."

Keir responded with a resigned nod. "I've already had a dram of whisky," he said. "If you've no objection, I'll take another."

"Certainly."

Merritt picked up his empty glass and took it to the sideboard. By the time she returned with the drink, Garrett had taken various items from her bag and laid them out on a clean cloth. After soaking a wad of absorbent cotton with antiseptic solution, the doctor swabbed around the wound.

So far, Keir had tolerated the process without comment. But as the doctor picked up a tiny glass syringe, unscrewed a little metal cap at the end, and attached a long, thin needle, it was clear he didn't like the looks of it *at all*.

"Whatever that is," he said, "I dinna need it."

"A hypodermic syringe," Garrett explained matter-of-factly. "I'm going to inject a solution into the wound to numb the area."

Keir reacted with a quick double blink. "No, you won't," he said firmly.

Garrett appeared momentarily nonplussed, then gave him a reassuring smile. "I know the prospect of an injection can seem a bit intimidating. But it's only a quick sting, and then it's done." Seeing the obstinacy on his face, she continued gently, "Mr. MacRae, I'm going to have to clean the wound before closing it with sutures. The process will be unpleasant for both of us if you won't let me give you a pain-relieving injection first."

"Do what you must," he returned, "but no injection."

Garrett frowned. "The choice is either one swift poke of a needle, or several minutes of excruciating pain. Which sounds preferable?"

"Excruciating pain," he said stubbornly.

Garrett's gaze met Merritt's in a silent plea for help.

"Keir," Merritt said gently, "you can trust Dr. Gibson. It will make her job easier if you're able to keep still."

"I'll be as still as a spiked gun," he promised.

"You're going to be poked by a needle anyway," Merritt pointed out.

"No' a hypodermic one." He cast a surly glance at the syringe, which Merritt had to admit privately did look rather menacing.

"I'm very experienced at administering injections," Garrett assured him. "If you'll just let me—"

"No."

"You won't even have to look at it. You can turn your head and hum a little song while I—"

"No."

"The hypodermic syringe has been in use for more than twenty years," Dr. Gibson protested. "It's safe and highly effective. It was invented by a brilliant physician who used the sting of a bee as his model." Trying to think of some way to convince him, she added, "A Scottish physician."

That caught Keir's attention. "His name?"

"Dr. Alexander Wood."

"From what part of Scotland?" Keir asked suspiciously.

"Edinburgh."

After cursing quietly beneath his breath, he let out a long sigh and said gruffly, "Go on, then."

Merritt bit back a grin, knowing exactly what Keir was thinking: He couldn't refuse the hypodermic injection if it had been invented by a fellow countryman—it would reflect badly on the honor of Scotland.

The two women shared a quick glance of relief over his head. Merritt handed Keir the glass of whisky, and he downed it while Garrett filled the syringe. At the doctor's request, Keir slid lower on the couch until he was laid out flat.

Merritt knelt beside the couch, while Keir rested his chin on his folded arms. She smiled slightly at his stoic acceptance of the situation. It reminded her a little of her father, who had always regarded complaining as the height of unmanliness.

Her attention was caught by the gleam of the thin steel chain around his neck. It led to the little gold object she'd noticed before . . . not a pendant, but a key. She touched it with her fingertip and gave him a questioning glance.

"A gift from my mither," he said.

"What does it unlock?" Merritt asked softly.

An unaccountably long hesitation followed before he replied, "I dinna know."

"Stay relaxed," Garrett said. "There'll be a bit of a burn at first, but it will fade quickly as the area turns numb."

Keir flinched as he felt the needle going in. His eyes half closed, and he held very still.

"Keep breathing," Merritt whispered.

He let out a controlled breath, his lashes lifting, and his gaze fastened on hers.

Very gently, Merritt reached out to push back a heavy lock of hair that had fallen over his forehead. She let her hand linger tenderly on the gold-shimmered waves, knowing if Garrett saw, she would never say a word to anyone.

"There," Garrett eventually said. "That should do it. I'm going to rinse the wound now. Let me know at once if you feel any discomfort."

As Garrett rinsed and cleaned the laceration, Keir turned his head to say over his shoulder, "You were right about the injection, Doctor. I can't feel anything."

"Excellent. Try not to move." Garrett picked up a pair of forceps and needle holders. "In my opinion," she mused as she began on the first suture, "the man who attacked you was no average street thief."

Keir frowned. "Why do you say that?"

"They're usually armed with a stout stick or club, not knives. And they rarely work alone—they prefer to rob in company. Then there's the knife itself: not some cheap blade stamped out by machine, but high-quality steel." Expertly she tied off the thread, snipped off the excess, and began on the next suture. "It's risky to use a knife against a big man; if you don't disable or kill him with the first strike, he'll turn on you. Moreover, the back is a difficult area of the body to attack effectively; the vital organs are fairly well protected. For example, if you aim for the heart from behind, you'd first have to slide the knife through the ribs. If you tried to sever the spinal cord, the blade would have to go between the vertebrae and lever to the correct angle."

"He could have tried to reach around and slit my throat," Keir said.

"Not an easy maneuver with an opponent your size. The most logical choice was to go for the kidney, which would kill you quickly, with the added benefit of having most of the blood remain in your body. Very little fuss or mess. And that appears to be precisely what he attempted. Fortunately, you made it difficult for him." Garrett wielded the forceps and needle with practiced dexterity. "But that leads to another point: The typical robber would have fled immediately, and searched for other, easier prey. One has to question why he persisted." She paused. "Do you know anyone who might want to kill you?"

"No one who'd put this much effort into it," Keir said dryly.

"With your permission, Mr. MacRae, I'd like to take the knife to my husband, who happens to be the assistant commissioner of the Metropolitan Police. As a former detective, he'll know what to make of it."

"Aye," Keir said. "Take the knife; I've no use for it."

"When will Ethan return from Scotland?" Merritt asked Garrett.

"Tomorrow, I hope. It's only a minor bit of investigative work." Garrett rolled her eyes briefly before continuing. "He could have easily sent one of his special agents to take care of it, but he was asked to go himself, and one can hardly say no to a duke."

"Duke?" Merritt looked at her alertly.

Realizing the slip she'd just made, Garrett muttered, "Bugger. You didn't hear that, either of you."

"I did," Merritt said, "I heard, and I insist on knowing who sent Ethan to Scotland. As far as I know, the only duke he's personally acquainted with is Kingston." Although Garrett refused to reply, Merritt detected the subtle hint of chagrin on her face. "It was," she exclaimed. "You must tell me what he's investigating. You know I won't breathe a word of it—the duke is like family to me." She would have persisted, but she noticed Keir's expression had gone taut and blank, like a freshly ironed bedsheet. "Do you feel the stitches?" she asked gently. "Are you in pain?"

He shook his head and lowered his chin to his forearm, staring at nothing.

After Garrett had finished the sutures and applied a bandage of adhesive plaster, she began to pack her supplies in the leather bag.

"Will you have a whisky before you leave?" Merritt asked.

The doctor looked wistful, but shook her head with a smile. "Thank you, but I can't. I'm in 'a hopeful way,' as Ethan puts it."

"Are you? How wonderful," Merritt exclaimed. "Congratulations, my dear!" Somewhere inside, she was relieved to discover that the private jab of heartache she'd always felt in the past upon hearing such news from friends and relations was now only a faint twinge. With a show of delighted interest, she asked when the baby was expected to arrive, and how Garrett was feeling.

Keir sat up and drew a blanket loosely around himself, listening to the conversation without comment. Glancing at him briefly, Merritt found his thoughtful gaze on her, taking in every nuance of her reaction. A flush of warm feeling spread over her as she realized he was concerned that Garrett's news might have been difficult for her.

After seeing Garrett out, Merritt returned to the parlor and began to gather Keir's discarded clothes. "I'll ask my maid to put these in to soak," she said, "and mend the slit in your coat. She's very skilled with a needle."

"I can't go home with no shirt to my back," he pointed out.

"Don't even think of putting those soiled clothes back over your nice clean wound," Merritt said, appalled. "We'll find something else for you to wear." She reached for his coat. "As for this, I'll clear out the pockets and give it to Jenny."

"Merritt," Keir said uneasily, rustling and stirring on the couch. "I'd rather—"

"It's no trouble at all," she said, emptying the inside pocket of the coat and setting the personal items on the table: a penknife, a few coins, the key to the flat, a map, a handkerchief, and a worn leather folding wallet with an outer pocket for tickets or notes. A folded slip of paper fell from the wallet, and she began to tuck it back in. "We'll keep all your things right here, and . . ." Her voice faded as she saw the imprint of typed letters on the parchment.

It was a carefully torn strip of the page she had typed at the office.

Mr. Keir MacRae Lady Merritt Sterling

"Oh," Merritt heard herself whisper, while her heartbeats went scattering like pearls from a broken necklace. It was only a scrap of paper and ink . . . but she understood what it meant.

Keir's face was partially averted, his color high. As the silence lengthened, he brought himself to meet her gaze with a faint, bleak smile.

"I shouldn't have come," he said.

Merritt knew he was right.

Common sense told her this couldn't be real—it couldn't be trusted. It was happening too fast. It wouldn't lead to anything that would be good for either of them.

Don't think, don't touch, talk, smell, or taste. Go into a dark room, lock the door, close the shutters against the sun.

But it was too late for any of that.

How long would it take, how many years, before she felt this way about someone again? Maybe five . . . maybe twenty.

Maybe never.

Fortunately, a woman of common sense always knew when to throw caution to the wind.

She went to Keir in a few strides, wrapped her arms around his neck, and pressed her lips to his.

Chapter 8

The moment Merritt had discovered the slip of paper from his wallet, Keir had expected her to react with outrage, or even worse, pity. Anything but this. Bewildered, he absorbed the feel of her, the tender mouth, the feminine warmth. The full, sweet curves of her body were covered in blue velvet trimmed with soft lace that tickled his bare skin.

His senses were filled with her. He had to have more of her weight on him, more closeness. Ignoring the pull of the cut on his back, he lifted one of his legs to the couch and settled her between his thighs. The pressure felt so good, there where he was hot and rigid, he couldn't hold back a low groan.

Mistaking the sound for pain, Merritt broke the kiss and tried to pull away, but he clamped a hand over her bottom to keep her there.

"Wait," she said breathlessly, "be careful—your back—you'll hurt yourself—" She reached down to adjust the folded linen compress, and the way she fussed with the placement of it, that attentive interest, aroused him even more. He pulled her higher against his body and locked his mouth to hers again. She began to breathe in rhythmic gasps, the way she would if he were inside her. The tip of her tongue ventured inside his mouth, a flick of sensation that went straight to his groin. He'd never been so hard in his life.

Somewhere in the molten cauldron that had formerly been his brain, Keir realized one of them had to put a stop to this, *now*. Since Merritt didn't seem inclined to do that any time soon, he would have to be the responsible one. It took a Herculean effort to pull his mouth from hers, but then she followed the movement, trying to maintain the kiss. Amused and steaming, Keir dove his face into the shadowed alcove created by her neck and jaw, and breathed in the fragrance of blood-heated perfume. He felt her quiver at the brush of his beard against her tender skin. *God.* He wanted to spend hours kissing every inch of her. Instead he lay still beneath her delicious female weight, fighting for control.

Merritt's head lifted. Her eyes were heavy-lidded, the black bristle of her lashes shadowing drowsy darkness.

She dampened her lips, and spoke as if she'd just awakened from a long sleep. "I've heard that Scots are the most passionate of men."

A slow smile crossed his lips. He let a fingertip play with the wisps of hair around her ear, delighting in her squirm of response. "Aye . . .'tis true that Scots have more passion than men of other lands. But I'll no' be the one to demonstrate it to you."

"What if . . ." Merritt paused to take an extra breath, her gaze slightly unfocused. "What if I wanted you to?"

He shook his head, knowing she wasn't thinking straight. "It would be a mistake."

"People should make mistakes," she said. "It builds character." She tried to kiss him again, but he pulled his head back.

"You dinna want to make this particular mistake with me, lass." Keir fingered the lobe of her ear gently. "I won't carry that bit of paper if you dinna wish it." He didn't need it: Her name had been permanently engraved on his heart.

The comment seemed to make her shy. "I don't mind if you want to keep it. But . . . why did you?"

Keir shrugged. "'Tis no' my way to take a feeling apart and examine the workings of it."

Merritt tilted her head, regarding him intently. "Did you want it as a trophy, perhaps? To remind you someday of a conquest you once made?"

Keir's smile vanished. He didn't think she really believed that, but the suggestion—the very idea of it—filled him with indignation. "*No.* I'm no' a brute who would think of you as a thing to be won."

Seeming to realize he was genuinely offended, Merritt said hastily, "Oh, I didn't mean to imply—"

"I may have rough ways, but I know how to be gentle with a woman—"

"Yes. Of course. I shouldn't have put it that way—"

"—and as for needing a *reminder*—" Keir's indignation deepened into outrage. "Do you think me so shallow-pated I'd need reminding of a woman I once held in my arms? How could I forget you? The most—"

He was interrupted as Merritt took his face in her hands and kissed him again. There was more he'd meant to say, but her mouth was too luscious to resist.

He opened to her, hungry for the sweet, damp softness, unable to keep from taking as much of her as he could. His erection awakened with fresh vigor. Dazed with lust, he closed his hand in the velvet skirts and began to pull them upward, then realized what he was doing.

He broke the kiss, gasping. "No more," he said hoarsely, "or I'm like to devour you on the spot."

Merritt nodded and lowered her flushed face to his chest, nuzzling her lips and cheek into the springy fleece. Her fingertips followed the fine chain around his neck, down to the little gold key, and she played with it idly. Her warm breath filtered through the curls, fanning his nipple, as she asked, "Are you hungry?"

"Aye, I've just said so."

Her cheek curved against his chest. "I meant for dinner."

Despite the pangs of desire, Keir's empty stomach reminded him that he hadn't eaten since breakfast.

"I'll have Cook warm some stew," Merritt continued before he could reply, "and I'll fetch a clean shirt for you. My footman accidentally dragged a sleeve through fresh ink last week, and even though we washed it twice, we couldn't remove the stain entirely. I think it's still in a basket of things we're collecting for the needy."

Keir let out a breath of amusement. "I believe I qualify."

Merritt began to lift herself away from him, hesitated, and gently drew her palm over his chest. A wash of color warmed her fair skin. "You're a beautiful man," she said a bit bashfully.

Her touch sent a thrill of pleasure through him. He had to steel every muscle to keep from arching against her hand. It was indecent, how much he wanted her.

In a hushed voice he replied, "'Tis glad I am you find me so, darlin'. But there's nothing in the world half so braw and lovely as you."

"Braw?"

"Something very fine. You're braw like sunlight on the sea, or a poem set to music."

Merritt smiled as she left the couch and restored her clothes. He adored the way she settled her bodice and skirts in place with deft little tugs. "Stay right there," she told him. "I'll have everything ready in just a moment."

She hurried off, a woman who loved arranging things.

Keir sat up and rubbed his face slowly. It was the worst mistake he'd ever made, agreeing to come to dinner at her house. It was madness.

And yet he was so damned happy to be here, with her, he could hardly breathe.

Chapter 9

THEY DINED AT A small round table in an upstairs parlor. The air was lit by candles and lamps with frosted glass shades. Thankfully, the room wasn't cluttered with little delicate figurines and ornaments. It was clean and simple, with oak paneling and windows swathed in blue velvet curtains. At least half of one wall was occupied by a long, low cabinet stocked with decanted liquor and glassware. Dishes of olives, almonds, and celery sticks on cracked ice had been set out.

Thanks to the injection Dr. Gibson had given him, Keir barely felt the wound on his back as he sat in a sturdy upholstered dining chair. The footman, Jeffrey, came to set covered dishes on the table, which had been overlaid with heavy white linen. After filling long-stemmed glasses with water and wine, the footman left them in privacy. Having expected him to hover around them during the entire meal, Keir was gratified to learn they would serve themselves.

He found himself relaxing deeply, steeped in Merritt's effortless charm. He'd never talked so much during a meal. The stew had been made with chunks of beef, potatoes, and turnips simmered in burgundy wine until they melted at the lightest pressure of the tongue. There was a salad of crisp lettuce greens and chopped mint leaves, and wedges of cottage bread, the interior laced with holes to catch every drop of salted butter.

As they talked, Merritt entertained him with stories of her childhood in Hampshire as the oldest of six siblings. Her father, the earl, loomed large in those stories, as a loving parent and a man of great authority and responsibility. His marriage to Lillian Bowman, an American heiress, had been an improbable match, but the union had turned out to be a remarkably happy one. Merritt's mother was a lively and lighthearted woman, the kind of mother who had romped outside with her children and splashed in puddles with them, and encouraged their flights of fancy.

At Merritt's coaxing, Keir told her about growing up on Islay, and a boyhood spent running about with a pack of rowdy friends. The group had frequently ended up in scrapes and misadventures that had earned all of them good hidings when they went home. All except Keir, whose father, Lachlan, had never laid a hand on him. His mother, Elspeth, had fretted over that: The neighbors had advised that without proper discipline, the lad would end up spoiled. But Lachlan always reasoned that a teenage boy had little enough good sense as it was; a clout upside the head might knock it right out of him.

One day when Keir had come home with bruises and a blackened eye from fighting with his friend Neil, Lachlan had said he reckoned Keir had already had enough battering, and he wouldn't add to it. But he did want an explanation. Keir had told him Neil had bragged that his father was the strongest man on the island and would win in a fight against anyone else's father. Especially Keir's father, Neil had added pointedly, who was older than everyone else's. So Keir had given Neil a thrashing to settle the matter. To Elspeth's annoyance, Lachlan had been so pleased, he hadn't even scolded the boy, declaring he'd been obliged to defend the family honor.

Merritt chuckled at the story. "You were an only child?" she asked.

"Aye. They were never able to have bairns of their own, so they . . . took me in."

"You were an orphan?"

"Abandoned."

Keir wasn't sure why he'd told her that. It was something he rarely, if ever, discussed with anyone. But those coffee-dark eyes were so warm and interested, he couldn't seem to hold back.

Merritt took a sip of her wine before asking gently, "Do you know anything about the woman who gave birth to you?"

"No, and I dinna need to."

Merritt's dark eyes seemed to look right inside him. "The gold key . . ."

Keir smiled slightly at her perceptiveness. "She left it with me at the orphanage. I wear it because . . . I suppose 'tis a small way of honoring her. I owe her that much at least, after the pain I caused her."

A tiny crinkle appeared between her fine brows. "Do you mean childbirth?"

"That, and the sorrow of having to give away her bairn." He paused reflectively. "I think I was one of many men who hurt her, one way or another. A lass who was protected and loved would no' have found herself in such circumstances."

An east wind gusted through a half-open window, whisking in the invigorating freshness of ocean brine and spindrift. It had begun to rain, the drops coming down with the weight of pennies.

Merritt went to the long cabinet, gesturing for Keir to stay seated. She brought back a coffee service on a silver tray. There was the pleasure of watching her prepare coffee for him, adding sugar and a dollop of heavy cream that billowed up to the steaming black surface. She passed the cup and saucer to him, along with a small plate bearing a yellow slice of marmalade cake.

As Keir ate every crumb and washed it down with coffee, he was steeped in the bittersweet awareness that for the rest of his life, the memory of this evening was the one he would return to over and over. Nothing would ever come close to the pleasure she gave him.

The mantel clock began a series of delicate chimes. Midnight.

Time had never been so unwelcome an intruder. But it was better that the night end now. With one hunger sated, his body was now ready to assuage another. He needed to remove himself from temptation.

"Merritt—"

"More coffee?" she suggested brightly.

Keir caught her hand as she reached for the pot. "I'll be taking my leave now," he said softly.

"But it's raining."

That kindled a faint smile. He forbore to point out

what she already knew: A Scot was hardly one to be daunted by rain.

He tried to say her name, but it came out as "Merry." A word of joy, shaped in longing.

Their hands folded together slowly, compactly, more thrilling than any physical connection he'd had in his life.

There was so much he wanted to tell her—all of it true, and none of it right.

A gust of rain came through the window as the storm burst with new vigor. The flame of a gas lamp sputtered and died, despite its protective glass housing. Keir sprang up and went to shut off the lamp valve, while Merritt rushed to the window. "The frame sticks from humidity," she said, struggling to close it, gasping a little at the rush of chilled wet air.

Keir came to help her, pushing the window down with one hand, while rain streamed over the glass. He left one hand braced on the sill, near her shoulder, while they both looked out at the turbulent night. He'd always loved storms, the charged air making his senses come alive. Shadows and ripples of light undulated across the sky as if they were viewing it from undersea.

"We're in for a brattle," he observed.

"Is that what you call it?" Merritt asked, turning to face him.

Gently he used the pad of his thumb to stroke away a raindrop near the corner of her mouth. "Aye, we have dozens of words for weather. If it comes in a soft shower, we call it a greetie."

Merritt's lips quirked. "In Hampshire, we say it's a roke." Her hands came to rest lightly at his sides.

Keir drew an unsteady breath as he felt her nestle closer to him. His body was hard and heavy, filled with a desire beyond utterance. Every cell clamored for him to take her, mate with her. Instead, he bent his head and laid his cheek against her hair. They stood together as the dark night sang a million notes of rain.

"At this moment," he whispered, "I'm as happy as any man who ever lived."

Her voice was muffled in the folds of his borrowed shirt. "Then stay."

Keir's heart jolted. She was being impulsive, he told himself. He didn't want to be something she might later regret. He didn't want to cause her one moment of pain or sorrow, when she'd already had her share of both.

"No," he muttered. "'Tis hard enough to leave you as it is—dinna make it worse."

"Stay for one night. Just one."

He'd never been so wildly aroused and frustrated. It would be so easy to let himself forget everything except the pleasure of her body. But one of them had to think of the consequences, and apparently that had to be him. There was no choice but to put a stop to this, now.

Letting go of her, he said brusquely, "You dinna know what you're asking for."

"I'm asking for the gift of a night with you."

Keir wanted to melt to the floor. For her to put it that way . . . as if making love would be a gift from him to her, instead of the other way around . . . she devastated him. With just a few words, she had taken ownership of him from head to toe.

He longed to tell her that. Instead, he decided to be

crude. If he had to offend her for her own good, so be it. He only hoped she wouldn't cry. Maybe she'd slap his face instead—he'd prefer that to tears.

"I dinna fook like a gentleman," he told her gruffly. "There'll be no pretty words and fine manners. I'll throw a leg over, start the bed to banging, and when I'm done, I'll give you a pat on the arse on my way out. If that's what you're after, tell me where your room is, and we'll go at it."

But there was no outrage. No face slap. Just a brief silence before Merritt said helpfully, "It's the last door on the right, at the end of the hallway."

She'd called his bluff. Her lips twitched at his expression.

Damn it.

Exasperated, Keir took her upper arms in his hands and held her apart from him. "If I stayed, no harm would come to me—only to you. I'd pay any price to have you, but I won't let you be the one to pay it."

"I'll take responsibility for my own decisions."

"Are you so daft, lass, that you think one night with me would be worth risking everything?" he demanded.

Merritt shrugged and lowered her gaze, but not before he saw the impish gleam in her eyes. "I'd like to find out."

Unable to stop himself, Keir jerked her close and kissed her roughly. She opened to him with sweet yielding, soothing the ragged edges of his passion until he groaned and stroked inside her mouth with his tongue. The kiss turned deep and languorous, sending waves of dizzying pleasure through him.

God help him, he would have died for what she was offering. To be inside her . . . to hold her for hours . . . he had to have this, no matter what happened afterward. Feverishly he kissed his way down her neck, feeling the movements of her throat as she gasped and swallowed.

Taking her head in a gentle clasp, he kissed her forehead and eyelids, and followed the slope of her nose down to the trembling bow of her upper lip.

"If that's what you want," he said hoarsely, "I promise you . . . the night will be worth it."

Chapter 10

KEIR HAD NEVER SUSPECTED it was possible for a woman to wear so much clothing. After they'd gone to Merritt's bedroom, he'd unfastened the back of her velvet dress and she'd stepped out of it to reveal a profusion of . . . Christ, he didn't know the names for them . . . frilly lace-trimmed undergarments that fastened with tiny hooks, ribbons, and buttons. They reminded him of the illustrations pasted on the walls of the Islay baker's shop, of wedding cakes decorated with sugar lace and marzipan pearls, and flowers made of icing. He adored the sight of her in all those pretty feminine things. His fingers itched to touch her. He was worried as hell for her sake, whereas she seemed almost cheerful about the whole thing, as if they were having a wee adventure instead of starting down the path to ruin.

Undressing with deliberate slowness, Keir let her look her fill, allowing her plenty of time to change her mind. When he was fully naked, he turned to face her.

Merritt's gaze traveled over him from head to toe, lingering briefly at his groin. Her eyes widened, and a tide of deep pink swept over her face.

Keir regarded her with a faint, wry smile as he approached her. "Merry . . . you've already given me the best night of my life. I could ask for nothing more." He lifted a hand to caress her cheek. "If you've second thoughts, I'll go now with a blessing on my lips."

She turned her face to nudge a smile into his palm, and said, "Don't even think of leaving. I'm only a little nervous, that's all."

Keir was almost shocked by the rush of tenderness he felt. "No, dinna be nervous with me." He took her against him, nestling her to his chest. "I would never harm you. You're safer in my arms than anywhere outside them." He caressed her shining dark hair, and ran his fingertips over her cheek and the neat curve of her ear. Her skin gleamed like a pearl in the light. "We dinna have to rush at it headlong," he murmured. "There's time enough to take it slow."

Merritt was still blushing, but to his delight, she glanced up at him with a little flirting grin. "You just said you were going to throw a leg over and start the bed to banging."

"I was trying to scare you off," he admitted. "For your own good."

"You could never scare me. I know what kind of man you are."

"Do you, now?" Keir asked, his breath shortening as he felt her small hands beginning to wander over him.

"You'd never use your strength to take advantage of someone weaker. And you're more of a romantic than you'd like to admit, which is why you feel guilty for sleeping with me. But you're going to do it anyway, because it's been a long time since you shared a bed with anyone . . . and you want me."

God, how he wanted her. It was the most delicious

sensation of Keir's life, standing there naked with her inquisitive fingers traveling shyly over him. He could barely think over the thumping of his heart. "What makes you say it's been a long time?"

"Just a guess." Merritt glanced up at him, her eyes sparkling. "Am I wrong?"

Keir's breath caught as she drew her palms over his backside.

"No' about that," he admitted, his eyes half closing. Her touch was almost too pleasurable to bear. "I live on an island, ye ken, where gossip never closes its wings. If there were a lass I tried to sneak up to a hayloft I'd soon find myself at the end of her father's twenty-bore." He paused as he felt her chuckle into the mat of hair on his chest. "But there is something you're wrong about."

"Oh?"

"I dinna feel guilty about bedding you." He bent to her lips, shaping them with a long, searing kiss until they clung and trembled. His voice thickened slightly as he continued. "I wouldnae bide the night with you just because I've gone lang without a lass. I'll stay because for the rest of my life, I want a memory of you to keep me warm on a cold night." He took her sweet mouth again, his fingers spreading over her back, her hips, as he molded her closer against him. The feel of her—all those deep feminine curves contained in stays and laces and layers of cotton—nearly drove him mad. As he sent his tongue deeper, the silky warmth of her was so satisfying he couldn't restrain a groan of pleasure.

He lifted her to the bed and climbed in after her. A

fine bed it was, made of cast iron and brass, with posts as thick as his wrist. It was so sturdy, it didn't creak beneath his weight. Experimentally he stretched out on it full-length.

Merritt propped up on her elbows and glanced over him. "You have very large . . ." She hesitated. ". . . feet."

Keir turned on his side to face her, a smile tugging at his lips. "That I do." He reached out to play with the lace trim at the neckline of her bodice. "Do you like a man with large feet?"

Her blush deepened until even her ears were red. "I'm not sure," she said, flustered, and his smile deepened.

"I'll be gentle," he promised, "every moment. As if you were a wee dove resting in my hands." He let his fingertips follow the lace to her shoulder. "What kind of shirt is this?"

"It's not a shirt, it's . . . a corset cover. To keep things smooth beneath the dress. It's difficult to unfasten, there's a—"

"No, dinna tell me. I'd rather find out for myself."

Keir found a row of tiny hooks that started beneath her arm and went down her side to her waist, and he undid them one by one. Eventually he eased the garment over her head and tossed it aside. He continued to undress her, gently rolling her body this way and that as he hunted for miniature unseen fastenings. Merritt was quiet except for an occasional gasp as Keir paused to caress newly revealed places . . . the curve of a knee . . . the taut shape of a calf . . . little pink toes.

He eased her drawers down, revealing smoothly

muscled thighs and a firm, round bottom. From years of horseback riding, he guessed, recalling she'd grown up on a hunting estate. The thought of how it might feel to have her straddle him, the grip of her thighs as she rode him, made him dizzy with lust. He caressed her legs, fondling his way up to the small triangle of neatly trimmed curls. Although he was dying to play with them, he continued to browse over her, marveling at the beautiful curves, the fine skin. Everywhere, her body was sweet from bath soap and touches of perfume.

"You're the bonniest thing I've ever seen, Merry," he said huskily, cupping one of her breasts and stroking his thumb over the tender peak. "You steal my breath away."

He moved with the care of a man handling some volatile substance, leaning over her to catch the tip of her breast with a slow, open kiss. She gasped, her hands coming to his head as he sucked the nipple into a hard, delicately textured bud. He framed both breasts in his hands and feasted on the lush curves, using his lips, tongue, the light grazes of his teeth.

Quivers ran along her body, and he followed them with his fingertips, his lips, down to the tender niche between her thighs. His fingers traced the softly closed slit until she panted and writhed. Staring into her dilated eyes, he realized she was already close to the edge.

"No' so fast, darlin'," Keir whispered. "Bide for a while, and let me love you longer."

He watched her lashes lower, trembling against her cheeks as she felt him part the folds of her sex, tickling the petaled edges. He stroked down to the entrance of her body and let his finger slip inside her by gradual degrees. The silky flesh pulsed and closed on his finger as if trying to draw him deeper, wetness emerging to ease his way.

She began to breathe in whimpers, trying to hold them back. He loved the sounds she made, her ladylike composure dissolving in sensation. Withdrawing his touch slowly, he bent to kiss her stomach. His lips skimmed down to the enticing triangle of curls, and her hands came to his head with an uneasy flutter as if to push him away.

"No, let me," Keir murmured between her thighs. "I love this part of you, like the sweet heart of a rose. Merry, honey-love . . . dinna ask me to spend the rest of my life never knowing the taste of you."

She subsided in a daze. He gripped the sides of her body carefully, keeping her in place as he parted her with his tongue and stroked the sides of the soft furrow. Entranced by the vulnerable shape of her, he lapped at the edges of softly unfurled lips and tickled them lightly. The delicate flesh was unbelievably hot, almost steaming. He blew a stream of cooling air over it, and relished the sound of her moan. Gently he licked up through the center, a long glide through silk and salty female dampness. She squirmed, her thighs spreading as he explored her with flicks and soft jabs. The slower he went, the more agitated she became. He paused to rest the flat of his tongue on the little pearl of her clitoris to feel its frantic throbbing, and she jerked and struggled to a half-sitting position.

Pausing, Keir lifted his head. "What is it, *muirninn*?"

Red-faced, gasping, she tried to pull him over her. "Make love to me."

"'Tis what I'm doing," he said, and dove back down.

"No—Keir—I meant now, *right* now—" She quivered as he chuckled into the dark patch of curls. "What are you laughing at?" she asked.

"At you, my wee impatient bully."

She looked torn between indignation and begging. "But I'm ready," she said plaintively.

Keir tried to enter her with two fingers, but the tight, tender muscle resisted. "You're no' ready," he mocked gently. "*Wheesht* now, and lie back. 'Tis one time you won't be having your way." He nuzzled between her thighs and sank his tongue deep into the heat and honey of her. She jerked at the feel of it, but he made a soothing sound and took more of the intimate flavor he needed, had to have, would never stop wanting. Moving back up to the little bud where all sensation centered, he sucked at it lightly until she was gasping and shaking all over. He tried to work two fingers inside her again, and this time they were accepted, her depths clenching and relaxing repeatedly. As he stroked her with his tongue, he found a rhythm that sent a hard quiver through her. He kept the pace steady and unhurried, making her work for it, making her writhe and arch and beg, and it was even better than he'd imagined, having her so wild beneath him, hearing her sweet little wanton noises.

There was a suspended moment as it all caught up to her . . . she arched as taut as a drawn bow . . . caught her breath . . . and began to shudder endlessly. A deep and primal satisfaction filled him at the sounds of her pleasure, and the sweet pulsing around his fingers. He drew out the feeling, patiently licking every twitch and tremor until at last she subsided and went limp beneath him.

Even then, he couldn't stop. It felt too good. He kept lapping gently, loving the salty, silky wetness of her.

Her weak voice floated down to him . . . "Oh, God . . . I don't think . . . Keir, I can't . . ."

He nibbled and teased, breathing hotly against the tender cove. "Put your legs over my shoulders," he whispered. In a moment, she obeyed. He could feel the trembling in her thighs. A satisfied smile flicked across his mouth, and he pressed her hips upward to a new angle. Soon he'd have her begging again, he thought, and lowered his head with a soft growl of enjoyment.

MUCH OF THAT night was a dark, sweet blur of sensuality, but some details caught in Merritt's memory like barbed quills, never to be dislodged. The smell of cold rain coming in through the window . . . the satiny locks of Keir's hair sliding through her fingers . . . the incredible fullness and heaviness of his possession.

He was so very gentle, despite his power and size, his fingertips sliding over her in light, beguiling patterns. His focus on her, his awareness of every sound, pulse, shiver, was absolute. His low voice tickled her ear as he murmured how beautiful she was, how good she felt, how hard she made him . . . and all the while, the thick shaft kept sinking deeper and deeper.

By the time he filled her completely, she was feverish with need. A little sob of anticipation escaped her as he began to move. But every thrust was long and agonizingly slow, withholding the last bit of stimulation she needed. He held her more closely now, his weight on her from pelvis to breasts, while his hips rolled and circled, drawing up new surges of feeling. His mouth lowered to one of her breasts, licking and gently gnawing at the erect nipple. Squirming in frustration, she pushed her hips upward, but he pulled back reflexively.

"No, love. I could hurt you."

"You won't. Please . . . Keir . . ."

"Please what?"

"I need more."

His laugh, a smolder of sound, could have come from the devil himself. "I dinna think you can take more than this, darlin'."

"I can." She strained against him.

"This deep?" he asked, reaching places in her that had never been touched before.

She shook at the pleasure of it. "Oh, God. Yes."

His hands grasped her hips, keeping them angled firmly upward as he pumped in a steady rhythm. Slow in . . . slow out . . .

"Faster," she said desperately.

"No' yet," he whispered.

"Please," she begged.

His low, dark voice curled in her ear. "There's a saying we have about whisky: Slow fire makes sweet malt."

She whimpered as he rolled his hips gently, his hardness caressing everywhere inside. The deliberate pace didn't alter, no matter how she tried to drive herself harder onto the rigid length of him. Every time she began to plead for more, his mouth came to hers in another one of those obliterating kisses.

None of this was what she'd expected. Her husband had been a considerate lover, doing everything she liked and giving her exactly what she wanted. Keir, however, was doing the exact opposite. He delighted in tormenting her until she didn't recognize herself in the frantic creature she'd become. He was absolutely wicked, shameless, making love to her in ways that felt unimaginably good, always holding satisfaction just out of reach.

"You give me so much pleasure, darlin' . . . more than a body can stand. The way you hold me so tight inside . . . like that . . . I can feel you pulling at me. Your wee, hungry body wants me deeper, aye? Put your hands on me . . . anywhere . . . ah, how I love your sweet touch . . ."

After what seemed like hours of sweet torture, he fell silent and pinned her down to keep her still, and she realized he was fighting to keep from climaxing. That excited her unbearably, and she couldn't stop her body from clamping and pulsing on the hard invasion, over and over.

Keir buried his face in the pillow with a primitive grunt, then he turned his head and told her, "Stop that, you wee wanton."

"I can't help it," she said faintly, which was true.

After a moment, he muttered, "Damn it, lass, you're like to pull the marrow from my bones." But his mouth curved against her ear.

His arms wrapped around her, and he rolled easily to his back, taking her with him.

Surprised and flummoxed, Merritt floundered a little as he gently pushed her up and arranged her legs to straddle him. "What are you doing?"

"Putting you to work," he said, "since you're so set on wringing me dry."

She looked at the brawny male beneath her and shook her head slightly.

A brief laugh escaped him as he saw her confusion. "You're a horsewoman, aye?" he asked, and nudged upward with his hips. "Ride."

Genuinely shocked at finding herself in the dominant position, Merritt braced her hands on his chest for balance. Her first tentative movement was rewarded by an encouraging lift of his hips. It sent him even deeper than before, the angle seeming to open something inside her, and she quivered in sensitive reaction. Hot and excited and mortified, she understood what he wanted. As she began to move, she gradually lost her self-consciousness and found a rhythm, her sex rubbing and pumping against his. Every downstroke sent pleasure through her, every sensation connected to the thick length of him.

Panting heavily, Keir reached up to cup her breasts, his thumbs stroking the stiff peaks. "Merry, love . . . I'm going to come soon."

"Yes," she gasped, a tide of heat approaching fast.

"You'll . . . you'll have to pull away, if you dinna want me to release inside you."

"I want it," she managed to say. "Stay in me. I want to feel you come . . . Keir . . ."

He began to pump fast and hard, his hands grasping her hips to keep her in place. His eyes half closed, the passion-drowsed intensity of his gaze pushing her over the edge. The release went on and on, new swells and crests washing over her, leaving her moaning and shivering in their wake. She felt his hands grip her thighs as he bucked beneath her once, twice, and held fast.

When he subsided, trembling like a racehorse held in check, she lay on top of him with their bodies still fused. Feeling euphoric, she nuzzled the dark golden fleece on his chest.

Keir let out a long sigh and relaxed beneath her. "Temptress," he said after a while, his voice low and lazy. "Are you satisfied, now you've had your way with a poor green lad from Islay?"

With great effort, Merritt levered herself higher on his body and touched her nose to his. "Almost."

Keir's chest moved beneath her as he chuckled. He turned until she was on her back, and carefully stroked a few loose locks of hair away from her face. Just before he kissed her, he whispered, "'Tis a good thing the night's not over, then."

THE BELLS OF St. George's were ringing. Keir blinked and emerged from sleep as he heard the sound, recalling they clanged at a quarter before six every morning, to awaken the East End workers. Time to leave, while he could still slip out unseen.

He lay still, absorbing the feel of Merritt snuggled against him from behind. Her knees were drawn up neatly beneath his, a slender arm draped across his waist. Her breath came in soft, even rushes against his back.

How sweet it felt to lie there with her warm little body tucked against him, his mind still full of the night's pleasures. A faint smile crossed his lips. He'd exhausted them both in his efforts to wrest a lifetime's worth of joy from a few short hours. And yet he still wanted her.

At first, he'd wanted, selfishly, to satisfy her so completely that she'd never forget him. To ensure he would always be the man she wanted most in her bed. But he'd been caught in a trap of his own making. *I'm the one who'll never forget. For me it will always be you, Merry, love, the woman I'll want until my last breath.*

Carefully he eased out of the warm bed and paused with a shivering stretch in the cold air. He hunted for his clothes, dressed in the semidarkness, and discovered his mended coat had been hung inside the door on the handle. His personal items had been tucked into one of the pockets. He checked his wallet, not for currency, but to look for the slip of paper with the typed names. To his satisfaction, it was still there.

A washstand had been built into the corner of the room. The pallid glow of an outside streetlamp slipped through the window as he drew back one of the curtains. He washed his face, brushed his hair, and rinsed his mouth with cold water. As he turned to the bed, his stomach felt leaden at the thought of saying good-bye. He didn't know what to say to her.

All he knew was that after he left, he'd have to learn how to live with his heart beating somewhere far away.

The first hint of daybreak frosted the shadowed room and gleamed on Merritt's bare shoulders and back. She lay on her stomach with her face turned toward him, and he saw that her eyes were open. A bittersweet smile curved her lips as she took in the sight of him standing there fully dressed.

Silently Keir willed her not to say something that would unravel him.

To his infinite relief, she said in a voice still thick from sleep, "Don't forget about my pat on the arse."

The touch of humor made him smile. He felt a rush of gratitude, realizing Merritt was not a woman to make a scene, or part with someone on an uncomfortable note. It was one of the many graces of her character that she would try to make this easier for him.

Keir approached the bed and slowly drew the covers aside to reveal her naked backside. He ran his palm over her bottom, bent to press a kiss on one full, sweet curve, and finished with the gentlest of pats.

After pulling the covers carefully back over her, he left without another word or glance. It was the most difficult thing he'd ever done, and it gave him as bad a feeling as he'd ever felt.

He walked through the chilled mist of morning, heading back to the warehouse flat to bathe and change into fresh clothes. Last night's storm had temporarily whisked away the city's haze of pollution, turning the sky soft blue and washing the roads clean of their usual pungent dust and debris.

In the past, whenever he'd slept with a woman, his mood was jaunty. Ready to take on the world. But not this time. Some protective layer had been removed, leaving his senses raw and sharpened. He was exhausted, and yet at the same time, unfamiliar energy vibrated through him as if he'd been strung with piano wires.

He went through the motions of the day, meeting with a spirit merchant, and later with the exciseman, Gruinard, who explained the procedure of transferring bonded whisky from the warehouse to the purchaser. Delivery forms and transfer applications to be filled out, assessments of duties to be paid, registries to be signed, permits and certificates to be issued.

As Keir struggled to pay attention to the mind-numbing details, he had to stifle a yawn that made his eyes water.

Gruinard chuckled, not unkindly, at the sight. "A bit 'sewn up,' as they say, after a night gallivanting about London? Can't say I blame you. I was once a young buck myself."

As evening approached, Keir went to the waterside tavern, where he saw some of the Sterling warehousemen he'd worked alongside. They called out to him heartily and insisted he sit at their table. A round of ale was poured, and someone handed him a glass filled to the brim.

"We always start with a toast to the good lady," one of them, an Irishman named O'Ceirin, told him.

Keir looked at him blankly. "The queen?"

The group laughed heartily, and O'Ceirin explained, "No, ye plank-noggin, we drink to the lady who saved our livings and kept her husband's company when she might have sold it." The Irishman raised his glass. "Fill up, lads, to the health and long life of Lady Merritt."

With a hearty chorus of approvals, the warehousemen drank deeply. Keir finished half his glass in one gulp, and tried not to show the utter gloom that had enveloped him. He was scarcely aware of ordering food, but a plate of green peas and flavorless boiled meat was set before him. After forcing down a few bites, he finished his ale and took his leave.

The warehouse was dark and quiet as Keir returned to his flat. After sitting heavily in the chair near the stove, he glanced morosely at the adjoining room, where the small, solitary bed awaited. It might as well have been a torture rack. How could he be so tired and yet so reluctant to go to bed? His body was cold everywhere except for the wound on his back, which glowed with heat. It was tender, oddly tight, pulsing with a precise and regular throb. He sat there, staring blindly at the little stove, and considered lighting it to warm the flat. No. Everything was too much effort.

Heaving a sigh, Keir finally let himself think about Merritt.

He couldn't believe he'd have to go the rest of his life without her. He wanted, needed, to see her one last time. Just for one minute. A half minute. Ten seconds. God, he was sick with longing. If he could just have a glimpse at her, he'd never ask for anything else in his life.

Maybe . . . he could go to her? *No, don't be a witless arse.* He'd barely managed leaving her once. Leaving her twice would be the death of him.

But even knowing that, Keir found himself rising to his feet and reaching for his coat. His heart thudded with anticipation. He would just ask after her well-being. Even if she didn't come to the door—if she were abed and he could only speak to the footman—that was still better than sitting here doing nothing.

He left the flat and began down the staircase leading to the outside door. But his steps slowed as he saw a cloud of smoke at the bottom of the stairwell.

Fire. A chill of alarm went through him in a flash, raising gooseflesh. He was stinging all over.

There was no such thing as a small warehouse fire. The stairwells and elevator shafts acted like chimneys, funneling flames and heat upward to spread the inferno across the wide-open floors.

With a curse, he barreled down the rest of the stairs and reached for the door handle.

It was gone.

Keir stared at the doorplate incredulously. The handle hadn't fallen off, it had been neatly removed, with the bolt turned to the locking position. Someone had deliberately trapped him in here.

A warehouse for bonded goods was designed to be as secure as a bank vault. The door, wrapped in steel sheets and attached with industrial hardware, could not be broken.

A dull roar came through the wall between the stairwell and the building's storage area. The sound of fire. Soon it would reach thousands of casks of whisky.

He was fucked.

Cursing, Keir turned and raced back up the stairs, taking them two and three at a time. He went back into the flat, fumbling slightly as he unlocked the door. He ran to the window, pulled back the fastening bar, and opened it wide. A glance down the side of the building revealed nothing in the way of stairs or fire escapes.

Three stories yawned between him and the hard-paved ground, with no way to break or soften his fall.

Very fucked.

He focused on a one-story transit shed, built approximately ten feet away from the warehouse. If he could manage to reach it, the distance of the fall would be cut by a third. But without a running start, Keir wasn't sure he could jump that far. And even if he could, he probably wouldn't survive hitting the shed's metal roof.

On the other hand, it was preferable to being roasted like an egg.

Breathing hard, Keir levered himself up to the window and stood carefully on the sill, gripping the jamb for balance.

It occurred to him that he'd probably end up being buried in England . . . far from his parents' graves and the island he loved.

Someone wanted him dead, and he'd never know why. The thought charged him with fury.

And he jumped.

Chapter 11

MERRITT STOOD IN HER bedroom as Jenny unfastened the back of her dress. It had been a long day, fraught with work she hadn't felt like doing. She hadn't been able to focus on anything for more than five minutes. Her mind had pulled back from every task like a cantankerous mule.

Her gaze strayed to the nearby bed, freshly made with pristine smooth sheets and blankets, the pillows nicely plumped. There were no signs of the torrid activity of the previous night. But for a moment, her mind conjured an image of a sleek golden body, broad shoulders rising over hers, the flash of the tiny key as it dangled from his neck and dragged gently between her naked breasts.

She gave a brief shake of her head to clear it. The bed was too large for one person, ridiculously so. She would get rid of it, she decided, and buy one half its size. Should she have the brocade counterpane cut down to fit the smaller bed? No, she would give it away and have a new one made. Perhaps something in blue—

Her musing was interrupted by a deep *boom* from outside, rattling the glass lamp housings and the crystal drops in the chandeliers.

"Holy Moses," Merritt exclaimed, "is that thunder?"

Jenny was frowning. "I don't think so, milady."

They hurried to the window and drew back the curtains. Merritt flinched at a blinding flash close to the horizon, instantly followed by another thunderous sound. It was coming from the direction of the docks, she realized. Her stomach turned to ice.

"Fasten my dress back up, Jenny," she said tensely. "No—first shout for Jeffrey and tell him to have the carriage readied, then help me with the dress."

Approximately ten minutes later, Merritt was hurrying downstairs. There was a hammering at the front door. Before she could reach it, someone shouldered inside without waiting for a response.

It was Luke, who wore no overcoat or hat. His face was set and grim as he said without preamble, "It was one of ours."

"The explosion? It was one of our warehouses? Which—"

"Yes—"

"Which one?"

"I don't know. I was at a card game at a club near the wharf. Someone came running in with the news."

"Why did you come here?" Merritt demanded, gasping with anxiety. "You should have gone to see if it was . . . if . . ." She couldn't speak for a moment. "Oh, God, Luke, do you think it was the bonded warehouse?"

Her brother's face was grim. "It was a bloody massive explosion," he said quietly. "The kind that would happen if fire reached a hundred thousand gallons of alcohol. I came straight here because I knew you'd rush to the scene, and it's as dangerous as hell. Listen to me, Merritt—I'm only letting you go there on condition that you stay close to me. You're not to leave my side without asking. Agreed?"

Merritt was both astonished and irritated by the tone of command she'd never heard from her younger brother before. Although she wanted to inform him that she had too much common sense to go dashing about the scene of raging fire, she didn't want to waste time. "Agreed," she said shortly. "Let's go."

They went out to a waiting hansom cab and headed toward the wharf at a breakneck pace. To Merritt's agonized frustration, the vehicle was forced to slow as they approached the main gate. A sea of onlookers had already amassed, filling the streets and making it difficult for the fire brigades' horse teams and steam engines to reach the docks. A cacophony of sounds filled the air, clanging bells, pumping steamers in the water, and people shouting.

"We'll have to stop here," Luke said, and paid the driver before helping Merritt out. He kept an arm around her, trying to protect her from the crush of bodies as they made their way through the crowd.

The flames illuminated the wharf with the brilliance of midday. A coughing sob broke from Merritt's throat as she saw the main source of the fire was indeed warehouse number three. She felt a hot slide of tears down to the edge of her jaw.

"He may not have been in there," Luke said immediately. "He might be at a tavern or . . . or the devil knows . . . a brothel or music hall."

Merritt nodded, trying to take comfort from the words. She blotted her wet cheek with the sleeve of her coat. It was a measure of her feelings for the man that she would have been overjoyed to find out he was at a brothel. Anything, *anything* other than being caught in that inferno.

"He could be wandering through the crowd right now," Luke continued. "If so, we'll have little chance of finding him."

"Let's search the area around the warehouse."

"Sweetheart, we won't be able to go anywhere near there. Just look at—no, you're too short to see over the crowd. There are at least a half-dozen steamers in the water, pumping at full force, and two rolling engines trying to extinguish it from the street."

"Maybe we can find out something from one of the firemen," Merritt said desperately. "Help me reach them." At his hesitation, she added, *"Please."*

"Damn it all," Luke muttered, and began to guide her through the jostling mass of bodies. Merritt could hardly see or breathe with so many people packed around them. A pungent, strangely sweet haze filled the air—the smell of whisky burning, she realized with piercing despair.

An anxious murmur went through the crowd as eerie blue flares began to shoot up from the warehouse like tentacles. Abruptly Luke hauled Merritt against him and covered her head with his arms. A fraction of a second later, she felt the ground shake from a brutal explosion. Heat seared her exposed skin as a massive fireball blossomed toward the sky. Screams erupted from the gathering, and people began to push and shove in panic.

As Luke and Merritt were swept along with the flow of bodies, she felt someone step on the hem of her cloak. She clutched at her brother to keep from falling. Perceiving the problem instantly, he ripped the cloak's fastening at her throat and let it drop. In seconds, it had been trampled by a battalion's worth of feet.

Merritt gave a little yelp of surprise as Luke picked her up bodily and threw her over his shoulder. She stayed still, trying to make it easier for him to carry her as he made his way toward a long shed near the burning warehouse.

Carefully Luke bent to set Merritt on her feet beside a brick wall, which provided some shelter from the blistering heat of the warehouse, about thirty yards away. "Stay right here," he said brusquely.

It was difficult to hear anything over the hissing and roaring of the steam engine nearby. Merritt squinted at their surroundings through a slow rain of bright cinders and ash that floated like black feathers. The shed contained shops belonging to the blacksmith, fitter, and wheelwright, with a shared work yard. Her attention was caught by a cluster of men standing near a large anvil, all staring at something on the ground.

"I'm going to try to talk to someone from the fire brigade and find out—" Luke fell silent as Merritt reached out with one hand to grip the lapel of his coat. He followed the direction of her gaze.

One of the men had moved, revealing a glimpse of a man's booted leg extended along the ground.

They were standing over a body.

Merritt felt her limbs turn to lead. The man she'd been intimate with only last night . . . the tender, passionate lover with laughing blue eyes and wicked hands . . . might be lying dead a few yards away from her.

She experienced a sensation she'd felt only twice in

her life. Once when she'd been kicked in the stomach by a pony that had spooked at an unexpected noise. The glancing blow had driven out her breath and filled her with nausea.

The second time was when she'd learned about Joshua's ship sinking.

With an incoherent sound, she started forward.

Luke caught her around the waist. "Merritt, no. *Stop.*"

She writhed in his grasp, focused only on the scene in front of her.

"Merritt," Luke persisted, grasping her chin and compelling her to look up at him. She blinked and subsided at the sight of her brother's strained face. He stared down at her with intense dark eyes, the same color as her own. "Let me go look," he said. "If it's him, it . . . you may not want to see." He paused. "Whatever happens, I'm here with you. Don't forget that."

Dazedly Merritt realized her younger brother, once a baby she'd helped to dress and bathe, and later a toddler she'd taught how to eat pudding with a spoon, had become a man she could rely on.

She set her jaw and nodded to let him know she wouldn't fall apart.

Luke let go of her and went to push his way into the gathering. He crouched on his heels beside the form on the ground.

Seconds passed as if they were years. Five . . . ten . . . fifteen . . . while Merritt stood like a cemetery statue.

Remaining in a crouch, Luke twisted and gestured for her to come.

Chapter 12

GALVANIZED, MERRITT RUSHED FORWARD as a few of the men shuffled aside to make room for her. She saw the gleam of golden-amber hair, and knelt beside the long body on the ground to look over him frantically.

It was Keir, and he was alive. At least for now. He was battered and filthy, but to her amazement, he didn't seem to have suffered serious burns. He must have been outside the warehouse when the fire had started, but close enough to have been caught in the explosion. She stripped off her gloves and gently touched his face. "Keir . . . Keir."

The thick lashes fluttered and lifted slightly, but he didn't open his eyes. He wasn't breathing at all well, his chest spasming in a struggle for air. After pulling a handkerchief from a skirt pocket, Merritt wiped at a trickle of fresh blood at the corner of his mouth. She longed to take him away from all this smoke and filth, and put him in a clean, soft bed, and make him well again.

As she moved to cradle his head in her lap, the change of position caused him to cough and gasp like a landed fish. Merritt held the handkerchief to his lips, and it came away spattered with blood. She glanced up at her brother, who had stood to talk to some of the men. "Luke," she managed to say unsteadily, "I need your coat to keep him warm."

Without hesitation, Luke unbuttoned the wool garment.

"Why can't he breathe?" Merritt asked desperately. "Is it smoke inhalation?"

"Broken ribs, maybe. Someone saw him jump from the window of the warehouse flat just before the first explosion."

Tears sprang to her eyes. "He suffered a three-story fall?"

"Yes, but not all at once. He landed on a shed roof about twenty feet down, and then the blast knocked him the rest of the way to the ground. A couple of lightermen risked their lives and went to haul him away from the building." Luke bent to drape his coat over Keir's supine form. "I'm going to find a cart or wagon," he continued, "and have these fellows help me move him. The question is, where to? The nearest hospital is Mercy Vale, but I wouldn't take my worst enemy there. We could try for Shoreditch Hospital, although—"

"My house."

After a brief silence, Luke replied, "You're not thinking clearly."

Merritt shot him a narrow-eyed glance. "My house," she repeated. She was going to protect and take care of Keir, not leave him to the mercy of strangers.

"Whether he survives or dies there, it's going to cause a bloody scandal."

Merritt shook her head wildly. "He's not going to die. And I don't give a damn about scandal."

"Maybe not now, but later—"

"Please, Luke," she said urgently, "let's not waste time arguing. Go find a wagon, quickly."

"I'LL TAKE IT as a good sign that he's still breathing," Luke commented later. "I was sure he was going to kick the bucket before we even reached the house."

Although Merritt didn't like the way her brother had put that, she'd had the same thought on the torturous ride back to Carnation Lane. She'd sat with Keir on the back of the vegetable wagon, keeping his head and shoulders on her lap, while loose turnips had rolled around them. The jarring of the wheels on rough road had drawn a few groans from him as he seemed to drift in and out of consciousness.

After Luke and Jeffrey had carried Keir to a guest room, the footman left immediately to fetch Dr. Gibson.

Luke stood at the foot of the bed, watching with a deep frown as Merritt removed the unconscious man's shoes. "I'll stay if you want me to help with him," he said. "But I'd like to go back to the wharf and find out if anyone else was injured. I also have to meet with the salvage corps and notify the insurance company."

"Go," Merritt said, stripping off Keir's wool socks. "I can manage until the doctor arrives."

"I'll come back as soon as I can. In the meantime, why don't you send for one of your friends in London to help you?"

"I'll consider it," Merritt said, but the only friend she would have liked to send for was Lady Phoebe Ravenel, who was in Essex.

Frowning, Luke came to look at the man on the bed. Keir was abnormally pale, his lips and fingernails blue-tinged. He was panting as if he couldn't take in enough air.

"God knows what injuries he might have," Luke said softly. "You'd better brace yourself for the possibility that he may not—"

"He's going to make a full recovery," Merritt interrupted. She felt like a vase someone had bumped into. Wobbly, about to tip over and break.

"He's a stranger, Merritt. Even if the worst happens, you don't know him well enough to fall to pieces."

Annoyed, Merritt was tempted to explain the folly of trying to dictate people's feelings to them, but she managed to hold her silence.

After her brother had left, Merritt did what she could to make Keir clean and comfortable. She resorted to cutting away the garments that couldn't be removed easily, and bathed him with a clean warm cloth. The strong, supple contours she'd become so familiar with, all those expanses of tough muscle, were now badly bruised. There was a lump on the back of his head. Every now and then his eyes flickered open, revealing a disoriented gaze, but he made no effort to speak.

To her relief, Garrett Gibson arrived quickly, striding into the guest room without even knocking. The footman, Jeffrey, followed close behind, carrying a leather case and a box of supplies. At the doctor's direction, he set them near the bed before leaving.

"Thank God you're here," Merritt burst out as Garrett went straight to the bedside. "Mr. MacRae can hardly breathe."

"The footman said he was injured during the warehouse fire?" Garrett rummaged through her medical bag. She pulled out a stethoscope and deftly fitted the earpieces into her ears. Her manner was so calm and assured, it seemed as if nothing bad could happen while she was there.

"Yes. There was an explosion. He—" Merritt couldn't prevent her voice from cracking into a higher register as she fought tears. "He jumped from a window and fell at least two stories."

Garrett held the drum of the stethoscope against various parts of Keir's chest, listening intently. After that, she set the instrument aside, took his pulse, and then spoke to him. "Mr. MacRae, are you awake?" At his lack of response, she gently took his face in her hands. "Can you look at me? Are you able to open your—there's a good fellow." She inspected his pupils, and gave him a reassuring smile. "I know it's hard to breathe," she told him sympathetically. "We'll do something about that in just a moment."

Merritt stood nearby, knotting her fingers together. Her lungs worked in strong pulls, as if she could somehow do Keir's breathing for him. She'd never felt so utterly helpless. She watched as Garrett went to the leather case, unlatched it, and began to fit a strange assortment of objects together . . . a steel cylinder approximately a foot and a half long, a bottle of clear liquid, a length of rubber tubing.

"What is that?" Merritt asked apprehensively.

"Oxygen apparatus," Garrett replied as she worked. "I've used it before to treat an asthmatic patient. I decided to bring it after Jeffrey described Mr. MacRae's symptoms." She connected a rubber bag to the contraption, turned a knob on the cylinder to start the oxygen flow, and fitted a cup over Keir's nose and mouth. He jerked and tried to turn his head, but she held the cup against his face persistently. "Breathe in," she coaxed, "slow and steady."

After only a minute had passed, the oxygen had wrought a near-miraculous change. Keir's color had lost its blue cast and returned to a healthy pink, and his desperate gasping had eased.

"There we are," Garrett said quietly, her slim shoulders relaxing. "Better?"

Keir nodded slightly, reaching up to grip her hand with the cup more firmly over his face as if fearing she might take it away too soon.

Merritt blotted her stinging eyes with a handkerchief and let out a shaking sigh.

The doctor glanced at her with a slight smile. "Go set yourself to rights, my friend," she suggested gently, "while I continue the examination. A cup of tea might do you some good."

Merritt realized the doctor wanted to protect her patient's privacy while she examined him. "Of course," she said, even though the last thing she wanted to do was leave Keir's side. "Ring the bellpull if there's anything you need."

Reluctantly she left the guest room, and found Jenny waiting in the hallway. The young maid gazed at her in worry. "Will the gentleman be all right, ma'am?"

"Yes," Merritt replied distractedly. "He has to."

"I'll help look after him, milady, if you need me to. I nursed my father through a fever once, and I know what to do in a sickroom."

"Thank you, Jenny. For now, if you would bring some tea to my room . . ."

"Right away."

Merritt wandered to her bedroom. The huge bed was pristinely made with fresh linens and blankets, the counterpane perfectly smooth. She glanced in her bedroom mirror, and was taken aback. Her face was soot-streaked, her eyes were red-rimmed, her hair was straggling down from its pins, and her dress was filthy. Grimacing, she pulled the pins from her hair and set them on her vanity table.

She could hardly catch up with her own thoughts. Her brain seemed to be working at twice its usual speed. She brushed her hair with vigorous strokes, twisted it into a simple chignon, and anchored it with pins. Although she still didn't know the extent of Keir's injuries, it was clear he would need a great deal of rest and care while he recovered. There would be a scandal if she kept him at her house. Perhaps she could take him down to the Marsden estate in Hampshire? *Yes.* It was safe and secluded there, and her family would help her. The idea was vastly comforting. She would take Keir there as soon as possible, depending on what Garrett said about his condition.

Jenny returned with the tea and helped her to wash and change into a clean dress. After gulping down a second cup of tea, Merritt glanced at the clock on the mantel. Forty-five minutes had passed since she'd left Keir with Garrett Gibson. Surely that was enough time to have finished examining him.

She went to the guest room and stopped at the closed door. Her heart leaped with gladness as she heard the sounds of conversation. Keir's familiar baritone was rusty-sounding and broken with coughing, but he was conscious and able to communicate.

Eagerly she knocked at the door with a single knuckle, pushed it open, and peeked around the edge. "May I come in?" she asked.

Garrett, who was sitting at the bedside, gave her a perturbed glance. "Yes, for a moment."

Merritt came to the bedside, while a mixture of joy, worry, and longing nearly overwhelmed her. Keir was partially propped up on pillows, regarding her with those cool, light blue eyes. Although battered and bruised, he appeared to be in remarkably good condition, considering what he'd been through.

"I'm so glad you're awake," she told him unsteadily.

Keir hesitated an unaccountably long moment. Instead of replying, he turned to Garrett with a raspy-voiced question.

"Who is she?"

Chapter 13

MERRITT'S STOMACH PLUMMETED.

Who is she? Was he joking? No . . . he was staring at her as if she were a stranger he didn't particularly want in the room with him. Was something wrong with his vision?

Garrett made a subtle patting motion in the air, signaling for her to stay calm. "Mr. MacRae," she asked, "do you not know this lady?"

His baffled, wary gaze returned to Merritt, and he shook his head. "Have we met?"

Her throat wouldn't work. She nodded, tried again to speak, and couldn't. Realizing she was still nodding dementedly, she forced herself to stop. *Yes, as a matter of fact, you spent most of last night in my bed, making love to me in every position except upside-down.* She still felt the trace of intimate soreness, and the strained muscles of inner thighs that had been spread for hours.

And he didn't recognize her.

"This is Lady Merritt," Garrett told him in a matter-of-fact tone. "You made her acquaintance a few days ago upon arriving in London."

"Sterling's widow," Keir said in that rough voice, frowning as if the effort to think caused him pain. "I beg your pardon, milady."

"That's . . . quite all right," Merritt managed to say.

Garrett reached over to adjust an ice bag beside his head. "Nothing to worry about," she said. "It's time for more oxygen." She turned the valves on the oxygen cylinder, fiddled with the tubing and attached wash bottle, and placed the cup against his mouth and nose. "Are you able to hold this while I speak to Lady Merritt for a moment?"

"Aye."

By tacit agreement, the two women went to the threshold. Merritt stood out in the hallway, while Garrett spoke softly through the partially open door. "First . . . there's a very good chance he'll survive."

"And recover?"

There was a worrisome hesitation before Garrett replied. "As far as I can tell, there are at least two ribs that are either fractured or badly bruised, but either way they'll heal. The lungs are a more concerning issue. There's a particular injury associated with explosions—I saw it once during my residency in France when a young soldier was brought to the hospital, and more recently when I treated a patient whose kitchen boiler exploded. Even though there's no obvious external damage to the chest, the force of the blast bruises the lungs. Mr. MacRae's case doesn't seem to be severe, however. With rest and good care, I would expect his lungs and breathing capacity to return to normal in ten to fourteen days."

"Thank God," Merritt said fervently.

"The more serious problem is the concussion—a trauma to the brain caused by a blow to the head. It's a good sign that he's had no seizures, nor is he slurring his words. However, I need to evaluate him more thoroughly before giving you a realistic prognosis. There could be lasting after-effects such as headaches, problems sleeping, difficulty with things like reading or tallying numbers . . ."

"And memory loss?"

"Yes. The good news is, he's perfectly cognizant of who he is and where he lives, and he's told me the names of family and friends, as well as a few details about his business. But, the last thing he remembers is departing for London. I estimate he's lost approximately a week's worth of memories."

Merritt sagged against the doorjamb and stared fixedly at the doctor.

A week, she thought numbly. A small loss, most people would say, all things considered. She might have said the same thing herself, not long ago.

But now she knew how important a week could be. A life could change course in a few days. In an hour. A single moment. People could gain and lose the world.

A heart could be broken.

FOR HOURS, MERRITT occupied a chair in the corner of the guest room and watched as Garrett took care of Keir. She did what she could to help, taking away used rags and towels, emptying basins of soapy water, and holding the oxygen mask over Keir's face while Garrett stepped out of the room from time to time.

"Why don't you go to your room and lie down for a bit?" Garrett had offered, around midnight. "I promise to wake you if there's any change in his condition."

"I'd rather stay, if you don't mind. You probably

think I'm very foolish, carrying on over a man I've known only a matter of days."

An odd little smile crossed Garrett's face. "Someday I'll tell you about my courtship with Ethan."

At approximately two o'clock in the morning, there came a tap at the guest room door, and Merritt heard her brother's voice.

"Merritt. It's me."

She sat up in the corner chair she'd occupied for hours, and rubbed her sore, tired eyes. "Come in."

The door cracked open to reveal Luke's grimy face. "Better not," he said ruefully. "I'm filthy, and I've been toasted like Welsh rarebit." He glanced around the edge of the door, surveying the scene.

Keir was sleeping on his side, while Garrett sat nearby, monitoring his condition and administering oxygen at intervals.

Merritt stood and stretched her sore back, and went out to the hallway to talk with Luke. He was sooty, muddy, and clearly exhausted, and his clothes reeked of smoke. "Poor old Buster," she said with a frown of concern. Luke had earned the affectionate family nickname as an energetic toddler, mowing down everything in his path and leaving broken teacups and vases in his wake. "What can I do for you? Are you hungry? I'll make sandwiches and tea. Do you—"

"First tell me how MacRae is."

She relayed everything Garrett had told her about Keir's condition.

"Naturally we'll make sure he has the best of care," Luke said. "But he can't stay here, sis. He really can't."

"It's not up to you, dear," Merritt replied gently.

"Hang it all, I know that. But you still can't—"

"Did you send word to the insurance company?"

"Yes, and then I went to the docks. The fire's under control now. The transit shed burned down, but the other warehouses are intact."

"That's a relief."

Luke nodded and rubbed the back of his neck wearily. "I saw Ethan Ransom there with the fire inspector, and I went over to talk with them."

Merritt blinked in surprise. Garrett's husband, Ethan, held a position of considerable power and authority in the Metropolitan Police. Even though the warehouse fire had been serious, an investigation would ordinarily have been handled by someone much lower down.

"Do they suspect arson?" she asked.

"Yes. It had to be. As I told Ransom, every Sterling employee knows the fire safety rules. They routinely check their pockets for stray matches every morning before entering the warehouse. No machinery was in operation, so it couldn't have been a stray spark. The only person who had access to the building was MacRae, and I can't conceive he would have been fool enough to start a fire in the flat. Furthermore, even if he had, it would have been contained in there, because the flat—and the stairwell leading up to it—were built with fireproof brick walls instead of frame." Luke paused. "Ransom asked if he could stop by here tonight to check on his wife and ask a few questions in the bargain. I told him I thought you wouldn't object."

"On the contrary, I'll be very pleased to see him."

"Good, because he'll be here soon." Luke paused

before asking hopefully, "Did you say something about sandwiches?"

Merritt smiled. "I'll bring a tray to the front parlor."

She went to the kitchen, fetched various items from the larder and pantry, and set the teakettle to boil. Although most ladies of her position rarely, if ever, set foot in the kitchen, Merritt had fallen into the habit of making small meals for herself on Cook's days off. It was faster and more convenient than waiting for things to be brought to her, and there was something soothing about puttering in her own kitchen. She made sandwiches with brown bread, ham, and mustard, and added hard-boiled eggs and pickles on the side.

By the time Merritt brought a tray out to the front parlor, she found Luke talking with Ethan Ransom.

"My goodness," she exclaimed, entering the room, "I didn't hear you arrive, Mr. Ransom. Luke, dear, if you'll take this and set it on the low table—" She handed the heavy tray to her brother and turned to Ethan. "I'm so very glad to see you," she said, giving him both her hands.

Ethan Ransom pressed her hands firmly in his and smiled down at her. "My lady." He was a good-looking man with black hair and dark blue eyes, his handsomeness agreeably roughened by a scar or two, and a nose that had once been broken. He had the perpetually vigilant gaze of a man who was all too familiar with the more dangerous streets and rookeries of London. But when he was among family and friends, he had a quiet, relaxed charm that Merritt liked immensely.

As the illegitimate son of the late Earl of Trenear,

Ethan was the most enigmatic member of the Ravenel family. Very little was known about his past, and he preferred to keep it that way. However, he was good friends with West Ravenel, who was married to Merritt's best friend, Phoebe, and Phoebe had told her a great deal about him.

"Ethan once worked as a government agent," Phoebe had said. "He was part of an intelligence force that was secretly funded by the Home Office. It had something to do with espionage and foreign intelligence, and one's better off not asking too many questions about it. But Ethan was a *highly* trained agent."

Bringing her thoughts back to the present, Merritt asked Ethan, "How long have you been here?"

"I've only just arrived," he replied.

"If you've come to retrieve your wife, I'm afraid we can't give her back yet," Merritt said with a wan smile. "She's the only reason Mr. MacRae has survived."

"How is he now?"

"Badly injured. He has a concussion and can't remember anything about the past few days."

"At all?" Ethan frowned, his gaze turning inward. "Damn," he muttered.

Luke, who had picked up a sandwich and was in the process of wolfing it down, volunteered with his mouth half full, "Dr. Gibson said the memory loss may be temporary."

Nonplussed by her brother's oafish manners, Merritt said, "Dear, why don't you make yourself comfortable on the couch?"

Luke gave her an unrepentant glance. "Sis, I know you'd prefer me to sit and eat like a civilized person.

But if you knew everything these trousers have been through tonight, you wouldn't want them on your furniture."

Ethan's lips twitched.

"I made several sandwiches," Merritt told Ethan. "You're welcome to have some if you'd like."

"Thank you, but first I'd like to see my wife."

"I'll take you up to her," Merritt said promptly, leading him out of the parlor.

Luke's muffled voice came from behind them. "I'll keep an eye on the sandwiches."

As they crossed the entrance foyer on the way to the stairs, Ethan stopped Merritt with a low murmur. "My lady."

She turned to him with an inquiring glance.

"Before we go upstairs," Ethan said carefully, "there's something I need to ask. I'm in the process of putting a puzzle together, and your help would be very much appreciated. Obviously, whatever you tell me will be kept in confidence."

"Is Mr. MacRae a part of the puzzle?"

He stared at her directly as he replied. "He's the center of it."

That gave Merritt a chill. "Has he been accused of something?"

"No," Ethan said with reassuring firmness. "Nor is he under suspicion of any wrongdoing. At the moment, my primary concern is keeping him alive."

"In that case, ask me anything."

"Last night, after Garrett left here . . . did MacRae end up staying for dinner?"

"He did."

"When did he leave?"

Merritt hesitated. It was no small risk to answer that question. Were it to be made publicly known that she'd spent the night with a man out of wedlock, her reputation would be ruined. She would become a fallen woman—as in fallen from the grace of God—and treated as an outcast by polite society. Even sympathetic friends would have no choice but to shun her or have their own reputations ruined by association.

She felt color flooding her cheeks, but she held his gaze as she replied calmly, "He stayed here the entire night, and left soon after the bells at St. George's rang."

It relieved her to see no trace of censure in Ethan's gaze. "Thank you," he said simply, acknowledging her trust. "Did he happen to mention where he was going?"

"He had business meetings. I'm not sure with whom, but . . ." Merritt paused as she heard a decisive knock at the front door. "Who on earth . . . ?" she said blankly, and went to answer it.

As the door opened, a gust of cold autumn wind blew in, causing the hem of the visitor's flowing black overcoat to flicker like a raven's wings. He cut a magnificent figure, looking as fresh and alert as if it were morning rather than the dead of night.

"Uncle Sebastian?" Merritt asked in bewilderment. It was unheard-of for a duke to wait on someone's doorstop. Usually a footman would first come to knock and make inquiries before the lord or lady descended from the carriage. Tonight, however, it seemed that Sebastian, the Duke of Kingston, had decided not to stand on ceremony. He smiled at Merritt.

"Darling girl," he said quietly. "May I come in?"

As soon as he was inside, Merritt went to Phoebe's father, and his arms closed around her in a brief, comforting embrace. She and her siblings had always known Kingston as the kind, handsome man with an abundant supply of funny stories, and always made time to play jackstraws or checkers with bored children. As Merritt had grown older, however, it had been impossible to avoid the gossip about his notorious past. She found it difficult to reconcile that version of him—the skirt-chasing scoundrel—with the devoted family man whose entire world centered around his wife. Whatever Kingston's past, he was like a second father, and she would have trusted him with her life.

The duke looked down at Merritt with a mixture of fondness and concern. "I'm sorry about the warehouse," he said. "Whatever you need, you have only to ask."

"Thank you, Uncle, but . . . how did you find out so quickly? And why are you here?"

For all Kingston's charm, he was a difficult man to read, habitually keeping his thoughts and feelings concealed. "I came to ask after the injured man," he said. "I happened to make his acquaintance at my club the day before yesterday."

"Yes, he told me about that."

Sharp interest flickered in the duke's gaze. "You saw him afterward?"

Merritt shrugged evasively, wishing she'd kept her mouth shut.

"And now you've brought him to your own home," he commented.

"The warehouse flat was destroyed," Merritt said, trying not to sound defensive.

"Tell me the nature of his injuries."

"Well, you see—wait, before we go into that, why have you taken such an interest in Mr. MacRae? And how—" Merritt stopped and looked up at Ethan, who had come to her side. She realized the two of them knew something about Keir that she didn't. "What's going on?" she demanded.

"I sent word to His Grace earlier this evening," Ethan replied, "as soon as I found out MacRae had been injured." He turned to Kingston with a slight scowl. "Sir, I thought I made it clear there was no need for you to come."

"You did," Kingston said calmly. "However, in light of the fact that over the course of two nights the lad was nearly carved up and roasted like a saddle of mutton, my involvement is obviously called for."

Luke spoke up then, having come from the parlor at the sound of the duke's arrival. "Hello, Uncle Sebastian. What did you just say? Carved up like a . . . did something happen to MacRae that I don't know about? Involving a knife?"

Merritt answered reluctantly. "Someone attacked Mr. MacRae in an alley the night before last, when he was on the way here for dinner. I sent for Dr. Gibson to come stitch him up."

"On the way here for dinner . . ." Luke repeated, and gave her a dark look.

Ethan, meanwhile, regarded the duke with thinly veiled exasperation. "With all due respect, Your Grace . . ." He paused to search for words.

After a few tense moments, Kingston let out a short sigh. "Ransom, everyone knows the phrase 'with all due respect' never precedes anything respectful whatsoever. Just speak your mind."

"Yes, sir. Your involvement at this point is only going to complicate the situation. It would be best for all concerned if you'd go home and wait for me to send word."

The duke leveled a cool glance at him. "You know why I'm not going to do that."

"*He* might know," Merritt burst out, "but *I* don't, and I'd like someone to explain what you're being so mysterious about."

Ethan looked apologetic as he replied. "I'm not at liberty to say, my lady."

She turned to Kingston. "Uncle?"

"My dear, as of yet there's nothing to tell, only unconfirmed suspicions. I'd rather not discuss it now." The duke focused on Ethan. "Ransom, what did you find out at the scene of the fire?"

"It was arson," Ethan said quietly. "The fire inspector found discarded kerosene cans by the road between the warehouse and the export sheds. And someone tampered with the exterior door to the bonded warehouse. The deadbolt was locked and the door handles removed. Whoever did it waited until MacRae was in the warehouse flat, and made sure he couldn't escape after the fire was set."

Merritt began to tremble with horror and rage. "Why would someone want to kill him?"

"I don't know yet," Ethan replied. "But I'll find out. In the meantime, he can't stay here."

Luke broke in triumphantly. "That's what I've been saying."

"We need to take him out of London," Ethan continued, "to a place where he can recover in safety while I find out who's behind this."

"I've already decided to convey Mr. MacRae to Hampshire," Merritt said, "to Stony Cross Park."

Her brother looked at her blankly. "Home? *Our* home?"

"Our parents' home," she said. "I'm sure they won't mind taking him in and helping me look after him."

"He's not a stray puppy, Merritt!"

Ethan intervened before an argument began in earnest. "My lady, since we don't yet know why MacRae is in danger, or who might be after him, I think it's better if you and your family are kept out of it."

"Ransom is right," the duke told her flatly. "You have more than enough to keep you occupied, and you have a reputation to consider. Don't worry about MacRae. You have my personal assurance he'll receive the best of care." He leveled a glance at Ethan. "He'll recuperate at my home in Sussex. My estate is large and well-guarded, and my wife and two youngest children are away on a trip to Paris."

"Uncle Sebastian," Luke asked in bemusement, "why do you want him? In fact, why are you here at all?"

Kingston ignored the questions, his attention remaining on Ethan. "I'll make the necessary arrangements for transportation," he said. "If the doctor says MacRae can be moved, I'll have him out of here by morning."

Ethan considered that, and agreed with a nod. "I'll tell Garrett there's no choice," he said quietly. "He won't be safe here, and neither will Lady Merritt, until he's gone."

Merritt was filled with anxiety as she realized the situation was now out of her control. Keir was being taken away from her. Decisions would be made for him, involving his safety and health, that she would have no part of. She couldn't let that happen.

"I'm coming with you," she burst out. "I insist. I *must*."

As all three men looked at her, she realized how odd her behavior must appear. She was far too agitated, too emotional, over the fate of a man she barely knew.

A curious, speculative expression flickered across the duke's face. "Why must you?" he asked softly.

Merritt took a deep breath, cleared her throat, and replied calmly, "You see, Mr. MacRae and I are engaged."

Chapter 14

A STUNNED SILENCE FOLLOWED MERRITT'S announcement. Then—

"Have you lost your mind?" Luke demanded. "You've only known him for three days!"

"It was long enough," Merritt said. "He spent last night here. I've been compromised, very compromised indeed. If he doesn't marry me, I could be thrown out of British society, and possibly driven out of England altogether. If you don't want me living in Prussia or Australia under an assumed name, you'll support my engagement." Which was overstating the case somewhat, but in these circumstances, she felt a little hyperbole was forgivable.

Dumbfounded, Luke rubbed the lower half of his face. "Before Keir MacRae arrived, everything was normal. Now there's been stabbings, explosions, and debauchery, and my sensible older sister is engaged to a Scottish whisky distiller. What's happened to you? You're supposed to be level-headed!"

Merritt tried to sound dignified. "Just because one is *usually* level-headed doesn't mean one is *always* level-headed."

"You won't be compromised if no one knows about it," Luke said. "And God knows none of us are going to say anything."

The duke intervened, his voice so dry one could have struck a match off it. "My boy, you're missing the point. Your sister wants to be compromised."

Ethan Ransom, who had been inching toward the stairs, ventured, "I don't need to be part of this conversation. I'm going up to see my wife."

Kingston motioned for him to leave with a graceful flick of his hand.

Luke was staring at Merritt with a deep frown. "I'm going to take you to Hampshire. The warehouse fire was a shock. You need rest and fresh air, and maybe a good long talk with Father—"

"The only place I'm going is with my fiancé," Merritt said.

Uncomfortable color rose in her brother's face. "Merritt . . . God knows I don't blame you for wanting . . . companionship. But you don't have to marry for it. Only a lunatic would decide to spend the rest of her life with a man she's just met."

"Not necessarily," Kingston said mildly.

Luke sent him an aggravated glance. "Uncle Sebastian, you can't approve of her marrying a stranger."

"It depends on the stranger." The duke glanced down at Merritt. "Apparently there's something special about this one."

"Yes," Merritt said, relieved that he seemed to be on her side. "He's . . ." But the words died in her throat as she noticed something she had missed until now.

Having known the duke for her entire life, Merritt had never thought about his looks. She was aware he was handsome, of course, but she'd never paid particular attention to his individual features or spent any time at all dwelling on them. To her he had always simply been Uncle Sebastian.

But in this moment, as she stared up at him, she was struck by the distinctive pale blue of his eyes, like a winter sky, like moonlight . . . like Keir's.

Shaken, she stared up at this complex, powerful man, who was so familiar . . . and yet so full of mystery.

"Let me stay with him," she whispered. "Take me with you."

Those light, piercing eyes stared into hers, kindly but not without calculation. Appearing to come to a decision, Kingston said slowly, "I'll send for Phoebe to stay with us at Heron's Point. Her presence will satisfy the proprieties, and I daresay you'll want to chat with her about . . . recent developments."

"Thank you," Merritt said, and let out an unsteady sigh of relief.

Their gazes held as they settled on an unspoken pact: When it came to the issue of Keir MacRae, Uncle Sebastian would be her ally, just as she would be his.

"I'd like a brief word with Dr. Gibson," the duke commented, "before I leave to make arrangements."

"I'll go up with you," Merritt said. She turned to Luke, who looked surly and exhausted. With a pang of affection, she went to him, stood on her toes, and kissed his cheek. "Will you stay in London to take care of Sterling Enterprises?"

Luke accepted the kiss but didn't return it. "Do I have a choice?"

"Thank you. If there's anything you need to ask, you know where I'll be."

"What I need is for you not to behave like a resident

of the local madhouse," he muttered. "Tell me, Merritt, if someone you knew were carrying on like this over a stranger—one of our sisters, God forbid—what would you say to her?"

At the moment, Merritt didn't feel like justifying her actions to anyone, least of all a younger sibling. But during the past year, she and Luke had formed a working partnership and friendship that made their bond unique. She would tolerate more from him than from nearly anyone else in her life. "I would probably caution her that she was acting impulsively," she admitted, "and advise her to rely on the counsel of those who love her."

"All right, then. I'm counseling you to stay in London and let Ransom and Uncle Sebastian decide what to do with MacRae. Whatever it is you feel for him, it's not real. It happened too fast."

In her weariness and strain, Merritt's temper had a lower flashpoint than usual. She could feel it beginning to ignite, but she grimly tamped it back down and managed a calm reply. "You may be right," she said. "But someday, Luke . . . you'll meet someone. And from one breath to the next, everything will change. You won't care whether it makes sense. All you'll know is that a stranger owns your every heartbeat."

Luke's mouth twisted. "God, I hope not." He heaved a sigh. "I'm going home for a few hours of rest. Tomorrow's going to be busy."

Merritt felt a strong twinge of guilt, leaving him to manage the company on his own at the worst possible time. "I'm sorry for abandoning you in the middle of a crisis," she said.

Luke looked down at her with a hint of reluctant amusement. "Don't worry, sweetheart. I can handle this. If I can't, I have no business running the company."

After her brother had collected his hat and coat and departed, Merritt went upstairs with Kingston.

As they ascended the staircase, the duke remarked, "You handled that well. I doubt Phoebe would have been able to summon as much restraint in the face of a younger brother's criticism."

"Well, you see," Merritt said ruefully, "Luke wasn't wrong. I . . . I think I have gone a bit mad."

The duke gave a soft huff of amusement. "I wouldn't worry. If you can say you've gone mad, or at least allow for the possibility, you're not."

They reached the guest room, and Merritt tapped on the door before opening it cautiously. In the dim light shed by a small lamp, Keir lay on his side, eyes closed, while Garrett stood at the bedside and talked quietly to Ethan.

Upon seeing Merritt and Kingston, Garrett came to the doorway and curtsied. "Your Grace."

"Dr. Gibson," the duke said. "A pleasure to see you, as always." His gaze went to the shadowed figure on the bed. "What is his condition?"

Garrett described Keir's injuries succinctly, and added with a frown, "I understand the necessity of moving him, but I certainly wouldn't recommend it. He's in considerable pain, and he needs rest and quiet."

"Can't you give him something?" Merritt asked.

"Not while his breathing is so labored. Morphine tends to depress lung function."

Kingston's attention seemed riveted on the injured

man. "I'd be obliged, Doctor, if you would make a list of what he'll require on the trip down to Sussex. You'll accompany us, of course."

Garrett frowned and caught briefly at her lower lip with her teeth before replying. "I'm afraid I must remain here. I have surgeries scheduled, and also . . ."

Ethan came to his wife's side and added, "My wife and I have an agreement that whenever one of us travels, the other will stay at home with the child. And I'll be away from London, working on the investigation."

"If you like," Garrett told the duke, "I can recommend a colleague, Dr. Kent, who has a practice near Heron's Point. He was trained according to Sir Joseph Lister's methods, just as I was, and will provide first-rate care to Mr. MacRae."

"Very well. I'd be obliged if you would contact him on our behalf. I want him waiting at the estate when we arrive."

"I'll wire him in the morning, Your Grace."

The duke took one last glance at Keir's sleeping form, his face inscrutable. But as he turned to leave, the mask of composure slipped to reveal a flash of anguished tenderness. Merritt blinked, and the expression vanished so quickly, she wondered if she'd imagined it.

Once they were out in the hallway, the duke told her, "You need pack only a few essentials. We'll send for more in a day or two."

"I should send a note to my family," Merritt said, trying to collect her scattered thoughts.

"You can write one on the way and dispatch it from Heron's Point." With a wry quirk of his lips, he added,

"I beg you to word it carefully. Despite my deep and abiding affection for your parents, I'd rather not be overrun by Marsdens for the time being."

"Neither would I," Merritt assured him. "Papa would ask a great many questions I have no wish to answer, and Mama . . . well, as you know, she's as subtle as a marauding Viking."

The duke laughed softly. "In the interest of self-preservation, I'll withhold comment."

The brief grin reminded Merritt of Keir, and nearly made her heart stop. "His expressions are so like yours," she said impulsively.

Kingston followed the abrupt turn of thought without needing explanation. "Are they?" he asked, glancing over his shoulder in the direction of the guest room. He turned back to her with a faint, pensive smile, and headed to the staircase.

Chapter 15

IN THE MORNING, GARRETT decided Keir's lungs had improved sufficiently to allow for a light dose of morphine. He was suffering from such a severe headache that he didn't object to the hypodermic syringe, and hardly even seemed to notice it. To Merritt's relief, the injection eased his misery enough to let him sleep.

"Poor chap," Garrett said quietly, settling an ice bag against his ribs. "He's in for a rough few days. He'll have to be up and moving before he feels like it, and in spite of the injured ribs, he'll have to do deep breathing exercises to prevent pneumonia."

"If you write out the instructions," Merritt assured her, "I'll see that it's done."

"I'm sure you will." Garrett smiled at her. "Don't neglect your own care, my friend. You'll need rest if you're going to be of any help to him."

THEY TRAVELED IN the duke's private railway carriage, a handsomely appointed vehicle trimmed with the blue and cream of the Challon family coat of arms. Merritt stayed at Keir's bedside to watch over him as he slept in one of the carriage's staterooms. Kingston, meanwhile, sat in the main compartment, poring over the instructions and medical records Garrett had sent with them.

Halfway through the journey, Kingston appeared at the stateroom's threshold. "May I come in?" he asked quietly.

Merritt looked up with a smile, trying to conceal her weariness. "Of course." She wrung out a cloth that had been soaking in ice water, and folded it in a long rectangle.

The duke approached the bedside. Very gently, he reached down to lay a hand across Keir's forehead. "He has fever," he commented.

"Dr. Gibson said the wound on his back will probably have to be cleaned and drained."

Kingston nodded with a frown. "I bloody hate fever," he muttered.

Merritt draped the cold cloth over Keir's dry, hot forehead. He made an incoherent sound and turned toward her, seeking the source of coolness. She murmured a few soothing words and used another iced cloth to stroke his face and throat. Keir subsided with a soft groan.

Kingston's eyes narrowed with interest as he saw the fine steel chain among the fleece of chest hair. "What's that?"

"A token from his . . . from the woman who bore him. He always wears it."

Kingston's long, elegant fingers slipped beneath the chain and carefully tugged upward. As the little gold key emerged, the duke's breath caught. He picked it up for a closer look, and he began to draw the chain over the sleeping man's head.

Merritt reached for it reflexively. "Wait."

"I need to borrow this," he said brusquely. "I'll return it to him safely."

"Uncle Sebastian—"

"You have my word."

"No."

To say the least, it was not a word the duke was accustomed to hearing. He went still, regarding her with an arched brow.

Merritt stared back at him calmly, doing her best to conceal how incredibly uncomfortable she felt at having to deny him something he wanted. But the key was precious to Keir, his only link to the mother he couldn't remember, and she couldn't allow it to be taken from him. Not for a day, an hour, or even a minute. Not while he was helpless.

She didn't let herself look away from those piercing light eyes, no matter how she wanted to cringe.

"This is a matter of personal significance to me," Kingston said coolly.

"I understand. But until Keir is able to give his consent . . . I'm afraid you'll have to wait."

The duke didn't like that, she could see. And she knew how easily he could have demolished her with just a few words. Instead, he said, "I'm the last person you need to protect him from."

"Of that I have no doubt, but . . . the key is sacred to him. He wouldn't want you to take it."

"Borrow," Kingston muttered.

Merritt made her voice soft and cajoling. "Of course, Uncle. But . . . it's important that you and he start off on the right foot, isn't it? What difference would a few days' wait make in the grand scheme of things?"

His mouth tightened. But to her vast relief, he let go of the key.

After another forty-five minutes, the train reached the station at Heron's Point, a seaside town located in the sunniest region in England. Even now in autumn, the weather was mild and clear, the air humid with healthful sea breezes. Heron's Point was sheltered by a high cliff that jutted far out into the sea and helped to create the town's own small climate. It was an ideal refuge for convalescents and the elderly, with a local medical community and an assortment of clinics and therapeutic baths. It was also a fashionable resort, featuring shops, drives and promenades, a theatre, and recreations such as golf and boating.

The Marsdens had often come here to stay with the duke's family, the Challons, especially in summer. The children had splashed and swum in the private sandy cove, and sailed near the shore in little skiffs. On hot days they had gone to a shop in town for ices and sweets. In the evenings, they had relaxed and played on the Challons' back veranda, while music from the town band floated up from the concert pavilion. Merritt was glad to bring Keir to a familiar place where so many happy memories had been created. The seaside house, airy and calm and gracious, would be a perfect place for him to convalesce.

A trio of railway porters came to collect their luggage, and a stocky young man, smartly dressed and carrying a doctor's bag, boarded the railway carriage.

"Good morning, Your Grace," the man said with a

pleasant smile. "I'm Dr. Kent. Although Dr. Gibson suggested I meet you at the estate, I thought I might accompany the patient directly from the station. I have an ambulance stocked with medical supplies waiting on the other side of the platform building. If the porters would help carry Mr. MacRae on a stretcher . . ."

"My footmen are at your disposal," Kingston said.

"Thank you, sir." Dr. Kent turned to Merritt. "And this charming lady . . . ?"

"I'm Mr. MacRae's fiancée," Merritt said before the duke could reply, and smiled serenely at the doctor as she added, "I'll be in charge of his care."

Although Kingston didn't contradict her, he sent her a glance of unmistakable warning.

Watch your step, my girl. I'll be pushed only so far.

Chapter 16

THERE WAS NO ESCAPING the pain, not even in sleep. It coiled in every jointure, bone, and ounce of flesh. Keir had never been sick like this before, in control of nothing, devolving into something less than human. Except when she was there.

She . . . her . . . He couldn't hold on to her name . . . it kept darting away from him . . . but he was aware of her soft presence, her voice like honey, her hands bestowing cool, sweet calm on his tortured body.

But for all her softness, there was steel in her. She was unrelenting when it came time to dose him with medicines he didn't want. She made him sip water or broth despite his struggles to keep anything down. There was no bloody refusing her. This was a woman who would keep him anchored safely to the earth, to life, with the force of her will.

During the worst of it, when Keir was maddened by suffocating heat, and every breath felt like someone was stabbing a peat knife into his chest, the woman packed ice around him, or bathed him all over with cool cloths. It mortified and infuriated him to lie there helpless and naked as a wee bairnie while she took care of his intimate needs, but he was too damned sick to do anything for himself. He needed her, both the softness and the steel.

She assured him that he would be better soon. He'd fallen, she said, and his lungs had been injured, but they were healing. A wound on his back was causing the fever, but that too would heal.

Keir wasn't so sure. The hot, pulsing place on his back seemed to be worsening by the hour, spreading poison through him. Soon he couldn't keep even water down, and instead of worrying about dying, he began to worry about *not* dying. He couldn't breathe, couldn't stop writhing from pain and nausea. He'd have welcomed any escape.

He felt a touch on his forehead and slitted his eyes open. A stranger stood beside him, tall and stern-faced, blindingly handsome, with silvery-gold hair. He looked like an angel. Not the kind offering comfort—the kind sent to smite people. Almost certainly this was the angel of death, and about time he appeared. Even hell would be better than this.

But instead of escorting Keir to the hereafter, the man pressed a fresh iced cloth to his forehead. As Keir writhed and panted in a red welter of fever, he felt the covers being drawn away, and someone began to lift the hem of his nightshirt. Riled by the indignity, he struck out blindly, trying to knock away the unfamiliar hands.

"Keir. Rest easy, boy." The stranger was leaning over him, speaking in a low, lulling voice that would have caused an entire sounder of wild boars to curl up like kittens. "We have to bring the fever down."

"Not you," Keir managed to gasp. "I want her."

"Lady Merritt has gone to bed for a few hours of badly needed rest. Do you remember me? No?

I'm Kingston. This fine old fellow beside me is Culpepper—he's been my valet for twenty-five years. Lie back now, there's a good lad."

Keir subsided warily while the odd pair—one golden and resplendent, one old and wizened—moved around him with quiet efficiency. The nightshirt was removed and a towel was draped over his hips. They cold-sponged his limbs, dressed him in a fresh nightshirt, and changed the sheets while he remained in bed. As Kingston reached around Keir and lifted him to a sitting position, he began to struggle.

"Calm yourself," Kingston said, sounding faintly amused. "I'm keeping you upright for a moment while Culpepper tucks the lower sheet around the mattress."

Having never been held by another male in his adult life, Keir would have balked, but he was too weak to sit up on his own. To his eternal humiliation, his head lolled forward onto the man's shoulder.

"It's all right," Kingston said, holding him securely. "Lean against me."

The man was remarkably fit, Keir would give him that. The form beneath the fine cotton shirt and soft wool waistcoat was sleek and rock-solid. And there was something so comfortable about his manner, so calm, that Keir relaxed despite himself. He tried to think, but his head was a maze of dead ends and trapdoors. Nothing about the situation made sense to him.

An onset of fever chills started his teeth chattering. "Why are you doing this?" he managed to ask.

It might have been his imagination, but Kingston's arms seemed to tighten a little. "I have sons who are approximately your age. If one of them were ill and far from home, I would wish for someone to do this for them."

Which wasn't really an answer.

"I'm going to lower you now," Kingston said. "Don't strain yourself—let me do the work." Carefully he settled Keir among the pillows and weighted him with blankets. He laid a hand over Keir's forehead. "Culpepper," he asked quietly, "when is the doctor scheduled to stop by?"

"This afternoon, Your Grace," the valet replied.

"I want him here within the hour."

"I believe he's on his rounds, sir—"

"His other patients can wait. Send a footman out to find him."

"Yes, Your Grace."

In a moment, Keir felt a cold compress on his forehead. "I dinna give a damn about the doctor," he muttered. "I want *her* . . . Merritt. Dinna have long."

"Nonsense," Kingston said with such cool conviction that Keir almost believed him. "I've survived fever worse than this. You'll pull through it."

But the next time Keir struggled up from the depths of sleep, he knew he was worse. The fever was raging, ruckling every breath and making him weaker than he'd ever been in his life. He was lying amid sharp angles of pain with no soft place to rest.

He became aware of the woman beside him, her pretty dark eyes filled with concern, her face tense and pale. He reached out, trying to pull her to him.

She hushed him gently and sat on the mattress, and stroked his hair with cool hands. The doctor was there, she said, to drain the wound and change the bandages, and Keir must stay still. He felt himself being turned to his front, carefully, but it sent a jolt of agony through his rib cage. The bandage on his back was removed, and he felt something prying at the searing, tender wound. A billow of pain provoked a rude churn of his stomach and a dry heave, and he growled wretchedly.

Merritt moved to cradle his head in her lap. "There, now," she soothed, while the jabbing and pressing continued. "Not much longer. Hold on to me. Let the doctor do his work, and then you'll be better. Almost finished . . . almost . . ."

Keir gritted his teeth, willing to tolerate anything for her. Shaking from the lancing pain, he focused on the feel of her soft fingers at the back of his neck.

There was a sting and burn on the right side of his arse, and then every sensation joined into one dull mass. He went numb in every limb, his mind floating. As the woman began to move away, he used the last of his strength to reach around her hips and keep her right there, his head in her lap. He was drifting aimlessly, cast loose in some uneasy current, and she was all that kept him from drowning. To his relief, she stayed, her fingers threading lightly through his hair.

Fearing she'd leave when he fell asleep, he told her he needed her to stay with him. Or at least, that was what he wanted to say. Words and their meanings were running together like paint on wet paper. But she seemed to understand. She murmured something, soft as the coo of a night bird, and he settled more heavily against her, letting the current carry him to some dark, silent place.

Chapter 17

"GO TO BED, CHILD," came Kingston's quiet voice as he entered the sickroom. "I'll look after him now."

Merritt, who was sitting beside the bed with her head and arms resting on the mattress, glanced up at him blearily. After Dr. Kent's visit, she'd stayed with Keir for the rest of the day and long into the night.

"What time is it?" she asked huskily.

"Three in the morning."

She groaned and rubbed her sore, scratchy eyes. "I can't leave him. He's at the crisis. His temperature hasn't gone below one hundred and four degrees."

"When was the last time you checked?"

"An hour ago, I think."

Kingston came to the bedside and leaned over Keir's still form. The light from a single lamp gilded both men's profiles, making it impossible to ignore their likeness, even with the thick beard covering the lower half of Keir's face. The long, straight noses, the high-planed cheekbones, the way their hairlines were shaped in a very slight widow's peak. Even the hand Kingston laid across Keir's forehead, the fingers long and blunt-tipped . . . that was familiar too.

The duke's face was inscrutable as he picked up a glass thermometer from the night table, deftly shook down the mercury, and tucked it beneath Keir's arm. Keir didn't even stir.

After lifting one of the ice bags, Kingston felt the slosh of water and proceeded to empty it in a basin. He refilled it with fresh ice from a lidded silver pail and settled it back in place.

"Does Aunt Evie know?" Merritt asked, too tired to guard her tongue.

"Know what?" Kingston asked, fishing a pocket watch from his waistcoat.

"That you have a natural-born son."

The duke's gaze remained on Keir. After a charged silence, he said evenly, "I have no secrets from my wife."

"Were you and she married when—" Merritt broke off as Kingston shot her an incredulous glance, his eyes flashing like sunlight striking off silver.

"Good God, Merritt. That you could even ask—"

"Forgive me," she said hastily. "I was only trying to guess his age."

"He's thirty-three. I would never betray Evie." Kingston took in a long breath and let it out slowly, working to bring his temper under control. "I should hope I'd never be so tedious. Adultery is only running away from one problem to create a new one." He flipped open the watch and reached down to press two fingers against the side of Keir's throat. "Why the beard?" he asked irritably. "Can't he bother to shave?"

"I like it," Merritt said with a touch of defensiveness.

"Every man should know the difference between 'enough beard' and 'too much beard.'" The duke stared at his watch for a half minute, then closed the lid with a decisive snap. He took his time about replacing it in his pocket. "Approximately a year ago," he said abruptly, "I received a letter from Cordelia, Lady Ormonde. Long ago, *before* I met Evie, I had an affair with her."

"Ormonde," Merritt repeated, staring at his taut profile. "I'm not familiar with the family."

"No, you wouldn't be. To my knowledge, Lord Ormonde hasn't been invited to Stony Cross Park for decades. Your father can't abide him."

"Why?"

"Ormonde is as vile as any man who's ever lived. I would call him a swine, but one hates to malign a useful animal. Cordelia was quite young when they married. She'd been impressed by all his boasting during the courtship, but after the wedding, she discovered what kind of man she'd married. Despite trying to produce an heir, they were still childless after four years. Naturally, Ormonde blamed Cordelia. For that reason and many others, he made her very unhappy." In a light, self-loathing tone she'd never heard from him before, he added, "And unhappy wives were my favorite."

Watching him with concern and fascination, Merritt prompted gently, "What was she like?"

"Charming and accomplished. She played the harp and spoke fluent French. Her family, the Roystons, saw to it that she was educated." Kingston paused, his gaze turning distant. "Cordelia was eager for affection, which I supplied in return for her favors."

Troubled by the lingering bitterness in his expression, Merritt pointed out, "It's common for married people to stray, especially among the upper circles. And they were her vows to break, not yours."

"Child." Kingston's head lifted, and he regarded

her with a wry smile. "Let's not be lawyerly. She couldn't have done it without a partner."

He reached down to Keir, gently took the thermometer from beneath his arm, and read it critically. "Hmm." After shaking down the mercury again, he tucked the thin glass cylinder beneath Keir's other arm. "Cordelia sent a letter from her deathbed," he continued, "to inform me she'd conceived a child from the affair all those years ago."

"That must have been a shock," Merritt said quietly.

"The world stopped spinning. I had to read the sentence five times over." Kingston's gaze turned distant. "Cordelia wrote that her husband had refused to accept my bastard offspring as his firstborn, and had forbidden her to tell me about her condition. He sent her to a lying-in hospital in Scotland to carry the baby to term in secret. After the birth, he would decide what was to be done. But Cordelia feared for the child's safety, and devised her own plan. She told Ormonde the baby had been stillborn. The head nurse of the maternity ward arranged for the boy to be smuggled out and given into the care of a decent family."

"Would Lord Ormonde really have harmed an innocent child?"

"He had two compelling motivations. First . . . Cordelia was an heiress. Her family had established a trust that would go to her husband if she died without issue. But if she had a child, all of it would go to him or her. Ormonde would never have allowed any possibility of the child inheriting."

"Is the trust so large it would make someone want to commit murder?"

"I'm sure Ormonde would be willing to do it for

free," the duke said dryly. "But yes, the portfolio includes commercial and residential properties in London. The annual rents bring in a fortune—and Ormonde desperately needs the income to keep his estate solvent." He paused briefly before continuing. "The second reason Ormonde wanted him dead is that regardless of who sired him, Cordelia was married to Ormonde at the time of Keir's birth. And therefore . . ."

"My God," Merritt whispered. "Keir is his legitimate son."

Kingston nodded. "Even if Ormonde marries again and produces a son by his new bride, Keir will still inherit his viscountcy. As long as Keir's alive, there's no chance Ormonde can pass down his family's title and estate to his own blood. It will all go to Keir."

"He won't want it," Merritt said. "Oh, he won't like this at all, Uncle."

"He doesn't have to know about that part until later, when he's ready to hear it."

"He'll never be ready to hear it." Groaning softly, Merritt rubbed her weary face with both hands. "How did Ormonde find out Keir was alive?"

"I'm afraid that was my doing." Kingston's mouth flattened into a grim line. "Cordelia named me as the executor of her will, and asked me to protect his rightful inheritance in the event he was still alive. The only way to keep the will in probate while I was searching for Keir was to provide a copy of Cordelia's letter to Chancery Court. From that moment on, Ormonde and I have each done our damnedest to locate Keir before the other one did." With a touch of annoyance, he commented, "I would have found Keir months ago, had I been able to hire Ethan Ransom, but he gave me some excuse about fighting an international conspiracy."

"From what I understand, he saved England," Merritt pointed out gently.

The duke waved away the comment like a bothersome gnat. "Someone's always plotting against England."

"As it turned out, you didn't have to find Keir. He found you."

Kingston shook his head with a faint, wondering smile. "He walked into bloody Jenner's," he said. "I knew who he was the moment I saw him. He has the look of a Challon, even with that scruffy crumb-catcher covering the lower half of his face."

"Uncle," she reproved softly. It was hardly a fair description of a handsome, neatly trimmed beard.

Carefully the duke took the thermometer from beneath Keir's arm and squinted at the line of mercury, holding it farther away from his face until the numbers were clear. After setting it aside, he glanced down at Merritt. "My dear, if you don't have some proper rest, you'll fall ill yourself."

"Not until the crisis has passed and Keir is out of danger."

"Oh, he is," came Kingston's matter-of-fact reply.

Merritt looked at him sharply. "What?"

"He's past the worst of it. His temperature has fallen to one hundred and two, and his pulse rate is normal."

She flew to Keir's side and felt his forehead, which was cooler and misted with sweat. "Thank God," she said, and let out a sob of relief.

"Merritt," he said kindly, "you're turning into a watering pot." He pulled a handkerchief from his coat and nudged her chin upward with a gentle forefinger. "Go to bed," he said, drying her eyes, "or you'll be of no use to anyone."

"Yes, but first may I ask . . . was Aunt Evie very upset when you told her about the letter?"

"No. Only concerned for the boy's sake, and mine as well."

"Many women in her position would consider him as . . . well, an embarrassment."

That drew a real smile from him, the first she'd seen from him in a while. "You know Evie. She already thinks of him as someone else to love."

Chapter 18

THE CLICK OF A china teacup on a saucer awakened Merritt from a deep sleep. She stretched and blinked, discovering the bedroom curtains had been drawn back to admit deep slants of afternoon sun. A blaze of coppery red hair caught her gaze, and she pushed up to a sitting position as she saw someone at the little tea table in the corner.

"Phoebe!"

Lady Phoebe Ravenel turned and came to her with a laugh of delight.

They had known each other their entire lives, growing up together, sharing secrets, joys, and sorrows. Phoebe was strikingly beautiful, as tall and willowy as Merritt was short and solid. Like Merritt, she had been widowed a few years ago, although in Phoebe's case, the loss had not been unexpected. Her first husband, Henry, had suffered from a prolonged wasting disease, and had passed away before the birth of their second son. Then West Ravenel had come into Phoebe's life, and they had married after a courtship so brief, it hardly even qualified as whirlwind.

"Oh, it's been too long," Merritt exclaimed as they embraced. "I've missed you so! Letters are never enough."

"Especially considering how seldom you write," Phoebe teased, and laughed at Merritt's expression.

"If you knew how hard I've been working! No time for letters, books, or tea with friends . . . no naps or shopping . . . I've been living like a medieval peasant."

Phoebe chuckled. "I meant to come sooner, but it's been madness at the estate. We're going into harvest, and I've been busy with the baby—"

"Where is she?" Merritt asked eagerly. She hadn't yet seen Phoebe's daughter, Eden, who'd been born six months earlier. "You've brought her, I hope."

"Had to," Phoebe replied wryly, gesturing to her button-front bodice, strained by the full bosom of a nursing mother. "She's not yet weaned. At the moment, she's with the nursemaid upstairs. I left the boys at home with West, but they may join us later, depending on how long I stay."

"I'm so glad you're here."

"Tell me what's been happening," Phoebe said, going to the small table. "I'll pour tea."

Merritt hesitated with a nonplussed laugh. "There's too much. I'm at a loss for words."

"You? You're never at a loss for words."

"I'm not sure how to start."

"Start with anything. No—start with the man you brought here. According to my father's note, he's a businessman who was injured in the warehouse fire. Which I was very sorry to hear about, by the way."

Merritt twisted to stack the pillows against the headboard. "Have you seen your father yet?"

"No, I've only just arrived. He's meeting with a pair of solicitors from London, and I told the butler not to interrupt him, and then I came straight to your room.

You're the one I wanted to talk with anyway." Phoebe brought her a cup of tea and went to perch on the corner of the mattress.

"You'll definitely want to talk with your father too, dear."

"About what?"

"Mr. MacRae, the injured man." Merritt paused to take a bracing gulp of tea. "He's a distiller from Scotland. One of the little islands off the west coast. He hired my company to ship and store his whisky in the bonded warehouse. But while my men were moving the cargo, a cask of single malt broke on a freight shed roof and soaked him. He came to my office in wet clothes, all muscles and smolder. I hardly knew where to look."

"I think you knew exactly where to look," Phoebe said, her light gray eyes sparkling with amusement. "Is he handsome?"

"A stunner. Tall and big-chested, with blue eyes and hair the color of summer wheat. And his accent . . ."

"Irresistible?"

"Oh, yes. There's something about a Scottish burr that makes it seem as if a man is either about to recite poetry or toss you over his shoulder and carry you away."

"Maybe both at the same time," Phoebe said dreamily, sipping her tea.

Merritt grinned and resumed the story, leaving nothing out. It was an incredible relief to confide in Phoebe, who would understand anything. But the torrent of words slowed when it came to telling her friend about the night she'd spent with Keir.

". . . and then . . ." Merritt said, her gaze carefully

averted, ". . . I asked him to stay the night. With me. In my bedroom."

"Of course you did," Phoebe said reasonably.

"You're not shocked?"

"Why would I be? You've occupied a solitary bed for a long time, and you were in the company of a ruggedly handsome bachelor with a Scottish accent. I'd be shocked if you *hadn't* asked him to stay." Phoebe paused. "My goodness, I hope you didn't think West and I were as chaste as unsunned snow during our courtship."

"No, but it's not quite the same. At least you knew West beforehand, and your families were acquainted."

Phoebe chewed lightly on her lower lip as she considered that. "I didn't know him all *that* well," she pointed out. "But I learned a great deal about him in a very short time. As you know, West is not what anyone would call shy and retiring."

Merritt smiled. "I adore men who talk. The taciturn ones are no fun at all."

Phoebe gave Merritt an expectant glance. "Well?"

"Well what?"

"Tell me about the night you spent together. How was it?"

Merritt felt color rise in her face as she pondered how to describe those intimate hours. Hesitantly she said, "I wouldn't want to compare him to my husband."

"No, one mustn't. It's different, that's all."

"Yes." Merritt paused. "It was astonishing. He was so assured . . . masterful . . . but very gentle. I was so lost in him and what he was doing, I stopped thinking at all. Phoebe . . . do you think it's possible to fall in love with someone in only a week?"

"Who am I to say?" Phoebe parried, taking the empty cup from her and going to replenish it.

"Oh, don't be waffly, tell me your opinion."

Phoebe glanced over her shoulder with lifted brows. "Aren't you the one who's always said opinions are tiresome?"

"Yes, when I had the luxury. But now I'm a businesswoman." Merritt's mouth pressed into a glum hyphen. "My interior life used to be flowers, party decorations, and quartet music. Now it's all purchase orders and typewriter ribbons and dusty office furniture."

"Surely not dusty, dear." Phoebe brought her a fresh cup of tea. "Very well, here's what I think: It's possible to have strong feelings for someone in only a week, but as for full-blown, deep, true love . . . no. There's been no courtship. You haven't spent enough time together. You haven't *talked*. Love happens through words."

"Drat." Recognizing the truth of that, Merritt scowled and drank her tea.

"Furthermore, the sleeping together is a complication. Once you've done it, it's almost impossible to talk without the interference of sensuality."

"What if he doesn't remember?" Merritt asked.

Phoebe gave her a baffled glance. "What?"

"If a tree falls in the forest and no one sees or hears, did it really fall?"

"Was the tree drinking?"

"No, it was a concussion." Merritt told Phoebe about the explosion on the docks, and finding Keir unconscious and injured, and Dr. Gibson's diagnosis.

"He's lost at least a week of memory," she finished, "and there's no guarantee he'll recover it. Now after talking with you, I'm beginning to think that may be for the best."

"You're not going to tell him you slept together?"

She shook her head. "It wouldn't be helpful at all. Just the opposite: He might think of it as a trap."

"Merritt, you're the catch of London. With your looks, wealth, and connections, there are countless men who would love to be caught in any trap you cared to set."

"Keir's different. He's not fond of town, to put it mildly. He's not impressed by luxury or appearances. He loves his simple life on the island, and doing things out in nature."

"And you dislike nature," Phoebe said sympathetically.

"'Dislike' is too strong a word. Nature and I have an understanding—we try not to interfere with each other. It's a peaceful coexistence."

Phoebe looked skeptical. "Dear, no matter how attractive this man is, I can't envision you existing happily on a remote Scottish island."

"It's possible," Merritt argued. "I'm a woman of many facets."

"You don't have a single facet that wants to live in a hut."

"I didn't say he lived in a hut!"

"Five pounds says it has a stone floor and no indoor plumbing."

"I never take bets," Merritt said loftily.

"Which means you think I'm right."

Merritt's reply was forestalled by the sound of muffled shouting and a thump or two—like something being thrown against a wall. It seemed to be coming from the direction of Keir's room. Instantly alarmed, she set aside her teacup and saucer and sprang out of bed.

"What in heaven's name is that?" Phoebe asked.

"I think it's Mr. MacRae," Merritt said in alarm.

Chapter 19

After donning her robe and slippers, Merritt sprinted along the hallway with Phoebe close behind. As they neared Keir's room, they saw Kingston approaching from the other direction.

"Father," Phoebe exclaimed.

"Hello, darling," the duke said pleasantly. "I didn't know you'd arrived."

"I didn't want to interrupt your meeting with the solicitors."

"We just finished." Kingston reached for the door. "What the devil is this all about?"

"I have no idea." Merritt hurried into the room.

They found Keir sitting up in bed, cursing at Culpepper, the duke's elderly valet. "You'll no' go by me again, you damned doaty auld ball sack!"

Merritt's heart was wrenched with worry as she heard the wheeze in Keir's breath. "What's the matter?" she asked, hastening to the bedside.

"I've been skinned like a hare for stewing!" Keir said wrathfully, turning to her.

Merritt was dumbstruck at the sight of his clean-shaven face.

Dear God. He was beyond handsome. The cushioning thick beard was gone, revealing the brooding masculine beauty of a fallen angel. His features were strong but elegantly refined, the cheekbones high, the mouth full and erotic. She could hardly believe she'd slept with this dazzling creature.

"They shaved off my beard while I was drooged," Keir told her indignantly, reaching out to clamp a hand on her skirts and tug her close.

The duke responded with an innocent look. "You'll have to forgive my valet," he said smoothly. "I instructed him to do a bit of grooming and tidying. It appears he assumed I meant a shave as well. Isn't that right, Culpepper?"

"Indeed, Your Grace," the old man replied dutifully.

"Culpepper tends to be impetuous," Kingston continued. "He needs to work on controlling his impulses."

Keir flushed with outrage. "He's no' a brash wee laddie, he's ninety-eight fookin' years old!"

"You may go now," the duke said to his valet.

"Yes, Your Grace."

Merritt focused all her attention on Keir. "Try to relax and take deep breaths," she said urgently, leaning over him. "Please. Look at me." Staring into his eyes, she inhaled slowly, willing him to follow. His gaze locked with hers, and he struggled to breathe along with her. To her relief, the rough panting began to ease. She dared to reach out and push back a heavy lock of hair that had fallen over his forehead. "I'm so sorry about your beard. I'm sure it will grow back quickly."

"'Tis the principle," he grumbled. "I was off my head and dinna know what was happening."

Merritt clicked her tongue sympathetically, her

hand sliding briefly to the hard, clean angle of his jaw. "They shouldn't have done such a thing without asking. If I'd been here, I wouldn't have allowed it." She was thrilled to feel him lean subtly into the pressure of her hand.

"In any case," she heard Kingston remark casually, "one can't deny it's an improvement."

Merritt twisted to send him a threatening glance over her shoulder, willing him not to antagonize Keir further. "It was a very nice beard," she said.

The duke arched a brow. "It looked like something I had to wrestle away from the dog last week."

"Uncle Sebastian," Merritt exclaimed in exasperation.

Keir's attention, however, was fixed not on Kingston, but on the frozen figure by the doorway. "Who's that?" he demanded.

Merritt followed his gaze to Phoebe, whose face was carefully blank. What a shock it must be for her, to be confronted with a man who looked so eerily similar—almost identical—to her father as a young man. "Dear," she said apologetically to Phoebe, "about that story I was telling you . . . there was a part I hadn't yet reached."

Her friend replied slowly, staring at the duke. "I think perhaps my father should explain it to me."

"I will," Kingston said, giving his daughter a reassuring smile. "Come with me." He ushered her from the room, saying, "We'll leave Merritt with her fiancé."

"*What?*" came Phoebe's bewildered voice, just before he closed the door.

In the raw silence, Merritt brought herself to meet Keir's baffled, accusing gaze.

"Fiancé?" he repeated. "Why did he call me that?"

Wishing she could throttle Kingston, Merritt said uneasily, "You see . . . I had to resort to . . . erm . . . a small prevarication."

Despite his weakened condition, Keir was easily able to pull her down beside him with a commanding tug. One of his hands settled beneath her arm to lock her in place. "I dinna know what that means," he said, "but it sounds like a fine-feathered word for lying."

"It is," she admitted in a sheepish tone. "And for that I'm very sorry. But saying we were betrothed was the only way I could accompany you here, to take care of you."

Keir leaned back against the pillows, leveling a surly glance at her. "Why?"

"It wouldn't be proper, since we're both—"

"No, I meant why did you want to?"

"I . . . I suppose I felt responsible because you were injured while staying in my company's warehouse."

"No one would ever believe I'd offer for you. 'Tis a daft notion."

Surprised and offended, Merritt asked, "Do you find me so unappealing?"

Keir seemed startled by the question. "*No*, of course not. You're . . ." He paused, staring at her as if mesmerized. The hand beneath her arm had slipped a bit lower, his long thumb beginning to stroke the side of her breast in a caress he didn't seem to be aware of. "You're as bonnie as a wild rose," he said absently. Merritt shivered beneath the gently erotic touch, the tip of her breast gathering into a hard peak. Suddenly realizing what he was doing, Keir snatched his hands from her. "But I'd never take a wife so far above me."

Merritt's heart was beating high in her throat, making it difficult to speak. "We're all woven from the same loom," she said. "That's what my father says. He married an American. My great-grandmother was a laundress, as a matter of fact."

Keir shook his head dismissively. "You're a high-born lady with fine ways."

Merritt frowned. "You make it sound as if I were some pampered creature who could barely lift a teacup. I've had to work very hard. I run a shipping company, a very large one—"

"Aye, I know."

"—and I've spent a great deal of time managing men who are far less civilized than you. I can be as tough as nails when the situation calls for it. As for the betrothal . . . I'll take the blame for breaking it off. I'll say I changed my mind."

Looking irritable, Keir reached up to stroke his jaw, and swore softly as he seemed to realize anew that his face was bare. "I need to see to the running of my own business," he muttered. "My men will have worrit when I dinna return on schedule. Do they know what happened?"

"I'm not sure. They may have sent an inquiry to the Sterling office. I'll ask my brother."

"I'll leave tomorrow," he decided, "or the day after."

"But you can't," Merritt exclaimed. "Your lungs need at least another week to heal. I have a list of breathing exercises for you to start on. And your ribs are either fractured or badly bruised. According to the doctor—"

"I'll heal as well at home as I would here." Keir paused. "Where is 'here,' by the way?"

"We're at the duke's estate in Sussex. In a seaside resort town called Heron's Point."

At the mention of the duke, Keir fastened a brooding gaze on the window, and let out a long sigh. "I look like him," he eventually said, his tone grim.

Merritt's reply was gentle. "Very much so."

"Does he think I'm . . ." Keir didn't seem able to finish the sentence.

"He's almost certain of it. He's had an investigator searching for evidence."

"I dinna care what he finds. I had a father. There'll be no replacing Lachlan MacRae."

"Of course not," she said. "He was your father in all the ways that truly mattered." She smiled absently as she recalled one of the stories he'd told her about his parents. "How could anyone replace the man who stayed up late to mend the cuff of your Sunday shirt?"

Keir had told her over dinner that when he was a boy, his mother had made him a shirt out of blue broadcloth, meant to be worn only to church or formal occasions. But Keir had disobeyed and worn it on a Saturday, when he'd gone to sweep and clean the coppersmith's shop for a shilling. He'd been trying to catch the eye of the man's daughter, and had hoped the new shirt would improve his chances. Unfortunately a cuff had caught on a nail while he was working, and had torn almost completely off the sleeve. Fearing his mother's disapproval, Keir had confessed the crime to his father. But Lachlan had come to the rescue, for he'd known how to sew.

"Dinna trooble yourself, lad," Lachlan had reassured him. "I'll stay up a wee bit later than usual, mend the cuff, and you can wear it to church tomorrow, with your mither none the wiser."

The plan would have worked brilliantly, except when Keir had dressed for church the next morning, he'd discovered that Lachlan had accidentally stitched the sleeve closed. It had been impossible to slide a hand through it. The shamefaced conspirators, father and son, had gone to confess to Elspeth. Her annoyance had soon been swept away in convulsive giggles as she'd inspected the sealed shirt cuff. She'd laughed for days, and had told her friends about it, and the story had been joke fodder among the women for years. But both Keir and Lachlan had agreed it was worth looking foolish, for Elspeth to have taken such enjoyment in it.

"How do you know about that?" Keir asked, his eyes narrowed.

"You told me, during dinner in London."

"We were at a dinner?"

"You came to my home. It was just the two of us."

Keir didn't seem sure what to make of that.

"We were exchanging stories about our families," Merritt continued. "After you told me about the shirt cuff, I told you about the time I spilled ink on a map in my father's study."

He shook his head, looking baffled.

"It was a rare two-hundred-year-old map of the British Isles," Merritt explained. "I'd gone into my father's study to play with a set of inkwell bottles, which I'd been told not to do. But they were such tempting little etched glass bottles, and one of them was filled with the most *resplendent* shade of emerald green you've ever seen. I dipped a pen in it, and accidentally dribbled some onto the map, which had been spread out on his desk. It made a horrid splotch right in the middle of the Oceanus Germanicus. I was standing there, weeping with shame, when Papa walked in and saw what had happened."

"What did he do?" Keir asked, now looking interested.

"He was quiet at first. Waging a desperate battle with his temper, I'm sure. But then his shoulders relaxed, and he said in a thoughtful tone, 'Merritt, I suspect if you drew some legs on that blotch, it would make an excellent sea monster.' So I added little tentacles and fangs, and I drew a three-masted ship nearby." She paused at the flash of Keir's grin, the one that never failed to make her a bit light-headed. "He had it framed and hung it on the wall over his desk. To this day, he claims it's his favorite work of art."

Amusement tugged at one corner of his mouth. "A good father," he commented.

"Oh, he is! Both my parents are lovely people. I wish . . . well, I don't suppose there'll be a chance for you to meet them."

"No."

"Keir," she continued hesitantly, "I'm not in a position to speak for the duke, but knowing him as I do . . . I'm sure he would never want to replace your father, or take anything from you."

No response.

"As for the duke's past," Merritt continued, "I don't know what you may have heard. But it would only be fair to talk to him yourself before making judgments . . . don't you think?"

Keir shook his head. "It would be a waste of time. My mind is set."

Merritt gave him a chiding smile. "Stubborn," she accused mildly, and took the empty glass from him. "You should rest for a bit. I'll find some proper clothing for you and come back later to help you dress."

His frown reappeared. "I dinna need help."

Thankfully, years of working in the rough-and-tumble environment of the South London docks had taught Merritt patience. "You've been ill," she pointed out calmly, "and you're recovering from serious injury. Unless you want to risk falling and causing yourself more harm, you should probably let someone assist you."

"No' you. Someone else."

That stung, but Merritt steeled herself not to show it. "Who, then?"

Keir heaved a sigh and muttered, "The auld ball sack."

"Culpepper?" Merritt exclaimed, baffled. "But you were so cross with him. Why would you prefer his help to mine?"

"'Tis no' proper for you to do it."

"My dear man, you're shutting the door after the house was robbed. There's not an inch of you I haven't seen by now."

His color heightened. "No man wants a woman to see him in the a'thegither when he's gone ill and unwashed for days."

"You have not gone unwashed. If anything, you've been water-logged. I've cold-sponged you constantly since we arrived." Smiling wryly, she went to the threshold and paused with her hand on the doorknob. "I'll send Culpepper later, if that's what you prefer."

"Aye." Keir paused before muttering, "Thank you, milady."

"Merritt."

"Merritt," he repeated . . . and gave her an arrested glance that jolted her heart.

Why was he staring at her like that? Had he remembered something? Her fingers clenched over the doorknob until her palm throbbed around the cool polished brass.

"'Tis a bonnie name," he finally said distantly, and turned his gaze to one of the windows, silently dismissing her.

Chapter 20

KEIR AWOKE THE NEXT morning just as a maid quietly left the room with the wood scuttle. A small fire snapped in the hearth, softening the night's chill. Sounds drifted from other parts of the house as servants went about their daily chores. He heard a few low-voiced exchanges, a delicate rattle of china or glass, shutters being opened, a carpet being swept. His nose twitched and his mouth watered as he detected the faint hint of something rich and salty frying—bacon, maybe?—and the sweetness of baking bread. *Breakfast soon*, he thought, his usual appetite asserting itself.

Carefully he got out of bed and hobbled to the washstand. The left side of his rib cage was as sore and tender as if it had been split by a plowshare. He had a headache and a come-and-go ringing in his ears. But worst of all were his lungs, weak and wheezy, like a ruptured blacksmith's bellows.

In a few minutes he made his way to one of the windows. Morning had come with frost on its back, turning the edges of the glass panes white and crystalline. The house was set on high ground above the Challon family's private cove, with grassy dunes belting the pale crescent of a sand beach, and a fetch of calm blue water. Far outside the estate at Heron's

Point, the busy world of smokestacks and railway terminals went about its business, but here within the boundaries of Kingston's domain, time moved at a different pace. It was a world—

That smell in the air was definitely bacon.

—a world where people had the luxury to read, think, and discuss high-minded subjects.

He needed to go home to Islay and fill his lungs with cold salt breezes off the sea, and sleep in the house where he'd been raised. Even if he couldn't manage to cook for himself yet, he had scores of friends and—

Salty, chewy bacon with crisp edges. God, he was starving.

—friends and neighbors who would welcome him to their tables. He would go back where he belonged, among his people, where everything was familiar. Not that anyone could rightly complain about recuperating in a duke's mansion. But a cage was no less of a cage for having been gilded.

Someone tapped at the door.

"Come in," Keir said.

A housemaid entered, carrying a tray fitted with little legs. "Will you take breakfast in bed, sir?"

"Aye, thank you." Realizing he was standing before her in nothing but a nightshirt, he hastened back to the bed. He drew in a sharp breath as he tried to climb in too quickly.

The maid, a dark-haired girl with a pleasant and capable air, set the tray on a table. "Try to roll into the bed with your back all stifflike," she suggested. "Me brother once cracked a rib after comin' back too beery from the tavern. Fell down the stairs. After that, if he forgot and twisted or turned, he said it was like Satan stabbin' him with a flamin' pitchfork."

"That's the feel of it," Keir agreed wryly. Following her advice, he half sat, half rolled onto the mattress, taking care to keep his torso and hips aligned, and pulled up the covers. His mouth watered in anticipation as she brought the tray to him and set it carefully over his lap.

The food had been prettily arranged on blue and white china and a lace-edged cloth. There was even a wee crystal bud vase with a single yellow chrysanthemum blossom. But the artful presentation of the breakfast didn't compensate for its stinginess. There was only a small plain custard, a few tidbits of fruit, and a slice of dry toasted bread.

"Where's the bacon?" Keir asked in bewilderment.

The maid looked perturbed. "Bacon?"

Maybe there was only a limited amount? Maybe it was intended for a special dish?

"Is there some for having?" Keir asked cautiously.

"There is, but . . . Lady Merritt wrote out a special menu for you, and there was nothin' on it about bacon."

"A man can't mend without meat," he said in outrage.

"If it pleases, sir, I'll ask for Lady Merritt's permission."

Permission?

"I'll have bacon and be damned to her," he said indignantly.

The maid took one glance at his face and fled.

In a few minutes, there came another tap at the door, and Lady Merritt ducked her head into the room. "Good morning," she said cheerily. "May I come in?"

Keir replied with a grunt of assent, sitting with his arms folded.

It was hard to keep scowling when he saw how pretty she was in a bright blue dress with white frills trimming the bodice and sleeves. And the way she smiled . . . he could literally feel the warmth of it, as if he were stepping from a shadow into sunlight. As she came to the bedside, her light fragrance brushed over his senses as softly as a veil made of tiny flower petals. Her skin looked so smooth, with a bit of a gleam, like textureless gauze. He wondered if it was like that all over, and felt an unruly stirring in his groin.

"Is there a problem with your breakfast?" she asked sympathetically, looking down at his untouched plate.

"'Tis no' a breakfast," he informed her curtly. "No meat, no eggs, no porridge? 'Tis a snack."

"Dr. Kent recommended only plain food for the next few days. He said rich fare might be difficult for you to manage."

Keir snorted at the thought. "Difficult for an Englishman, maybe. But I'm after having for a full Scottish breakfast."

Her dark eyes twinkled. "What does that consist of?"

Unfolding his arms, he settled back against the pillows with a nostalgic sigh. "Bacon, sausage patties, ham, fried eggs, beans, potatoes, scones . . . and maybe a bit of sweet, like clootie dumpling."

Her brows lifted. "All that on one plate?"

"You have to build a mountain of the meat," he explained, "and arrange the rest around it."

"I see." She regarded him speculatively. "If you're *very* sure you can keep it down, I suppose you could try one or two strips of bacon."

"I want a full rasher," he countered.

"Three strips, and that's my final offer." Before he could argue, she added, "I'll even throw in a coddled egg."

"What's coddled?"

"Steamed in a little cup."

"Aye, I'll have some of those."

"Lovely. After that, the duke's valet will come around with some clothes, and if you're feeling up to it, you and I might take a few turns around the upper floor of the house. Later, we'll make a start on the breathing exercises."

"What about the duke and Lady Phoebe?" Keir asked. "What will they be doing?"

"They're going out to have lunch with friends and visit some shops along the local esplanade." Lady Merritt paused, her gaze seeming to wrap around him like velvet. "I told them I wanted to spend a day with you," she said. "There are sensitive subjects to discuss . . . and I thought it might be better coming from me."

Keir frowned. "If you're going to tell me all the whisky was destroyed, I already expected that."

A fortune, literally vanished into thin air. Badly needed profits, all gone. After spending five years paying off the distillery's debts, he was financially strapped once again.

"Would it help if I said the loss was covered by the warehouse insurance policy?" Lady Merritt asked gently.

"What about the tax due on it?"

"If the government won't release you from the tax obligation, the insurance company will have to pay it. Sterling Enterprises' legal department is quite firm that the tax liability counted as an insurable interest. They may want to litigate in court, but we'll almost certainly win."

Keir nodded slowly as he thought that over. "Even if I had to pay the tax," he said, "it wouldn't be the ruin of the distillery, as long as the rest of it was covered."

"Good. If you have any difficulties in that regard, I'm sure I can find ways to help."

Keir stiffened. No matter how well-intended, the offer of help from a wealthy woman rankled. "I dinna want your money."

Lady Merritt blinked in surprise. "I didn't mean I was going to hand you a sack of cash. I'm a businesswoman, not a fairy godmother."

The sudden edge to her tone, subtle though it was, was keen enough to lacerate.

Seeing how her radiance had vanished, Keir felt a chill of regret, and his first thought was to apologize.

Instead, he kept his mouth shut. It was better not to grow close to her.

After taking over the distillery upon his father's death, the first decision Keir had made was to install new safety equipment and procedures. There were too many dangerous elements in a building where drink was made from grain: dust, alcohol vapor, heat, and sparks from static or friction. The only way to avert disaster was to keep those elements as separate and controlled as possible.

All his instincts warned him to do the same in this situation . . . create a distance between himself and Lady Merritt . . . before they started an inferno.

Chapter 21

"YOU'RE USING YOUR CHEST," Merritt said later that day, glancing down at Keir as he reclined on a long, low couch.

"Aye," he said dryly. "'Tis where I keep my lungs."

Merritt stood over him, a medical book in one hand and a stopwatch in the other, while Keir lay flat on his back. He felt more than a little foolish, not to mention frustrated. The breathing exercises, which had sounded simple in the beginning, had turned out to be unexpectedly challenging, mostly because Merritt seemed to want him to breathe in a way that was anatomically impossible.

They were in an upstairs family parlor, a wide and spacious room divided into separate areas by groupings of furniture and potted palms. Two sets of French doors opened to an outside balcony that ran almost the full length of the house.

Earlier, Culpepper had brought Keir a selection of spare clothes belonging to the duke's two grown sons, Lord St. Vincent and Mr. Challon. The garments were finer than anything he'd worn in his life. Not fancy, but incredibly well made. With the valet's help, Keir had chosen a shirt made of Egyptian cotton with mother-of-pearl buttons, and a silk-lined waistcoat, stitched so the hem was perfectly smooth instead of curling upward. The trousers were fluid and slightly loose, tailored to allow for greater ease of movement.

"You're supposed to take in air from lower down, in the belly," Merritt said, consulting *The Thorax and Its Viscera: A Manual of Treatment*, which Dr. Kent had provided.

"The belly is for filling with food, not air," Keir said flatly.

"It's a special technique called diaphragmatic breathing."

"I already have a technique. 'Tis called in-and-oot."

She set the book aside and fiddled with the stopwatch. "Let's try again. Inhale for four seconds, and exhale slowly for eight. As you breathe out, control the air flow by pursing your lips. Like this." Her mouth cinched into a round, plush shape, the sight throwing his brain into chaos . . . *soft, tender, rose blossoms, cherries, sweet currant wine* . . . he couldn't help wondering how they would feel on his skin, stroking downward, parting as her sweet tongue flicked out to taste him—

"Now you try," Merritt said briskly. "Pucker your lips. Pretend you're pouting about something."

"I dinna pout," he informed her. "I'm a man."

"What do you do when you're angry but can't complain?"

"I toss back a dram of whisky."

That drew a grin from her. "How surprising. Pretend you're blowing out a candle, then." She held up the stopwatch, thumb poised over the crown stopper. "Are you ready?"

"I'd rather be sitting up."

"According to the book, lying flat helps to focus on the expansion and contraction of the abdomen while increasing the vertical capacity of the chest." A decisive click of the watch. "Start."

Dutifully Keir inhaled and exhaled at her count.

Click. Merritt assessed him like a drillmaster determined to train a raw recruit. "Your ribs moved."

"They dinna!" he protested.

Ignoring him, she clicked the watch. "Again."

Keir obeyed. Deep breath in, slow breath out.

Click. Lady Merritt stood over him, shaking her head. "You're not even trying."

Exasperated, Keir muttered, "I *am* trying, you wee bully."

Instantly her face changed, her eyes widening.

Keir was startled by the feeling of having already experienced this exact moment, as if he'd just fallen through a trapdoor connecting the present and the past.

"I've called you that before," he said huskily.

"Yes." Merritt sounded breathless. "Do you remember anything else?"

"No, only saying those words to you, and . . ."

His heart had begun to thud, the force of it ricocheting everywhere inside and gathering at his groin. Alarm seized him as he realized he was turning hard, his cock stiffening in a series of swift jumps. He sat up with a muffled curse, pain searing through his ribs.

"What is it?" he heard Merritt ask in concern. "Do be careful—you'll hurt yourself—here, let me—"

Her hands were on him, one at his shoulder, the

other at his back. The pressure of her palms, gentle but firm, flooded him with lust. Another door seemed to open in his brain, and for a moment all he could think of was being in bed with her, the rush of her breath against his ear, the clasp of female flesh, amazingly silky, supple, powerful pulses working his shaft as he pushed deep and felt her squirm—

"Dinna touch me," he said, more roughly than he'd intended.

Her hands snatched back.

Keir leaned forward, bracing his forearms on his thighs. She was standing too close, her delicately perfumed scent feeding the hard ache of arousal. He was light-headed, suffocating from lack of oxygen. Grimly he focused on the pain of his ribs, letting it tamp down the flare of lust.

No . . . he had never been in bed with her. She'd never have let him do such a thing, and God knew he'd never have tried.

As he fought to bring the unruly desire under control, he became aware of a reedy squalling that grew more and more insistent. A baby's cry. Lifting his head, he looked at the doorway, where Lady Phoebe Ravenel stood with a fussy infant in her arms.

Bugger me, he thought grimly.

The long, involved conversation he'd had with Merritt after breakfast had been full of revelations about the duke's long-ago affair with Cordelia, Lady Ormonde, and its consequences—one of which was very likely Keir himself. Which meant the red-haired woman at the threshold could very well be his half sister, and the wailing imp in her arms his niece.

Having been raised by elderly parents, Keir had never expected a sibling. His rowdy pack of friends were his brothers, and the men at the distillery were his extended family. It was strange to think of having a sister. It shocked him, in fact, to realize that for the first time in his life, here was someone . . . a woman . . . with whom he might have a blood tie. And not just any woman, but an aristocratic lady. There was nothing for them to talk about, no experiences they had in common.

But as he stared at Lady Phoebe, she seemed like any ordinary young mother on Islay, who hadn't had quite enough sleep and couldn't always tell what her baby wanted. There was a smart, bright look about her—canty, a Scot would say, a word that suggested the dancing flicker of a candle flame.

"I'm so sorry," Phoebe said, with a comical grimace, trying to soothe the fretting baby. "I thought we might stop by for a brief visit, but my daughter seems to have made other plans. Perhaps we'll try again later."

She was nervous, Keir thought. Just as he was. His gaze moved to the infant, squirming unhappily amid a bundle of white ruffles, her plump stockinged legs churning like a windmill. One of her little white shoes was missing. He couldn't help smiling at the large pink bow on her head, which had been fastened around a wild tuft of carroty-red hair in a valiant attempt to tame it.

"Dinna rush off yet," he said, and rose to his feet.

ANXIOUS TO HELP, Merritt hurried to Phoebe and the baby. "Is she hungry?" she asked.

Phoebe gave a frustrated shake of her head. "No, I

fed her recently. Sometimes she has these spells, and there's nothing to be done about it." Looking rueful, she added, "Apparently I was the same."

"Let me take her," Merritt suggested. "I'll walk her up and down the hallway while you and Mr. MacRae chat."

"I think we'll all be better off if I cart her off to the nursery." Phoebe cast a regretful glance at Keir as he joined them. "I do beg your pardon, Mr. MacRae. The baby's out of sorts and I can't—"

"What's her name?" he asked.

"Eden."

To both women's surprise, Keir reached out for the baby. Phoebe hesitated briefly before transferring the infant to his arms.

Keir settled the baby comfortably against one broad shoulder and began patting her tiny back in a steady rhythm. "Poor wee bairnie," he murmured. "Now, now . . . dinna fret ye . . . dinna greet . . . fold your wings, birdikin, and nestle wi' me for a bit . . ."

Merritt's jaw dropped as she watched the big, rugged Scot begin to wander about the room with the baby. Merritt and Phoebe exchanged a look of astonishment as Eden's wailing broke into snuffles.

A low sound caused the hairs on the back of Merritt's neck to lift and tingle, and she realized Keir was singing softly to the baby in Scots. A haunting melody, sung in a dark and tender baritone that turned every bone in Merritt's body molten. It was a miracle she didn't sink into a puddle on the floor.

The baby went quiet.

"My God, Merritt," Phoebe whispered with a wondering smile. "He's marvelous."

"Yes." Merritt felt almost ill with yearning.

It was only now that she finally accepted the impossibility of ever being with him. Any faint, foolish hope she'd nurtured dissolved like a cloud of smoke. Even if every other obstacle between them were somehow overcome . . . Keir would want a family. Seeing him with the baby made that clear. He would want his own children, the one thing she could never give him. And even if he were willing to make such a sacrifice, she would never allow it. This man deserved a perfect life.

Especially after all that had been taken from him.

As Keir made his way back to them, Merritt painstakingly tucked away all signs of her despair, although it kept threatening to spill out like clothes from an overpacked valise.

"Thank you," Phoebe said fervently at the sight of her daughter slumbering against the crook of Keir's neck.

"Sometimes a new pair of arms does the trick," Keir replied matter-of-factly.

"How did you learn to do that?" Phoebe asked.

"I have friends with bairnies of their own." Keir paused, his expression a bit sheepish as he continued. "I suppose I have a knack for putting them to sleep. There's no magic to it. Only a bit of patting and singing and walking."

"What were you singing?" Merritt asked. "A lullaby?"

"An old song from the islands, about a selkie." Seeing the word was unfamiliar, he explained, "A changeling, who looks like a seal in the water but takes the form of a man on land. In the song he woos a human maiden, who gives birth to his son. Seven years later, he comes back to take the child." Keir hesitated before adding absently, "But before they leave, the selkie tells the mother he'll give the boy a gold chain to wear on his neck, so she'll recognize him if they meet someday."

"Are she and her son ever reunited?" Merritt asked.

Keir shook his head. "Someone brings her the gold chain one day, and she realizes he's dead. Shot by—" He broke off as he saw Merritt's face begin to crumple. "Och," he exclaimed softly. "No . . . dinna do that . . ."

"It's so terribly sad," she said in a watery voice, damning herself for being emotional.

A chuckle broke from Keir as he moved closer. "I won't tell you the rest, then." His hand cupped the side of her face, his thumb wiping at an escaping tear. "'Tis only a song, lass. Ah, you've a tender heart." His blue eyes sparkled as he looked down at her. "I warn you, no more tears or I'll have to put you on my shoulder and pat you asleep as I did the bairnie."

It left Merritt temporarily speechless, that he sincerely seemed to believe she would regard that as a threat.

She heard a quiet sound of amusement from Phoebe, who knew exactly what she was thinking.

"Let's sit by the fire and chat," Phoebe suggested brightly, "and I'll send for tea. I want to hear about your island, Mr. MacRae, and what it was like growing up there."

Chapter 22

On the fourth day after Keir had recovered from the fever, he was well enough to walk down to the beach cove with Merritt. A sunken lane led from the house to a path that opened onto a beach of fine sand, spread beneath a blue taffeta sky. Farther on the west side, the shore graded to pebble and shingle before rising into a white chalk cliff. The beach had a well-tended look, as if someone had sifted and cleaned the sand, and filed the edges of the tide pools. Even the grasses of the dunes were orderly, as if someone had run a giant comb through them.

Although Keir would always prefer his island to anywhere else in the world, he had to admit this place had its own magic. There was a softness about the air and sun, a trance of mist that made everything luminous. Lowering to his haunches, he ran his palm back and forth over the fine golden sand, so different from the caster-sugar grains of the beaches on Islay.

At Merritt's quizzical glance, he dusted his hands and smiled crookedly. "'Tis quiet," he explained. "On the shore near my home, it sings."

"The sand sings?" Merritt asked, perplexed.

"Aye. When you move it with your foot or hand, or the wind blows over it, the sand makes a sound. Some say it's more like a squeak, or whistle."

"What makes it do that?"

"'Tis pure quartz, and the grains are all the same size. A scientist could explain it. But I'd rather call it magic."

"Do you believe in magic?"

Keir stood and smiled into her upturned face. "No, but I like the wonderments of life. Like the ghost fire that shines on a ship's mast at storm's end, or the way a bird's instinct leads him to his wintering grounds each year. I enjoy such things better for no' understanding them."

"Wonderments," Merritt repeated, seeming to relish the word.

As they walked idly along the shore, while sandpipers darted and pecked at the tide wash, Keir was filled with an ease he hadn't known since boyhood. A holiday feeling. He'd never gone this long without working in his adult life. But he knew the sense of well-being came mostly from the woman beside him.

Talking with Merritt was like slipping into one of those silk-lined borrowed coats from the Challons. Comfortable, luxurious. She was whip-smart, understanding the details, the unsaid words. She had a way of wrapping people in empathy that extended to everyone from the duke down to the young assistant groundskeeper. It was the kind of charm that made people feel wittier, more attractive, more interesting, in her reflected glow. Keir was doing his level best to resist her lure.

But he was so drawn to her, so damned besotted.

He adored her fancy words . . . "prevarication" . . . "resplendent" . . . her easy smiles . . . her perfumed wrists and throat. She was like a beautiful gift that begged to be unwrapped. Just being near her made the blood sing in his veins. Last night, the mere thought of her naked, along with just a few strokes of his own hand, had been enough to bring him to a shuddering, bone-jarring climax—an experiment he'd regretted when his ribs had instantly burned as if someone had taken a sledgehammer to them. And yet he still craved her, worse now than yesterday.

To protect himself, he tried to keep barriers between them. He did his best not to confide in her, nor did he invite confidences. He was friendly but polite, surrounding his heart with steel-plate armor and hoping that would be enough to keep it safe. If not . . . he'd end up ruined for any other woman.

He had to leave soon, or it would be too late. It might already be.

IN THE AFTERNOON, Keir spent time with Phoebe in the family parlor. She played with the baby on a quilt spread across the floor, while Keir occupied a comfortable chair nearby. He'd taken an immediate liking to Phoebe, who was friendly and straightforward, with a sharp edge of humor. She shared the running of an Essex estate with her husband and could talk so easily about ordinary subjects, like farming and husbandry, that Keir could almost forget she was the daughter of a duke.

"I thought you might want to see this," Phoebe said, nudging a weighty leather-bound book across the low table in front of him.

"What is it? A scrapbook?"

"A photograph album of my family." She paused before correcting herself. "*Our* family."

Keir shook his head, refusing to touch the album. "I dinna see the need."

Her brows lifted. "You're not the least bit curious about your own relations? You have no questions? You don't even want to *look* at them?"

"We may not be kin. No one can put it to hard proof."

"Hogwash." Phoebe gave him a sardonic glance. "A preponderance of circumstantial evidence meets the legal standard of proof, and in your case, there's more than enough to erase all reasonable doubt." She paused before adding gently, "As you'd already know, if you would just talk with Father."

Keir frowned and reached out to a lamp on a table beside his chair, playing with the beaded fringe trim on the shade. He'd had little interaction with Kingston so far, and never just the two of them, for which he was thankful. He wasn't ready for the uncomfortable and inevitable conversation that awaited them.

Fortunately, the duke hadn't been inclined to press the issue, probably because his days were too damned busy as it was. Every morning he read a mountain of reports and correspondence, dictated to a private secretary, and dispatched a footman to post letters and telegrams. In the afternoons, there were meetings with tenants, tradesmen, or estate managers, and sometimes with people who'd come from London or beyond.

At the end of the day, however, all business was set aside, and it was time for relaxation. They would all gather for dinner at a table weighted with silver and crystal and lit with abundant candles. White-gloved footmen would bring out marvelous dishes . . . platters heaped with succulent red-and-white shrimp, called pandles by locals, still smoking-hot from the gridiron . . . tureens of bisque sprinkled with tender shreds of Chichester lobster . . . Amberley trout spangled with toasted almond slices, served directly from the pan onto the plates. There were endless varieties of fresh vegetables, and salads chopped as fine as confetti, and bread served with newly churned butter, and platters of local cheese and hothouse fruit for dessert. Keir had never eaten so well in his life.

The invalid menu, of course, had been swiftly discarded. Keir had filled his plate with defiantly generous portions, his gaze daring Merritt to object, and she had only smiled wryly, letting him have his way. Ah, he liked her so damned much. She might be a wee bully when it came to certain matters, but she was never a nag.

"Are you going to talk to Father?" Phoebe persisted, bringing his thoughts back to the present.

"He hasn't asked me to," Keir muttered.

"He's waiting for *you* to ask."

"I dinna know what he wants. He has enough sons. There's nothing I could give him he doesn't already have, and nothing I need from him."

"Must it be a transaction? Can't you simply accept the relationship, and enjoy whatever it turns out to be?"

"Oh, aye," he said sarcastically, "I'll enjoy it like a trout being guddled."

"Guddled?"

"'Tis when you stand in a stream, near a boulder or steep bank, and ease your bare hand into the water beneath the trout. After a while, you start to tickle his belly and chin with your fingertips. When you've won his trust, and he relaxes to your hand, you shove your fingers into the gills, haul him out, and soon he's in a hot pan with butter and salt."

Phoebe laughed. "My father . . ." she began, and paused. "Well, I suppose he is something of a guddler. But you won't end up in the pan. Family is *everything* to him. When he was a young boy, he lost his mother and four sisters to scarlet fever, and was sent away to boarding school. He grew up very much alone. So he would do anything to protect or help the people he cares about."

She hefted the album into Keir's lap, and watched as he began to leaf through it dutifully.

Keir's gaze fell to a photograph of the Challons relaxing on the beach. There was Phoebe at a young age, sprawling in the lap of a slender, laughing mother with curly hair. Two blond boys sat beside her, holding small shovels with the ruins of a sandcastle between them. A grinning fair-haired toddler was sitting squarely on top of the sandcastle, having just squashed it. They'd all dressed in matching bathing costumes, like a crew of little sailors.

Coming to perch on the arm of the chair, Phoebe reached down to turn pages and point out photographs of her siblings at various stages of their childhood. Gabriel, the responsible oldest son . . . followed by Raphael, carefree and rebellious . . . Seraphina, the sweet and imaginative younger sister . . . and the baby of the family, Ivo, a red-haired boy who'd come as a surprise after the duchess had assumed childbearing years were past her.

Phoebe paused at a tintype likeness of the duke and

duchess seated together. Below it, the words "Lord and Lady St. Vincent" had been written. "This was taken before my father inherited the dukedom," she said.

Kingston—Lord St. Vincent back then—sat with an arm draped along the back of the sofa, his face turned toward his wife. She was a lovely woman, with an endearing spray of freckles across her face and a smile as vulnerable as the heartbeat in an exposed wrist.

Keir's gaze lifted to Phoebe's classically beautiful face, with clean-chiseled angles inherited from her father. "You favor him more than her," he said.

"You favor him more than anyone," she replied gently. "The resemblance is too close to be coincidence. You can't deny it."

Keir let out a quiet groan. "I'm nothing like him or the rest of you. My world is different than yours."

Phoebe's mouth twisted. "One would think you'd been brought up on a pirate ship, or another planet. You're Scottish, that's all. You were only raised a few latitudes north of here." She paused. "I'm not even sure you're technically Scottish."

Keir gave her a blank look.

"The only Celtic ancestors on the Challon side are Welsh," she explained. "I've looked up your mother's family, the Roystons and the Plaskitts, and according to *Debrett's Peerage*, there's no Scottish blood in either lineage."

"I'm no' a Scot?" he asked numbly.

Whatever Phoebe saw in his face caused her to say hastily, "I've only gone back two generations."

Keir dropped his head in his hands.

"Is something wrong with your lungs?" Now she sounded worried. "You're wheezing."

He shook his head, breathing through his fingers.

"I'll look farther up on your family tree," he heard Phoebe say firmly. "I'll find a Scottish ancestor. I have no doubt you're as Scottish as . . . as a leprechaun wearing a kilt, riding a unicorn through a field of thistle."

Keir looked up long enough to tell her dourly, "Leprechauns are Irish," before he dropped his head again.

Chapter 23

By THE END OF the second week at Heron's Point, Keir was chafing to go home. He was tired of relaxing, tired of soothing scenery and luxurious rooms and days of unrelenting sexual frustration. He wanted a blast of cold sea air in the face, and chimney smoke fragrant with peat, and the sound of familiar accents, and the sight of rocky hills with their shoulders in the clouds. He missed his distillery, his work, his friends. He missed the old version of himself, a man who'd known exactly who he was and what he wanted. This new version was riddled with uncertainty and torn loyalties, and wracked with desire for a woman he could never have.

Dr. Kent had stopped by on his rounds yesterday and pronounced that Keir was healing remarkably well. The back wound had almost closed up, his lung capacity was back to normal, and according to Kent, his ribs would be fully mended within six to eight weeks.

But before Keir could broach the subject of his departure with any of the Challons, Phoebe beat him to the mark.

"It's time for me to return to Essex," Phoebe announced at the breakfast table one morning. A regretful smile touched her lips as she glanced first at

Merritt, then Keir. "It's been a lovely visit. I hate for it to end, but I've been away long enough."

Kingston, who'd paused in the middle of opening a newspaper, received his daughter's announcement with a slight frown. "Your mother returns from Paris in a matter of days. Can't you stay until then?"

"I miss my husband and sons."

"Tell them to come here."

Phoebe rested her chin on her hand and smiled at her father. "And who would manage the estate? No, I'm leaving this afternoon on the three o'clock express to London, and then the five o'clock to Essex. I've already told my maid to start packing."

"I'll go with you as far as London, if you've no objection," Keir said abruptly.

Silence.

Aware of all three gazes on him, Keir added, "I can stop there for the night and go on to Glasgow the next morning." He set his jaw, silently daring anyone to object.

"It may have slipped your mind," Kingston commented acidly, "that whoever nearly succeeded in spreading you across the South London docks like so much chum still hasn't been found."

"No one knows I survived the warehouse fire," Keir pointed out. "They won't be after me now."

"Has it occurred to you," Kingston asked, "that running back to Islay and firing up the stills will tip them off?"

Keir scowled. "I can't bide here for months, wearing silk trousers and eating off fancy plates while my life turns into a shambles. I have responsibilities: a business to be run, men to be paid. A dog I left in the care of a friend. I'm no' asking for permission."

"Uncle," Merritt interceded, her face unreadable, "we can hardly blame him for not wanting the situation to go on indefinitely."

"No," Kingston allowed, settling back in his chair, leveling a cool glance at Keir. "But I'm afraid you're going to have to muster a bit more patience and stay here. The day after you pop up at your distillery alive and kicking, someone will come to finish you off."

"Let them try," Keir shot back. "I can defend myself."

The duke arched a mocking brow. "Impressive. Only a matter of days ago, we were celebrating that you were able to drink through a straw. And now apparently you're well enough for an alley fight."

Keir was instantly hostile.

"I know how to keep up my guard."

"That doesn't matter," Kingston replied. "As soon as your arm muscles fatigue, your elbows will drift outward, and he'll find an opening."

"What would a toff like you know about fighting? Even with my ribs cracked, you couldn't take me down."

The older man's stare was that of a seasoned lion being challenged by a brash cub.

Calmly he picked up a small open pepper cellar from the table and dumped a heap of ground black pepper in the center of Keir's plate.

Perplexed, Keir glanced down at it, as a puff of gray dust floated upward. His nose stung, and in the next breath, he sneezed. A searing bolt of agony shot through his rib cage. *"Aghhh!"* He turned away from his plate and doubled over. "Devil take your sneakit arse!" he managed to gasp.

Through the ricocheting pain, Keir was aware that Merritt had jumped up and rushed over to him, her hand coming lightly to his back. "Shall I fetch your medicine?" she asked, her voice vibrant with concern.

Keir shook his head. Gripping the edge of the table for leverage, he sat up and shot Kingston a baleful glance.

The duke regarded him unapologetically, his point made. He pushed back from the table. "Come with me."

"What for?" Keir asked warily.

"We're going for a walk." Kingston's mouth twisted impatiently at Keir's lack of response. "An ancient method of travel, performed by lifting and setting down each foot in turn while leaning forward." His gaze flickered over Keir's casual clothing, the wool sack jacket and broadcloth trousers. "You'll need to change those leather shoes for canvas ones. Meet me at the back of the house, by the door closest to the holloway."

The holloway. The bastard intended for them to walk down to the cove, then.

Although Keir was tempted to tell him to bugger off, he held his tongue and watched him leave. Clasping a hand to his sore ribs, he stood and looked down at Merritt, who had remained beside him. He felt a flash of regret, knowing his impulsive leave-taking must have struck her like a bolt from the blue.

But there was no accusation or sign of distress in the quiet dark pools of her eyes. Her composure was ironclad. She had the dignity of a queen, Keir thought in admiration.

"I can't stay here any longer," he told her.

"I understand. But I'm concerned about your safety."

"I'll be safe on my own territory," he said. "I have friends to guard my back, and a watchdog who'll let me know if a stranger comes within a mile of my property."

"Wallace," Merritt surprised him by saying.

He blinked in surprise. "Aye, that's his name. I told you about him?"

"Yes, over dinner. Wallace likes to attack your broom when you're sweeping. And he can retrieve a penny-piece from a field of standing corn."

His prickly annoyance melted away, and Keir felt a smile spread across his face as he stared down at her.

"Poor lass," he said huskily. "I must have jabbered your wee ear off that night."

Merritt smiled faintly. The surface of her lips was plush and fine, like the velvet skin of orchid petals. "I did my share of the talking."

"I wish I could remember."

She laughed, a pretty sound with a fractured crystal edge. "I'm glad you can't."

BEFORE KEIR COULD ask what she'd meant, Merritt coaxed him to leave the breakfast room and change his shoes for the walk to the cove.

She returned to the table and sat beside Phoebe, who wordlessly reached out to take her hand. The tight clasp was nothing less than a lifeline.

Merritt was the one to finally break the silence. "You're about to tell me it's too soon to be sure how I feel," she said huskily, "and after I spend some time apart from him, my perspective will change, and I'll stop hurting. I'll find someone else."

Phoebe nodded, her gaze soft with concern.

"All that would be the right thing to say." Merritt squeezed her friend's hand before letting go. Her cheeks felt stiff and resisting as she tried to smile. "But ten years from now, Phoebe, I'll still say it was love. It was love from the beginning."

WHEN KEIR MET Kingston at the back of the house, he was glad to discover the family dog, Ajax, was going to join them on the excursion. The boisterous black and tan retriever helped to ease the tension as they walked along the holloway, a narrow sunken lane that had once been an ancient cart path. Slender trees bracketed the high banks on either side, forming a delicate canopy overhead.

Casually Kingston said, "You mentioned you have a dog. What breed?"

"A drop-eared Skye terrier. A good rabbiter."

Ajax bounded ahead of them and emerged onto the beach, where high tide had turned the shallows into a froth of white and brown. Farther out, the water thickened into bands of green and blue, darkening to blue-black where the distant shape of a steamer inched across the horizon. The cold, salted morning breeze winnowed its way through tussocks of marram grass and bindweed on the dunes.

Barking in excitement, Ajax dashed off to chase foraging birds on the shore. Kingston shook his head and smiled as he watched the happy retriever cavorting. "Witless animal," he said fondly, and went to a painted storage shed near a bank of dunes. After taking out a few supplies, he gestured for Keir to follow him to a pit that had been dug in the sand and rimmed with large stones.

Realizing Kingston intended to build a fire, Keir asked, "Should I collect some driftwood?"

"Only a few knots for kindling. For the rest of it, I prefer birch—there's a rick on the other side of the shed."

They spent a few minutes making a proper fire, starting with dried grass and seaweed, adding a layer of driftwood knots, then a stack of split birch logs. The familiar process, something Keir often did with friends on the island, eased the tension in his neck and back. He lit the fire with a Lucifer match, watching in satisfaction as flames rushed through the kindling, and caught at the driftwood with flashes of blue and purple.

Kingston seemed in no hurry to talk. He removed his shoes and stockings, rolled his trouser legs to his ankles, and lounged on one of the wool blankets he'd brought from the shed. Keir followed suit, sitting on his own blanket, and extended his bare feet toward the fire's radiant heat. In a few minutes, Ajax came padding up to the duke, wet and sandy, holding what looked like a round stone in his mouth.

"God, what is that?" Kingston asked ruefully, extending his hand.

Gently the retriever dropped the object into his palm. It turned out to be a disgruntled hermit crab, withdrawn tightly in its shell. In a moment, a set of tiny legs and a pair of eye stalks emerged as the crab investigated its new terrain.

A faint smile touched the duke's lips. He stood in

a limber movement and went to set the hermit crab at the edge of a nearby tide pool. Carefully he positioned it close to a rock crevice where it could easily duck for cover.

As Kingston returned to settle by the fire, he said wryly, "Stay, Ajax. You've harassed the local wildlife enough for now."

The retriever plopped down beside him, and Kingston stroked the dog's head as it rested on his thigh, his long fingers playing idly with the floppy ears.

Keir had watched him with growing interest, having assumed Kingston would toss the unlucky crab aside, maybe fling it toward the sea. Any of Keir's friends would have thought nothing of chucking it into the path of a foraging herring gull. But to show consideration for an insignificant beastie . . . take the trouble to carry it to a safe place . . . it revealed something wholly unexpected about the man's character. A regard for the fragile, the vulnerable.

Now Keir wasn't sure what to make of Kingston. An aristocrat of staggering wealth and position, notorious for his decadent past . . . a devoted father and faithful husband . . . there seemed no way to reconcile those two versions of him. And here was yet another version, a man lounging casually next to a fire on the beach with his dog, his bare feet dusted with sand, as if he were an ordinary human.

Keir's thoughts were interrupted as a footman emerged from the holloway and approached carrying a small polished wood chest.

The duke reached up to take the box from the footman. "Thank you, James."

"Your Grace, shall I—"

"No, I'll take care of it," the duke said pleasantly.

"As you please, Your Grace." The footman bowed smartly and made his way back to the holloway with sand-filled shoes.

Kingston opened the latch of the chest and pulled out a small whisky decanter. He held it up with a questioning lift of his brows. "Too early?"

Keir smiled, thinking the morning was improving rapidly. "No' for a Scot." He watched with anticipation as Kingston proceeded to pour the whisky into a pair of crystal tumblers.

After taking the pleasantly weighty glass, Keir studied the glowing amber color appreciatively. He gave it a swirl and bent his head to take in the aroma.

His breath caught. His fingers tightened on the glass. Dazedly he wondered how it was that a smell could go straight to the part of the brain where memory lived.

The whisky was from the special forty-year-old batch his father had made.

"You brought samples to Jenner's," he heard the duke say. "I happened to be there that day, and we spoke briefly. Do you remember?"

Keir shook his head. To his horror, his throat had gone very tight, and hot pressure was accumulating at the corners of his eyes.

"My steward placed an order for all two hundred and ninety-nine bottles of Lachlan's Treasure," Kingston continued. "To my regret, it was destroyed in the warehouse fire. But we still had the samples."

A long silence passed, while Keir struggled to gain control of his emotions. Breathing in the dry, woody, smooth fragrance of his father's whisky made him feel as if Lachlan were close by. He could almost see the craggy face, and black eyes snapping with humor. He could almost feel the wiry, compact arms that had once held him with such strength.

When Keir was finally able to lift his head, the duke gestured with his glass. "To Lachlan MacRae," he said simply.

Bloody hell, Keir thought. He'd just been guddled.

He drank, the mellow heat of the whisky sliding over the hard lump in his throat . . . and noticed something in Kingston's eyes he'd missed before. A quiet glow of understanding and concern. A paternal look. Being the focus of it felt . . . not bad.

After taking a swallow, Kingston spoke carefully. "Had I been told about you, Keir . . . I would have taken you in and raised you with all the care and devotion a father could give a son. You would have been a joy to me. From the moment I received that letter from your mother, I've run the gamut from fury to fear, wondering what your life had been like. My only consolation in all of it has been hearing that MacRae was a loving father. For that, if he were still alive, I would kiss his feet."

Keir grinned crookedly, staring into the contents of his glass. "You wouldn't say that if you'd ever seen his feet."

He heard Kingston chuckle, and he found himself relaxing. And as they sat there on the beach listening to the endless rustle of waves, with the taste of Lachlan MacRae's whisky on their lips . . . they were finally able to talk.

Chapter 24

MERRITT HAD NO ILLUSION that Uncle Sebastian would be able to persuade Keir to stay at Heron's Point. She'd seen the tension in Keir's posture, the way he'd gripped one hand inside the other. It was the look of a man whose nerves had been chafed raw. Short of chaining him to a heavy article of furniture, there was no way to keep him from leaving, regardless of what danger awaited him.

She supposed she should make plans for her own departure. She would leave tomorrow morning.

A feeling of utter gloom rolled toward her like a bank of storm clouds. She couldn't let it engulf her.

Before she returned to London, she would go to Hampshire. She needed to see her family, especially her mother, who would surround her with inexhaustible warmth and vitality. Mama would hug her tightly, and demand to hear every detail, and send for a tray of sweets from the kitchen, and ask the butler to bring wine, and they would talk for hours. By the end of it, life would seem bearable again. Yes, she would go home to Stony Cross Park tomorrow morning.

Clinging to her resolve, Merritt wrote a telegram and dispatched a footman to post it, and went to find a quiet place to read correspondence. She settled on the tapestry room, a cozy wood-paneled space hung with glowing French tapestries. Sitting at a small gilt-wood desk positioned in front of a window, she read a detailed letter from Luke about meeting with insurance executives, and putting a vessel into dry dock for repair, and getting a builder's estimates on constructing a new bonded warehouse.

What a fine manager Luke was turning out to be, she thought with pride. Reliable, attentive to detail, confident in charting a difficult path. A natural leader. She couldn't imagine leaving the company in better hands than his as she went on to the next stage of her life . . . whatever that turned out to be.

She could stay in London, surround herself with people, go to dinners and parties, and become a patroness of worthy causes. But that would be far too similar to her life with Joshua. She'd outgrown all that. She wanted something new, something challenging.

Before she made any decisions, perhaps she should travel abroad. Italy, Germany, Spain, Greece, China, Egypt . . . She could visit the seven wonders of the world and keep a journal. What *were* the seven wonders? She tried to recall the poem a governess once taught her to help remember them. How did it go? . . . *The pyramids first, which in Egypt were laid . . . Next Babylon's garden, which Amytis made* . . . Now that she thought of it, who had made the list in the first place? In a world full of wonders, seven seemed an awfully stingy number.

Gloom started to creep back over her again.

I'll compile my own list of wonders, she decided, *far more than seven*. She would become an adventuress.

She might even try mountain climbing. Not a large, life-threatening mountain, but a friendly mountain, with a nearby resort that served afternoon tea. Being an adventuress didn't mean one had to suffer, after all.

A sound at the threshold caught her attention, and she turned in her chair.

Keir had come to the open doorway. He leaned a broad shoulder against the jamb with his hands tucked in his trouser pockets. He was rumpled, sandy, his form loose-limbed and athletic. The outdoor air had heightened the color in his face until the brilliant light blue eyes were almost startling in contrast. The carelessly disheveled layers of his golden-wheat hair practically begged to be smoothed and played with. Too handsome for words, this man.

As Keir stared at her intently, Merritt felt her insides turn clattery and heavy, like a drawer of jumbled flatware. This was it, she realized. The moment he would leave her for good. Again.

She felt her face arranging itself into the expression of a woman far too well-mannered to fall to pieces. "How did it go?" she asked.

"Better than I expected," Keir admitted, and paused. "He was crabbit after I told him I wouldn't change my mind about leaving. But he said he wouldn't stand in my way if I agreed to stay at his club tonight. He says I'll be safer there."

"You will," Merritt assured him. "Jenner's is well guarded."

"I also had to promise I'd let one of the night porters go with me to Islay," Keir said with a scowl. "And let the porter stay close by until Ethan Ransom says I'm no longer in danger."

"I think a bodyguard is an excellent idea."

"But a porter's no' a bodyguard . . .'tis a waiter, aye?"

"Not always," Merritt said. "There are very unsafe areas in St. James, and so the porters at Jenner's—night porters in particular—have been trained to deal with all kinds of situations. Many of them are former constables or security men."

Keir didn't appear impressed by the information. "Devil knows where I'll be putting him," he muttered. "He'll have to sleep in the cowshed."

Merritt stood and smoothed her skirts. "Did the conversation end on a pleasant note?" she asked hopefully. "Are you and Uncle Sebastian on better terms now?"

Keir shrugged uncomfortably and came farther into the room, gazing over the tapestries. "I dinna know," he admitted. "He wants to make up for lost time. And I think he may have a notion of turning a rough diamond into a polished stone."

"But you don't want to be polished?" Merritt asked gently.

"I'm no' a diamond in the first place."

She smiled as she went to him. "I disagree on that point." An earthy but appealing mixture of scents clung to him, smoke, sea air, a hint of wet dog, the sweet tang of whisky on his breath.

"I'm no' inferior," Keir said, "only different. My life suits me—why change it?" Shoving his hands deeper in his pockets, he frowned and paced. "I told Kingston to end the probate," he muttered. "If I renounce the trust, which I never wanted in the first place, Ormonde will have no reason to get rid of me."

"But the trust is your birthright," Merritt protested. "Your mother wanted you to have it—"

"That's what Kingston said."

"—and Lord Ormonde may still try to have you killed regardless."

"He said that too." Looking surly, Keir ducked his head and scrubbed his fingers through the short hair at the back of his neck. "But I told the duke if I went back to Islay and disavowed any connection to the Challons, that would likely put an end to it."

"Oh, Keir," she said softly. How that must have hurt Uncle Sebastian.

"Then he reached in his waistcoat and took out a wee lock on a watch chain."

"The one from your mother?"

"Aye. He asked if I wanted to try the key on it."

"And did you?" Merritt asked gently.

Keir shook his head, his color rising, his gaze troubled and guilty.

Tenderness washed through her as she reflected that through no fault of his own, he'd been thrown into a situation with no easy choices. "I'm sure you're worried about all the things that key might unlock," she said. "How could you not be? Since you arrived in England, you've had to endure more upheaval and pain than any of the rest of us. What you need is time to recover and reflect on all of it. Eventually you'll know the right thing to do."

His shoulders relaxed, and he turned to face her fully. "What will you do?"

Merritt summoned a smile. "You needn't worry about me. I expect I'll be making plans to travel abroad. My brother Luke will take care of all the issues related to the warehouse insurance, and make sure you're reimbursed."

Keir gave a brief shake of his head to indicate he wasn't concerned about that.

The half-hour chime of the desk clock floated through the air as delicately as a soap bubble. Merritt felt her heart sinking, anchoring her so deeply in this moment of loss, it seemed she would never be able to move on to another feeling. "You'll have to leave soon," she said, "if you're going to reach the station in time."

"The duke said Culpepper would pack for me. All I have to do is wash up."

She smiled at him blindly. "Let this be our good-bye. I hereby release you from our engagement. You were a very nice fiancé"—she paused to give him a mock-reproving glance—"although I do think you might have tried to kiss me at least once."

"'Tis only that I know better." Keir smiled slightly, his gaze traveling over her, collecting every detail. "Scotland has a long history of border warfare, ye ken. There are many ways to attack a fortified hold: battering rams, siege towers, cannons . . . but the best strategy is to wait." He reached out to touch a loose tendril of her hair and stroke it gently behind her ear. "Sooner or later," he continued, "the drawbridge has to be lowered. And that's when the invaders force their way through." His eyes held her fast in silver heat. "If I let you slip past my guard, Merritt . . . I'd be leveled to the ground."

"Then we're fortunate that didn't happen," she managed to say.

He took both her hands and lifted them to his lips. "Lady Merritt Sterling . . ." His voice was slightly hoarse. "I'm glad to have met you. I owe you my life. And though I shouldn't say it . . . you're everything

I've ever wanted in a woman, and more." His fingers tightened briefly before letting go. "'Tis the 'more' that's the problem."

"I THINK WE would all agree it was a peculiar visit," Phoebe told Keir dryly, as the carriage rolled along the drive leading away from the estate at Heron's Point. They were followed by another carriage conveying the nanny, nursemaid, and footman. She cuddled Eden on her lap, gently shaking a carved wooden rattle in front of her. The baby's gaze followed the toy with rapt attention. "I do wish my mother had been there," Phoebe continued. "You would have liked her tremendously. But I suppose it's soon for you to start meeting the rest of the family."

"I may never want to meet them," Keir said. "Or at least, no' for a while."

Phoebe regarded him pensively. "Merritt said anyone in your situation would feel overwhelmed, and we must let you set the pace." She smiled. "But I hope you don't think I'm going to let you vanish into the proverbial Scottish mist, never to be seen again. You need a sister, and I happen to be excellent at sistering."

Keir responded with a distracted nod. The mention of Merritt's name had infused his blood with restless, uneasy energy.

After saying good-bye to her in the tapestry room, Keir had gone to bathe and change into the traveling clothes Culpepper had laid out for him. *Only* for traveling, the valet had emphasized, as they were made of heavier, darker fabrics designed to withstand the rigors and filth of the journey.

When it was time to depart for the railway station,

Kingston had gone out to the front drive to see them all off. He'd helped Phoebe and Eden into the carriage, then turned to Keir.

"I'll visit you on Islay soon," Kingston had said in a tone that would brook no argument. "Naturally I'll send information from Ethan Ransom as soon as I receive it. In the meantime, you're to take no chances, and you'll hold to our agreement about the porter. I've already wired one of the club managers, and he's making the arrangements." To Keir's surprise, the duke had handed him his familiar folding wallet. "This is yours, I believe."

It had been filled with a thick wad of Bank of England notes.

"What's all this?" Keir had asked blankly.

"You'll need cash for the journey. No, for God's sake, don't argue, we've done enough of that today." The duke had seemed pleased that Keir had dutifully tucked the fat wallet inside his coat. "Be safe, my boy. Look sharp, and don't let down your guard."

"Aye. Thank you." They had exchanged a handshake, a good solid grip that had imparted a surprising measure of reassurance.

Keir glanced out the carriage window as the team of horses pulled them along the graveled drive with gathering momentum. He felt uncomfortable in his own skin. Tangled up in something, the way kelp, with all its leathery strings and straps, could snare an unwary swimmer off Islay's shore. Random muscles in his arms and legs twitched with the need to walk or run, but all he could do was sit.

"What are you going to do about Merritt?" Phoebe asked.

"Nothing," he said gruffly. "What needs doing?"

"You're not going to write to her? Visit her?"

"I bid her farewell, and that's the end of it."

"I suppose that's for the best. Although the two of you did seem to have . . . what's the word . . . an affinity?"

Keir sent her a dark glance. "Some birds can swim and some fish can fly. But they still dinna belong together."

"Yet another fish analogy," Phoebe marveled.

The bulk of the overstuffed wallet was bothersome. Keir reached into his coat and fished it out. Brooding, he began to sort through the cash in the wallet, discovering a variety of denominations . . . one-pound notes, fivers, tenners . . . so much that it wouldn't allow the wallet to stay folded. He would give some of it to the footmen and carriage drivers, he decided, and began to remove a wad of notes.

A little slip of paper fell from the side pocket of the wallet, fluttering to the carriage floor like the slender leaf of a rowan tree. With effort, Keir clasped one hand to his ribs and bent to retrieve it. He sat up and regarded it curiously.

Mr. Keir MacRae   Lady Merritt Sterling

The names had been typed . . . but why? . . . what for? . . .

Bits and pieces of memory whirled in his head . . . thoughts wheeling just beyond reach. As he struggled blindly to catch hold of something, make sense of the tumult, he heard Merritt's voice . . . *stay for one night just one* . . . and there was the smell of rain and the cool darkness of night, and the warmth of a bed . . . the tender plump curves of a woman's breasts, and the hot clasp of her body pulling at him, squeezing in voluptuous pulsation, and the sweet, wracking culmination as she cried out his name. And there was the sight of her in candlelight, flames dancing in guttering pools of wax, catching glimmers from her eyes, hair, skin . . . and the glorious freedom of yielding everything, telling her everything, while inexhaustible delight welled around them. And the despair of leaving, the physical pain of putting distance between them, the sensation of being pulled below the surface of the sea, looking up from airless depths to an unreachable sky. *Tap.* He saw Lady Merritt's fingertip pressing a typewriter key. *Tap. Tap.* Tiny metal rods flicked at a spool of inked ribbon, and letters emerged.

Keir was panting now, clutching the slip of paper, while his brain sorted and spun, and pin tumblers aligned, a key turned, and something unlocked.

"Merry," he said aloud, his voice unsteady. "My God . . . *Merry*."

Phoebe was looking at him with concern, asking something, but he couldn't hear over the wild drum of his heartbeat.

Turning too quickly in his seat, Keir ignored the stab of discomfort in his ribs as he hammered the side of his fist on the panel of the driver's box. As soon as the carriage stopped on the drive, he told Phoebe brusquely, "Go on without me."

Before she could reply, he climbed out of the carriage and headed back to the house at a full-bore run.

Chapter 25

After Phoebe and Keir had departed for the railway station, Sebastian went back into the house, intending to finish reading reports from his estate managers. But he hesitated at the threshold of his study, reluctant to return to his desk. Frustration gnawed at him. It had gone against every instinct to let his son leave the sphere of his protection while still recovering from his wounds. Keir was a target, and if there wasn't someone hunting for him now, there would be soon. Lord Ormonde would make certain of that.

Thinking of the selfish hatchet-faced bastard, and the hell he must have made Cordelia's life, and most of all how he'd almost succeeded in killing Keir, Sebastian was filled with a cold white flame of fury. It was an unholy temptation to go find Ormonde and personally beat him to a pulp. However, murdering Ormonde, while highly satisfying, would result in consequences Sebastian wasn't particularly fond of.

Why was Ethan Ransom taking so bloody long to report to him? Why hadn't the hired assassin been caught and interrogated by now? He couldn't have disappeared into thin air.

Brooding, Sebastian flexed the tense muscles of his shoulders and reached up to rub his tight neck.

Damn it, he thought wearily, *I miss Evie.*

When she was away, which thankfully was seldom, the world stopped spinning, the sun went dark, and life devolved to a grim exercise in endurance until she returned.

At the outset of their marriage, Sebastian had never dreamed a shy, awkward wallflower, who'd spoken with a stammer since childhood, would turn out to have such fearsome power over him. But Evie had immediately gained the upper hand by making it clear he would have nothing from her—not her affection, her body, or even her thoughts—unless he'd earned it. No woman had ever challenged him to be worthy of her. That had fascinated and excited him. It had made him love her.

Now he was left counting the remaining nights—four, to be precise—of waking in the middle of the night blindly searching the empty space beside him. And the hours—ninety-six, approximately—until Evie was in his arms again.

Christ, it was undignified to pine over one's own wife.

He was the one who'd encouraged Evie to accept the invitation from their friends Sir George and Lady Sylvia Stevenson, the newly appointed British ambassador and his wife. The Stevensons and their children had recently settled in the magnificent embassy on the rue de Fauborg Saint-Honoré, only a few doors down from the Élysée Palace. *You must bring Seraphina and Ivo as well*, Lady Sylvia had written. *My children will be so happy to have familiar friends visit their new home, and Paris in autumn is beautiful beyond compare.*

Although a stream of cheerful postcards and letters had arrived from Evie for the past three weeks, they were a poor substitute for the sound of her voice, and her good morning kisses, and the quirks only a husband would know about. The adorable way her toes would wiggle in her sleep whenever he touched her foot. And the way she would bounce a little on her heels when she was especially happy or excited about something.

God, he needed her back in his bed. He needed it soon. Meanwhile, he would try to exhaust himself into not thinking about Evie.

He decided to go for a swim.

AFTER THE CARRIAGES had departed, Merritt retreated to the privacy of her room and sat in a cozy corner chair, having what her mother had always referred to as a "two-hanky wallow." She wept, and mopped at her welling eyes, and blew her nose gustily. In a few minutes, the worst of it had passed, and she relaxed back in the chair as a sense of dull peacefulness settled over her.

"There," she said aloud, clutching a sodden handkerchief. "All done. Now I must find something to do." Perhaps she would work on her list of wonders. She would add the Great Wall of China to the itinerary. To her chagrin, a new sob caught in her throat, and another tear slid down. Fresh sorrow had escaped, ready to rampage again.

Holy Moses, she had to stop this.

She stood and went to the dresser for a fresh handkerchief, and paused as she heard a commotion from somewhere in the house. Good God, had someone been injured? Was it a brawl? There was the bang of a door being thrown open . . . feet pounding the stairs . . . a hoarse shout that sounded like her name.

She whirled around in alarm as someone burst into the room without knocking.

It was Keir, huge and disheveled, panting with trip-hammer force, as if he'd been running for his life. He stopped in his tracks, his fixed stare raising every hair on her body.

"What happened?" Merritt asked, utterly bewildered. "Why are you here? You . . . you'll miss the train."

"Merry."

Chills of astonishment went down her spine. She couldn't make a sound, only watched with wide eyes as he came to her.

Breathing raggedly, Keir reached for her hand and pressed something into her palm. Her gaze fell to the trembling strip of paper in her hand, and she saw their typed names.

The paper fell from her nerveless fingers. She looked into his eyes, light and burning like twin stars. Oh, God, he'd remembered.

"Keir," she said, trying to sound very calm, "it doesn't matter now. Everything's been settled. That night was a diversion for both of us, a lovely one, but . . . there's no need to make a muckle into a mickle." She paused, thinking she might not have said that right. "Keir—"

But the words were blotted out as he pulled her against him, his mouth seizing hers.

Somewhere outside this room, life rushed by like scenery outside a railway carriage, melting into a mad watercolor blur. But here in the compass of his arms, time had stopped. The ticking minutes caught fire and vanished into smoke. There was only the urgency of Keir's embrace, the rough, vital kisses, the strength of him all around her. She'd never expected to feel this again.

Her hands groped around his neck, her fingers lacing through the thick shorn locks at the back of his head. The hard, clean contours of Keir's face rubbed against hers, a different feeling than the coarse tickle of his beard. But the mouth was the same, full and erotic, searingly hot. He consumed her slowly, searching with his tongue, licking deep into each kiss. Wild quivers of pleasure went through her, weakening her knees until she had to lean against him to stay upright. As her head tilted back, a forgotten tear slid from the outer corner of her eye to the edge of her hairline. His lips followed the salty track, absorbing the taste.

Keir cradled her cheek in his hand, his shaken whisper falling hotly against her mouth. "Merry, love . . . my heart's gleam, drop of my dearest blood . . . you should have told me."

Merritt heard her own weak reply as if from a distance. "I thought . . . in some part of your mind . . . you might have wanted to forget."

"No." Keir crushed her close, nuzzling hard against her hair and disheveling the pinned-up coils. "Never, love. The memory slipped out of reach for a moment, is all." His hand coasted slowly up and down her spine. "I'm so damned sorry for the way I've been trying to keep you at a distance. I dinna know you were already inside my heart." He paused before adding wryly, "Mind, I did have to jump from a three-story window, with little to break the fall but my own hard head." Taking one of her hands, he pressed her palm over his pounding heartbeat. "But you were still in here. Your name is carved so deep, a million years could no' erase it."

Completely undone, Merritt buried her face against his chest. "This is impossible," she said in despair. "You shouldn't have come back. We have no future. I wouldn't be happy in your life, and you wouldn't be happy in mine."

Although the words were smothered in his shirtfront, Keir managed to decipher them.

Softly he asked, "Would you be happy without me?"

Merritt swallowed hard. "No," she admitted wretchedly. "We're doomed, separately or together."

Keir cupped a hand over her head and gathered her deeper into his embrace. She felt a tremor run through him, and for a moment she thought he might be weeping. But no—he was *laughing.*

"You find this amusing?" she asked indignantly.

He shook his head, swallowing back a chuckle and clearing his throat. "I was only thinking if we're doomed either way . . . we may as well stay together, aye?"

Before she could reply, he bent and caught her lips with his, coaxing a response she couldn't hold back. Nothing was under her control. She was as reckless as a girl in her teens, overwhelmed with new emotions and ready to throw away everything for the sake of love.

Except even as a teenage girl, she'd never felt anything like this.

Keir was kissing her harder now, ravishing slowly, letting her feel his hunger, his need.

Unbelievably long, sensuous kisses . . . sometimes languid, sometimes fierce . . . kisses that made impossible promises.

A breath rasped in his throat as he let his lips wander gently over her face. "Merry, lass . . . I have to tell you what that night meant to me. How beautiful it was . . . how you quenched a thirst in my soul."

"Keir," she managed to say, "we must be careful not to confuse the physical act with deeper feelings."

He drew back to look down at her with a frown. "I dinna mean when we fooked."

Merritt flinched as if he'd just dashed cold water in her face. "For heaven's sake, please don't put it that way."

His brows lifted slightly at her vehemence. "How should I say it, then?"

After sorting through various possibilities, she suggested, "Sleeping together?"

Keir looked sardonic. "Neither of us slept a wink."

"Then . . . 'when we had relations.'"

He snorted, obviously loathing that suggestion. "My word means the same thing, and 'tis shorter."

"The point you were about to make . . . ?" Merritt prompted.

"Oh, aye. What made the night special was how we talked for hours, just the two of us. The ease of it . . . like floating on salt water." A soft distance entered his gaze as he continued. "We were in our own world. I'd never felt that with anyone before, but I knew I could tell you things I'd never told anyone. And when we slept together . . . that was part of the conversation, only without words."

Merritt was speechless.

He had to stop saying wonderful, endearing things in that accent, and standing there with that stray lock of gold-burnished hair falling over his eyes . . . how was a woman supposed to think straight?

She went to him, pulled his head down to hers, and silenced him with her lips. Only as a necessary measure to stop him from talking. Not because she wanted him. Not because the silky, delicious warmth of his mouth was impossible to resist.

Keir's arms went around her reflexively, his lips sealing over hers. He explored her with avid hunger, stroking and teasing, awakening deep pangs of delight. One of his hands slid low on her spine, keeping her pressed close and tight. His body was so hard, the aggressive shape of him nudging against her, and she went hot all over at the remembered sensation of him filling her.

Mortified by the awareness that she'd gone wet, her intimate flesh throbbing, Merritt struggled out of his arms.

Keir set her free with a breathless laugh. "Careful, lass. One stray jab of your wee elbow would send me to the floor."

She went to the window and pressed the burning side of her face to a cool glass pane. "This is madness," she said. "This is how lives are ruined. People are caught up in the pleasure of the moment without stopping to consider the consequences. There are so many reasons we shouldn't be together, and only one reason we should, and it's not even a good reason."

"'Tis the only reason that matters."

"You know that's not true, or you wouldn't have tried so hard to keep from forming an attachment to me."

"'Tis no' an attachment," he said brusquely. "You're in my blood." He came to the window and propped one of his shoulders against the frame. Mellow autumn light gilded his inhumanly perfect features.

"I wouldn't have left on that train today, Merry. I'd have come back even if I hadn't remembered that night. No' a minute after the carriage started on the drive, I was ready to leap out of my skin. It felt wrong to be leaving you. Unnatural. My body can only bide so much distance from yours."

Merritt forced herself to turn away from him and go to the washstand. Clumsily she poured cold water onto a linen hand towel. "I've always prided myself on my common sense," she muttered. "I've always had definite views of marriage, and I waited for years until I found a man who met the requirements on my list."

"You had a list?"

"Yes, of qualities I desired in a partner."

"Like shopping?" From his tone, it was obvious he found the notion entertaining and nonsensical.

"I was organizing my thoughts," Merritt said, holding the compress against her sore, swollen eyes. "You wouldn't give a dinner party without first writing out a menu, would you?"

Keir approached her from behind, reaching around her to brace his hands on either side of the washstand.

"I've never been to a dinner party," he said. He bent to kiss the back of her neck, and she felt the shape of his smile against her skin. "How well do I suit your list?" he asked, his breath stirring the tiny wisps of hair at her nape. "Not at all, I'd wager."

Merritt set down the compress and turned to lean back against the washstand. "The list doesn't suit you. A whisky distiller from a remote Scottish island was not what I had in mind."

He grinned at her. "But you couldn't help yourself."

"No," she admitted. "You're perfect as you are. I wouldn't want to change you."

"Life changes everyone," he pointed out. "I'm no' proof against that. None of us knows what's in store."

That reminded Merritt of a subject that needed to be brought up. She folded her arms against a sudden chill. "Keir," she asked, "has all your memory returned, or only part of it?"

"'Tis coming back in pieces, like a puzzle. Why?"

"The day I showed you to the warehouse flat, we talked about why I hadn't had children with Joshua. Do you remember what I told you?"

Keir shook his head.

"I'm barren," she said flatly, her fingers flexing into her upper arms. "Just before my husband died, I visited a London specialist to find out why I hadn't been able to conceive." She paused, recalling the term the doctor had used . . . *uterine fibroids* . . . but at the moment it wasn't necessary to go into such detail. "After the examination, he said I had a condition of the womb—it wouldn't endanger my health—but it's virtually impossible for me to have a baby. If I'd wanted to become a mother, he said, I should have tried much sooner, and there might have been a chance. By the time I finally married, however, it was too late."

Keir was expressionless. After a long silence, he asked gently, "What did your husband say?"

"Joshua was overwhelmed with sadness. It was difficult to accept he'd never have children of his own. No son to inherit the business he'd built. He didn't blame me in the least, but it was the greatest disappointment of his life. It sent him into a deep melancholy. I tried to comfort him, but it was impossible, since I was the cause of his grief. That was why he went on that last trip—he thought perhaps spending a little time away from me, and seeing family and old friends in Boston might lift his spirits. So in a way, his death was—"

Merritt paused, surprised by the words that had nearly sprung out.

My fault.

In the days and weeks after her husband's passing, she'd discovered grief wasn't a single feeling but one made of many layers, mortared together with *if-onlys.* If only she hadn't turned out to be barren. If only she'd done a better job of consoling Joshua and lifting his depressed spirits, he wouldn't have gone on the trip. If only she'd never married him in the first place, he would have married someone else, and he'd still be alive.

She knew logically that she hadn't been to blame, it had simply been an accident.

Joshua's ship hadn't been the first to go down at sea, nor would it be the last. But deep down she'd harbored a sliver of guilt, like one of those splinters so small it could stay lodged in a finger for years.

Keir's alert gaze took in every tiny variation of her expression. His chest rose and fell with a long breath, and he pushed away from the washstand with startling abruptness. He began to pace around the room, not like someone deep in thought but like a caged lion.

Merritt watched him in growing confusion. Was he sorry for her sake? Was he bitterly disappointed, as Joshua had been?

No . . . from the way he raked his hands through his hair, from his deepening flush and darkening scowl . . . and the twitching muscle in his clenched jaw . . .

"Are you angry?" she asked, bewildered. "With me?"

Chapter 26

For years, Sebastian's morning ritual had started with a swim, which not only kept him fit and flexible, but helped him face the day in a state of calm alertness. In summer, he preferred the open water at the cove, but in the colder months, the only option was to swim indoors. In a resort town filled with therapeutic and recreational baths, it had been an easy matter to find contractors to install a saltwater swimming bath in one of the Challon mansion's wings.

The bath was thirty by sixty feet, surrounded by a platform of pitch pine and intricate mosaic tile floors. Pipes leading from the kitchen ran beneath the pool to take the chill from the water, while louvers in the glass roof could be adjusted for ventilation. Rows of stained-glass windows in white, green, and blue admitted light while maintaining privacy. For the comfort of family and guests, there were changing rooms, lavatories, shower baths, and lounge areas with upholstered wicker furniture.

Sebastian stripped off his clothes beside the bath and tossed them onto a nearby chaise longue. He dived in cleanly and began swimming laps with a smooth, efficient overhand stroke. The steady back-and-forth cleared his mind, and soon he was conscious only of moving through the water in a steady forward propulsion.

After twenty minutes of hard swimming, his muscles were burning. He hoisted himself out of the water, breathing heavily, and went to fetch a towel from a stack on a table. As he dried himself vigorously, he caught a glimpse of someone standing by the other end of the swimming bath. He went very still at the sight of rose-copper hair . . . pink cheeks and round blue eyes . . . and lavish curves contained in a fashionable striped wool dress. Every filament of his nervous system sparked with an infusion of joy.

"Evie?" he asked huskily, afraid he was imagining her.

She glanced at the water, remarking innocently, "You were swimming so hard, I thought there might be a sh-shark."

It took all Sebastian's concentration to reply casually. "You know better than that, pet." He wrapped the towel around his waist and tucked in the overlapping edge to fasten it. "I *am* the shark."

He went to his wife in no apparent hurry, but as he drew closer his stride quickened, and he snatched her up with an ardor that nearly lifted her feet from the floor. She gasped and clutched his shoulders, and lifted her smiling mouth to his.

Glorying in the taste and feel of her, Sebastian kissed her thoroughly, eventually finishing with a soft, provocative bite at her lower lip. "Evie, my beauty, did you remember to bring back our children?"

"I did. Ivo has gone in search of Ajax."

He arched a brow. "I've been eclipsed by the dog?"

Evie's lips twitched. "I told the children I wanted to see you privately first. Seraphina was quite happy to change out of her traveling clothes and lie down for a nap." Her palms curved over the bulging muscle of his upper arms, and she made a little hum of appreciation. "If you keep exercising like this, I'll have to alter your shirts."

"It's been my only recourse," Sebastian said darkly. "I've roasted in a hell of sexual deprivation since you abandoned me."

"Abandoned?" she repeated in surprise.

He gave her a severe glance. "You vanished in the middle of the night."

"It was morning," she protested.

"Without saying a word about where you were going."

"You arranged for the t-tickets!"

"I didn't even have a chance to say good-bye."

"You *did*," Evie protested. "You took two hours, and nearly made me miss the train."

Sebastian muffled a quiet laugh against her glowing curls. "Oh, yes. I remember that part." He smoothed back a few ruddy wisps of her hair and began to kiss her forehead, then jerked his head back abruptly. Frowning, he drew a finger across her forehead and down her nose, and examined his fingertip for cosmetic residue. Nothing.

"What happened to your freckles?" he demanded. *"Where are they?"*

His wife looked vastly pleased with herself. "Sylvia and I went to visit a celebrated Parisian cosmetician. She gave me a sp-special cream for my complexion."

Sebastian was genuinely appalled. "You know how I loved those freckles."

"They'll come back by summer."

"This is an international outrage. I'm going to lodge a formal complaint with the embassy. There may be war, Evie." He took her face in his hands and gently tilted it this way and that, finding nothing but smooth, creamy whiteness. "Look what they've done to you," he grumbled.

Her blue eyes twinkled with amusement. "I may have a few left," she confided.

"Where?"

"You can look for them later," she said primly.

"I must have proof. Show me now." He tugged her toward the upholstered chaise, while she resisted with a burst of giggles.

"Not here," she exclaimed, and distracted him by applying her mouth to his. After a long, savoring kiss, she drew back to meet his gaze. "Tell me what happened while I was gone," she urged gently. "I decided to return a f-few days early after I read your last letter. I could tell something wasn't quite right."

"I worded it carefully, damn it."

"That's how I knew."

A rueful grin worked across his face. He pulled her close and nuzzled into her hair, close to her ear. "Evie," he said softly, "I found him."

There was no need to explain who "he" was. Evie looked up at him in amazement. "More accurately," Sebastian continued, "he found me. He stayed here for a fortnight, and left today just before you arrived. I wouldn't be surprised if your carriage passed his."

"How wonderful," Evie exclaimed, beaming. "I'm so—" She broke off, an odd look crossing her face. "Wait. Is his name MacRae?"

"Yes." He gave her a questioning glance.

"As our carriage approached the house," she explained, "we saw a man sprinting along the drive. He ran right up to the front door and dashed inside. By the time we entered the main hall, there was no sign of him. But the butler said he was a guest of yours—a Scottish gentleman by the name of MacRae."

"Keir MacRae," Sebastian said absently as he pondered the information. "He must have come back. I expect he went to find Merritt."

"*Our* Merritt?" Evie looked bemused. "She's here? How is she acquainted with Mr. MacRae?"

Sebastian smiled. "We have much to talk about, love." Deliberately he tugged at the ends of the lace scarf that had been tucked into her bodice. "But first, about those freckles . . ."

Chapter 27

KEIR STILL HADN'T SAID a word, only stalked around the confines of the bedroom.

"I wish you'd stop pacing like that," Merritt commented uneasily. "If we could sit and talk—"

"No' when my birse is up," Keir muttered.

"Birse?"

"Like a brush made from a wild boar."

"Oh, bristle; you mean you're bristling. But . . . you're not blaming me for being barren, are you?" She stared at him, stricken. "That's not fair, Keir."

Looking outraged, he reached her in two strides and took her by the shoulders, as if he wanted to shake her. But he didn't. He only held her, opened his mouth to say something, snapped it shut, and tried again. "Why would I give a damn if you're barren?" he burst out. "Who do you think you're bluidy talking to? My parents loved me as much as they would a blood-born son. They took no less pride in me for all that I was brought to them a bastard. From the moment they took me in, I was theirs, and they were mine. Are you saying that wasn't real? That we were no' a true family?"

"No, I would never say that. You know I wouldn't! But most men want sons to carry on the family name and bloodline."

"I'm no' one of them," Keir snapped.

He wasn't shouting, precisely, but his intensity unnerved Merritt. She hesitated, unsure how to reply.

"I'm sorry," she said humbly. "I assumed you would feel strongly about having children of your own blood—and I'll never be able to give that to you."

"I dinna need a broodmare, I need a wife."

At the sight of her woebegone face, Keir's impatience vanished. With a soft groan, he pulled her into the tough, warm haven of his embrace. He smoothed her hair and pressed her head to his shoulder. "Blood is no' what binds a family. Love is." His warm breath filtered down to her scalp. "How many bairns do you want? We could have a dozen if it pleases you. 'Tis the same as loving any other child. And you'd be such a fine, good mither—the beating heart of the family." His fingers slid beneath her chin to angle it upward. "As for your late husband," he continued, "I liked the man, and I dinna wish to speak ill of someone who can't defend himself. But I'll say what I would have told him while he was still living: It was no' the time to be leaving you when he did. His loss was no greater than yours. You were the one who most needed comforting."

"I had family and friends for that. Joshua knew they would help me through it."

"It was a husband's place to help you through it as well."

"You don't know what you would have done, if you'd been in his place."

"I do," Keir said firmly. "I would have stayed with my wife."

"Even knowing there was nothing you could have done for me?"

His gaze didn't move from hers. "Staying there doing nothing would have been doing something."

Merritt felt her face contorting as she struggled to control her emotions. "Sometimes . . ." She had to pause and clear her throat before continuing. ". . . I find myself wishing he'd married another woman who could have given him children. Then he'd still be alive."

"Lass, you dinna know that. He might have taken the same ship, on that same day, for a different reason. Or he might have married a woman who could have given him bairns but made his life a misery." Keir cupped her cheek in his hand. "If he could, I think he'd tell you what a joy you were to him, and ask you no' to remember him with guilt." His blue eyes, the lightest color of sky, stared into her watering ones. "Ah, love," he said gently, "I'd die in his place, if bringing him back would stop you from blaming yourself."

She stiffened in horror at the thought. "Don't say that."

His thumb eased over the tiny, tense muscles of her jaw in gentle circles. "Soft, now," he murmured. "None of it was your fault. Promise me you'll be as kind to yourself as you'd be to someone else."

Closing her eyes, she nudged her cheek into his palm and nodded.

"Say it," he prompted.

"I promise to try," Merritt said, and let out a wavering sigh. "But what's to be done now?"

"About us? We'll come to the right decision, you and I. Later. For now . . . let's go to bed."

Her eyes flew open. She gave him a dumbfounded look. "Here? Now?"

"My arms ache to hold you," he said. "No' just for a little while. For a long time."

"Oh, I don't think . . ." Floundering, Merritt lowered her forehead to his shoulder. "It wouldn't solve any problems."

He made a sound of amusement in his throat. "It would solve at least one of mine." His lips slid lightly over the outer edge of her ear. "I'll do some begging, if that would sway you."

"Keir, it was a mistake the first time we did it."

"Aye, and I'm after making it again."

She drew her head back to give him a scandalized glance. "In the middle of the afternoon?"

There was a dance of mischief in his eyes. "There'll be no one to hear us. Thursday is when the servants polish the silver downstairs in the dining room."

"They'll still know," Merritt said, wincing at the thought. "With all the commotion we've made, it's hardly a secret that we're alone in my bedroom."

"Merry, honey-love . . . I want you too badly to give a damn who knows." Keir smiled down at her with a charm that cast sunspots across her vision. "Come to bed with me, my heart. There are worse ways to spend an afternoon."

It would have taken a woman made of far sterner stuff to resist him.

Merritt went to lock the door and turned to find Keir undressing beside the bed. Her heartbeats tumbled together like a row of ninepins as she watched him unbutton the half placket of his shirt. He lifted the garment over his head, revealing a torso that was sleek and layered with muscle, his chest covered with a light mat of glinting hair. She was amazed by how beautiful he was. But as she saw him wince while lowering his arms, she frowned in concern.

"You're still healing," she said. "Is it too soon for this?"

"No."

"I think it's too soon."

His eyes glinted with mockery. "Maybe you should go fetch Dr. Kent's book and see what it says."

That drew a reluctant grin from her. "I don't recall seeing a chapter on this particular subject."

"Just as well." Keir reached out with one arm and pulled her against his brawny chest. "You might have brought the stopwatch as well, and I dinna want to be rushed."

Her chuckle was caught between their lips as he kissed her soundly. Dressed only in trousers, he padded barefoot to a chair where he had set his clothes. To Merritt's amusement, he folded the shirt carefully before setting it on top of the neat stack of garments.

Seeing her quizzical gaze, he explained, "It makes Culpepper crabbit if I wrinkle the clothes after he's worked hard to press them."

"You're on better terms with him now?"

"Aye. He and I talk a bit every morning, when he gives me a shave." Keir came back to her and turned her to face away from him, and a ripple of excitement chased down her spine as she felt him unfastening the back of her dress.

"Why do you let him keep shaving you?" she asked. "I thought you would have started growing the beard back right away."

Keir sounded slightly sheepish as he replied. "There's always an ackwart stage of growing a beard, when the stubble grows longer but the rest hasn't filled in. 'Tis patchy like a pasture after the goats have grazed it."

"And you didn't want Uncle Sebastian making comments?"

"No, I dinna give a damn about that—he couldn't say anything worse than the lads back on Islay. There's no mercy when one of us is growing a beard—we'll call him a 'duck in molt,' or . . . no, the rest isn't fit for your ears."

"If you weren't worried about Uncle Sebastian's opinion, then what was it?"

"I dinna want you to remember me with a beard that looked to be trimmed with a hand mower."

"You stayed clean-shaven for me?" A smile spread across Merritt's face, and she turned around to face him. "Whatever stage of beard you happen to be in, you're irresistible." She leaned close to brush her nose, lips, and chin through the luxuriant fluff of his chest hair.

One of his hands slipped into the open back of her dress and found her bare upper shoulder. "I'll have to shave from now on," he said. "Your skin is as soft as a petal. After a night with me, you were scoured from head to toe."

"Not *scoured*," Merritt said, blushing. "You don't have to give up your beard for my sake."

"As often as I plan to bed you, milady, I think I'd better."

She sent him a flirtatious glance. "That's rather presumptuous, don't you think?"

Keir shook his head, smiling. "Only hopeful."

By the time he'd undressed them both, the yolk-colored light of deep afternoon had pushed through the partially closed wooden blinds, and slid across the bed in a row of golden ribbons. They reclined on the bed, and Keir stretched out on his side with Merritt in the crook of his arm. His mouth worked slowly on hers, tasting, softly tugging, then sealing tight and sending his tongue deep.

"I have an idea," Merritt said breathlessly, when he began to kiss his way down her throat. "Let's try to make this as mediocre as possible. We'll cure ourselves of each other. We'll be dull and clumsy and inconsiderate, and then we'll never want to do this again. What do you think?"

His soft laugh collected in the deep valley between her breasts. "I think there's nothing you could do to cure me of you."

Merritt ran her fingers through the heavy locks of his hair, savoring the rich feel of it. "I'm going to lie still and be very boring," she said. "That will be sure to ruin your fun."

"The only way you could ruin it," came his muffled voice, "is by making me sneeze."

A giggle burst from her lips, and then she fell silent as his free hand wandered over her, kneading gently, stroking, teasing tenderly. She was too vulnerable. He knew too much about her now. A shock of pleasure went through her as his mouth captured the tip of her breast, nibbling and sucking. Her closed thighs spread easily at his touch, as if her body had decided to follow his commands instead of her own.

Through the mad pounding of the heartbeat in her ears, she heard his quiet murmurs as he kissed and licked all down her front. "The feel of you . . . so sweet . . . I never want to stop . . . every night, I need this from you . . ."

The air was cool against the thin hot skin of her vulva. It was embarrassing to be swollen and wet before he'd even touched her there. His hands were so strong, but his fingertips traced the intricate shape of her with unbelievable delicacy. She whimpered as he played with her. Such tantalizing caresses, parting the dark curls, spreading the tender lips. If he touched the peak, with just the slightest graze of his fingers, she would climax harder than she ever had in her life.

But he didn't. His fingertips glided lightly between the humid folds, down to circle the wet entrance of her body, then tickled their way up to the tight little pearl, circling tenderly without touching it. Oh, God, she remembered how he liked to make it last a long time. He couldn't do that tonight; she couldn't endure it. Her face and body were hot, she was sweltering, she would die without relief soon.

"Keir . . . we shouldn't draw this out. Your ribs . . . too much exertion . . . you'll hurt yourself."

He lifted his head, his blue eyes laughing at her as he said gently, "We've only been at it for five minutes."

"It's been longer than that," she said, squirming. "I'm sure it has."

"Dinna worry about my ribs. We'll try this and that, and find out what's best." He bent to kiss her stomach, so low that his chin brushed the triangle of curls. The tip of his tongue touched her skin, painting a delicate pattern. Her hips undulated, trying in vain to coax him lower, her entire body begging, *Please down there down there.* She felt as helpless as a jointed doll.

Different parts of her were quivering, tensing, trembling, while her insides closed frantically on emptiness.

He changed their positions with a quiet grunt of discomfort, until they were both lying on their sides, his head toward her feet. She felt him pull her top leg up and across, and then he relaxed with what sounded like a purr. As she felt him breathing between her thighs, she moaned, panted, licked her dry lips, wanting to say his name but afraid she might scream it. She tensed at the touch of his fingers, stroking lightly across the wet entrance of her body.

All her consciousness focused on what he was doing, the fingertip that dipped very slightly into the pulsing cove. A teasing finger slid all the way inside and began to thrust in the slowest, gentlest rhythm possible, while her intimate muscles clenched and squeezed at the invasion, and her belly writhed. His breath rushed against the hard, tender bud of her clitoris in feathery tickles. It was heaven. It was torture. She wanted to kill him. He was the meanest, wickedest man who'd ever lived, the devil himself, and she would have told him so if she'd had the breath to spare.

He added another finger, and a deep glow began at her core. The feeling spread through every limb and swept upward, until it burned in her face and throat, even at the lobes of her ears. It was beneath her arms, between her toes, at the backs of her knees, a radiant heat that kept climbing. His fingers curved gently inside and held her like that, and then, finally, she felt his mouth at her sex, his tongue stroking in catlike laps. It sent her into a climax unlike anything she'd ever felt, pure ecstasy without a precise beginning or end, a long open spasm that went on and on.

A new surge of wetness emerged when his fingers finally withdrew. His tongue was strong and eager as he hunted for the taste of her, making her writhe. Her head came to rest close to his groin, her cheek brushing the satiny skin of his aroused flesh. Languidly she rubbed her parted lips along the rigid length, making him jolt as if he'd received an electric shock.

Encouraged by his response, she took hold of the shaft with one hand and drew her tongue along it. When she reached the tip, she fastened her lips over the silkiness and salt taste, and sucked lightly. He groaned between her thighs. With his fingers, he spread her furrow wider, and nibbled at the taut, full center, flicked at it. She moaned, the sound vibrating around the head of his shaft.

Keir pulled away suddenly, gasping and laughing unsteadily. "No' yet . . . *ahh* . . . wait, Merry . . . I want more of you." He climbed from the bed and pulled her to the edge of the mattress, arranging her until she was bent over with her feet on the floor. He widened the spread of her thighs and stood between them.

Merritt turned red, her hands clenching into the bedding. She felt exposed, maybe slightly ridiculous, presenting to him like this, in a posture reminiscent of the farmyard. Uneasily she wondered what it meant that he would ask this of her, or what it would mean for her to allow it.

A gentle palm ran down her tense spine. "Easy, my heart. Do you no' prefer it like this?"

"It's . . . I've never tried it."

"Do you want to?"

Merritt considered that, relaxing slightly under his soothing hand. The fact that he was sensitive to her discomfort, that the choice was entirely hers, eased her worries.

"Yes," she said, and let out a wobbly laugh. "Although I've never felt so undignified."

Keir leaned over her, his forearms braced outside of hers, the warm fur of his chest brushing the sensitive skin of her back. It felt good, as if he were protecting her from something. She heard the trace of a smile in his voice.

"There's no dignity in any of this," he said, "for either of us. That's the fun of it."

It was, she realized. Here was a man, a lover, with whom she could have true intimacy, and share a deeply private act without shame. She relaxed even more.

Keir kissed the back of her shoulder. "If you dinna like it," he said, "you'll tell me right away, aye?"

"Yes."

His weight lifted, and his hand reached between her thighs, stroking and opening her. She felt a nudge, an adjustment as he aligned himself, then steady pressure at her entrance. He was so hard, his flesh like steel, but he was gentle and controlled, taking his time. She gasped as her muscles gave way and the broad tip pushed inside, stretching her, keeping her open. He held still, his hands stroking her hips and bottom.

All her nerves tingled and sparked in anticipation, knowing how good it was going to be. She pressed back against him, and he sheathed himself in a slow, wet plunge, all the way inside, deeper than she'd ever been filled before. He went in at just the right angle, pressing where she most wanted. Her body gripped him, or tried to, except the invasion was so thick, her muscles only fluttered and throbbed instead of clenching down. She felt almost as if she were at the brink of release. And to her astonishment . . . she was. She was about to tip over into a sea of mind-dissolving pleasure.

"Wait," she heard Keir say through the clamor of her heartbeat. His hands were on her hips, keeping her close and tight. For some reason it aroused her intolerably, knowing he was trying to stop her from climaxing. She tried to drive herself back on the hard shaft inside her, unable to get enough of it even though she was stretched to the limit. Raising up on her forearms, she writhed and pushed desperately against him.

Keir's husky laugh caressed her ears as he leaned over her. He held her hips snugly against his, allowing only a sense of motion, a subtle grinding that wasn't nearly enough. Very gently, he closed his teeth on the side of her neck and soothed it with his tongue. "Tell me how good it feels," he whispered.

Merritt fought for the breath to reply. "It feels too good. I want to come . . . I want to spend . . . oh, please, Keir . . ."

"Spend," he repeated, and smiled against her shoulder. "I like that word for it." He withdrew just an inch, and rolled his hips upward. "Aye, I want your pleasure. Spend it all on me."

She sobbed and squirmed, able to feel the motion of him deep in her belly, but it wasn't enough. "Harder. Please."

The rhythmic drives grew longer, more aggressive. "No one else could ever feel this good to me," he said. "No other woman in the world. Only you." He reached beneath her to cup the round weights of her breasts, and began to pinch and tug at her nipples. Not sharply but not softly, the little flashes of discomfort somehow magnifying her pleasure. His hand slid down her front and between her thighs, finding the taut peak of her sex. The gently massaging fingers, the steady pumping, set off an explosion of pleasure that spread to every part of her body and kept unfolding and renewing itself. The release was so powerful, it left her dazed and too weak to move. She was only vaguely aware of Keir's climax, the quiet growl he pressed against her skin, the rough shudders that ran through him.

His sweetness afterward was almost better than the lovemaking, as he kissed up and down her body, praising and caressing her. Eventually he lit a lamp near the bedside and went to the washstand. He returned with a glass of cool water and a damp cloth. Merritt drank thirstily, and lay back as he washed her intimately. She could have done it herself, but it was delicious to be taken care of, and she felt utterly limp, as if all her bones had been soaked in honey.

After seeing to his own needs, Keir got into bed and tucked Merritt against his good side. She snuggled into the crook of his arm and frowned in curiosity as she saw a small envelope in his hand.

"What is that?" she asked.

"Someone slipped it beneath the door."

"We've been found out," Merritt said, seeing that his name had been written on the envelope, even though it had been delivered to her room. An embarrassed chuckle escaped her, and she hid her face on his chest. "But how? We've been so discreet."

With a snort of amusement, Keir opened the letter. "It's from Kingston," he said, and fell silent as he read.

Merritt lifted her head. "What does it say?" she asked, unable to interpret his expression.

"The duchess, Seraphina, and Ivo arrived from Paris this afternoon."

"They came back early? I wonder why."

"It doesn't say. But it seems they're tired from the journey and will have an informal supper in the family parlor—leaving us to our own devices."

"Thank heaven," Merritt said gratefully. "I couldn't have gone down to dinner. I'll ask for a tray to be brought to the room." She winced a little as she brought herself to ask, "Did Uncle Sebastian write anything about . . . this?"

"No, he only asks that I come to breakfast tomorrow morning. He wants to introduce me to the duchess."

Merritt let her hand wander lightly over his chest and toyed with the fine steel chain. "Are you dreading it?" she dared to ask.

"Partly," he admitted. "But I'm also curious. Whatever else you can say about Kingston, 'tis obvious he puts a store by his wife."

"He does. And she's a dear, kind woman. There'll be no unpleasantness with her, I promise."

His chest rose and fell in a measured sigh.

"You're worrying what the coming days will bring," Merritt guessed.

Keir took her hand and kissed the backs of her fingers, and drew them along the edge of his jaw. "I'm no' giving any of it a thought tonight," he replied, and set the letter aside. "No' with you in my arms. 'Tis all that matters to me."

"KEIR. KEIR, WAKE up *now*." Merritt sat up and leaned over him and shook him gently, and patted his cheek with an urgent flutter of her hand. "We've slept late. The sun is up, and—oh dear, it must be almost ten o'clock. No one came to stir the grate or bring tea. I suppose they didn't know what to do, since you're—and I didn't—"

"Wait," he said groggily, reaching up to touch her lips with his fingers. "Too early. Too many words."

"But it's *not* early. That's what I'm trying to tell you. You should be going down to breakfast now. I'm sure Culpepper has already gone to shave you and found only an empty bedroom. This is all very mortifying. I'm not sure what to—what are you doing?"

His long arm curled around her, and he pulled her down into an embrace of heat and hardness and hairy limbs. "How bonnie you are, all tuzzled and soft wi' sleep."

"Did you hear anything I just said?"

"I've never known such a night," he murmured, kissing her throat and cupping one of her naked breasts. "You put me to hard use, lass. 'Tis a wonder I survived."

"You were the one who kept waking me up," she reminded him, and gasped as she felt the scrape of his unshaven bristle against the tip of her breast.

"Poor flower," Keir said contritely, and covered the

chafed spot with his mouth. The wet velvety tug sent a shot of pleasure down to her toes. "You shouldn't tempt me so."

Merritt slid her fingertips lightly across his injured ribs. "Are you sore?"

"A wee bit," he admitted, pressing light kisses to the curve of her breast. "'Tis only to be expected, after all your wildness."

"My wildness?"

"I was ridden like a stolen horse," he claimed, and grinned as she wiggled beneath him.

"Let me out of bed," she exclaimed, trying not to laugh. "Your version of morning-after talk is appalling."

Keir pinned her beneath him and settled between her thighs. "Lass, I'm a whisky distiller. If you wanted pretty words, you should have slept with a poet."

Her eyes widened as she felt the hot, aroused length of him against her belly. "Again?"

"'Tis a persistent ailment," he told her.

"Apparently incurable." She slid her arms around him and kissed his shoulder. "Keir . . . we have to get out of bed. It's so terribly late."

He rested his head on the pillow and whispered near her ear. "How could it be late, when you're the sunrise? There's no morning sky or lark-song before you appear. No butterfly would dare unfold its wings. The day waits on you, my heart, just as the harvest waits the reaper."

As Merritt considered revising her opinion of his morning-after talk, he widened the spread of her legs and nudged against her in the suggestion of a thrust. A tingling pleasurable ache began deep inside.

"Give me one more seeing-to," he coaxed.

"Don't start that," she protested. "There's no time."

"Fifteen minutes."

Thinking of his usual leisurely pace, she gave him a skeptical glance. "You need to shave, and wash, and dress . . ." As she squirmed beneath him, her pulse quickened and her temperature rose. It was impossible to resist the allure of a hot, hard, virile male who happened to be naked in bed with her. "Would it really take only fifteen minutes?" she asked weakly, and saw his quick grin.

"Where's your stopwatch? You can time me." He reached down between their bodies, and she felt the smooth head of his shaft stroke up and down between her thighs, parting her dampening flesh, while the silky-coarse hair of his chest teased her breasts, and suddenly nothing in the world mattered except having this feeling go on. She wanted his naked body forever against hers, his scent and weight, the way he flexed and moved.

Holding on to his shoulders, she gave a little satisfied moan as he began to enter her, gently working inside the pliant opening, stretching her slowly. Her senses were so occupied with him and what he was doing, she was slow to register the brisk tap at the door.

The door opened with a startling burst, and Keir reacted swiftly, pulling Merritt farther beneath him and guiding her face to his chest. A hiss of discomfort escaped him at the sudden motion.

"Merritt, darling," she heard a familiar voice exclaim. "I know this is a surprise but—*Oh.*"

Blinking in bewilderment, Merritt peeked out from within Keir's embrace. "Mama?"

Chapter 28

"WHAT THE DEVIL ARE you doing here?" Sebastian asked as Marcus, Lord Westcliff, entered the morning room. He set his newspaper on the breakfast table and sent his old friend a puzzled, irritable glance. "You couldn't wait to be announced?"

There was hardly any man more feared or respected than Marcus Marsden, Lord Westcliff, who'd inherited one of the oldest peerage titles in England. His earldom was so ancient and venerated, in fact, that Westcliff outranked Sebastian, even though Sebastian was a duke.

Their friendship went all the way back to their days at boarding school, and although it had acquired its dents and scars, it still thrived. No one, not even the two of them, could explain why, when they were so different in character. Westcliff was honorable and reliable, a problem-solver with a strong moral compass. Whereas Sebastian, a former rake, had always lived by a far more flexible code.

Over the years, their families had spent so many holidays and summers together that their children thought of each other as cousins. As a result, there had been no romantic involvements between any of the Marsden or Challon offspring, who all claimed to find the idea somewhat incestuous.

Now it seemed a marital alliance between the Marsdens and Challons might be forged after all. But Westcliff was probably going to be rather less than enthused about the prospect of a union between his cherished daughter and Sebastian's illegitimate son.

Westcliff came to the table with a scowl. Although the passing years had threaded the once-black hair with steel and deepened the lines bracketing his nose and mouth, the earl was still vigorous and robust. He was not a tall man, only an inch or two above average height, but the bull-like strength of his shoulders and legs, combined with a naturally tenacious disposition, made him an opponent no sane man would take on. Having once been soundly thrashed by Westcliff—deservedly so—Sebastian had no desire ever to repeat the experience.

"Where's my daughter?" Westcliff asked.

"She's here."

"Unharmed? Not ill?"

"She's perfectly fine," Sebastian said. "What's put you in such a damn tither?"

"Yesterday morning I received a telegram from Merritt, stating she would arrive at Stony Cross on the evening train. She wasn't on the train, nor did she send any word." Westcliff went to the sideboard, laden with hot dishes protected by silver covers, crystal bowls of cut fruit, and a platter of bread and pastries. He picked up a china cup from a neat stack and proceeded to fill it with coffee from a silver urn. "Why did she change her plans?"

Sebastian pondered various ways to answer that. "She . . . decided to retire to bed early." And as far as he knew, she'd stayed there with Keir for the entire afternoon and all through the night. Sebastian had decided not to object, understanding there were some issues best solved with time, privacy, and a bedroom. He could only hope Keir had awakened at a decent hour and gone back to his own room.

"Have you seen Merritt this morning?" Westcliff asked.

Sebastian shook his head. "She may still be abed."

"Not for long. Lillian has gone in search of her. She went to ask one of the servants which room she's in."

Alarm whistles shrilled in Sebastian's brain. "Lillian's here? Running loose through the house? Good God, Westcliff, don't you think this is a bit of an overreaction to a missed train?"

"If that were the only issue, I would agree. However, Lillian and I are both concerned about a rumor that reached us two days ago." After stirring cream and sugar into his coffee, Westcliff turned with the cup in hand and leaned back against the sideboard. "I was comfortable allowing Merritt some leeway when she wrote she'd be staying here to help care for Mr. MacRae. Although the situation was unorthodox, I trusted her judgment. Of all my children, Merritt is the most level-headed and—Kingston, why are you staring at the ceiling?"

"I'm wondering which part of the house Lillian's in," Sebastian said distractedly. Were those her footsteps overhead? No, it was quiet now. Where was she? What was she doing? God, this was unnerving. "What was the rumor?"

"That this MacRae is something more than a business client. There was a suggestion of personal involvement, even an engagement, which is absolute rot. No child of mine would descend to the idiocy of agreeing to marry a virtual stranger."

"People have reasons—" Sebastian began defensively, but broke off as another question occurred to him. "How the devil could a rumor travel from Sussex to Hampshire that fast?"

Westcliff looked sardonic. "We live in the modern age, Kingston. With railways and efficient mail service, a rumor can cover the whole of England in the blink of an eye. One of your servants may have mentioned something to a deliveryman, who told a shopkeeper, and so forth. More to the point: *Is it true?*"

"You just said it was rot," Sebastian replied cagily, glancing at the ceiling again. His nerves crawled with unease in the knowledge that Lillian was prowling overhead. "I wouldn't dream of disagreeing with you."

"You used to be a better liar than this," Westcliff commented, now starting to look concerned. "Who is this man, and what has he been doing to my daughter? Is he still here?"

Mercifully, they were interrupted by Evie's voice. "Good morning, my lord."

Westcliff's expression softened as Evie came into the room, looking fresh and beautiful in a daffodil-yellow dress.

"What a l-lovely surprise to find you here," Evie exclaimed, beaming. She rose on her toes to press her cheek against his.

"Forgive the intrusion, my dear," Westcliff said, his dark eyes smiling down at her.

"It's nothing of the sort, you're family."

"I didn't expect to find you here," Westcliff commented. "Have you returned early from Paris, or does my memory fail me?"

Evie laughed. "Your memory never fails, my lord. I am indeed back early."

"How are Sir George and Lady Sylvia?" Westcliff asked.

"Settling in nicely." Evie would have said more, but Sebastian touched her elbow lightly. She turned to him with a questioning glance.

"Lillian's here, darling," he told her. "Running through the house unsupervised." Meaningfully he added, "She's looking for Merritt."

He saw from the slight widening of Evie's eyes that she understood. "I'll go find her," she suggested brightly. "We'll all breakfast together."

Lillian's voice came from the doorway. "Capital idea! I'm famished."

She cut a dashing figure in a scarlet traveling dress and black cloak, with a plumed red hat set at a jaunty tilt on her head. Even after having given birth to six children, Lillian was still slender and coltish, with the same high spirits and confident stride she'd had as a young woman.

Evie and Lillian hurried to each other and embraced warmly. The two of them, along with Lillian's sister Daisy Swift, and the vivacious Annabelle Hunt, had begun a lifelong friendship more than three decades ago. They had all been downtrodden wallflowers, consigned to sitting in a row at the side of a ballroom while everyone else danced. But instead of competing for male attention, they had made a compact to help each other. And throughout the years, they had championed and saved each other, time and again.

"Did you find Merritt?" Westcliff asked as Lillian came to the breakfast table with Evie.

Lillian replied with brisk cheerfulness, even as telltale banners of bright pink ran across her cheekbones. "Yes, she was in bed. Sleeping. Very soundly. Alone, of course. She'll come down soon."

Holy hell, Sebastian thought grimly. He was positive she'd seen Keir with Merritt. No doubt in some spectacularly compromising position.

However, as a devoted and loyal mother, Lillian would keep her mouth shut. She might criticize one of her children in private, but never in public. She would go to any lengths to protect them.

"I was just asking Kingston," Westcliff told Lillian, "about Merritt's business client, Mr. MacRae."

"Is he still here?" Lillian asked, a little too innocently.

"As a matter of fact, yes," Sebastian replied smoothly. He seated Evie at the table, while Westcliff did the same for his own wife.

As Lillian settled into her chair, she darted a look at Sebastian that said: *You do not have long to live.* He pretended not to notice.

Westcliff sat next to Lillian and rested a hand on the table, drumming his fingers lightly. "Why did Merritt bring MacRae here to recuperate from his injuries?" he asked Sebastian. "I would have expected her to take him to Stony Cross Park."

"It was at my request."

"Oh?" Westcliff studied him closely. "What connection do you have to him?"

Sebastian smiled slightly, reflecting that of all the things he'd ever broken, lost, or left by the wayside, he was grateful to have kept this man's friendship. Something about Westcliff's steady, logical presence made any problem seem manageable.

"Marcus," he said quietly. They never usually went by first names, but for some reason it slipped out. "This has to do with that matter I told you about last year. The one involving Lady Ormonde."

Westcliff reacted with a quick double blink. "This is *him*?"

Lillian shook her head in confusion. "What are you talking about?"

"I'll explain," Sebastian said. As he tried to think of how to start, Evie's slim hand crept to his, their fingers weaving together. He looked down at their joined hands and stroked his thumb across a golden freckle on her wrist. "First," he said, "let me remind everyone that in my youth, I was by no means the angel I am now."

Lillian's mouth twisted. "Believe me, Kingston . . . no one's forgotten."

Chapter 29

SEBASTIAN EXPLAINED HOW HE'D found out about the existence of an illegitimate son, and went on to describe the events following Keir's arrival in London. The only part of the story he left out was Merritt's personal involvement with Keir, which in his opinion was no one's business but theirs.

Somewhere in the middle of it, Lillian interrupted. "Wait just a minute," she said. "All three of you have known about this for a year, but no one told me?" As she read the answer in their faces, her brows rushed down in a scowl. "Evie, how could you leave me in the dark about something like this? It's an utter betrayal of the wallflower code!"

"I wanted to tell you," Evie said apologetically. "But the f-fewer people who knew, the better."

Westcliff regarded his wife quizzically. "What's the wallflower code?"

Lillian glowered at him. "Never mind, there is no wallflower code. Why didn't *you* tell me Kingston had a natural-born son?"

"He asked me to keep it a secret."

"It doesn't count if you tell your wife!"

Sebastian broke in. "I decided not to confide in anyone other than Evie and Westcliff," he said flatly.

"I knew that telling you would only confirm all your worst opinions about my character."

"And you thought I would use it against you?" Lillian asked incredulously. "You assumed I'd say hurtful things during a time of personal distress and turmoil?"

"I didn't think it outside the realm of possibility."

"After all we've been through . . . all the time our families have spent together . . . you think of me as an adversary?"

"I wouldn't put it that way—"

"I would have been kind to you," Lillian snapped, "had you told me. You should have given me a chance. I gave *you* a chance all those years ago, and—no, I don't want another blasted apology, I'm pointing out that I set aside past grievances for the sake of your friendship with my husband. If I'm not worthy of your trust after that, I'll be damned if I'll try any longer."

"Try to what?" Sebastian asked, mystified. As he stared into her infuriated face, and saw the hurt in her eyes, he asked slowly, "Lillian, are you saying you want to be friends with me?"

"Yes, you self-absorbed, dull-witted lobcock!" Lillian jumped to her feet, obliging the men to stand as well. "No, don't get up," she said. "I'm going for a walk. The three of you can finish the discussion without me. Apparently that's how you prefer it."

She strode from the room, and Westcliff began to follow.

"Wait," Sebastian said to him urgently. "This is my fault. Let me make peace with her. Please."

Westcliff swore quietly and relented. "If you upset her any more than she already is—"

"I won't. Trust me."

At his friend's reluctant nod, Sebastian left the morning room and saw Lillian heading toward the back entrance of the house. "Lillian. Wait." He caught up to her swiftly. She turned away from him, folded her arms, and went to a bank of windows overlooking a small garden.

"I'm sorry," he said. "I was an ass. You deserve far better than that from me."

She didn't look at him. "Apology accepted," she muttered.

"I'm not finished yet. I should have given Westcliff leave to say something to you. Selfish bastard that I am, it didn't occur to me that I was putting him in a damned difficult position by asking him to keep a secret from his wife. I beg your forgiveness for that. You're entirely worthy of my trust, and I wouldn't have minded at all if he'd told you."

Lillian's shoulders relaxed, and she turned to give him a wry glance. "Marcus would never break a confidence," she said. "He always tells the truth and keeps his word. You have no idea how trying it is."

Sebastian's lips twitched. "I might. I have my own issues with Evie. She insists on being kind and trying to see the good in everyone, every damn day. I've had to live with it for decades."

He was gratified to hear Lillian's reluctant snort of amusement. In a moment, he went to stand beside her at the window. Together they contemplated a bed of purple heliotrope and cascades of pink ivy geranium on lax stems that trailed over the border edging.

After an awkward but not unfriendly silence, Lillian

ventured, "It must have been a nightmare to learn you had a grown child you were never told about. It could have just as easily happened to Marcus, you know."

"Hard to imagine."

"Not really. No matter how careful one is, there's always a risk. As the mother of six children, I ought to know."

Sebastian sent her a bleak glance. "I always knew I'd have to pay for my sins in some future cosmic reckoning. But in my arrogance, it didn't occur to me that a man never bears the cost of his sins alone. The people around him—especially those who love him—have to pay as well. That's the worst part of it."

It was the most vulnerable he'd ever allowed himself to be with her.

When Lillian replied, her voice was uncommonly gentle. "Don't be unduly hard on yourself. Ever since you married Evie, you've tried to be the man she deserves. In fact, you've inhabited the role of a good man for so long, I think you may be growing into it. We become our choices, eventually."

Sebastian regarded her with a touch of surprise. "Throughout this entire godforsaken mess, Lillian . . . that's possibly the most comforting thing anyone has said to me."

She looked smug. "You see? You should have told me at the beginning."

His lips twitched, and his gaze returned to the window. "I'm sure I'll regret asking this," he said, "but was Keir in Merritt's room when you found her?"

"Yes," Lillian replied dourly.

"Were they—"

"Yes."

Sebastian winced. "That must have been a shock."

"I wasn't shocked by what they were doing so much as I was by Merritt's recklessness. Taking a man into her bed in broad daylight? It's not at all like her. She's behaving as if scandal can't touch her, and she knows better than that."

"So does Keir. But they're both moonstruck. You remember how it is in the beginning."

She grimaced. "Yes, a state of derangement with chapped lips." Folding her arms across her chest, she heaved a sigh. "Tell me about this young man. Is he a silk purse or a sow's ear?"

"He's pure gold. A big, fearless lad . . . engaging and quick-witted. Admittedly, the manners are a bit rustic, and I can't speak as to hygiene: so far, grooming him has been a collective effort. But all in all, a fine young man."

"And how is he with Merritt?"

Sebastian hesitated before replying. "No one outside a relationship can ever know its inner workings. But from what I've seen, it has the makings of something durable. They talk easily. They pull together in adversity. Many marriages have started with far less, including mine."

Lillian nodded, seeming deep in thought. "Is marriage on the table? Would he be willing to do the right thing by her?"

"He'd cut off a limb if she asked him to."

"Good. She'll need the protection of his name. Or someone's name. Merritt has flouted convention one too many times since she became a widow. Rumors of this affair will be the final drop that makes the cup runneth over. As we all know, there's nothing society loves more than tearing down a respectable woman who's broken the rules." She hesitated. "I'm afraid for her sake."

In all the years of their acquaintance, Sebastian never heard Lillian admit to being afraid of anything.

"Nothing will harm Merritt," he said. "A score of eligible men would offer for her tomorrow if she'd have them. But I think she wants this one."

Lillian shook her head distractedly. "My God, Sebastian. She chose her first husband with such exacting care, and now it seems likely she'll end up with a man she hardly knows and has nothing in common with."

"Common interests can be acquired," he pointed out. "What matters most is having similar values."

"Oh? What values do you and Evie have in common?" But the question sounded teasing rather than mocking.

Sebastian thought for a moment. "She and I have both always wanted me to be happy." As Lillian laughed heartily, he offered an arm to her. "Shall we rejoin the others?"

"No, I'm going to walk out to the cove and do some thinking. You may tell the other two I've regained my sweet temper and am no longer breathing fire. And don't fret over things you can't change. 'Life must be lived forwardly.' That's from a philosopher Marcus has taken to quoting lately, I can never remember the name.'"

"Kierkegaard," Sebastian said. "Life can be understood only by looking back, but has to be lived forwardly."

"Yes, that's it."

"I'll keep it in mind."

Impulsively Lillian gave him her hand, and he held it in a brief, warm clasp.

"Pax, old friend?" Sebastian asked gently.

Her lips quirked. "After thirty years, we may as well give it a try."

Chapter 30

KEIR SAT NEXT TO the firepit at the sandy cove, watching shore birds feed. Dunlin, plovers, and stints ran delicately across the wet sand to peck and probe for mollusks. They whistled plaintively and kept a wary eye on a gull digging for a buried shellfish.

Before long, he thought wryly, he would be driven to forage for mussels right alongside them. He was hollow with hunger. All he'd had so far that day was the cup of tea Culpepper had brought before shaving him.

The valet had told him that Lord and Lady Westcliff were breakfasting with the duke and duchess. Assuming Keir would join them, Culpepper had brought an elegant morning coat and vest, and trousers made of striped gray wool for him to wear. Keir had assured him emphatically that he had no intention of going down for breakfast. He was heading to the cove, and would need casual clothes and canvas shoes. Although the old valet obviously hadn't liked that idea, he'd brought a new set of garments after the shave.

Keir felt like a coward, slinking out of the house rather than face the Westcliffs, but he had no intention of meeting them *and* the duchess all at once.

"Perhaps you should lie low," Merritt had suggested to Keir, "while I go downstairs and assess the situation."

Keir had thought that was a good plan, in light of the fact that Merritt's mother had just caught them in bed together. He'd told Merritt he would probably walk out to the cove, as the weather was mild and no one else would be out there.

If only he weren't so hungry.

Sighing, he poked at a birch log. It sank heavily into a blaze of collapsing kindling, pluming the air with smoke and sparks. Through a dance of light-flecks, he saw a figure emerging from the holloway.

It was a woman wearing a black cloak. She stopped at the sight of him, seeming disconcerted to find someone else at the cove.

Keir rose to his feet, reaching up awkwardly to remove his hat before remembering he wasn't wearing one.

The woman crossed the beach toward him with an easy, energetic stride. As she approached, he saw she was beautiful, with heavy dark hair, an oval face, and merry brown eyes. She was an elongated, less bosomy version of Merritt, as if someone had carefully stretched her about five inches north and south.

Lady Westcliff, he thought, and a blaze of embarrassment raced over him.

"Is that a signal fire?" she called out in breezy manner, her accent distinctly American. "Are you in need of a rescue?" She had Merritt's smile, the one that started with a little crinkle of her nose and made her eyes tip-tilted.

Keir's trepidation began to fade. "Aye," he said, "but I'm no' sure what from yet."

She was about to reply, but she stopped in her tracks with startling abruptness, her astonished gaze sweeping down to his feet and back up again. "Flaming fuckbustles," she exclaimed under her breath.

Keir looked at her blankly, having never heard such language coming from a woman.

Lady Westcliff snapped her mouth shut. "I'm so sorry. It's just that you look like—"

"I know," he said with a touch of chagrin.

"*So* much like him," she said, still disconcerted, "particularly as he was in a less-than-charming period before he married Evie." She frowned. "But that has nothing to do with you, of course."

Keir nodded, unsure how to reply.

The conversation collapsed like a pricked balloon. They both stood there pondering how to breathe life into it.

"Milady . . . did you want to speak with me?" Keir asked.

"Actually, I came out here to do some thinking. I didn't expect to find anyone at the beach."

"I'll leave," he offered. "I'll stoke up the fire for you and—"

"No, please stay." She paused. "What are you doing out here?"

"Hiding."

That amused her. "Not from me, I hope."

Her laugh sounded so much like Merritt's that he felt his heart lean toward her like a garden seeking the sun. "You're no' the only one I was trying to avoid."

"I'm avoiding them too."

"Would you like to sit by the fire with me?"

"I would," she said. "Let's pretend we've done all the small talk, and go straight to a real conversation."

"NOT LONG AGO, you made up your mind never to marry again," Merritt's father reminded her as they walked along the holloway to the cove. They had talked for at least an hour after breakfast, just the two of them, lingering over tea in the morning room. It was always a relief to unburden herself to Papa, who was pragmatic and sympathetic, and had an uncanny ability to quickly grasp the details and implications of a problem.

Now Merritt had set out to find Keir, carrying a small lidded basket with a few tidbits from the sideboard. Her father had asked to accompany her, suspecting his wife had encountered Keir at the cove.

"That's true," Merritt admitted. "I couldn't fathom why I'd want to take a husband after Joshua. There was no reason. But then I met this man, and . . . he was a shock to the system. No one's ever had this effect on me before. I feel ten times more alive." She laughed self-consciously. "Does that sound silly?"

"Not at all. I understand. Your mother had the same effect on me."

"Did she?"

The earl let out a gravelly chuckle as he thought back to those days. "She was a fearless, free-spirited beauty with all the self-restraint of an unbroken horse. I knew she wasn't suited to the only life I could offer her. But I was mesmerized by her. I loved her enthusiasm and warmth, and everything that made her different from me. I thought if we were both willing to take a chance on each other, we might have a good marriage. It's turned out to be an extraordinary one."

"No regrets, then?" Merritt dared to ask. "Even in the privacy of your own thoughts?"

"Never," he said promptly. "Without Lillian, I would never have known true happiness. I don't hold with the common wisdom that a couple must have the same tastes and backgrounds. Married life would be dull indeed without some friction: one can't light a match without it."

Merritt smiled. "I adore you, Papa. You've made it nearly impossible for me to find a man who doesn't suffer in comparison to you."

They reached the cove, and saw her mother and Keir sitting on the beach next to a crackling fire. To her delight, they appeared to be talking companionably. As Keir went to pick up a split birch log and toss it onto the fire, flames leaped with new vigor and burnished him with light. He was a breathtaking sight, golden and godlike, his long-limbed form sensuously lean and powerful. He belonged in this natural setting of sun and salt water, the gilded layers of his hair ruffled by a sea breeze.

"Somehow," her father said dryly, "I think that fellow will survive the comparison to me." He paused before adding beneath his breath, "Good God. There's no doubt as to his sire."

Lillian remained seated on a wool beach blanket, grinning as they approached. "Hello, dears. My lord, this is Keir MacRae. We've been having the most delightful chat."

"A pleasure, MacRae," the earl said, with a precise bow, which Keir reciprocated. "It appears there's something we need to discuss, in light of a rumor I've heard."

"Sir?" Keir asked warily.

"Kingston mentioned you're an angler."

Keir relaxed visibly. "Aye, now and then I'll take a brown trout from one of the lochs on Islay."

"I occasionally try my luck at dry-fly casting on a Hampshire chalk stream." The earl glanced at Merritt and smiled reminiscently. "My daughter has accompanied me a time or two. She has excellent aptitude but little interest."

"I lose patience with the fish," Merritt said. "They take too long to make up their minds. I prefer going shooting with you—it takes far less effort."

"Are you a good shot?" Keir asked.

"I'm not bad," she said modestly.

"She's the best shot in the family," Lillian said. "It drives her brothers mad."

The earl went to his wife and lowered to his haunches until their faces were level. "My lady," he said, his voice softening with a warm, tender note, "I came to ask if you'd be willing to listen to some groveling."

"How much groveling?" Lillian asked, sounding interested.

"A one-man symphony. 'Grovel in D minor.'"

Lillian chortled. She gave him her hands and let him pull her to her feet with him. "I'll settle for a short overture," she said. Rising on her toes, she kissed her husband impulsively.

Despite the impropriety of the gesture, the earl returned the kiss soundly. Keeping an arm around his wife, he said, "We'll continue our discussion later, MacRae."

"I look forward to that," Keir replied.

As her parents walked away, Merritt went to sit on

the blanket. The radiant heat of the fire sent a pleasant shiver through her. "I hope my mother didn't shock you," she said as she watched her parents walk hand in hand to the holloway.

"She's a charming woman," Keir replied, sitting beside her. "I like her very well. She dinna shock me, although . . . she swears like a Scottish golfer."

"Oh, dear. Are Scottish golfers really that profane?"

"Aye, the worst language you'll ever hear is from a Scot in a sand bunker."

"Is there golf on Islay?"

Keir nodded. "A neighbor by the name of Gordon Catach laid out a nine-hole course on his property."

"Golf is a civilized sport," Merritt said. Perhaps it was grasping at straws, but she was happy to learn about any kind of culture on Islay. "I find that encouraging."

He laughed. "I dinna want to give you a false impression. The course is ruggit and patchy with muckle stones, and we usually have to clear the livestock off the fairway before we play."

"It's still nice to learn there's a golf course." She reached into the basket she'd brought and unearthed an enameled tin flask with a lid.

"What's this?" Keir asked as she handed it to him.

"Tea with honey." Merritt reached in again and withdrew a napkin-wrapped parcel. "And I thought you might want these."

Unwrapping the napkin, Keir discovered a trio of sausage pasties, miniature pies with sausage filling. A brilliant smile crossed his face. "Merry . . ." He reached out, curved a hand around the back of her neck, and guided her head to his. He kissed her ardently, trapping her laugh between their lips.

After he had devoured the pasties and drained the flask of tea, he wrapped his arms around Merritt and coaxed her to lean back against him.

"Isn't this uncomfortable for you?" she asked in concern.

"No' if you stay still," he said. "How my arms love the feel of you, lass."

She smiled, her eyes heavy-lidded as she stared into the fire, the flames shivering and snapping at the breeze. One of his hands drifted over her gently, coming up to stroke the side of her throat and twine a stray lock of hair around his finger.

After a contented silence, Keir said lazily, "When this business about Lord Ormonde is settled, and all is safe . . . will you visit Islay with me? You could have a look at the island, to help decide if you could make a life there."

"Do you think I would be happy on Islay?"

"'Tis no' for me to say what your needs are. 'Tis for you to say, and me to listen."

"First, I need you."

She felt him smile against her hair. "You already have that," he said. "What else?"

"I need a comfortable home with enough rooms for my family and friends to visit."

"My house is too small for that," he said regretfully. "And although 'tis comfortable for me, I dinna think you would find it so."

Her fingers slid into the cuff of his sleeve, reaching far enough to play lightly with the glinting hair of his forearm. "What if I wanted to build a house for us on the island, with my money? Would you be too proud to live in it?"

Keir made a quiet sound of amusement. "I've sacrificed my pride for worse reasons. I'll live wherever you want, my heart. But we may no' have to spend your money. I think I may be able to pay for it."

Carefully she turned her head on his chest to give him a questioning glance.

His lips brushed her temple before he explained. "I told you before that I wanted to renounce my trust and let Lord Ormond have it. But that was when I thought I was leaving you for good. Now I've thought better of it. I'll take the inheritance my mother intended for me and try to do some good with it. We can start with a house."

"I think that's a fine idea," Merritt said.

But Keir sounded less than enthusiastic as he commented, "The trust comes with commercial leaseholds that have to be managed. I'll no' be giving up my distillery to collect rents and spend my days with contractors."

"Of course not," Merritt said. She sat up and maneuvered to face him, running her palm up and down his chest as if to soothe away his worries. "We can hire managers and keep close oversight." Leaning closer, she brushed her lips over his, feeling the heat of his mouth afterward as if she'd been softly branded. "We'll find the answers together."

He caught her wrist and looked at her with a wicked gleam in his eyes. "Lass, if you're after calming me by stroking me with your wee hand . . . 'tis having the opposite effect. You'd better stop if you dinna want to be ravished right here on the beach."

Merritt crinkled her nose and laughed. "You wouldn't do that," she said. "Not out in the open."

Keir dragged her hand down his body to the hard, aroused ridge behind the front placket of his trousers. "There's something you need to learn about Scotsmen," he said. "We never back down from a challenge."

Chapter 31

KEIR WAS JOKING. HE had to be. Except he'd started to kiss her in a way that meant business. Teasing at first, but soon deepening into a slow, molten exploration. Her eyes closed, a slight pinch of concentration between her brows as she was inundated with too much feeling, seeming to come from every direction. The warm pressure of his hand cradled her cheek and jaw, carefully angling her face as he caught her mouth at a deep angle. He tasted like tea and honey and the fresh, subtle flavor she'd come to recognize as his alone.

Her arms went around his shoulders, but the position was awkward. She was heaped between his thighs, her walking skirt twisted and bunched all around her. The spoon busk of her corset, with its bottom edge curved slightly inward, dug into her abdomen. Perceiving her discomfort, he rearranged their position and hiked up her walking skirts in handfuls. As he guided her knees to the outside of his, she realized he wanted her to kneel astride him.

"Keir," she began to protest, glancing uneasily around them.

"Sit on my lap," he wheedled. "Just for a few minutes."

"What if someone sees?"

"No one will come out here."

"But they might," she persisted.

His teeth closed on her earlobe in a gentle nip. "Then we'd best be fast."

"Keir . . ." Merritt squirmed and dissolved into giggles. "This is not the place . . . No, really . . ."

"'Tis the perfect place," he said, nuzzling her throat. "Kiss me."

She gave in to temptation and fastened her lips to his, and Keir responded with lusty enthusiasm. Beneath her skirts, his hands were busy, tugging and rearranging unseen garments until the waist of her drawers sagged to her hips, and the seams of the crotch were spread wide open.

Merritt pulled her head back to look at him, an objection hovering at her lips. But his eyes were sparkling with boyish mischief, and he was too enticing to resist.

"There's no one here to pay us mind," he said. "I'll be able to see if someone comes from the holloway." One of his hands slipped between her thighs, gently fondling. "You've never done this outside?"

The light caresses sent shocks of heat through her, making it difficult to speak. "The idea has never even occurred to me."

"'Tis different out in nature, with the wind and sun on your skin."

"And sand in my drawers."

Keir laughed softly. "We'll keep to the blanket." He stroked her intimately, tickling the edges of closed lips, the soft folds and petals. The delicate sensation drew a fullness to her groin and lit her veins with anticipation. A finger entered by tender, halting degrees, wriggling with each slight pause as if he were easing it into a glove. Her flesh closed around the invasion, again and again, and he pushed deeper each time she relaxed, until finally the palm of his hand cupped snugly over the triangle of dark curls. He kneaded her, his finger stirring and undulating languidly inside.

Merritt's vision became slightly unfocused. "We're going to be caught," she whimpered, writhing on his lap.

Slowly his finger withdrew. "Then dinna tarry," he said huskily. "Undo my trousers."

"We should wait until later."

"I've gone through worlds of waiting," he said, nuzzling her cheek. "And that's just since this morning."

Merritt hesitated and glanced bashfully over her shoulder at the empty beach.

Keir grinned at her indecision. "Be brave, Merry," he coaxed with a note of teasing. "There are five buttons between you and what you want. Just reach down and . . ." He drew in a rough breath as he felt her grasp the erect shaft and guide him into place. "Aye," he said gruffly, "feel that . . . 'tis all for you. Come take your pleasure of me."

He steadied her hips as she sank down on him. She concentrated on relaxing to let him in, yielding to the thick, heavy glide of him inside her. When she'd taken all she could, she paused, trembling, her face level with his. She felt pulses and throbs, sensation and echoes of sensation, all centered in that naked, concealed place where they were joined. He curved his hand beneath her bottom to support her, and stared at her with those singular eyes, the cool blue so brilliant it appeared to be throwing off sparks.

Merritt touched his face, her fingertips as light as a whisper as she traced the high planes of his cheekbones, the elegant hollows beneath, the squared-off jaw. She leaned close to kiss the firm, beautiful shape of his mouth, the lower lip more deeply curved than the upper. The altered angle of her body sent a zing of delight through her, but provoked a quiet grunt from him as if she caused him pain.

"Oh—I'm sorry—" she began, but he shook his head with a breath of amusement.

"No, love—you dinna hurt me—" He lowered his forehead to her shoulder, gasping. "You nearly unmanned me, is all."

She began to lean back, but he gripped her hips and kept her there. "Merry," he begged desperately, laughter threading his voice, "for the love of all that's holy, dinna move."

Merritt turned her face against the rich amber and gold of his hair and held obediently still. It was difficult, when her body demanded that she grind and thrust against him. She tried to stay relaxed, but every now and then her inner muscles clamped strongly on the hard pressure, eliciting a faint groan from him. How strange and delicious it was to sit here like this, entwined and filled, while sea breezes rustled through the marram grass on the dunes and quiet waves lapped at the shore.

Eventually Keir lifted his head, his eyes very light in his flushed face. "Put your legs around my waist," he said. He helped to rearrange her limbs until they were pressed together closely in a seated embrace, with his bent knees supporting her. It was surprisingly comfortable, but didn't permit much movement. Instead of thrusting, they were limited to a rocking motion that allowed only an inch or two of his length to withdraw and plunge.

"I don't think this is going to work," Merritt said, her arms looped around his neck.

"Be patient." His mouth sought hers in a warm, flirting kiss. One of his hands searched beneath her skirts to settle on her naked bottom, pulling her forward as they rocked rhythmically.

Feeling awkward, but also having fun, Merritt experimented by bracing her feet on the ground and pushing to help their momentum. The combination of pressure and movement had a stunning effect on her. Every forward pitch brought her weight fully onto him, in deep steady nudges that sent bolts of pure erotic feeling through every nerve pathway. The tension was building, compelling her toward a culmination more intense than anything she'd ever felt. She couldn't drive herself hard enough onto the heavy shaft, her body taking every inch and clenching frantically on each withdrawal as if trying to keep him inside. Nothing mattered except the rhythmic lunges that pumped more and more pleasure into her.

Keir's breath hissed through his teeth as he felt her electrified response, the cinch of her intimate muscles. His hand gripped over her bottom, pulling her onto him again, again, again, until the relentless unfaltering movement finally catapulted her into a climax that was like losing consciousness, blinding her vision with a shower of white sparks and extinguishing every rational thought. When she emerged from the euphoria, she was locked tightly to Keir, who was still a hard presence within her. She rested her head on the shoulder of his coat, wishing she could feel the warmth of his skin and the hair on his chest. His hand coasted over her hips and bottom, slowly chasing the last few shivers that raced over her skin. He kissed her neck, letting her feel the edge of his teeth, the heat of his tongue. He began the rocking motion again, his powerful thighs tensing and relaxing, his hand guiding her hips.

Merritt moaned, too weak and shaky to move. "Keir, I can't—"

"I'll do it all," he murmured against her neck. "Just hold on to me, darlin'."

"This is only for you," she managed to say. "Can't come again . . . too tired . . ."

"I know."

But the patient rhythm didn't cease. As she sat implanted on that hard, unyielding flesh and felt its altering pressures inside with each back-and-forth sway, the tension began again. She started to move with him, her breath hastening with renewed effort. He braced one hand on the ground and slid the other low on her backside, pulling her into each thrust. She jerked as she felt one of his fingers accidentally slip into the crevice between the halves of her bottom. A guttural sound escaped his lips as her body clenched tightly around his shaft. The finger teased deeper, and she responded with a little squeal of protest, clamping down hard on him again. Keir groaned in pleasure and kept thrusting, while she yelped and writhed to avoid that impudently delving, stroking finger, her muscles squeezing over and over until she stiffened with a climax that stole her breath away. Somewhere in the midst of the white-hot shudders, she was aware of Keir finding his own release, his entire body turning to iron beneath hers. She subsided on him in a limp heap, panting, and gradually realized he was lying flat on his back. His chest vibrated with drafty chuckles that made her head bounce. Oh, he was pleased with himself.

"Did that hurt your ribs?" she asked.

"Aye," he said, still snickering.

"Serves you right," she said tartly. "Keir, if you don't remove that hand from my posterior in the next three seconds—"

He pulled it away obligingly, and lifted his head to grin at her. "Merry, my bonnie, heartsome, lively lass. 'Tis my jo, you are, and will be 'til my last breath."

"Your jo?"

"My joy . . . my lover . . . my dearest companion and the spark of my soul. 'Jo' is a small word of large meaning . . . perfect for the woman who means everything to me."

Chapter 32

OVER THE NEXT TWO days, Keir was in an unfamiliar state of acute happiness mingled with occasional unease. "Gleamy" was the Scots word for weather like this: sunshine interrupted by clouds or showers. There were no threads of continuity between his old life and this one, no rough edges anywhere. No recognizable faces or voices. Even the clothes he wore were new and strange. And yet it was all so comfortable and beautiful, he couldn't help liking it immensely.

In a way, it would be easier if the Challons and Marsdens put on airs around him, or pretended he was beneath their interest. That way, he could preserve his sense of separateness, and remain a stranger in a strange land. But no, they had to be warm and friendly and interesting. He was especially charmed by the two youngest Challons, Ivo and Seraphina, both of them engaging and warm, but also possessing their father's knack for a perfectly timed witticism—a *bon mot*, Merritt called it.

They asked countless questions about Islay, his friends, his dog, and the distillery, and they entertained him with stories of their own. To Keir's relief, neither of them seemed to have difficulty accepting him as a half brother, despite the vast differences in their ages. They had been brought up in an environment filled with so much abundance, it didn't occur to them to feel threatened by anyone.

The Challons were nothing like the noble families Keir had heard of, in which the children were raised mostly by servants and seldom saw their parents. These people were close and openly affectionate, with no trace of aristocratic stuffiness. Keir thought that was in no small part due to the duchess, who made no pretense about the fact that her father had made his start as a professional boxer. Evie was the anchor who kept the family from drifting too far in the dizzying altitude of their social position. It was at her insistence that the children had at least a passing acquaintance with ordinary life. For example, it was one of Ivo's chores to wash the dog, and Seraphina sometimes accompanied the cook to market to talk with local tradespeople.

Although Evie was far quieter than the rest of the family, everyone paid close attention whenever she spoke. For all her gentleness, she possessed a core of inner strength that had made her the center of the Challons' world. And she was so kind that Keir couldn't help but like her. When they'd first met, the duchess had stared at him for a moment of wonder, and then had smiled and embraced him with tear-glittered eyes, as if he were her own long-lost child instead of Kingston's.

On the second day after the Westcliffs' arrival, Keir sat in the morning room with the other men, having an early breakfast. He found much to admire in Merritt's father, a man's man who loved to hunt, ride, fish, and shoot. Like Kingston, Westcliff had long ago foreseen the need to develop sources of income other than farming rents from his estate. He'd invested in industry and commerce, and had become financially powerful at a time when other ennobled families were destitute.

In the middle of breakfast, the butler entered the morning room and brought a message on a silver tray to Kingston. Having never seen a telegram with a seal on it, Keir watched alertly as Kingston opened and read it.

The duke frowned slightly. "Ethan Ransom will arrive this afternoon."

Westcliff drained his coffee before commenting, "It's about bloody time."

Keir glanced at the telegram in Kingston's hand. "Did Ransom say they caught the man from the alley? Or whoever set the warehouse fire?"

The duke shook his head and handed the piece of paper to Keir.

"Are we assuming one man committed both crimes?" Westcliff asked.

"Not necessarily," Kingston replied. "Although if you're hiring someone to commit murder, it's better to keep it to one."

Westcliff's dark eyes glinted with amusement as he remarked blandly, "You say that with unsettling authority."

Kingston's lips twitched. "Don't be absurd, Westcliff. If I wanted to murder someone, I'd never deny myself the pleasure of doing it personally." He reached for a water goblet and idly rubbed his thumb over the cut crystal surface. "I'd lay odds Ransom still hasn't caught the bastard," he said, and frowned as he glanced at Keir. "It's been almost a year since Cordelia's death. As the executor of her will, I'm due to appear at the High Court the day after tomorrow. Once I tell the Chancery judges I was able to locate you, Ormonde's lawyers will try to cast doubt on the fact that you're Cordelia's son."

"Will I need to be there?" Keir asked.

"No, I'd prefer you to stay out of sight for the time being. My solicitors will present evidence of your identity, including hospital records, witness statements, and as many of the facts surrounding your birth as we can provide . . . at which point I'll also have to publicly reveal that I'm"—Kingston hesitated—"the one who sired you."

"Ah," Keir said softly, while a sick feeling came over him. He set down his fork, having immediately lost his appetite. The news would be a sensation far beyond London. An overwhelming amount of unwanted attention would be focused on him, Kingston, and the rest of the Challons. He shrank inwardly from the idea of instant notoriety, especially for the sake of an inheritance he didn't want in the first place.

"After I reveal your existence to the court," Kingston continued, "Ormonde will know you survived the warehouse explosion. And his only hope of acquiring Cordelia's trust will be to kill you before Chancery reaches a judgment in your favor."

"How long will that take?" Westcliff asked.

"Two days, I'd guess. Unless they want to call in witnesses for questioning—that could draw it out to a week."

"Let the lawyers negotiate," Keir suggested. "I'd settle for dividing the London properties and giving him half."

Kingston's face hardened. "Like hell you would. It was your mother's dying wish for you to be given the trust. Besides, even if you handed over the whole bloody inheritance to Ormonde, he'll still hunt you like a bag-fox. He'll never stop."

"Why?" Keir demanded, baffled. "What motivation would he have after the will is settled?"

"My boy," the duke said quietly, "we're all subject to a system of descent and distribution that's been in place for a thousand years, based on handing everything down to the eldest son. It's called primogeniture. You're not going to like what I'm about to say. However, as soon as the court acknowledges you as Cordelia's legitimate issue, you'll be established as Lord Ormonde's rightful heir. You're the first and only male offspring, which means you're next in line for his viscountcy. He'll do everything in his power to keep that from happening."

Keir was so aghast, he could hardly speak. "But you'll have just told the court that I'm *your* son. How could they turn around and rule that I'm Ormonde's son?"

Westcliff broke in to explain, his expression grave but kind. "Your mother was married to him when she gave birth to you. Therefore, you're legally Ormonde's son, even though you're not of his blood."

"But . . . everyone will know it to be a lie. I've never even met the bastard!"

"The law has its limitations," Westcliff said ruefully. "Something can be legal without being true."

"I'll refuse the title and estate."

"You can't," Kingston said curtly. "Peerage titles don't work that way. You may as well try to change your eye color. It's *who you are*, Keir."

Keir was filled with panic and fury as he felt his future closing around him like the jaws of a steel trap. "*No.* I know who I am, and it's no' that. A *viscount*? Living in a big dank house with too many rooms and . . . God help me, *servants*, and . . . far away from Islay . . . I can't do it. I won't." He stood and tossed his napkin onto the table. "I'm going to talk to Merry," he muttered, and walked away with ground-eating strides.

"What are you going to tell her?" he heard Kingston ask.

Keir answered in a growl, without looking back. *"That I have too many fookin' fathers!"*

Chapter 33

In the afternoon, the Challons and Marsdens gathered in the upstairs parlor to await Ethan Ransom's arrival. Seraphina and Ivo had gone to attend an informal dance at a friend's home. The event, a combination of afternoon tea and dancing, was called a *thé dansant* . . . a phrase which, as Ivo had remarked dryly, was never used by actual French people, only English people who wanted to sound French.

When Ethan finally arrived at Heron's Point and was shown into the parlor, Merritt was a bit concerned by his appearance. He was obviously exhausted, with sleepless shadows beneath his eyes, and uncharacteristic grooves of strain carved into his face. Ethan's iron constitution and Napoleonic ability to go without sleep had always been a source of ready humor among the Ravenels. But he was still a young man who shouldered a weight of worldly responsibilities that would have crushed nearly anyone else. And this afternoon, it showed.

"You look like an ill-scraped haggis," Keir said bluntly as he shook hands with Ethan.

Merritt winced, wishing he'd worded it more diplomatically.

Ethan grinned, however, taking no offense. "We can't all lounge in the lap of luxury," he retorted.

Keir nodded ruefully. "Aye, I've been treated like a

king, but I need to go back to work as soon as possible. My distillery's been shut down for too long. By now my men have all gone soft."

"My men are probably conspiring to lock me in a basement," Ethan said dryly. "And I wouldn't blame them. I've pushed them hard."

"No luck with the search?" Merritt asked softly.

Ethan's mouth flattened in a grim line, and he gave a quick shake of his head. "Not yet." He went to exchange pleasantries with the rest of the group, and soon they all settled in front of one of the parlor's two hearths.

Keir took a place beside Merritt on a settee, a hand resting close to hers in the space between them. Their fingers tangled gently, concealed by the mass of her skirts.

Kingston stood beside the fireplace mantel, his face bathed in fire glow. He glanced at Ethan expectantly. "Well?"

"The man we're searching for is Sid Brownlow," Ethan said without preamble. "We found the name through the identifying number on the cavalry knife MacRae recovered from the alley. According to War Office records, the knife was one of a limited series issued to a special unit within the 1st Dragoons."

"A distinguished regiment," Westcliff remarked. "They saw action at Balaclava during the Crimea."

"Yes," Ethan said. "Although Brownlow enlisted long after that. He was a skilled marksman and won an inter-regimental shooting match two years in a row. But he was discharged with a pension before his term of service was even half over."

"Why?" Kingston asked. "Was it a medical disability?"

"The War Office pension list doesn't explain the reason for the discharge, or the pension, which is highly unusual. However, one of my men searched through muster rolls and disciplinary actions until he uncovered evidence that Brownlow was twice put in a regimental cell for malicious conduct toward other soldiers in his company. After his discharge, he returned to Cumberland, where he'd been raised. His father was a gamekeeper at a grand estate, and helped secure a job for him at the stables."

Kingston's jaw hardened, his eyes turning ice-cool at the mention of Cumberland. "Who owns the estate?" he asked, although he seemed already to know the answer.

Ethan nodded in confirmation before replying. "Lord Ormonde."

A few soft exclamations broke the silence.

Merritt glanced at Keir's expressionless face. He didn't speak, but his hand moved to enclose hers.

"Unfortunately, that's not enough to implicate Ormonde," Ethan continued. "We'll need testimony from Brownlow. I'd hoped to apprehend and interrogate him by now, but we've run out of leads. I personally questioned Brownlow's father, who claims to have no knowledge of his whereabouts, and I'm inclined to believe him. Ormonde wouldn't agree to an interview, but he allowed me to question most of his household staff, and none will admit to having witnessed any interaction between him and Brownlow. Nor can I find evidence of any incriminating financial transactions in the bank records."

Lillian spoke then. "You've had men watching the ports?"

"Ports, railway stations, thoroughfares, and border

crossings. I've assembled a force of special constables, detectives and waterguard, in a coordinated effort. My agents have been combing through ship manifests, train schedules, and guest registries at every conceivable kind of lodging house. We've even checked with public stables and coaching services. It's like trying to find a flea in a coal-pit."

Evie spoke then. "Do you th-think he's left the country?"

"Your Grace, my sense is that Brownlow is still in England, and will turn up eventually." After a long pause, Ethan turned his gaze to Keir. "With your cooperation, MacRae . . . we may be able to set a trap for him."

Before Keir could reply, Kingston said curtly, "Absolutely not."

Keir regarded the duke with a frown. "You dinna know what his plan is yet."

"I know enough to be certain you're the bait," Kingston said. "The answer is no."

Keir turned to Ethan. "Tell me what you have in mind, Ransom."

"You would be the bait," Ethan admitted.

"Go on," Keir said.

"I'd like you to return to Islay, one or two days from now," Ethan told him. "Kingston will go to Chancery and reveal your identity and location to the court, and Ormonde will immediately send someone to dispatch with you. However, two of my agents and I will be there to protect you. As soon as Brownlow or some other hired thug sets foot on your property, we'll apprehend him."

Kingston interrupted acidly. "These would be the

same agents who've failed to apprehend Brownlow so far?"

"We've already surveilled the MacRae land and distillery," Ethan said. "It's surrounded by open fields covered in low vegetation, with no hills or woodland to offer concealment. Furthermore, it's situated on a peninsula on the west side of the island, and connected by a narrow isthmus. You couldn't design a more effective situation to corner someone."

"Still," Westcliff said, "you're proposing to set up MacRae like a plaster duck in a carnival shooting gallery, when he's unable to defend himself. He's still recovering from injured ribs, and furthermore—"

"I can defend myself," Keir protested.

Kingston gave him a speaking glance. "Son, let's not start that again."

"Also," Westcliff continued, "MacRae can't shoot."

Ethan regarded Keir blankly. "At all?"

Keir was slow to reply, which Merritt thought was due to his surprise at hearing Kingston call him "son." Although it had been imperceptible to everyone else, she'd felt the little jerk of his hand. "My father kept only one gun," he told Ethan. "An old Brown Bess, which he took out once a year to clean and oil. We tried shooting it once or twice, but neither of us could hit a target."

"A muzzle-loading flintlock?" Ethan asked in bemusement. "No sights on the stock . . . shooting only roundballs from a smoothbore barrel . . . I doubt I could hit anything with that either. And with a high risk of accidentally blowing off half your face, I'd be terrified to try."

"The point is," Westcliff said, "you're proposing

to put MacRae in harm's way while he's injured and unarmed. I'm no more comfortable with that than Kingston."

"I understand," Ethan said. He looked at Keir and said frankly, "I can't give you an ironclad guarantee that nothing will go wrong. I can only promise to personally do everything in my power to keep you safe."

Keir nodded, looking troubled. He released Merritt's hand and went to stand at the other end of the fireplace mantel, facing Kingston. The sight of them, their incredible likeness, was stunning.

"Sir," Keir said to Kingston quietly, "if I dinna take the risk now, I'll have to spend every minute looking over my shoulder for God knows how long, wondering when someone will come after me. And 'tis no' feasible to have a half-dozen guards, or even a brace of them, biding with me indefinitely. I can't live that way."

"Let me go with you," Kingston said.

Merritt could tell from Keir's expression that he was surprised and moved by the offer. The smile-lines deepened at the outer corners of his eyes as he said, "Thank you, sir . . . but I can't imagine you living in a wee hut with a stone floor for weeks or months."

As Merritt glanced around the room, she found Mama's fond but incisive gaze on her. There was little doubt in Merritt's mind about what her mother would do if she were in the same circumstances. As a parent, Lillian had always been lively and playful, prone to leaving clutter in her wake, sometimes talking too loudly in her enthusiasm, and always demonstrative in her affection. A let's-try-it-and-see-what-happens sort of mother. If Merritt had been forced to offer a criticism, it would have been that as a child, she'd sometimes been disappointed about all the rules her mother hadn't known and couldn't have cared less about.

When Merritt had asked her the proper dinnertime etiquette for when one discovered something like a bit of bone or a cherry stone in a mouthful of food, Mama had said cheerfully, *"Hanged if I know. I just sneak it back to the edge of the plate."*

"Should I use a fork or fingers?"

"There's not really a right way to do it, darling, just be discreet."

"Mama, there's always *a right way."*

In retrospect, however, her mother's irreverence might have been one of her greatest gifts as a parent. Such as the day when Merritt had run crying to her because a group of boys hadn't wanted her to play rounders with them.

Lillian had hugged and comforted her, and said, *"I'll go tell them to give you a turn."*

"No, Mama," Merritt had sobbed. *"They don't want me to play because I'm not good at it. I mostly can't hit the ball, and when I do, it doesn't go anywhere. They said I have baby arms."* The indignity of that had been intolerable.

But Mama, who'd always understood the fragility of a child's pride, had curved her fingers around Merritt's upper arm and said, *"Make a muscle for me."* After feeling Merritt's biceps, her mother had lowered to her haunches until their faces were level. *"You have very strong arms, Merritt,"* she'd said decisively. *"You're as strong as any of those boys. You and I are going to practice until you're able to hit that blasted ball over all their heads."*

For many an afternoon after that, Mama had helped her to learn the right stance, and how to transfer her weight to the front foot during the swing, and how to follow through. They had developed her eye-hand coordination and had practiced until the batting skills felt natural. And the next time Merritt played rounders, she'd scored more points than anyone else in the game.

Of the thousands of embraces Mama had given her throughout childhood, few stood out in Merritt's mind as much as the feel of her arms guiding her in a batting stance. *"I want you to attack the ball, Merritt. Be fierce."*

Not everyone would understand, but *"Be fierce"* was one of the best things her mother had ever told her.

Suddenly the right course of action became clear in Merritt's mind. She switched her attention to Ethan Ransom. "Ethan," she asked, "are you carrying a pistol?"

"I might be," he said.

"Would you come out to the balcony with me, please?"

Ethan followed readily as Merritt headed to one of the sets of French doors. The balcony, furnished with a few pieces of wicker furniture woven in filigree designs, extended the entire length of the house's main section.

Ethan came to stand at the railing with her, surveying a paved terrace with steps that led to acres of velvety green lawn. A stone retaining wall extended from the house, finishing in an urn-shaped planter spilling over with ivy. There was a fountain surrounded by stone benches, and a collection of decorative objects . . . a reflective gazing globe on a wrought iron base . . . a pair of French style obelisks . . . a bronze armillary on a sandstone pedestal . . . and a whimsical pair of pottery rabbits set on the stone wall.

As Keir came to Merritt's other side, she glanced up at him with a faint smile before turning her attention back to Ethan. "May I see the pistol?" she asked.

Looking perplexed, Ethan reached into his coat and pulled out a revolver with a short barrel and heavy cartridge. Deftly he opened the cartridge gate, pulled out an extractor rod, and removed the cylinder and its central pin from the frame. He handed the frame to her and set the cylinder and pin on the balcony railing.

The revolver was chambered for .442 rounds, which meant there was only room for five. "These are large caliber bullets for such a short gun," Merritt remarked.

"It's designed to stop someone at close range," Ethan said, absently reaching up to rub a spot on his chest. "Being hit by one of those bullets feels like a kick from a mule."

"Why is the hammer bobbed?"

"To keep it from catching on the holster or clothing, if I have to draw it fast."

Keeping the muzzle of the gun pointed away from him, Merritt reassembled the revolver, slid the extractor rod into place, and locked it deftly.

"Well done," Ethan commented, surprised by her assurance. "You're familiar with guns, then."

"Yes, my father taught me. May I shoot it?"

"What are you going to aim for?"

By this time, the others had come out from the parlor to watch.

"Uncle Sebastian," Merritt asked, "are those pottery rabbits on the stone wall valuable?"

Kingston smiled slightly and shook his head. "Have at it."

"Wait," Ethan said calmly. "That's a twenty-yard distance. You'll need a longer-range weapon." With meticulous care, he took the revolver from her and replaced it in his coat. "Try this one." Merritt's brows lifted slightly as he pulled a gun from a cross-draw holster concealed by his coat. This time, Ethan handed the revolver to her without bothering to disassemble it first. "It's loaded, save one chamber," he cautioned. "I put the hammer down to prevent accidental discharge."

"A Colt single-action," Merritt said, pleased, admiring the elegant piece, with its four-and-a-half-inch barrel and custom engraving. "Papa has one similar to this." She eased the hammer back and gently rotated the cylinder.

"It has a powerful recoil," Ethan warned.

"I would expect so." Merritt held the Colt in a practiced grip, the fingers of her support hand fitting neatly underneath the trigger guard. "Cover your ears," she said, cocking the hammer and aligning the sights. She squeezed the trigger.

An earsplitting report, a flash of light from the muzzle, and one of the rabbit sculptures on the wall shattered.

In the silence that followed, Merritt heard her father say dryly, "Go on, Merritt. Put the other bunny out of its misery."

She cocked the hammer, aimed and fired again. The second rabbit sculpture exploded.

"Sweet Mother Mary," Ethan said in wonder. "I've never seen a woman shoot like that."

"My father taught all of us how to shoot and handle firearms safely," Merritt said, giving the revolver back to him grip-first.

Ethan reholstered the gun and stared into her face for a long moment. He nodded slightly, understanding the reason for her demonstration. "It's up to him," he said, his gaze flickering to the man just behind her.

Merritt turned to Keir, who was staring at Ethan, his eyes a chilled light blue. "She's no' going to Islay with me," he said flatly.

"I can do more than hit targets," Merritt said. "I can pursue and hunt game while moving behind cover. I'm comfortable with using telescopes and field-glasses, and I'm good at calculating distance even on open terrain. And, unlike Ethan and his agents, I can literally stay within arm's reach of you most of the time, including at night."

Her mother's voice came from beside the French doors. "Merritt darling, you know I'm usually the first to say to hell with proprieties. But it falls to me to point out that you can't stay at the home of an unmarried man without . . . well . . ."

"I've already thought of that," Merritt said. "We could stop at Gretna Green on the way, just as Uncle Sebastian and Aunt Evie did."

"First," Keir said coolly, "I have no' proposed yet. Second, there are no border weddings in Scotland now.

They changed the law twenty-five years ago. People have to bide in Scotland for at least three weeks before they're allowed to wed."

Merritt frowned. "Drat," she muttered.

Uncle Sebastian cleared his throat. "Actually . . ." He pretended not to notice as Keir sent him a damning glare.

"Yes, Uncle?" Merritt prompted hopefully.

"There's an ancient Scottish tradition called marriage by declaration," Sebastian continued, "that's still legal. If you state in front of two witnesses that you both freely consent to become husband and wife, the local sheriff will have it registered."

"No waiting period?" Merritt asked.

"None."

"And it's legal outside of Scotland?"

"Indeed."

"How perfectly convenient," Merritt said in satisfaction.

Keir's expression had turned thunderous. "You're no' going with me," he told her. "I'm putting my foot down."

"Darling," she said reasonably, "you can't put your foot down, I've already put my foot down."

His eyes narrowed. "Mine is bigger."

"Mine is faster," Merritt said. "I'm going to start packing."

She fled before he could reply, and he followed at her heels.

AFTER THE PAIR had left, and Ransom had gone to write some telegrams, Sebastian remained in the parlor with Westcliff, Lillian, and Evie.

Westcliff went to Lillian and slid his arms around

her. "Well," he asked, "would you advise locking her in her room, or should we threaten to cut off her allowance?"

A rueful smile crossed Lillian's lips. "I couldn't help but wonder if you regretted having taught her to shoot so well."

"For a moment," Westcliff admitted. "But MacRae won't capitulate. I could see it in his face."

"I pity the lad," Sebastian commented. "In her ladylike way, Merritt is a sledgehammer."

Wryly, Westcliff commented, "All three of my daughters are hellbent on making decisions for themselves. They always have been."

"Mine as well," Sebastian said. "Much to my dismay." Noticing the way Lillian and Evie glanced at each other and smiled, as if at some shared reminiscence, he asked, "What is it?"

"I was remembering the conversations we used to have with Annabelle and Daisy," Evie told him, "about the things we wanted to teach our daughters."

Lillian grinned. "The first point we all agreed upon was, 'Never let a man do your thinking for you.'"

"That explains a great deal," Sebastian said. "Evie, my sweet, don't you think you should have asked me before filling the girls' heads with subversive wallflower philosophy?"

Evie came to him, slid her arms around him, and tucked her head beneath his chin. He could hear a smile in her voice as she said, "Wallflowers never ask permission."

KEIR FOLLOWED MERRITT into her room and closed the door with a little more force than was necessary.

She turned to face him, her lips parted, but he held up his hand in a staying motion before she could get a word out. He was angry and worried and filled with agitation, and he didn't want to be soothed or cajoled. He needed her to understand something.

"Sit," he said gruffly, pointing to a chair next to a little table.

Merritt complied, arranging her skirts and folding her hands neatly in her lap. She watched calmly as he paced back and forth in front of her.

"Since I came to London," he said, "I've been twisted and spun about like a bobbin winder. I lost the entire whisky shipment, along with every last bottle of Ulaidh Lachlan. I was stabbed and almost blown to smithereens. I gained a new father I'm no' sure of yet, and a fake father who's trying to have me murdered. I learned I'm about to acquire a great load of real estate I dinna want, and if I live long enough, a peerage title I already hate. And I learned I'm no' even Scottish. And more important than any of the rest of it . . . I've fallen in love for the first time in my life." He gripped the arms of the chair and lowered to his knees with his thighs spread to bracket hers. "I will love you, Merry, until my last breath of life. You understand me well enough to know it would destroy me if the least bit of harm came to you. How could I let you risk yourself for my sake? How could you even ask such a thing?"

"I ask because I love you." Her lips trembled. "And I want to be your partner."

"You are."

"Not if you're planning to leave me behind the way Joshua did. That's not what a partner does. He tried to protect me by going away to solve a problem on his own, when we should have faced it together."

"'Tis no' the same," Keir said in outrage.

"It feels the same."

"There's nothing wrong with a man protecting the woman he loves."

"Can't I protect the man I love? No one could dispute that you'll be safer with me there."

"I thunderin' well dispute it!"

"What if someone enters the house at night while you're sleeping?"

"I'll have the dog with me. He'll let me know. And Ransom's men will stop an intruder long before he comes in."

"What if the intruder manages to sneak by them? What could you and Wallace do if he has a weapon?"

"I'll learn how to shoot one."

"That's not something you can learn in an afternoon. You need many, many hours of practice, and even then, there's an enormous risk of accidents when you're in a situation filled with that much pressure and uncertainty." She leaned forward to clasp her hands on either side of his face. "Let me go with you," she said earnestly. A faint smile tugged at one corner of her lips. "I'll be the extra rib that protects your heart."

Keir pulled back abruptly. The motion sent a stab of pain through his ribs, and he swore. Rising to his feet, he sent her a glance of mingled torment and frustration. "You can't, Merry."

The hint of a smile had vanished. "Because you doubt my abilities," she said rather than asked.

Keir shook his head. "Because you *are* my heart." He turned and left the room while he was still able.

Chapter 34

KEIR WANDERED AIMLESSLY AROUND the house, brooding. If Merritt were able to recognize what an impossible situation she'd put him in, everything would be so much easier. His refusal to take her to Islay had nothing to do with his respect for her, which was enormous. Her well-being would always take precedence over his, because she was what he valued most. Because of who he was as a man. Because he loved her.

He found himself meandering down the hallway that led to the study, and heard the sound of voices coming from the open door. Without making a conscious decision, he paused at the threshold and glanced inside. Kingston and Westcliff were talking with the comfortable ease of old friends, a tray bearing a brandy decanter and crystal glasses between them. Keir missed sitting at the tavern talking with friends, or lingering with some of the men after work to finish the day with a taste of whisky, or "dramming," as they called it.

Kingston looked up and smiled as he saw Keir. "Come in, my boy."

It was disarming to see the change in the duke's expression, the elegant features softening and warming. And in response, Keir was surprised by a feeling of kinship, and relief, and the expectation of a good conversation. He realized he was starting to like the man's company.

As he entered the room, he paused in front of Westcliff, knowing something had to be said about his relationship with Merritt. "Sir," he said, and cleared his throat uncomfortably. "Earlier . . . Merritt gave the impression that a certain question had already been asked and answered. But I would no' do so without first discussing it with you."

The earl's expression was difficult to read. "A father's consent isn't necessary in the case of a widow marrying for the second time."

"'Tis necessary to me, milord," Keir replied. "If you're of the opinion she'd be ill-served to have me as a husband, 'tis your right to say so, and my obligation to pay attention."

Westcliff regarded him thoughtfully. "There's no need to enumerate the obvious challenges you and she are facing. I'd rather ask how you're planning to handle them."

Kingston picked up his brandy and stood. "Good God," he said with amusement, "if it's turning into *that* sort of conversation, I'm going to pour the lad a brandy. Take my chair, Keir."

Keir complied, and sat facing the earl. "I dinna have an actual plan yet," he admitted. "But I would do everything possible to protect her and take care of her feelings. She would never go wanting. I would listen to her opinions, and treat her as a beloved companion, always. I'll work very hard, and sacrifice what I must.

If she's no' happy living on Islay, I'd live somewhere else."

The duke gave him a glass of brandy, and half sat on the heavy mahogany desk nearby.

Westcliff seemed struck by the last words. "You'd move away from the island? You're that convinced she's worth it?"

"Of course. There is but one Merritt. And no' one minute of the day does she cease to be a joy to me."

That drew the widest, most natural smile Keir had seen yet from Westcliff. "If you can say that after her determined display this afternoon, I think you'll do well together."

"'Tis proud I am that she's such a fine marksman," Keir assured him. "But it was no' necessary for her to prove. There was never a chance I would allow her to go into danger with me."

"You're a fine young man," the earl said. "For what it's worth, the union has my full support. However, marrying a Marsden can be a knotty proposition, even with one as amiable as Merritt. If I may share a bit of hard-won wisdom . . ."

"Please," Keir said readily.

"I do a fair amount of riding on my estate," Westcliff said. "With every single horse I own, I often lay the reins on his neck and let him move forward to find his own natural balance and gait. I've seen far too many overbearing riders constantly manage and adjust the horse to force its obedience. Every little toss of the head or momentary hesitation is corrected. A variety of torturous bits, spurs, and straps are employed to make it submit. Some horses endure such treatment, but far more are ruined by it. Their spirits are broken, and their temperaments permanently soured. Always let a horse be a horse." He paused. "Do you take my meaning?"

"Aye, milord."

"Was an analogy really necessary, Westcliff?" Kingston asked. "You could have simply said, 'Please be kind to my headstrong daughter and don't break her spirit.'"

"Force of habit," the earl said. "None of my sons pay attention unless it's horses." He swallowed the last of his brandy and set the empty glass aside. "I'll take my leave and let the two of you talk," he said, and stood. On the way to the threshold, he added, "Incidentally, if it's ever mentioned that I used that analogy for handling my daughter, I'll have no choice but to say it's a vicious lie."

"I understand," Keir said, and drowned a grin in his brandy.

Kingston remained half-sitting, half-leaning on the desk. "If you don't mind my asking," he said after Westcliff had left, "how was it left with Merritt?"

Keir gave him a resigned glance. "If I don't take her to Islay, it somehow proves I don't value her as a partner."

"That's the Marsden streak," Kingston said dryly. "Not a single one of Westcliff's brood doesn't fantasize about saving the day in one way or another."

"'Tis *because* I value her that she can't go."

"She'll come to understand."

"I hope so." Keir took another swallow of brandy and sighed shortly. "She'll have more than enough opportunities to save the day in the coming months and years."

The duke crossed his long legs and idly regarded the tips of his polished shoes. "Keir . . . I believe I understand some of what you're feeling. Particularly the part about facing a mountain of responsibilities for which you've never prepared. However, you're absolutely capable of handling it all, and eventually you'll find the right people to manage your affairs. Meanwhile, I can think of no other woman more perfectly suited to help you through it than Merritt."

"What about the people in her circles? The fancy folk."

"What of them?"

"Will they give her a hard time of it, for marrying below herself?"

Kingston appeared mildly startled. "Below? Your rank and pedigree are superior to hers. Not only are you the son of a duke, but on your mother's side, you're descended from an ancient Saxon family."

"But manners, bearing, education—"

"Irrelevant. Above all, society respects lineage. Therefore, you'll find their expectations of you and your behavior will be most elastic. If you descend into lunacy, they'll call you delightfully eccentric. If you act the dullard, they'll praise your refreshing lack of pretense."

A reluctant grin spread across Keir's face.

"Whatever you may need," Kingston said, "in the way of advice, connections, capital, or anything else, do not hesitate to come to me. I'm always at your service." He paused. "Later, when there's an opportunity,

I want to introduce you to your two remaining siblings. You would enjoy their company. You and Gabriel, in particular, are much alike in temperament. He married into the Ravenel family, and his wife is a thoroughly charming woman—"

"Oh, Pandora is my favorite!" came a new voice from the doorway, and they both glanced at the threshold where Seraphina was standing. "She's very witty and fun, and a bit odd in the nicest possible way." With her slender form clad in a green dress, and her brilliant golden-red hair trailing over her shoulder in a thick braid, she reminded Keir of a mermaid. "May I interrupt just for a moment?" she asked, beaming at them both. "I have something important to show Keir."

Kingston gestured for her to enter, and Keir started to rise to his feet.

"No, sit right there," Seraphina urged, and took the chair next to his. She held a folded length of parchment in her lap. "Phoebe left a note asking me to go through our family genealogy books to see if we had any Scottish ancestors. She found none on your mother's side at all, and she said you'd be disappointed if there were none on Father's side."

Surprised and touched by both sisters' concern, Keir shook his head with a smile. "Dinna worry about that, Seraphina. I decided 'tis enough to be Scottish in my heart."

"Still, you wouldn't *mind* if I told you we have some Scottish blood, would you?" she asked, her eyes twinkling. "Because I've discovered that we *do* in fact have a Scot in our family tree! It's been overlooked because he's not in our direct line. I had to trace the connection through some female ancestors instead of going only through the male lineage. But we are very clearly *indisputably* descended from a Scot who was our great-great-great-great-great . . . well, let's say eighteen-times-great . . . grandfather. And just see who it is!" Seraphina unfolded the parchment, which was inscribed with a long vertical chart of connected names. And at the top—

ROBERT I
King of Scots

"*Robert the Bruce?*" Keir could feel his heart expanding in his chest.

"Yes," Seraphina said gleefully, leaping up and bouncing on her heels.

Keir stood, laughing, and bent to kiss her cheek. "One drop of Robert the Bruce's blood will do the job. I could no' be happier. Thank you, sister." He tried to hand the chart back to her, but she shook her head.

"Keep that if you like. Isn't it wonderful news? I have to go tell Ivo we're Scottish!" She left the room triumphantly.

Keir chuckled as he folded the paper and slid it into his pocket. He glanced at Kingston, who had managed to quell his own smile long enough to finish his brandy.

"I'll say good-bye to you in private now," Keir said. "I'll be leaving at first lark song."

The duke looked at him alertly. "A day early?"

"'Tis easier that way," Keir said, and paused bashfully. "I want to thank you for safeguarding the trust on my behalf. You've fought for a year without even knowing if you'd find me."

"I knew I'd find you," Kingston said quietly. Turning abruptly businesslike, he walked to the other side of the desk and opened a drawer. He pulled out a calling card, took up a pen from a carved agate holder, and unstopped an inkwell. "I'm giving you my London address," he said, writing on the engraved card, "and also the name of a manager at the club, who always knows my whereabouts. Send a telegram if there's anything you need. Anything at all. I—" He broke off, set the pen down, and took a moment to discipline his features. "It's difficult to let you leave, knowing Ormonde is going to send someone after you."

"I'd rather be shot at," Keir said, taking the card from him, "than spend all day in court as you'll be doing."

Kingston responded with a mirthless chuckle.

Keir hesitated for a long moment, and came to a decision. Feeling self-conscious and vaguely idiotic, he reached down past the collar of his shirt, hooked his finger on the chain around his neck, and tugged until he'd fished out the gold key. He cleared his throat and tried to sound casual. "I wondered . . . if you still . . ." His voice trailed into silence as he saw Kingston reach for his waistcoat pocket. The man's usual adroitness seemed to have deserted him as he worked to unfasten the watch chain. " 'Tis only a formality," Keir muttered.

"If it doesn't unlock," Kingston said calmly, his face averted, "it's unimportant. For all we know, she could have sent the wrong key."

"Aye." But Keir's heart had begun to pound fast and

hard, resonating high in his throat. Kingston gave him the chain with the heart-shaped lock dangling from it. As Keir took it, he was chagrinned to discover his hands were shaking a little. He fumbled to insert the key, and twisted.

Click.

The tiny, definite sound pierced him. The lock fell open and detached from the chain, as Keir had expected it would. There was no reason to make a fuss. But he kept his head down as his eyes and nose stung and the room became a watery blur. His throat clenched until he had to clear it.

In the next moment, he felt himself caught in a secure, roughly affectionate grip, one hand at the nape of his neck, the other clamping on his shoulder to bring him close in something that wasn't quite an embrace, but felt like one. And through the ramshackle pattern of his own breathing, he heard Kingston's vibrant and unsteady voice.

"You'll always be Lachlan MacRae's son. But you're mine too." A pause, and then he added hoarsely, "You can be mine too."

"Aye," Keir whispered, while an unexpected sense of peace stole over him.

MERRITT EMERGED FROM heavy layers of sleep. She was filled with such lassitude that it was difficult even to turn over in bed, as if the blankets had been sewn with lead weights. Her mind awakened by slow degrees, still occupied with a dark, velvety dream of Keir making love to her.

Except . . . it hadn't been a dream . . . had it? No,

he'd come to her room in the middle of the night, hushing her when she'd tried to speak, kissing every inch of her skin as he'd removed her nightgown. Her eyes blinked open. As she glanced around the room, she caught sight of her neatly folded nightgown on the nearby chair. Wondering if the maid had seen it, Merritt sank a little lower beneath the covers. To her relief, the housemaid soon left wordlessly and closed the door.

Merritt was naked and profoundly relaxed, the tip of her breasts a little chafed. The soft flesh of her vulva was filled with lingering sensitivity after having been caressed, kissed, bitten, teased, invaded. Remembering the pleasure Keir had given her, she writhed a little and felt her toes curl. He'd lain on top of her, between her thighs, his weight nudging her pelvis with each deliberate thrust. He'd felt so powerful, his body claiming hers, invading her with deep, delicious strokes, and it had gone on forever. She'd been exhausted afterward, but she'd mumbled that they had to make plans and talk, and spend the day packing and preparing for their trip to Islay, and she was sorry if he was unhappy that she insisted on going with him. Keir had hushed her and held her against his hard, hairy chest, until she hadn't been able to stop sighing and yawning. That was the last thing she remembered.

The sunlight pressing in through the shutters was very bright. How late had she slept?

She stretched and began to roll over—

—and twitched at the unfamiliar feeling of something sliding down her arm. She felt for it, realizing it was a chain.

A bracelet?

Hastily Merritt climbed out of bed, snatched up her nightgown, and pulled it on. She hurried to the windows and opened the shutters, and stared down at the bracelet in a flood of sunlight. It was a gold watch chain, fastened around her wrist by the tiny gold padlock.

She was shaken by a confusing mixture of emotions, all wrapped in panic.

Keir had left without her.

She wanted to break something. She wanted to cry. How could he leave without telling her? And what was she going to do about it?

Her mind summoned three words.

"Be fierce, Merritt."

Chapter 35

MERRITT HAD TOLERATED THE long railway journey to Glasgow quite well. It was after a sail on a mail packet down Loch Fyne, however, and then another packet steamer down the loch of West Tarbert, that she began to feel tired and a bit queasy. It was a pity she couldn't enjoy the trip down the freshwater loch on the handsome black and white paddle ship, adorned with a striped awnings over the deck seating. But she'd made the mistake of starting out in the large ladies' cabin down below, and the subtle rocking had set her system in revolt. She left one of the deck chairs and went to the railing, hoping the rush of cold air over her face would help to calm her unsettled stomach.

"Milady?" she heard someone ask hesitantly, and she turned to see an elderly couple approaching. The woman, stout and attractive in a striped skirt and dark green traveling cloak, was a stranger, but the man with her, wizened and lean, with a shock of silver hair beneath a flat cap, looked vaguely familiar. As she stared at him, she remembered he'd been one of the distillerymen who'd first come with Keir to London.

"Mr. Slorach," he said, tapping his chest, "and 'tis my wife Fia."

"Mr. Slorach," Merritt exclaimed, summoning a weak smile. "How delightful it is to see you again. And Mrs. Slorach . . . a pleasure . . ."

"I cannae believe my eyes," the man exclaimed, "to see such a grand lady on a steamer from Tarbert!"

Grimacing, Merritt turned back to the water. "Oh dear," she said thickly. "Not so grand at the moment. How mortifying, I'm so . . ." Leaning over the railing, she panted and sweated.

Mrs. Slorach came to stand beside her, producing a white linen cloth from somewhere and handing it to her. "Now, now, poor lass," she said, patting Merritt's back gently. "A wee brash of the heaves is nothing to worry about. Dinna fash. Go on and let it oot."

To Merritt's everlasting embarrassment, she did just that, retching helplessly over the railing. When the spasms were over, she used the cloth to wipe her mouth. She apologized profusely as the couple guided her to an empty section of deck seating. "Thank you, Mrs. Slorach, I'm so sorry—"

"Fia." The woman looked over her kindly. "There was no' much to come up," she remarked. "Hae you eaten today, lass?"

"I had a slice of toast for breakfast . . ." The very thought of it made her ill.

"Ye need more than that for your inwards. Never set off on an empty stomach." She rummaged in a basket she'd been carrying over her arm, and took out a little napkin-wrapped parcel. "Nibble on one of these, dearie, and it will set you to rights."

"How kind. I'm not sure—what is it?" Merritt recoiled as Fia unwrapped a little stack of square-shaped beef sausage without casings, the slices fried and cooled. "Dear heaven, *no,* please, that will be the death of me."

"A wee nibble. Just one." A sausage square, held in a napkin, followed the movements of Merritt's face as she tried to avoid it.

Having no choice but to surrender, Merritt suppressed a gag and bit off a tiny corner.

Mercifully, the sausage was bland and slightly dry. She forced it down. To her astonishment, the nausea began to fade miraculously. She took the patty and began to consume it slowly.

"That's the way of it," Fia said, a smile crossing her round face. "Common beef sausage is what aye put me to rights when I was in your condition."

"Condition?" Merritt repeated, nibbling and chewing.

"Why, biggen with bairn, of course."

"Oh." Merritt's eyes widened. "I don't think . . . no, I'm quite sure that's not it."

Mr. Slorach spoke then, telling his wife, "Lady Merritt is a widow, you ken."

"Ahhh." But Fia looked over her speculatively, as if cataloging details. "Are you gang to Islay, then?"

"Yes." With each bite of cold fried beef, Merritt felt better and better. In fact, it was giving her a surge of new energy.

When Merritt finished the sausage slice, Fia gave her another, while Mr. Slorach viewed her with increasing concern.

"May I ask who're you after visiting on the island, milady?" he inquired.

"Mr. MacRae," Merritt replied.

Slorach nodded slowly. "He came back hame only yesterday. I've not seen him yet, as Fia and I were off to visit our daughter in East Tarbert." He hesitated. "Is there a problem, Lady Merritt? Aught I can help with?"

"I wouldn't call it a problem," she said. "Mr. MacRae and I struck up an acquaintance during his stay in England. He left rather suddenly, and . . . I need to speak to him about a personal matter. Perhaps you could tell me how to find transportation to the distillery once we reach Port Askaig?"

The husband and wife stared at each other with thunderstruck expressions, evidently coming to some dire conclusion about why she would be traveling alone to find Keir after his abrupt departure from England. "I told you, Fia," Slorach exclaimed in a low voice. "I should ne'er have left him to gallyvant and strollop about that wicked toon. 'Tis corrupted him, London has, as I said it would."

Fia nodded and told Merritt stoutly, "Dinna be feart, milady, we'll see to it the lad does the dacent thing by you. We owe it to Elspeth and Lachlan, God rest their souls."

AS THE SLORACHS accompanied Merritt across the island in a cart pulled by drays, she was struck by Islay's remote, stark beauty. There were northern and western hills covered with open fetches of heath and arable land, clean white shores scoured by waves, and deep lochs cutting through the rugged terrain. But there were also villages with neat rows of whitewashed houses, and streets overrun with ducks and geese. People milled around shops or stood around wayside taverns talking in small groups. "'Tis always Saturday afternoon on Islay," Slorach told Merritt cheerfully.

They approached the distillery, a set of large whitewashed buildings built on low-lying peninsular rock, with a perfect view of the cold blue sea. Merritt's heart began to pound as they followed a drive around the distillery and reached a small, neat house with a gray slate roof, and a fenced-in kitchen garden just visible in the back.

The carriage stopped, and Slorach helped his wife and Merritt down. They started on a path of stepping stones leading to the house. Before they even reached the front door, it opened and a small, silver-gray terrier came bounding out. He stopped a few yards away from Merritt and growled.

"Hello, Wallace," she said with a faint smile, and stood still as he came to her. The terrier circled around her, sniffing at her skirts. In a moment he gazed up at her with bright eyes and a wagging tail, and let her pet him. "What a handsome boy you are," she exclaimed, smoothing his fur.

"Merry," she heard, and looked up to find Keir striding toward her.

"Don't be angry," Merritt said, her lips trembling as she tried to smile.

But if there was anger mixed in with Keir's emotions, it was far outweighed by concern, love, and longing. He stepped forward and pulled her into his arms, and clasped her head against his chest. "My heart, what are you doing here?" he asked in a low voice. "How did you . . . My God, dinna tell me you came alone. I know you did. *Damn it*, Merry . . ."

Slorach spoke up then. "Fia and I met her on the way back from Tarbert. She was ill on the packet."

Keir turned pale, and guided Merritt to look up at him. "Ill?"

"Just a bit seasick," she assured him.

Slorach gave Keir a dark glance. "Fia is of the mind the lass is in a hopeful way."

Fia nodded firmly, ignoring Merritt's sputtering protest. "Look at the palms of her hands," she said. "See you how pink they are, a bit paler in the centers? And do you ken what calmed the heaves? *Beef sausage*, that's what." She gave an emphatic nod, as if that proved a point.

Keir smoothed Merritt's hair and looked down at her. "You're a willful lass," he muttered. "Traveling here by yourself? Of all the crackbrain, reckless notions—" He broke off, scowling. "We're going to have words over this, Merry, and a sore hearing it will be for you." But his hands cradled her face as he spoke, and he couldn't stop himself from kissing her forehead, cheeks, chin, and the tip of her nose.

"I had to come," Merritt said reasonably, thrilling to the feel of his arms around her. "You forgot to leave the key to the lock. I had no way of removing the bracelet."

"I meant it to stay on you," he told her, and pressed his cheek to hers. "To remind you whose heart is in your keeping."

"I don't need reminding of that," she whispered. He ducked his head to kiss the side of her neck.

"Young MacRae," Slorach demanded, "do you mean to make it right for this puir lady you did wrang by?"

"I do—" Keir began, and paused as someone emerged from the distillery. Following his gaze, Merritt saw Ethan Ransom approaching.

Ethan smiled at her. "I told MacRae I thought you'd show up here, no matter what he or anyone else said."

"Why?" she asked sheepishly. "I suppose I must strike you as remarkably obstinate?"

He shrugged and shook his head. "It's only that my wife would have done the same thing."

Keir kept his arm around Merritt as he turned more fully toward Ethan. "Ransom . . . I'd be obliged if you'd send one of your men to fetch the sheriff. Before we're beset by assassins, it seems we have the small matter of a wedding to take care of."

Chapter 36

After Keir collected Merritt's leather valises, she went into the cottage with him. Wallace followed, panting happily. The home's interior was brighter and airier than Merritt had expected, with white plastered walls and windows with diamond-shaped panes to let in the light. A broad brick fireplace with a polished copper hood warmed the main room. Although the floor was paved with hard gray slate, it was neatly swept and softened by colorful handmade rugs. The far end of the room opened to a small kitchen with a stove and a plumbed sink.

Keir carried the valises into a small, sparsely furnished bedroom with a fine four-poster bed with fluted columns.

Merritt unpinned her traveling hat and set it on the bed. She ran her fingertips lightly over a beautifully quilted coverlet. "Did your mother make this?" she asked, feeling oddly bashful.

"Aye, she was great on sewing." He turned her to face him and unfastened her traveling cloak. "If there was anyone I trusted to take you back home," he said, "I'd put you on the next steamer back to Glasgow. I dinna want you traveling alone again, Merry. You shouldn't have come."

"I know," she said contritely. "I'm sorry."

His mouth twisted. "You're no' sorry," he said.

"I'm sorry you're not happy about it."

His brooding gaze swept over her. "What's this about being ill on the ship?"

"It was just a moment of queasiness. I'm quite well now."

After removing her cloak and laying it on the bed, Keir took her shoulders in his hands. "Are you willing to wed me?"

"It's what I want more than anything," she said.

He continued to frown. "Dinna complain to me if you change your mind later."

She smiled up at him. "I won't change my mind."

Hearing muffled conversation from the main room, and the sounds of someone bustling in the kitchen, Keir reluctantly released her. "'Tis best to say as little as possible about Ransom," he told her. "I told Slorach he's representing a well-heeled whisky merchant who's after buying land on Islay and laying out a links course. Ransom is to go around the island and look over the ground."

"Is Ethan staying here?" she asked. "With us?"

His lips twitched. "No. That would be a bit crowdit. He and his two men are staying down the road at a wee auld change-house."

"Change-house?"

"Ale-house, you could say, where a man can stay for a penny-fee if his wife has denied him her bed."

"Why did Ethan bring only two men?"

"'Tis all that's needed, he says."

"That's not enough," Merritt said, frowning. "Not

nearly. What could he be thinking? It's a good thing I'm here to protect you."

With a long-suffering expression, Keir took her back to the main room, where the Slorachs were busy in the kitchen. Fia had put a kettle on the stove, and was carrying items from the kitchen worktable to a cupboard.

Slorach was peeking into a group of baskets and crocks that remained on the table.

"Ranald," Fia warned her husband, "dinna touch one morsel of that. 'Tis food the neighbors brang for Keir, now that he's returned from his travels."

"So have I returned from my travels," Slorach protested, "and I'm hungert."

"Keir's travels were to England," Fia said tartly. "You went only as far as Tarbert."

Keir intervened with a grin. "Let him have a bite, Fia."

While the other three talked, Merritt went to a tea table and chair, positioned in front of a window that revealed a view of the sea and a distant lighthouse. She sat in the cushioned chair, and Wallace came to rest his chin on her knee, his round dark eyes twinkling at her. Her hand moved gently over his head. It was darkening outside, and she shivered pleasurably at the comfort of being in a warm house.

Keir came from the kitchen with a mug of tea and set it before Merritt. She glanced up at him in mild surprise, and smiled. "Thank you." As she took a sip, she realized he'd made it exactly how she liked it, lightened with milk and just the right amount of sugar.

Staring down at the terrier, Keir asked softly, "What do you think, Wallace? She's one to be keepit, aye?"

The long, silky tail fanned vigorously from side to side.

Soon Ethan arrived with the sheriff, a ruddy-faced giant of a man with abundant red hair and a handsome thick mustache.

"Lady Merritt," Keir said. "'Tis our sheriff, Errol MacTaggart."

"A reet winsome lady, she is," MacTaggart exclaimed, grinning. "I was told English ladies were pale and sickly, but here you've found a dark beauty with roses in her cheeks."

Keir smiled briefly. "Let's no' make this langsome, MacTaggart. Lady Merritt is weary, and as you know, I'm no' one to stand on ceremony."

"'Tis a haisty affair, aye?" the sheriff observed, some of his good cheer fading as he looked around the room. "No flowers? No candles?"

"No, and also no ring," Keir informed him. "Let us say our pledge, give us the certificate, and we'll have done with it in time for supper."

MacTaggart clearly didn't appreciate the younger man's cavalier attitude. "You'll be having no signed paper until I make certain 'tis done legal," he said, squaring his shoulders. "First . . . do ye ken there's a fine if you've no' posted banns?"

"'Tis no' a church wedding," Keir said.

"The law says without the banns, 'tis a fine of fifty pounds." As Keir gave him an outraged glance, the sheriff added firmly, "No exceptions."

"What if I give you a bottle of whisky?" Keir asked.

"Fine is waived," MacTaggart said promptly. "Now, then . . . do the rest of you agree to stand as witnesses?"

Ethan and the Slorachs all nodded.

"I'll start, then," Keir said briskly, and took Merritt's hand. "I, Keir MacRae, do swear that I—"

"*No' yet,*" the sheriff interrupted, now scowling. "'Tis my obligation to ask a few questions first."

"MacTaggart, so help me—" Keir began in annoyance, but Merritt squeezed his hand gently. He heaved a sigh and clamped his mouth shut.

The sheriff resumed with great dignity. "Are the both of you agreeable to be wed?"

"Aye," Keir said acidly.

"Yes," Merritt replied.

"Are the both of ye single persons?" the sheriff inquired. When they both nodded, he pressed, "You're no' brother and sister?"

"No," Keir said curtly, his patience wearing thin.

"Nor ooncle and niece?"

"MacTaggart," Keir growled, "you know thunderin' well I have no nieces."

The sheriff ignored him, focusing on Merritt with a deeply searching gaze. "Milady, has this man used force or false representation to carry you away against your will?"

Merritt blinked in surprise.

"What's the matter with you, MacTaggart?" Keir demanded. "Of all the goamless questions—"

Fia interrupted. "This lass has no' been abducted, sheriff."

Keir glanced at her over his shoulder. "Thank you, Fia."

"She's been debauched," Fia continued primly. "Drawn away from the path of virtue by the temptations this lad exerted upon her."

Keir was thunderstruck. *"Debauched?"*

MacTaggart stared at him gravely. "Do you deny you've lain with this lass, MacRae?"

"I deny 'tis any of your fookin' business!"

Ranald Slorach shook his head glumly. "'Twas London," he said. "That wicked city put lewd ideas into the lad's head and corrupted his mind."

Merritt pressed her lips together and lowered her head, holding in a helpless giggle while the Slorachs and the sheriff continued to discuss the ruination of Keir's moral character while tarrying too long in the unwholesome environment of London, and the degenerate atmosphere of England in general. She stole a covert glance at Ethan, who was struggling manfully to conceal his own amusement.

"Sheriff," Ethan broke in, "now that the damage has been done, I believe only marriage will correct it."

"'Tis right, you are," MacTaggart said decisively. "The lad must be hob-shackled right away, for the saving of his character." He looked at Keir. "Go on then, MacRae. Speak your vow."

Keir turned to face Merritt fully, and took both her hands in his. As he stared into her eyes, his expression changed, softening with tender warmth. "I take you for my wife. I vow I'll try every day to be the man you deserve. And I'll love none but you, my heart, until my last waking moment."

She was caught in that diamond-bright gaze, while every part of her was alive with awareness of him . . . her skin, her body, her pulse, the marrow of her bones . . . all harboring the recognition of him not as a separate being, but as part of herself. She'd never imagined such intimacy was possible, an intimacy that had nothing to do with ownership.

I'll be the extra rib that protects your heart.

You can't. You are my heart.

She smiled up at him, burning and weightless with joy, wondering how gravity could still be anchoring her to solid ground. "I take you for my husband. I'll love you with all that I am and all that I have, forever."

His mouth came to hers.

SHE NEVER REMEMBERED anything specific from the next few minutes, what words were exchanged, or what time it was when everyone else left and she and Keir were finally alone. She did recall he'd heated a hot bath for her, and when they'd climbed into bed, the sheets had been ice-cold, but Keir's body heat had warmed her rapidly. And she remembered him leaning over her with a lazy smile, his hand moving gently down her body as he said, "Ransom told me we'll have to confine ourselves mostly to the house and thereabouts for the next few days."

"That won't be a problem," she'd whispered, and drawn his head down to hers.

Chapter 37

By the time Keir and Merritt emerged from the house the next day, it was early afternoon.

The weather was cool and gray—dreich, Keir called it—but Merritt's wool walking dress and sturdy shoes kept her comfortable, and a thick cashmere shawl protected her from the wind. Wallace raced back and forth, playing fetch-the-stick with Keir as they walked.

The distillery and house covered three acres of ground, all of it overlooking the sea. Although the property appeared to exist in romantic isolation, it was only about two miles from Port Charlotte, which, according to Keir, was filled with shops, gardens, and terraced houses.

Wallace followed as Keir took Merritt into the distillery for a tour. She was amazed by the size and complexity of the operation, which used a combination of machinery and gravity to move enormous quantities of grain and liquid. Barley was hoisted to two- and three-story lofts, and funneled to various places in the distillery through iron shoots. There were upper malting floors connected to a massive kiln by gangways, along which bags of dried malt were carried. That had been one of Keir's early jobs when he was a boy, as he could scurry quickly back and forth along the gangways. After being ground in a giant mill, the dried malt was conveyed by elevator to a grist loft, and eventually mixed with hot water in a sixteen-foot diameter tun that stirred the mash.

"Once the malt is mixed with water," Keir said, "it cuts down on the grain dust and lowers the risk of explosions."

Merritt looked at him with wide eyes. "Like the kind that happens in flour mills?"

He nodded. "'Tis the same. But we connected a large metal pipe between the grist elevators and the roof, so most of the explosion's force would go up into the sky. And we installed fire hydrants and plugs, reels, and hose wherever we could." He kept Merritt's hand in his as they wandered past a towering row of copper stills. "There's little danger of that now, as the distillery's been shut down for nigh a month. But 'tis still no' a good idea to light a match or smoke a cigar anywhere around the distillery."

"Or fire a gun, I suppose," Merritt said.

"Or that," Keir agreed ruefully. He hesitated before asking warily, "You dinna bring a revolver to Islay, did you?"

"Of course I did. I borrowed one from Uncle Sebastian's gun room. I came here to protect you, remember?" She reached into the pocket of her walking skirt, where a small but weighty Bulldog revolver rested against her hip. "If you'd like to see—"

Keir groaned and shook his head, pulling her between the copper stills. "No, dinna show me." He backed her up against a cool copper surface. "I dinna need you to protect me," he informed her. "I need you for other things."

"I can do those too."

His mouth moved over hers in a long, savoring kiss, not stopping until she was clinging to him weakly, her legs unsteady.

They broke apart as Wallace ran up to them, carrying something in his mouth, his tail wagging.

"What did you find?" Keir asked, reaching down to take the object from him.

Merritt felt a sharp pang of worry as she saw that it was a man's wool flat cap. "Dinna fash," Keir said immediately, "it belongs to one of Ransom's agents. Duffy, I think. He's probably somewhere in here."

Merritt continued to frown. "Are they hiding from us?" she whispered.

"No, only trying to stay out of our way." He dangled the flat cap near Wallace's nose. "Let's go find him, laddie."

The terrier trotted away, glancing repeatedly over his shoulder to make sure they were following.

"Does Wallace know when Ethan or one of his men are nearby?"

"Aye. He met them—Duffy and Wilkinson are their names—before you arrived. I introduced them, and gave them each a bit of carrot to feed him. Wallace counts them among his friends, so he won't bark at them. But if a stranger is nearby, he'll tell us."

They went to a large multi-story rackhouse, where filled whisky casks were stored horizontally on racks, stacked four high.

"Duffy?" Keir called out cautiously.

Merritt tensed, her hand creeping surreptitiously to her skirt pocket as they waited for a reply.

"Mr. MacRae?" A young clean-shaven man with

dark hair came walking from the other side of the rackhouse. Keir gave the hat to the terrier, who dutifully carried it to Duffy. "Thank you, Wallace," the man said, scratching him behind the ears. "I was looking for that." Glancing at Merritt, he bowed respectfully. "Milady."

She smiled and curtsied in return. "Mr. Duffy."

The young man's gaze went to Keir. "If you're going to tour the rackhouse with Lady Merritt," he offered, "I could patrol another area in the distillery."

"Aye," Keir said.

They waited until Duffy had left before they began to walk among the racks, with Wallace following. "How old do you think he is?" Merritt whispered, slightly disgruntled.

"Two-and-twenty?" Keir guessed.

"I was estimating about twelve."

Keir gave a shake of his head, dismissing her concern, and turned her to look at the stored casks. "Look at these racks—we installed them last year. Before that, we had to store the casks standing upright, which exerts too much pressure on them and causes leaks. Keeping them sideways is easier on the casks, and it lets more air circulate around the sides and ends."

"Why do you want air to circulate?"

"Improves the flavor."

"How do you move the casks in and out of the racks?"

"It still takes brute force to lift them up," he admitted, "the same as with vertical storing. But to take them down, 'tis a simple matter of pulling the levers at the end of each row. It releases the stops, and the barrels come rolling out."

"That could be exciting," she said dryly, looking at the endless rows of barrels waiting to tumble.

Keir reached out and eased her against him, and nuzzled a few kisses beneath her jaw and along her throat. "Have you seen enough of the distillery for now, love? I could do with a wee nap."

She slid her arms around his neck and lifted her mouth to his for answer.

Aside from that brief encounter with Duffy, they saw no sign of Ethan or his men. They were so absorbed in each other, relishing the novelty of being able to do whatever they pleased with no concern about anyone's schedule, that the hours slipped by without their notice. They cooked a simple meal, drank wine, made love, and had a long, relaxed conversation before the fire. In the evening, they took Wallace for a walk around the property, and looked out at the sea through binoculars as dolphins cavorted.

Merritt had never been so happy, but at the same time, the lurking, nagging worry about potential danger was ever-present. And there was also the question of what was happening in court. It had been two days since Kingston had appeared at Chancery to reveal he'd located Keir, but so far there had been no word of any legal developments.

"He'll telegram when there's something to report," Keir said. "Or Ransom will find out and tell us."

As it turned out, Ethan knocked at the front door early the next morning. Keir dressed hastily and went to let him in while Merritt hurriedly put on a robe and set a kettle on to boil.

Ethan looked tired and tense as he entered the

kitchen and held his chilled hands over the stove to warm them. "I have shocking news," he said, rubbing his hands briskly to distribute the heat. "Do I have to broach it carefully, or can I simply come out with it?"

"Is it shocking in a good way or a bad way?" Merritt asked.

Ethan considered that. "Not bad, on the face of it. But I don't know the details yet."

"What is it?" Keir asked.

"Lord Ormonde was found dead in his home late last night."

Chapter 38

A SENSE OF UNREALITY CAME over Merritt. She struggled to wrap her brain around the information and decide what it meant, but her usual thought process seemed to have been disassembled. She glanced at Keir, who had turned to busy himself with measuring tea into the teapot. His face was difficult to read, but she knew he had to be stunned and profoundly worried by the fact that everything was falling on his head at once . . . inheriting the trust and almost certainly the viscountcy and estate as well.

"Was it natural causes?" Keir asked calmly.

"I don't know yet. He was certainly of an age for that possibility. I have to leave for London immediately and oversee an investigation." Ethan went to a basket of food, lifted a cloth, and took out a bannock. He took a bite of the dry, crumbly oat bread without seeming to taste it. "I want to take Wilkinson with me and leave Duffy here, if you don't object."

Merritt frowned. "I might object."

Ethan glanced at her speculatively and swallowed the bite of bannock. "With Ormonde's death," he said, "there's no motivation for Brownlow to come all the way here and carry out the wishes of a dead man. It's unlikely MacRae will be troubled by him again."

"Unlikely," Merritt said, "but not impossible."

"Which is why I'm leaving Duffy with you," Ethan said evenly, eating more of the bannock.

Keir slid his arm behind Merritt's back and patted the side of her hip. "We'll be all right," he said. "We'll stay safe in the house and plan of what to do next. There's the distillery needing to be started up again, the trust properties needing to be managed . . . and an estate in . . . where is it?"

"Cumberland," Merritt replied.

"Cumberland," Keir repeated, and went to pour hot water into the teapot. He spoke while facing away from her, sounding wry. "If only I could divide myself into three men, each doing a job well, instead of being one man doing three jobs badly."

"Three of you," Merritt mused, her natural sense of humor asserting itself. "That would be rather too much for me to manage. Depending, of course, on how many of you would want me as your wife."

Keir turned to glance at her over his shoulder, his hair tousled, his blue eyes glinting with a smile. "My heart," he said, "there's no version of me that would no' choose you as my wife. 'Tis the first thing I would do." His gaze held hers, and he added softly, "The very first thing."

AFTER ETHAN AND Wilkinson had left for London, Duffy went back to the change-house to rest in preparation for his solitary night watch. Merritt spent the afternoon talking with Keir, the two of them cuddled together on a very small settee. She would have to order one at least twice this size, she thought, when it came time to build a new house on the island. She watched with amusement as Wallace paced restlessly around the overloaded settee, obviously trying to calculate how he too could sit there.

"Wallace," Keir said dryly, "I dinna know where you think you'll find a blessed inch of empty space."

The terrier persisted, however, hopping up near their feet and painstakingly crawling over their bodies.

"Wallace will come to London with us, of course," Merritt said, reaching out swiftly to steady the dog as he wobbled. She pulled him onto her lap and leaned back against Keir. "As soon as Ethan says it's safe, we'll stay at my—our—home there, and meet with your father." She paused, disconcerted. "I'm sorry, I meant with Kingston."

"I dinna mind," he said in a matter-of-fact tone. "He is my father, whether I call him that or no'."

Merritt smiled and gently scratched Wallace's head and ears until he sighed and slumped across her lap. "He'll explain how we should proceed with the trust, and we'll meet with all the solicitors and bankers and so forth."

"'Tis no' the trust I'm worried about," Keir said morosely. "'Tis the estate and title. I have no connection to those lands—nor to the people who farm it—and I dinna think I can live in a place where my mother bided in such misery." He paused. "Can I no' give any part of it away?"

"One can't give away a title, I'm afraid. And perhaps there's a tiny percentage of land you might be able to sell, but most of it's probably entailed. That means it has to be kept all together, along with the house, to pass down to the next generation. You won't really own it so much as you'll be its caretaker until the next Lord Ormonde. Certainly you wouldn't want to evict the current tenants, who are good, hard-working people." She thought for a long moment. "However . . . that doesn't mean the manor house itself can't be used for some other purpose."

"Such as?"

"A school?" she suggested.

"A school for what?"

"For boys and girls who are disadvantaged and need a good education as well as a healthy, happy place to live."

Keir pressed his lips to her head. "I like that idea," he said. "Very much."

"It's not the same as running your distillery of course, but there might be aspects you would find interesting and rewarding."

"'Tis about more than making whisky, my distillery," he said reflectively. "The part I like the most is that my men and I, we're all working together to make something good. Something we're proud of. I think . . . I could feel some of that for a school."

Merritt smiled and nestled more tightly against him.

They talked into the evening, until they were both tired and ready for bed.

"Let's bathe first," Merritt suggested.

Keir parted his lips to reply, when Wallace suddenly leaped off the settee and ran uneasily from the main room to the bedroom and back again. His small body quivered with excitement, and his wiry fur stood on end.

"What is it?" Keir wondered aloud, going to the window. Merritt turned down the lamp to reduce the glare of reflected light.

All three of them jumped as they heard a jarring sound from the distillery, a mingling of groaning metal and broken glass, as if something had smashed.

Then the night was silent.

Wallace erupted in furious barking, until Keir laid a gentle hand on his head, quieting him.

"An accident with machinery?" Merritt suggested. "Perhaps one of the copper stills fell over?"

Keir shook his head, staring intently out the window.

Something was wrong. Merritt felt her insides turn hollow. She went to the bedroom, took the Bulldog revolver from the leather valise where she'd been keeping it, and turned the lamp down in that room as well. As she glanced through the window at the whitewashed walls around the distillery, she couldn't detect any movement.

Soon Keir came into the bedroom, his face grim. "Duffy would have come in to say something about it by now, if he were able."

"Let's go out together and look for him," Merritt suggested.

Keir shook his head. "Stay here in the bedroom with the dog, keep the revolver with you, and lock the door. Wallace will growl if a stranger tries to come in."

"What are you planning to do?"

"I'm going to look for Duffy outside, and if he's no' there, I'll look in the distillery."

"Keir, *no*—I'm coming with you. You're not armed, and I—"

"You can't shoot in the distillery, darlin', or you might blow it to kingdom come. I can find my way through the distillery in the dark if need be, Merritt. I know it much better than he does. Dinna go in there—wait for me here. I'll come back. I promise." His lips twitched as he added, "And dinna shoot my dog by accident."

After Keir had left the house, Merritt watched from the bedroom window for at least fifteen minutes. The distillery's many roofs and walls, and the long machair grass surrounding the whole of it, were eerily illuminated by the blue light of a cloud-ghosted moon. Her breath caught as she saw Keir go through one of the side arches leading into the main building.

Wallace, who was standing beside her with his front paws braced on the windowsill, wagged his tail, and licked and panted.

Another minute passed, and another, as they continued to watch.

A growl came from the dog's throat, so quietly menacing that every hair on Merritt's body stood on end. In a moment, she saw movement near the archway . . . a man following Keir into the distillery. He appeared to be heavier, broader than Duffy.

"Oh, no you bloody don't," Merritt whispered, electrified with fear and urgency. Wallace remained at the window, staring outside. She couldn't risk taking him with her.

Quietly she left the bedroom and closed the door, keeping him safely inside. With the revolver in hand, she went outside and made her way past the distillery walls. After hesitating at the main building, she followed an instinct and skirted around to the gigantic racking-house. The main door was ajar. She nudged past it and eased inside.

The maze of racks and casks was only faintly illuminated by fingers of blue light that crept in through a few high, small windows. After sidling against a wall, Merritt held very still, hearing the sounds of quiet footsteps. Another, slightly different set. Walking, stopping, walking . . . stopping. It was difficult to tell where any of them were coming from. She ventured farther into the rackhouse, keeping to the shadows and straining to see through the darkness.

A man was walking several rows away from her. Suddenly, she was startled by the feel of a gentle hand covering her mouth, and she inhaled sharply. Her heartbeat went out of control, cluttering her chest with its wild pounding until she could hardly breathe. But the strong, warm fingers were familiar. She relaxed at the scent and feel of her husband. His hand slid down her arm, closed over the gun, and gently removed it from her grip. After sliding it into her skirt pocket, he took her hand and pulled her along with him.

She could hear the other man's footsteps again, this time much closer. Keir drew her with him to the end of a row. He ducked his head around one side of the rack and then the other, but both corridors were empty.

Merritt felt him lift one of her wrists up to his mouth. There was a slight tug as he bit through the threads affixing a tiny decorative button to the cuff. He took the little button between a thumb and finger, and tossed it into one of the corridors between the racks.

In response to the sound, the footsteps came closer,

until Merritt could tell the man was heading toward them. Her hand inched toward her skirt pocket, but Keir caught it gently and guided it to a wooden lever attached to the rack.

"Push it down on three," he whispered, almost inaudibly, and he reached for a higher lever on the rack.

She waited, sweat breaking out as the footsteps came closer. Keir's fingers tapped on her arm. One . . . two . . . three. She shoved the lever down with all her strength.

The entire rack shuddered, and casks began to roll with the sound of thunder. Seeing Keir pull another lever, and another, Merritt reached to help him. She glanced into the corridor, and saw the stranger staggering between the heavy plummeting casks.

Then the man was quiet, groaning as he was pinned beneath the weight of a barrel.

Keir went into the corridor and looked at the man incredulously. "He's no' the one from the alley," he said.

A FEW MINUTES later, Merritt sat in the kitchen with Agent Duffy, dabbing gently at his bruised and lacerated temple with a cold, wet cloth. She and Keir had found him outside one of the distillery walls, where he'd been knocked unconscious by the intruder. After they'd helped him into the house, Keir had gone to fetch the sheriff.

"I'm so sorry," Merritt murmured, as the young man flinched and drew in a hissing breath. "I do wish you'd take that dram of whisky Keir poured for you."

"Ransom wouldn't like it," Duffy said. "I'm still on the job."

Merritt nudged the glass toward him. "I won't tell."

Duffy reached for it gratefully. After a bracing swallow, he let Merritt press a cold compress to his forehead. "I should be handling the situation," he said. "Where's Mr. MacRae?"

"He's gone to fetch MacTaggart," she said.

"The suspect—where is he?"

"We left him in the rackhouse, after we bound him up with baler twine."

The stranger had been dazed and battered, putting up only a feeble struggle before Keir had subdued him. After the man's hands had been fastened behind his back and his legs tied together, Keir had searched his pockets and found a revolver and a set of brass knuckle dusters. Merritt had pulled out a knife from a sewn-in sheath in the shaft of his boot.

She'd been perplexed by how ordinary the hired assassin's appearance was. There was nothing of the stage villain about him, nor did he seem mad, desperate, impoverished, or any of the things that might drive a man to crime. He was a well-dressed man in his twenties, with a face that could have belonged to a shopkeeper or a business clerk.

As the man sat propped up against a wine cask, his hard, empty eyes had unnerved Merritt. He'd refused to speak, only stared at them with that emotionless gaze, as if he were turning to stone in front of them.

"Whether you tell us or no'," Keir had said wryly, "'tis no great mystery about who sent you, and what you were after doing." As the stranger maintained his cold silence, Keir had stared at him with curiosity and a hint of pity. "I dinna know what made you so broken, but life must have gone hard for you. Why kill a man you have no quarrel with? Only for money? Had you come to me as a stranger needful of work, I'd have offered you a good honest job."

That had provoked a reaction, the calcified façade cracking to reveal molten scorn. "I'd never work for a sheep-shagging Scot."

Outraged, Merritt had been about to tell him exactly what she thought of him, but Keir had smiled at the insult and rose to his feet, pulling her up with him. "Is that the best you can come up with?" he'd asked. "My friends and I call each other much worse after a round at the local tavern."

Merritt's thoughts returned to the present and Duffy as he gingerly gripped his sandy head in his hands and stared down at the table. "I'm not cut out for this kind of work," he said glumly. "I should have stayed with teaching."

She looked at him alertly. "You're a teacher?"

"Assistant master of science at Cheltenham College. And I was good at it."

"Why did you go into law enforcement?" Merritt asked.

"I thought it was more exciting. And important."

"Dear boy, there's nothing more exciting or important than teaching."

"Platitudes," he muttered.

"Not at all," she said earnestly. "Teaching makes people who they are. Perhaps it even *shows* them who they are. If done well, it's . . . magical. A good teacher is a guide to the wonderments of life."

Duffy folded his arms and lowered his head to them.

"It doesn't matter now," came his muffled voice. "The position at Cheltenham has long since been filled."

Merritt leaned forward to reposition the compress against his forehead. "If that's what you want, I'll see what I can do to help." She smiled. "Or perhaps a new opportunity will present itself."

Keir returned with Sheriff MacTaggart and a deputy, and Duffy went with them to the distillery rackhouse. In the meantime, as dawn approached, the small house was overrun by friendly strangers, some of them neighbors, some distillery workers and their wives, and some of them friends of Keir's since childhood. They were all excited and outraged by the news of an intruder having been caught at the MacRae distillery, and were full of colorful opinions about what to do with him.

Even if Merritt had been well-rested and prepared for visitors, the deluge would have been overwhelming. As it was, she found herself wandering distractedly among the crowd, smiling and nodding, and repeating names in an effort to remember them. Someone brought a basket of hot morning rolls directly from the baker and began handing them out. Someone else filled the tea kettle and set it on the hot stove plate.

Amid all the bustle, Merritt found herself gently shepherded to the settee. Gratefully she sat, and Wallace hopped up beside her. The terrier licked his lips and stared at the morning roll in her hands. It had been split open, with a curl of cold butter beginning to melt inside. Slowly Merritt consumed the roll and broke off a few small pieces to feed to Wallace. With his solid, warm body cuddled up to hers, and her stomach comfortably full, it took only a few blinks before exhaustion overtook her.

"Merry," came a low, familiar voice, and she opened her eyes to discover Keir leaning over her. He smiled and stroked back a loose lock of her hair, and glanced down at Wallace, who extended his short legs in a trembling stretch.

She had no idea how much time had passed as she'd dozed in the corner of the settee, but the daylight was much brighter now, and many of the visitors seemed to have departed.

"Poor weary lass," Keir said, sitting beside her and gathering her close.

Merry yawned against his shoulder. "The first time I meet your friends and neighbors . . . and I fall asleep in front of them."

"They understand, love. They're full of good wishes. Soon they'll take their leave, and we'll have a proper rest." Keir patted her hip. "When I told everyone you followed me into the distillery with your wee pop-gun to protect me, they all said you were as brave as a Scotswoman. 'Tis a great compliment, ye ken."

Merritt's lips twitched at his description of the high-caliber revolver as a "wee pop-gun."

"MacTaggart took the man to a holding cell in Port Charlotte," Keir continued, settling her more comfortably in the crook of his arm. "We found out his name is John Peltie."

She glanced up at him in surprise. "You made him talk?"

"No, it was Duffy. He convinced him it would go better for him if he cooperated. Peltie admitted that

Lord Ormonde hired him to finish the job after Brownlow failed at it."

Wallace hopped off the settee, simultaneously yawned and whined, and padded across the room to the door.

"I'll take him out," Keir said.

"I wouldn't mind stretching my legs," Merritt said, reaching for a shawl draped over the back of the settee. "I'll go with you." She drew the shawl around herself and knotted it loosely over her front.

Before they went outside, however, Sheriff MacTaggart met them at the threshold, having just returned from Port Charlotte. "MacRae . . . and milady . . . I received a telegram from Commissioner Ransom that you'll be wanting to know about." With a slightly theatrical flourish, he took the message from his pocket. "It says Mr. Brownlow was apprehended last night at the Charing Cross station while attempting to board a train. Brownlow confessed to Ransom that he killed Lord Ormonde, after Ormonde fired him and wouldn't pay what he owed him."

"To be fair," Keir said reflectively, "I can see Brownlow's side of it. He did a fine job of setting fire to the warehouse and shutting me in. By all rights, I should have been scowdered and burnt to a crisp."

"I could have warned him you were a daft numptie who'd jump oot the window," MacTaggart said, and they exchanged a grin.

The dog pawed impatiently at the door.

"Sheriff," Merritt said with a slight smile, "if you'll excuse us, Wallace has his priorities."

MacTaggart stepped aside and opened the door for

Wallace with a show of deference, and the terrier trotted out.

Keir took Merritt's hand. They paused at the threshold, blinking in the bright daylight.

There was so much ahead of them, Merritt thought, feeling momentarily overwhelmed. So much to be done.

She glanced up at Keir, who smiled as if he could read her thoughts.

"Let's start with a walk," he suggested, and bent to steal a kiss. "We'll figure it out from there."

And together, they walked out into the morning.

Epilogue

THE SCENTS AND SOUNDS of Christmas filled the mansion at Stony Cross Park, Lord Westcliff's renowned Hampshire estate. Rich smells wafted from the kitchen . . . standing rib of beef, ham, turkey, smoked oysters, Yorkshire pudding, every imaginable kind of pie. Greenery and flowers bedecked every horizontal surface, and the fresh acrid pungency of a towering Christmas tree exerted its magic through the main hall and beyond. Servants hurried through the hallways on frantic errands to make everything ready for the Christmas Eve dance that evening. Children's happy screams echoed through the halls as they scampered everywhere during a game of hide and seek.

"Mama," one young voice was heard to whine, "why must I sit here and play carols when you know I abhor it? Why don't *you* do it?"

"Because," an older female voice retorted with a laugh, "my mother never loved me enough to force me to learn the piano."

The reply was accompanied by dramatic musical chords of a distinctly antagonistic interpretation of "God Rest Ye Merry Gentlemen." "Mama, I wish you loved me just a little . . . tiny . . . smidgeon . . . less!"

Dazed by the general uproar, Lord Westcliff closed

the door of his study and handed Sebastian a brandy. "This is the only safe place in the house," he said. "I'd barricade the door, but there are still a few unfortunate men fighting their way through. I would hate to deny them their last chance of survival."

"It's every man for himself," Sebastian said, taking a sip of brandy and settling into a comfortable chair. "If our sons and sons-in-law didn't have the good sense to avoid the main hall, they deserve to be trampled."

"Such a loss," Westcliff said regretfully, pouring a brandy for himself. "Ah, well . . . I have some news to share about MacRae and Merritt."

"I already know," Sebastian said smugly. "They're going to arrive tonight instead of tomorrow morning."

Westcliff, who loved knowing things other people didn't, smiled even more smugly. "It appears you haven't been told *why,* however."

Sebastian's brows lifted.

Ceremoniously Westcliff took a folded letter from his pocket. "Lillian shared this with me. After I read it, I told her I had to be the one to tell you. I begged, as a matter of fact. She refused, and then I had to promise . . . no, we won't even go into what I had to promise. However, she said I could give you the news as long as we're able to act surprised when they announce it."

"Good God, Westcliff, you're positively giddy. Give that to me." Leaning forward, Sebastian took the letter. He scanned it quickly, and a grin broke out on his face. "Well, naturally. Keir is descended from my line. Our virility is unmatched."

Westcliff tried to look severe. "You realize, Kingston, that my first grandchild has been sired by your illegitimate offspring."

"Yes, yes, who cares about legitimacy. This child will be magnificent. With my looks and your brains . . ."

"It could have my looks and your brains," Westcliff pointed out.

"Don't be such a pessimist. Bring the brandy bottle over here, and we'll start making plans."

And the two old friends grinned at each other as they clinked their glasses.

Author's Note

Dear Friends,

I must confide that my much-adored husband, Greg, will no longer accompany me to Costco. As he points out, no matter how short my shopping list is, I start to wander up and down the aisles in a daze, adding very large boxes and tubs of unnecessary things to the cart.

To my chagrin, this is also a pretty good description of my book-researching habits. While I was writing *Devil in Disguise*, there were so many fascinating subjects to learn about—*Islay!—whisky distilling!*—that hours would fly by with too much reading and not enough writing. Helpfully, Greg would occasionally stick his head into my office, perceive my lack of progress and shout "Stay out of Costco!" (Well, maybe he didn't shout; it was more of a vigorous exclamation.)

But if I hadn't let myself wander a little here and there, I wouldn't have found out about Victorian Sippy Cups. I mean, mustache cups. The Victorian era was a time of elaborately styled and curled mustaches that required wax to keep their shape. And when that waxed facial hair came too close to a cup of tea or coffee, the wax would melt into the beverage. Euw. In the 1860s, however, this mortifying dilemma was solved by the British potter Harvey Adams, who invented a cup with a little ledge set inside the rim to shield a man's upper lip from heat.

The expression "barm-leavened" refers to bread that's been leavened by foam from ale. Some very old bread recipes call for barm as one of the ingredients. The meaning of the word "frothy" is why silly or not-quite-sane people were sometimes referred to as "barmy."

In 1853, the Scottish physician Alexander Wood invented the hypodermic syringe with a hollow needle, using the sting of the bee as his model. It was a huge leap forward in pain relief and, of course, has been used in countless other applications, including vaccinations. Thank you, Dr. Wood. (And thank you, bees.)

The British Bulldog revolver, introduced by Philip Webley of Birmingham, England, in 1872, is a deceptively small handgun. It was designed to be carried in a coat pocket, with a barrel that's only 2.5 inches long, but it has enough stopping power to knock someone off their feet. In 1881, a disgruntled lawyer assassinated President James Garfield with a Belgian-made British Bulldog revolver.

I based the MacRae distillery on Bruichladdich, a renowned distillery on Islay. After Greg and I watched a fascinating documentary titled *Scotch: A Golden Dream* (I think it's still available on Amazon) I was instantly taken with the idea of creating a hero who made whisky. (Spelled "whiskey" in the US and Ireland, but "whisky" in Scotland and Canada.) There's a romance and art to distilling whisky, and the flavor is influenced by the water that goes into making it, the kind of wood used for the cask, how long it's been matured, and a thousand other factors.

Slàinte Mhath (slan-ge-var), my dears—that's a toast to your health. I've relied on your friendship and support so much this past year, and I never take any of you for granted. Much love to all!

Lisa

THIS IS A LOAF of sunshine, based on Victorian era loaf cake recipes. It's perfect for breakfast, teatime, or dessert. (Lady Merritt suggests using actual marmalade instead of "fruit spread.")

Ingredients:

- $^3/_4$ C butter, softened
- $^3/_4$ C sugar
- 3 eggs
- 4 tablespoons marmalade
- juice of 1 orange (about $^1/_2$ C)
- zest of 1 orange
- 1 $^1/_2$ C flour
- 2 tsp. baking powder
- 1 tsp. salt

Glaze:

- 4 tablespoons marmalade
- 1 tablespoon butter

Preheat oven to 350 degrees. Grease a 9x5-inch loaf pan—put a little rectangle of parchment paper on the bottom if your loaf pan isn't nonstick.

Whisk softened butter and sugar together. (If it's your cookmaid's day off, use an electric mixer.) Add eggs, marmalade, orange juice, and zest; mix until combined.

In a separate bowl, whisk together flour, baking powder, and salt. Add to the butter mixture and mix until just combined. Don't overmix! Also don't worry if it looks lumpy.

Bake for 55 minutes, or until a toothpick is inserted and comes out clean. If it starts to look too brown during the baking, lay a piece of foil over the top.

Cool for 15 minutes and ease the loaf out of the pan. Melt the other four tablespoons of marmalade with a tablespoon of butter and spread over the top of the warm cake, then let it cool completely before slicing. (If you have that much self-restraint, which, sadly, my family does not.)

A Word of Caution:

When serving this treat to a prospective suitor, remember to have a chaperone present.

We all know what scandal can lead to.

Don't miss the rest of the Ravenels series . . .

Available now from

PIATKUS

PIATKUS